Darkest Fears T

Freed
By Him

Clair Delaney

REVIEWS FOR FREED BY HIM

"The term 'Never let me go' was never so aptly used as it was in this, on both their counts. I truly loved and connected with how this played out. I'm kind of a wreck as I wobble on the final book. Can't wait!" **Goodreads**

"Hot! Hot! Hot! This author knows how to write hot steamy sex! Plus, it was just as gut wrenching as the first book. I really love Coral and Tristan. I laughed and I cried, and then the climax at the end was just awesome. This trilogy is going to go far in the romance world, and this author is going to have a stellar career." **LibraryThing**

"Brilliant sequel to the first book, I was as equally hooked into the story. After the end of Fallen For Him, I couldn't wait to get into Freed By Him. It's one of my most memorable reads for years." **Amazon**

"Coral and Tristan share an amazing chemistry together, but Tristan's past hides an enormous secret that threatens their future together, it was a joy to read. The steamy parts were well written and I loved the dialogue. Thumbs up." **Amazon**

"Intense and very engaging romance, I was so easily pulled into the steamy relationship between Coral and Tristan. Another great read that delivered on both the dramatic and erotic fronts. Love the characters and the story. Looking forward to the conclusion in Forever With Him." **Amazon**

"One of the best series I have read in a long time. After finishing the first book, I just had to read the second. I loved the love scenes and how powerful the story was. This book was just as good as the first and I cannot wait for the third." **Barnes & Noble**

'The story just pulled me in. So sexy, anticipating! Writing was so smooth. Was bummed when it ended. I need more!' **iBooks**

'I fell in love with Tristan and Coral, a great captivating read I just couldn't put down.' **iBooks**

'Love, love, love these books!' **iBooks**

'This trilogy just gets better and better. Very well written, heart meltingly warm, brilliant second novel.' **Kobo**

ALSO BY CLAIR DELANEY

Fallen For Him
Darkest Fears Trilogy Book One

Forever With Him
Darkest Fears Trilogy Book Three

A Christmas Wish
Darkest Fears Christmas Special Book Four

CONTENTS

Prologue 1
Chapter One 3
Chapter Two 15
Chapter Three 30
Chapter Four 45
Chapter Five 59
Chapter Six 77
Chapter Seven 93
Chapter Eight 108
Chapter Nine 121
Chapter Ten 135
Chapter Eleven 150
Chapter Twelve 163
Chapter Thirteen 177
Chapter Fourteen 192
Chapter Fifteen 205
Chapter Sixteen 219
Chapter Seventeen 236
Chapter Eighteen 250
Chapter Nineteen 268
Chapter Twenty 285
Chapter Twenty-One 304
Chapter Twenty-Two 319
Chapter Twenty-Three 336
Chapter Twenty-Four 353
Chapter Twenty-Five 382
Chapter Twenty-Six 402
About the Author 425

PROLOGUE

HE IS OBLIVIOUS. He doesn't understand. I have loved him for so long now. I was so close to reuniting us until we came to Brighton…and he met her. It is not allowed. I have waited for so long. I was finally going to make him mine. I am angry he has made me wait. He is denying our love. He is denying me what is rightfully mine. He is afraid.

I see him, he is different with her, but he cannot have her.

I won't allow it.

It cannot happen.

He is mine.

I've been watching her. I see her. She is not worthy of him. She is a freak.

He is mine.

I am his.

I will stop her.

I follow her down to the Marina when it's dark. Does she know I am watching her? Will he care if I kill her? She can't have him. He is mine. I don't understand why he likes her. She is nothing. I am everything.

He is mine.

And I am his.

But he will pay for what he has done to me.

The metal feels heavy in my hand. I practice with it. I lift my hand and aim it at her. It is dark. She is walking too fast and is too far away.

I silently move closer in the shadows.

I wait until she is standing still.

He is mine.

Bang, bang!

You're dead.

CHAPTER ONE

I HEAR THE PATIO door slide open and instantly stop crying. *Who the hell is that?* I don't want anyone to see me like this! I lean up from my slumped position, listening intently. Maybe I should call the police? *Shit, my bag is downstairs!*

"Coral?" I hear Tristan's voice shout, making my heart pound against my chest. *Oh no!* What is he doing here? I hear the bathroom door open and close as he tries to find me.

"Coral, answer me!" He demands. *Oh no! I don't want him here. I don't want him to see me like this.* His footsteps come barreling up the stairs, his eyes bleak and wide, searching for me.

"Coral!" He gasps as he reaches the top of the stairs and sees me.

"Go away!" I croak and squeeze my eyes shut.

"No baby, no!" He says, sounding appalled. The next thing I know I'm in his arms, and he's crushing me to him. I try to push him away, but it's useless. "Baby, tell me what's wrong? Why did you leave?" He asks rocking me slowly.

"Tristan, please go." I croak.

"No!" he barks. "I'm not leaving you in this state."

"Please..." I whimper.

"Why?" He asks in his husky voice.

"B-because..." I choke back the tears that threaten to fall again. "Tristan, I...I can't do this, I can't be what you want, what you deserve." I croak.

"You are what I want." He states clearly. "I love you just the way you are." I finally look up at his deep, hypnotic eyes. "Don't you know that?" He questions.

I sniff loudly – It's really not attractive.

3

"But '– "No buts baby, come home with me." He pleads.

"No," I grumble. I just want to be left alone. I don't want to face my fears, and I don't want to see the look in his eyes when I freak out because he's sexually touched me. I squeeze my eyes shut, trying to block out the horror within.

"I don't want you on your own baby. You don't even have to be in the same room as me, I'll sleep downstairs, just come home." I think about what he's asking – *Can I do that?*

"Please…" he begs again. "Look Coral, I think we'd be crazy if we let this go. What we have…is so very special, I've never felt this way before."

"Tristan…" I look up at him feeling full of remorse and guilt.

He gently wipes a couple of stray tears away with his thumbs.

"You don't have to tell me anything, just come back with me." I can tell by the look in his eye that he's not going to give in. "I told you, baby, I won't stop fighting for you no matter how hard you push me away, no matter how many times you leave me. You're all I've ever wanted. I've never loved anyone like I love you." He leans forward and kisses my temple. He keeps his lips there; pressed hard against my skin.

A lump forms in my throat. He came back for me, he came back…I think about the piercing pain that lanced through me just moments earlier, and how it seems to have magically vanished. I think about how I felt when I thought I would never see him again, just moments ago, yet here he is cradling me in his arms – *Why? Why does he care so much for me?*

"Why are you here Tristan, I…I left you," I croak.

"I know," he sighs heavily. "And it was the worst moment in my entire life." He trembles.

I gasp and look up at him. "I don't ever want to feel that pain again, so don't run from me…please. I'll be whatever you want me to be, just don't…leave me. " He crushes me to him again – *Oh Tristan! That's just how I felt!*

What a stupid thing I did, especially given the fact that this feels so right, like he's meant for me. I finally relent and wrap my arms around him, resting my head against his chest, listening to his racing heart. I don't know how long we stay there for, five minutes, an hour, I'm not sure, but my tears slowly subside, and I start to feel calmer.

"Come home with me?" He whispers, rocking me gently. I think about his request and realise I don't want to be alone. I don't want to be without Tristan – even though it's scaring me to death.

I take a deep breath and slowly blow it out. "Ok," I tremble. I'm still not sure if I'm doing the right thing here.

His whole body seems to sag with relief. "Good…that's good." I look up at him just as he lifts my hand to his lips. "You're trembling," he says and kisses my knuckles.

"I'm scared," I whisper croakily.

"So am I." He admits. He rocks me gently again. "Jesus Coral…don't do that to me again," he says, his heart beating madly – I close my eyes and surrender. Feeling his arms wrapped around me is like being in seventh heaven. I never want to feel like that again, which is really fucking scary, because I know it means facing my fears.

"Shall I get the car?" He murmurs.

"The car?" I question.

"Yeah, I went for a drive…" He solemnly shakes his head. "It's not far away, shall we walk there or' – "No, can you go get it?" I interrupt. "I still feel shaky. I don't think my legs would carry me."

"Yes, I can. But I need you to do something for me," he says.

"What?" I whisper.

"I need you to give me your word you'll be here when I get back." I nod silently to him. "Say it Coral," he says more sternly.

"I'll be here," I whimper.

He kisses my temple once more, releases me and slides off the bed. "I won't be long," he tells me. I smile weakly at him and watch him walk away from me. *Crap!*

Now I have no choice. Sighing heavily, I climb off the bed and slowly make my way down the stairs. Stepping into the bathroom, I take a good look at myself.

Christ, what a mess!

I walk back into the living room find my toiletries, and makeup bag, and head back into the bathroom. I slowly cleanse my face then try my best to re-apply some mascara - It's a trying feat with red, puffy eyes. When I'm done I stare at myself in the mirror, trying to find some courage from somewhere – Tristan's going to want to know why I freaked out earlier, I know he is.

I close my eyes for a moment, take a deep breath and head back into the living room. Just as I bend down to repack my bags, Tristan walks into the studio. He's breathing hard and sweating; I guess he ran back here to make sure I didn't disappear on him again.

"Hey." He says and walks over to me.

"Hi, did you want some water?" He shakes his head at me. "Ok." I look down at my hands that are twisting together in anxiety, unsure of what to say or do.

"Shall we?" He says I nod in reply, so he bends down and picks up my weekend bag. I throw my handbag over my shoulder and find my sunglasses to hide my puffy eyes. Our eyes catch again as I slide them on, he silently reaches out and caresses my cheek.

"Ready?" I nod silently to him. He takes a deep breath and silently holds his hand out to me. I place my hand in his open palm, and we silently head home...

AS WE REACH THE gates to the house, Tristan turns and clutches my hand in his, giving it a gentle squeeze as he does. He pulls up outside the house, switches off the engine and turns in his seat. It feels very strange being back here, considering I only left a short while ago – I try not to panic.

"Ok?" he softly asks. I smile weakly at him.

I still don't know if I'm doing the right thing here.

"Ok." He nods his head once, almost as though he understood my unspoken answer, and steps out the car. Reaching my side, he opens my door and holds out both his hands. I place my hands in his, and he gently pulls me to my feet. Then he bends down and swiftly kisses my forehead as he swiftly shuts the door behind me.

"I'll get the bags, why don't you let yourself in?" He softly says.

I shake my head at him. I don't want to go inside that house without him.

"You ok?" He asks.

I nod mutely again. He reaches out and runs a cool finger down my cheek, calming me. Then he walks round to the boot, collects my bags and walks back over to me. I take his outstretched hand, and we walk to the front door – this feels so surreal.

Taking his key out he unlocks the door, and pushes it open, gesturing for me to go first. With trembling legs, I take a step inside the house, then another and another, until I'm stood inside the huge entrance hall.

I hear Tristan follow, shut the door behind him and drop my bag to the floor.

"Do you want anything baby?" I put my handbag down, take off my sunglasses, and slowly turn to look at him.

He puts his hands in his pockets and gazes back at me. He looks lost, very wary, and slightly uncomfortable. I hate that I've made him feel like this. He's beautiful and sweet, caring and attentive and I love him. *Why the hell did I walk out on him?*

I grit my teeth at myself, take the two steps needed and crush myself against his chest, wrapping my arms tightly around his strong, muscular back.

"I'm so sorry," I choke. He hesitantly wraps his arms around me and gently rocks me.

"It's ok baby. You don't have to be sorry." He softly says.

"But I walked out on you," I choke.

"Yes, I know," he shudders. "What do you want Coral? Do you want to be alone, or do you' – "No, I want to be with you," I interrupt, closing my eyes and inhaling his intoxicating scent.

"Oh baby, I want to be with you too." Tristan kisses my hair several times. "Coral, what do you need?"

"You," I whisper.

I hear his soft chuckle and look up at him. "I need you too," Tristan says, finally smiling at me. He reaches up and takes my face in his hands. "You don't have to tell me anything you don't want to, ok?"

I nod once and swallow hard.

"You didn't eat much earlier. Are you hungry?" I shake my head. "Thirsty?" I shake my head again and start to smile, Tristan's grin widens in response.

"Hmm... what to do?" He says.

"Stay here," I reply, squeezing him tighter. I may not like

strangers touching me, but ever since I came to realise that Gladys wasn't bad, I always loved her hugs – they made me feel safe, loved. Just like Tristan's hugs, only Tristan's are so much better.

"I have a better idea." He says, smiling broadly now.

"You do?" I squeak, looking up at those mesmerising chocolate eyes of his.

Tristan nods once, his serious expression is back. "Dance with me?" He asks.

"Now?" I squeak. Tristan nods once. "Here?"

He nods again, looking down at me with such a loving expression, that I have only one answer. "Ok," I shrug. "But we don't even have any music?" I add.

"Stay there." He grins and walks over to the kitchen.

Moments later I hear a guitar rift begin. I instantly recognise the tune – Hero, Enrique Iglesias. My heart starts manically beating...*oh, the words...this song... it's so beautiful...*I feel very overwhelmed and have to fight to stop myself crying.

Tristan walks over to me, his eyes wide, and his hand held out. I place my hand in his, without a word, he pulls me into him, and spins us around a couple of times, making me smile. Then we slowly dance our way around the empty space of the living area, Tristan is so good at this.

"Hero?" I whisper, looking up at him.

He nods solemnly and twirls us around again.

"You wanna be my hero?" I ask.

Tristan stares down at me and nods once more. *Oh, Tristan!*

"Oh," I smile up at him, feeling shy.

He stares down at me with wide, sincere, serious eyes. "Always," he whispers.

My heart swells with love again, love for this man. I cradle my head under his neck and surrender to it. I close my eyes just as Tristan sings in my ear, *'I can be your hero baby, I can kiss away the pain, I will stand by you forever, you can take my breath away.'*

I practically melt in his arms. What a beautiful thing to do, what a song to pick!

The beat comes in, loud and clear and Tristan really starts to twirl us around, singing to me again. Tears pool in my eyes as I look up at him. *He wants to be my hero!*

I feel some of my barriers break down, and my heart stitch

back together; just that little bit more…*Oh, Tristan, what are you doing to me?* The song ends, but Tristan is still swaying us around, then he stops, and we gaze at one another.

"You ok?" He smiles.

"Yes, I am now," I say smiling back.

"Wine?" He asks – *Hell yes! I think I need it.*

"Please." Tristan goes to move, but I stop him. "Stay here, just a little while longer," I beg.

"Anything for you," he softly whispers. I hold him to me for a few more minutes until I'm feeling calm and brave enough to let him go.

"Want to go watch the sunset?" He asks huskily, bringing me back to him.

"Yeah, that would be nice." I look up at him.

He slowly and hesitantly reaches down. His lips millimetres from mine, waiting to see if I respond. I reach up onto my tiptoes and plant my lips against his, they mould with his, it's almost as though they were made for each other. *Perfect!*

He kisses me back, gently, softly, but it's enough to make my head swim, I feel so lightheaded. I stop kissing him, my lips going limp against his.

"You ok?" He asks.

I open my eyes and the room swims and sways – *Why do I feel faint?*

"I feel faint," I whisper. In the next breathe I am up and into his arms. I wrap my arm around his neck, cradle my head under his chin and inhale deeply.

"That's because you haven't eaten much," he scolds as he carries me into the kitchen.

"No," I shake my head, keeping my eyes closed. "It's you, you take my breath away."

"Ditto," he whispers. Tristan sits me down on the breakfast bar, his arms gripping me tightly. "Open your eyes baby." I do as he asks, but this time I feel more stable, the world has stopped spinning.

"I'm sorry about earlier," I whisper again.

Tristan smiles at me. "I'm not." He replies.

I frown up at him. "What do you mean?"

"I'm not sorry I pushed. It made you leave, and that, in turn, has made me realise a few things," he says.

"Like what?" I whisper, with wide eyes.

He shakes his head at me. "Later." I pout at him, he laughs at me then his serious face is back. "Maybe you shouldn't have wine if you're feeling faint; you should have some food instead."

"No," I bark.

He smirks at me. "How about some orange juice?" I raise an eyebrow at him sardonically. "Ok, wine," he says, smiling and shaking his head at me.

Tristan pours us both a glass of wine and places them next to me on the breakfast bar. Then he picks up the other beanbag, walks out onto the patio and makes a makeshift lounger with the one I'd left out there. Then, he comes back to me with his arms open. I go to take his hands to stand, but he simply shakes his head and lifts me up into his arms.

I roll my eyes at him. "I can walk you know," I say dryly.

He smiles wryly at me. "Humour me." He walks outside and places me down on the beanbags, then he heads back inside and returns with our wine.

Placing them down on the floor next to the beanbags, he sits behind me, his back against the sliding door, his legs stretched either side of me, and pulls me gently against his chest.

"This ok?" he softly asks.

"Yes," I whisper. Handing a glass to me, he then picks up his glass and wraps his free arm around my waist. I feel contented, that warm glow flows through me from the dream again.

"This is nice," he whispers and takes a sip of wine.

"Yeah, it is." I agree. I really, really hope Tristan meant what he said; that he won't ask me about what happened earlier – because right now, I feel on top of the world. *What a difference to how I felt just a short while ago?*

WE SIT IN COMFORTABLE silence, both brooding I think, but the setting sun is a welcome distraction. I quietly sip my wine and try to keep my mind clear of all thoughts, good and bad. I watch the sky change from scorching oranges and blazing yellow, to a darker ominous mix of deep pinks, and aquamarines.

I decide the silence has become too deafening, so I rack my brains for something to say, other than the obvious. "Did you have a good week?" I ask.

"A good week?" He questions.

"Yes, when you left on Wednesday. Was it a productive week work wise?"

Tristan chuckles, kisses my temple, and thankfully starts telling me about what he's been doing for the few days we've been apart…

THE SUN HAS SET ON OUR perfect little piece of heaven, and the stars are out in full force. I shiver slightly, a cool breeze has picked up, so of course, my over-sensitive body has developed goosebumps all over.

"Cold?" Tristan asks, running his hand up and down my arm trying to generate some heat.

"A little," I answer.

"Want to go in? We could put the fire on?" He suggests.

"Won't you get too hot?" Tristan already feels toasty against me.

"I don't care. Whatever you want beautiful, it is yours." He says in that sexy, low voice.

"Ok I'm convinced, a fire would be nice." He stands, takes my hands and gently pulls me to my feet. "May I?" he asks, his arms open wide.

"Tristan, I'm fine now," I say trying to placate him.

"Coral' – "Tristan, I'm not feeling faint anymore, so you don't need to carry me into the house, ok?" His lips set into a hard line. I roll my eyes at him. "I need a bathroom break. Why don't you take the bean-bags in and get the fire going?" I suggest.

"Fine!" He huffs, then picks up the bags and heads inside. I smile internally at his overprotective ways. I collect our empty glasses, place them on the breakfast bar and head off to the downstairs bathroom. When I return I notice he has the fire going, its orange glow filling the room, creating a warm, romantic atmosphere.

"Mmm…that's nice," I say huddling in front of it, warming up my arms.

"Would you like a jumper?"

"No, I'm ok thanks."

Tristan comes and stands behind me, places his hands on my arms and gently rubs up and down. "You feel cold."

I close my eyes to the feeling. His skin against mine does strange things to me. It heats my blood and sets my heart racing. I don't understand it?

"I'll be fine," I breathe.

"Want a drink?" he asks. "I have a really nice Cognac?" he adds.

The same kind of brandy George gave me? *I'm in!*

"Yes please." I smile up at him, and there it is; that feeling.

I can feel it surrounding us, a strange bubble, like a bright white light, making me feel safe, turned on, dizzy with wanting and longing. Whatever it is, it's strong, really strong. Almost tangible, like I could reach out and touch it. The room is so dark, except for the orange glow of the fire, but I can't stop looking at him.

He smiles nervously at me then loses the grin. "Thank you for coming back, for trusting me."

I swallow hard. Is this just lust? Or do people really fall in love and feel like this about each other?

Tristan moves closer, his lips parting slightly and kisses me softly on the lips, then he runs a cool, soft finger down my cheek. "You are so beautiful."

I swear to god if he keeps saying that he's going to have me convinced that I am. I slowly exhale at his touch. It sears me, weakens me and at the same time, it makes me mad; because I don't want to fall in love, but I think it may already be too late.

"Shall we have some music?" I can't find my voice, so I nod my head. "I won't be a moment," he softly adds. Tristan returns with his MP3 Player and his portable speakers. "Why don't you find something," he says handing them to me.

"Ok." I smile shyly at him – *Why am I feeling shy again?*

Shaking my head at myself, I switch on the player and plug in the speakers. When it fires up, I notice it's a Cowon, the same as mine. It's freaky how many things we have that are the same. I start scrolling through his list of albums, and I'm gob-smacked– again! Tristan returns and sits on one of the beanbags, placing the Brandy's in front of the fire.

"This is freaky," I tell him, still scrolling through the albums.

"What is?" he asks.

"We have so many of the same albums," I answer.

"We do?" he says in surprise.

"Yeah, it's weird. What do you fancy?" I ask.

"There's a new album I put on yesterday, I made my own mix of songs." He smiles enigmatically at me. I pass him the player so he can find it.

"What?" I grin back.

"They all remind me of you," he tells me and presses play.

Gabrielle Aplin's soft voice fills the room with The Power Of Love – I feel all the blood drain out of my face. It's such a haunting, heavy track. Tristan picks up the Brandy's offering one to me. I shake my head at him, I don't want mine yet. He nods once and sits back on the beanbag, sipping his drink.

I stay sat, several feet away from Tristan, in the safe zone.

My backside hurts sitting on the cold, porcelain floor, but the fire is a welcome relief, warming my arms, my body. As I listen to the song, I feel myself getting overwhelmed–she sings this song so well.

I turn and gaze at Tristan, he's watching me carefully as he slowly sips his Brandy. I turn away and stare at the fire, watching the flames lick and bite each other, battling for the biggest flame.

I close my eyes, letting the song wash over me. *Is this what Tristan is to me?* Is he going to cleanse my dark soul? He's made it pretty clear what he feels for me. He wants to love me, protect me, be my hero, that much is obvious.

Love is an energy Gabrielle sings – *Yes, it is, one I don't know or understand, not like this.*

I wrap my arms around my legs and continue to stare at the fire. The song ends, and it's quickly followed by James Morrison's You Make it Real. It's a little more upbeat thank heavens; and my favourite song of his.

I turn and smile at Tristan.

"You like?" he asks.

I take a deep breath and crawl across the floor. He seems nervous as I approach him, but as I do, I slowly lean forward and kiss him, being careful not to get too carried away.

"My favourite," I whisper against his lips.

"Mine too." He murmurs, then kisses me back, his tongue slowly lapping against mine. I feel myself getting tearful and overwhelmed by the moment again. *What is wrong with me?*

"Oh, baby…" Tristan pulls me into his lap and wraps his arms around me.

"Sorry…" I choke. "I just can't get over…" I stop myself and take a deep breath.

"I know," he says, softly stroking my back. "This already feels very heavy and deep…permanent. Kind of took us both by surprise."

"Yeah…" I croak a little laugh escaping.

Tristan leans forward, picks up my glass, and hands it to me. "To us," He says.

"To us," I breathe, and we clink glasses. I lay against Tristan's chest again, enjoying the songs, and the sound of his heart beating in my ear.

"Coral, I have something for you." He says, his voice sounding nervous.

I turn my head and gaze up at him. "For me?" I squeak.

"Yes," he breathes. "I was going to give you this earlier…" He breaks off momentarily, a flash of pain crosses his face.

It makes me cringe inwardly, knowing I put it there. He reaches down beside him and picks up an A5 sized jewellery box. It's dark blue, brushed velvet, and it's got a big red bow on it.

CHAPTER TWO

I SIT UP FROM MY slumped position, my mouth gaping open and my heart slamming against my chest – *Shit! He's bought me a present!* – I hate presents.

Gladys and Debs have always been awful at this. Buying me things I either don't want or need, and the impossible moments that have to follow of saying thank you, and smiling as though you like it are cringe-worthy.

"Here," Tristan gestures for me to take it.

I look up at his warm eyes not really knowing what to do. Tristan gently takes hold of my hand and places the box in it. I can see the apprehension on his face, I feel myself tighten up with anxiety – *What if I don't like it?*

"Open it," he orders, his eyes crinkling sweetly at the corners.

Tentatively, I pull on the satin ribbon that's been tied into a bow and lift the lid. *Wow!*

I am both surprised and elated. Inside is a bracelet, a very old, antique looking bracelet. As I look closer, I see that it has dragons engraved on it. There are four segments, each with a dragon, and a Chinese symbol hanging down as a charm. It's quite chunky and is almost a gunmetal grey, just the kind of thing I like – I look up at Tristan in astonishment.

"How did you?' – "You have several dragon ornaments in your bedroom. I saw this and thought you might like it," he softly says.

I shake my head in wonder and smile at him. This is the first piece of jewellery I have been given that I will actually wear

– Gladys gave up years ago, after noticing I wouldn't wear what she bought me.

"It's antique. A miracle dragon bracelet, they're quite rare," he tells me.

I'm awestruck. Not only did he get the dragon part right, but I have a thing for antique jewellery. The stuff you see in most of the jewellers just seems same-o, same-o, to me. Antiques are just well…different. I peer down at the bracelet, I'm nervous to touch it, it looks so delicate.

"Here baby." Tristan takes it out of the box, and carefully clips it around my right wrist, it's a perfect fit.

"Tristan…I don't know what to say…thank you," I choke.

"Do you like it?" He questions.

"Yes," I gush, smiling down at it. "Thank you," I say again.

He lifts my chin to look at him. "You're very welcome, I'm really glad you like it," he says smiling broadly.

"Oh, I do…" I gush, then lean forward and softly kiss him.

He chuckles against my lips. "You really like it?" he says a little smugly.

"Yes, I do. How did you know I'd like an antique?" I ask, feeling a little dazed by it all.

"You don't wear any jewellery, and you're anything but traditional Coral, so I took a chance," he says wrapping his arms around my waist again.

"I love it," I tell him, gazing at it again. It's not to everyone's taste, but it's just so different. "What does the symbol mean?" I ask in wonder.

Tristan chuckles and kisses me again. "You're going to love this part," he says tucking my hair behind my ear.

"I am?" I say feeling giddy with excitement.

"Yes." He smiles his deep, wide-grinned sexy smile at me.

"Tell me," I squeak.

He reaches up and gently strokes my cheek. "Karma," he whispers. I lose the grin and swallow hard. *How can he get so much right with one piece of jewellery?*

"I…" I swallow again. "Is that just luck or..?"

Tristan shakes his head. "No. I liked the dragons, and I thought you would too, but when I was told the symbol meant Karma, I knew it was meant for you."

"That's just, wow...thank you," I gush again, feeling tears prick the corners of my eyes.

"Hey now, there's no need for that," he says, brushing the fallen tears away.

I reach up, lean my forehead against his and close my eyes – I still don't get what I've done to deserve him. "You're a wonderful man Tristan Freeman," I breathe.

He reaches up, puts his hands either side of my face and pulls my head up.

I open my eyes and gaze back at him.

"And you're a beautiful, challenging woman," he says. I smile, he smiles in return. I kiss him once more and lie back against him, staring down at my new bracelet. "I really like the quilt cover you picked," he tells me, pulling me from my musing.

"Yeah?" Tristan seems to like neutral colours – like me. So I picked mocha; it goes with the rest of the room.

"You must let me pay you back," he tells me.

I turn and look up at him. "I thought you said you wanted this to be *'our'* place?" I question.

"Well...yeah I did, but'- "No buts Tristan, you have to let me contribute," I tell him sternly.

"No!" he barks, I frown at him. "Coral, you have a mortgage and bills of your own to pay. Please don't get buying anything else for this place, it all comes out of my pocket. Understand?" Tristan is mad, his eyes have narrowed, and the way he's looking at me tells me there's no argument to be had.

"Fine!" I huff. *How ridiculous, I can't even buy anything for the house!*

"Which reminds me," he says, getting up and walking over to his suit jacket that's hanging on one of the breakfast stools. I watch him pull out his wallet and walk back over to me. Sitting down, he opens it up and pulls out a card. "Here, this is for you."

I cock one eyebrow up at him. "Why are you trying to give me one of your cards?"

"It's not mine," he tells me, opening my hand and placing the card in it.

I look down and see my name printed on it – *What the fuck?*

"Um...why...Tristan, what's going on? I don't understand?" I say, scowling at him.

"Anything you want just put it on that card, it's a joint account," he tells me artlessly.

"A what?" I gasp in shock. I can't believe he's done that! I wouldn't do that! Not from only knowing someone a few days, but then I do have trust issues. "Are you crazy?" I shriek. "You don't know me, yet you give me this card?" I shake my head at him, I can't believe...

"Coral, you want to buy something, anything...some clothes, pay a bill, or maybe you're out and you see something you like for this place, just use the card. Ok?"

I shake my head in wonder, I feel like I've been given the keys to the bank.

"I trust you," he tells me pulling my chin up, his eyes boring into mine.

"I still think you're crazy," I say, half choking on my own words.

Tristan chuckles at me. "I think I'm a pretty good judge of character, I don't see you running off with my millions," he says.

I roll my eyes at him. "Have you ever done this before?"

"No, well...apart from my folks," he answers, his voice soft with warm memories. "Want to see a picture of them?" he asks, his eyes crinkling at the corners.

"Of course," I say, wondering if it's going to upset him to do this. Tristan opens his wallet, pulls out a faded photograph and hands it to me.

It's a small, square, black and white photograph- *God knows how old it is!*

I handle it carefully and stare at the young couple smiling back at me with their arms wrapped around one another. Tristan looks just like his very handsome Grandfather, and his Granny is very pretty. Her hair is curled and pinned back, just as they all used to wear it back then, and she's smiling. Her eyes look bright, they both look so happy.

He hands me another. Tristan is in the photograph with them, he's in the middle with his arms wrapped around each of them. They are all smiling, they all look so happy. He looks younger though, maybe in his teens?

"When was this taken?" I ask softly.

"It was my 21st." He tells me, his eyes darkening. "I wish I'd have met you while they were still alive, they'd have loved you so much. I know they would," he says his voice breaking as he does, making my heart ache for him, I wish I could take his pain away.

"Tristan," I whisper putting my arm around his back and resting my head on his shoulder. I sit staring at the photos when suddenly inspiration hits. "Can I borrow these?" I ask.

Tristan frowns at my request. He doesn't seem to want to let them go, which is understandable.

"Not now," I add, handing them back.

"Sure," he says and places them back in his wallet.

"You look like your Grandfather," I tell him cheerfully, trying to lighten the mood. "And your Grandmother was so pretty, I can see why your Grandfather fell for her," I add.

Tristan smiles, but it doesn't reach his eyes. I feel nervous again, so I take a sip of my brandy. It warms and burns me, as it slowly makes it way to my stomach. I'm starting to feel a little drunk, my head is slightly spinning - *This is strong stuff.*

I gaze at Tristan who is staring blankly ahead at the fire, no doubt thinking about his folks. I try to understand what that would have felt like, to lose your parents at such a young age, even more so, to lose parents that loved and cherished you, took care of you. I want to take his pain away, to make him feel better. I move carefully and slide over him, so I'm straddling him.

He looks up at me in confusion. "Coral, what are you' - "I'm sorry," I whisper, placing my hands on his cheeks. I lean down and kiss him softly. "It's not fair," I add. Tristan doesn't say anything, he just gazes up at me. "I'm guessing you miss them, so much," I add.

"Yes, I do," he sighs, so I kiss him again, trying to take away his pain, but a flame ignites within me. I want to take this further, so I don't stop.

I kiss him more passionately forcing his lips apart, finding his tongue as a slight moan escapes me. Tristan seems very hesitant, then finally I hear a deep groan of longing reverberate from deep within him, his lips press harder against mine, and his breathing picks up.

He wraps his arms around me and crushes me hard against him, sending shivers all over my body. We roll onto the floor, Tristan on top of me, the length of his body stretched out on top of mine. I feel his erection hard and heavy against my abdomen, only this time, I don't freak out...*oh, I want him...so badly.*

I force my hands into his hair, pulling his lips harder against mine, then I wrap my legs around him, using my heels to push his backside, his erection deeper into me. I want to feel him inside me.

Tristan suddenly freezes. "Stop!" He shouts, staring down at me with dark eyes. He sits up, pulling me with him so I'm straddling him again.

We stare at each other, almost nose to nose, both panting heavily.

"Did I do something wrong?" I ask.

"No." He shakes his head. "I just...." He runs a hand through his hair then gazes at me for a moment. Without a word, he strokes my cheek, his face looks torn like he doesn't know what to say or do.

"What is it?" I ask placing my hand against his as it rests on my cheek.

"You freaked out earlier, then you left me," he says darkly. "I don't know why I just don't want you to feel like you have to do anything you're not ready to do' – I place my finger against his lips to silence him.

"I was ready then," I tell him, but he still looks concerned.

"I can't take that chance," he says, shaking his head.

"Take what chance?" I squeak.

"Of you, leaving me again," he breathes.

"But'– "Coral, I'm not going to do anything until you're ready to tell me." He says his voice firm, his dark chocolate eyes seeing straight through me.

I sigh heavily. "You're not going to let this go, are you?"

Tristan shakes his head at me. *Great!*

So he's not going to have sex with me unless I tell him why I freaked out earlier. I shake my head in annoyance. I don't want to tell him, but I want him, and I want it to stop. I want to stop freaking out about it.

"You're not going to like it," I tremble, pulling my gaze away from his.

"I want to know," he tells me softly. "You can tell me anything baby."

"You're going to regret you said that," I choke out nervously.

"Am I?" he says, gripping my face in his hands, so I have to look at him. His face is contorted as though he's in pain. "Tell me," he orders.

And just like that, all my defences fall down, and I blurt it out. "I was raped," I whisper.

Tristan's eyes narrow for a moment then widen with shock. In a flash, he is up on his feet glaring down at me. His jaw is set, his teeth grinding together, and his hands are clenched into fists; the tendons and veins in his forearms sticking up in response. His breathing is heavy, eyes dilated, almost black. He looks really, really, angry – *Shit!*

I can't let this come between us – I can't lose him because of this.

"Tristan," I beg holding my hand out to him. "Please don't let this change how you feel about me, I'm begging you." He silently holds up his forefinger in response, so I stop talking and wait.

Once his breathing has calmed down, he finally speaks to me. "Give me a minute," he says and storms off to the downstairs bathroom – *Fuck what have I done, I knew this would happen.*

I grip my head in my hands and start to rock myself. The angry tears are back, I fight against them, but they silently fall against my cheeks. It seemed like the right thing to do, George said I should tell him, and if we had ended up staying together, I know I would have eventually told him – *Fuck, what have I done?*

Strong arms envelop me from behind. I snap my head up just as Tristan crushes me to him, so hard, in fact, I have to tell him.

"Tristan...c-can't....b-b-breath....." He relaxes his grip a little but still says nothing. My heart slowly relaxes, he came back, I haven't lost him – *Well, at least I don't think I have?*

"Tristan," I whisper, turning around and gripping onto his vest, crushing myself harder against him. "Please...say something."

He doesn't respond with words. He just crushes me harder against him, his arms wrapped tightly around me, and starts rocking me back and forth, staring blankly into the fire.

"Don't feel sorry for me," I croak.

He freezes, then glares down at me. "What? What kind of thing is that to say?" he asks in astonishment.

"I...I just don't want it to change how you feel for me," I squeak out.

"Well, it has!" He answers sharply, gripping me tighter.

I wrap my arm around his neck, caressing the hair at the nape of his neck. "Please come back to me," I whisper kissing his ear, his sideburn, his cheek.

Tristan looks down at the floor, then back at the fire, contemplating his response.

Finally, he glares back at me. "I want to know who. I want to know when. I want to know everything. His name, what he looked like, everything...you will tell me," he says, his voice low and menacing.

My breath catches in my throat – *Does Tristan have a dark side?*

"I' – "Coral!" Tristan shakes his head, so subtlety than it sends a shiver of fear running down my spine.

"Ok, you're scaring me now," I choke, wanting to get up and out of his arms.

His eyes slowly close, and he takes several deep breaths to calm himself. "I'm sorry," he softly says. He opens his eyes, and I can see my Tristan is back, his eyes the colour of milk chocolate.

"It's ok," I answer, kissing him lightly on the lips, but he doesn't reciprocate. I pull back, frowning deeply at him, at his behaviour. Feeling angry, I scramble out of his arms and up onto my feet. "So this is it! This is how it's going to be? I let you in, opened my heart to you, and this is your reaction? I knew I shouldn't have come back, I knew I shouldn't have told you!" I screech as I pace up and down, my hands clenched into fists.

Tristan stands in one fluid movement and moves towards me. "Coral," he reaches his hand out to me.

"Stay away from me," I choke, turning my back on him.

He doesn't want me. So this is what rejection feels like? My legs tremble, and I hit the floor, choking back angry tears. I feel his arms wrap around me again, my back to his front. I try to struggle free, but it's useless.

"Stop Coral...stop! I'm sorry baby. I reacted badly, that was the last thing I expected to hear," he says, trying to soothe me. "Please baby, calm down...please." Tristan squeezes me tighter.

"Coral, listen to me. Nothing's changed, nothing's changed at all. Please believe me, I still want you, I still want to be with you. I just didn't know how to handle..." Tristan breaks off again.

I finally turn my head, and our eyes meet. I can see his anguish, his pain for me. I turn my body around and launch myself against his chest.

His arms wrap around me, making me feel safe and secure. "I'm so sorry baby," he whispers into my ear.

I close my eyes and surrender to the feeling. I've never allowed myself to be vulnerable with anyone besides George, so I relish the feeling and let a few stray tears fall. For some reason, I know it's ok, and Tristan isn't going to turn me away. If anything, he'll be more protective of me. I'm starting to realise I kind of like that.

"I still want you to tell me," he croaks, rocking me gently.

"I think it's best' – "Coral' – "No don't Coral me," I argue leaning back to look at him. "It happened two years ago on a Sunday night, he said he was from London, but I doubt that anything he told me was true' – "Do you remember his name?" He sternly interrupts.

I close my eyes for a second. "I didn't tell you so you could drill it out of me you know," I say gritting my teeth.

Tristan sighs heavily. "But we might be able to catch him' –"He did give a name," I interrupt. "But when I looked him up, there was no one by that name living in any area of London."

Tristan exhales slowly, gritting his teeth in annoyance.

"Believe me, I checked just in-case I did find him. Besides, you know how the system works, even if we catch him it's my word against his, and it happened so long ago Tristan, there's no evidence…" I drift off.

Tristan winces knowing exactly what I mean. "If we find him, it doesn't have to go through the system. I'll make his life hell, he'll wish he'd never been born. If I find the fucker, I'll have him tortured, they can knee-cap him first then slowly pull his fucking fingernails off, one by one!" he rants.

"Stop," I shout. "Please no more," I say weakly.

I don't want to think or talk about him anymore. I stare back at Tristan's big chocolate eyes, I can see he's still angry about it. His jaw tenses several times, then he looks down at the floor, takes a deep breath, and slowly exhales it.

"Better?" I ask.

"No, not really," he says looking down at me. "But no more," he adds repeating my words.

I close my eyes in relief. I feel Tristan pull me to him, crushing me against his body again.

"Thank you," I whisper.

"Oh baby," he coos, rocking me again, then he takes my hand and leads me over to the beanbags. We sit watching the fire again, quietly sipping more brandy. Tristan hasn't said anything more about it, which I'm thankful for. I don't want to re-live it, I don't want to remember – I just want to get better.

I WAKE UP STARTLED. It's pitch black outside, so the only light is from the fire that's still on, keeping us warm. Tristan's music is still playing. Rumer is singing Slow. I turn and see Tristan is softly sleeping. *Wow, he looks so cute and sexy at the same time!*

As I watch him sleeping, I listen to the words of the song. I wonder if this is how I make Tristan feel because it's how he makes me feel, word for word. Suddenly, his eyes flutter open, and he gazes up at me. I smile, feeling shy that he caught me watching him; he silently reaches up and strokes my cheek.

"You ok?" He croaks.

"Yes, we fell asleep," I whisper.

"Yeah, I guess we did." He smiles, then yawns.

"Come on, let's go to bed." I stand and hold my hands out to him, he smiles enigmatically at me, places his hands in mine, and I pull him to his feet.

"Why don't you go up," he says. "I'll switch everything off."

"I'll stay," I whisper, not wanting to be apart from him. I don't like big houses with dark rooms, they scare me.

He cocks his head to the side. "You don't want to go up?"

"No, not without you," I whisper.

"Why?" He asks, his eyebrows pulled together.

I stare down at the floor. "I don't like dark, empty places, reminds me of being a kid." I shudder slightly and wrap my arms around myself.

Tristan frowns and nods once. "I can understand that," he softly says.

I smile up at him, feeling shy again. His eyes darken, and

that magnetic pull fills my stomach again. Slowly, he reaches out, takes my face in his hands and softly kisses me, making my stomach flutter madly, then he lets go, bends down, and switches of the fire and the music.

Taking my hand, we pad into the kitchen. "Would you like a glass of water?" He asks.

"Please." He fills two glasses and hands one to me. "Oh! My bags," I squeak, remembering them.

"I'll get them," he says passing me his water. I watch Tristan walk across the hallway, pick up my overnight bag, my handbag, and walk back over to me.

"I have to say, it doesn't suit you," I giggle.

"What?" He questions.

"The handbag," I say cocking an eyebrow up.

He looks down at the bag on his shoulder. "Yes, I have to agree, here." He pulls the bag off his shoulder and hands it to me. I throw it over my shoulder and giggle up at him.

"Yes, definitely suits you more," he says leaning down to kiss me. I can't help giggling again. "I love that sound," he adds.

"What sound?" I laugh.

"You, giggling, it's very sweet," he says, tucking my hair behind my ear, then he leans down and kisses my forehead. "Shall we?" he says, gesturing for me to go first.

"Yes." I smile up at him, and we silently head up the stairs.

As we reach the master suite, Tristan flicks the light on. I eye the big bed with renewed appreciation. Placing my glass on the floor, I collapse onto the bed and smile. *Mmm, it's so comfortable.* Tristan reaches into his overnight bag and pulls out two glass looking objects, flicks them in his hands, and they start to glow, like candles.

"What are those?" I question.

"Electronic candles." He smiles wryly at me.

"You and technology," I chuckle.

"Well…there safer than candles, and they last a long time." He says as he switches off the main light.

The room suddenly takes on a warm, romantic atmosphere. Tristan smiles at me then heads off to the bathroom. I lie on my back staring up at the ceiling, watching the strange shadows flickering from the candles. The bathroom door opens, and Tristan comes walking over to me, stripping his vest as he does, and throws it on the floor. *Wow, he really is an Adonis.* He has the perfect v shape and no chest hair, his body is just so…perfect. He must work out a lot.

My heart starts to beat erratically, just as butterflies swarm in my stomach and in that moment, I know – I'm going to bed him, and I don't feel nervous about it –*I want him so badly, and I want him now* – I've decided.

Sliding off the bed, I make my way to the bathroom. I quickly brush my hair and strip my sweats off. Then I pad back into the bedroom. Tristan is lying on his back, watching me walk towards him.

"You're a sight for sore eyes," he tells me in that sexy husky voice of his.

I reach the bed, and without a word, I straddle him; he looks so confused.

"Coral, what are you' - "I want you," I tell him. "So badly," I add leaning down to kiss him hard, forcing his lips apart, lapping my tongue against his.

I run my hands across his chest, down his abdomen and into his sweats, my eyebrows raise in surprise. "Commando." I smile.

"Yeah," he croaks.

"I like that," I tell him, kissing him again.

"Coral…" Tristan takes hold of both my wrists and sits up, so we are nose to nose. "Don't do this because' – "Stop!" I say. "And let go." Tristan instantly releases my wrists. I can see he is very, very hesitant about this, so I decide to give him a challenge. Taking a deep breath, I rest my hands on his broad shoulders.

"Tristan," I whisper closing my eyes for a moment. "I love you," I say opening them up to see his reaction. He looks shocked, in awe, and kind of schoolboy bashful that he would hear this from me.

"I haven't with anyone since…and that was two years ago. I'd really like to replace all those negative emotions, with positive ones, and I want you to be the one to do it. I know you can, I love you, I trust you, I feel so safe and protected with you, and I'm so crazy about you. I have been from the very beginning…" I shake my head at myself, surprised at what I am saying, but I can tell Tristan is still hesitant.

"If I had a pound for every time I've pictured you naked, I swear I'd be a very rich woman by now." I add.

Tristan's lips quirk up at the corners, as he stares back at me in wonder.

"Please," I beg. "I want this, and I want you more than I've ever wanted anyone in my entire life." I can see I'm getting through to him, but he's stalling.

"Coral' - "Please…" I beg again and start kissing him. Tristan's tongue laps slowly and smoothly against mine, I pull back and stare down at him. "Don't hold back," I tell him. "Be like you would be if I hadn't told you." Grabbing hold of my vest top, I pull it up and yank it over my head.

Tristan stares down at my full breasts, my nipples standing to attention just aching for his touch. I take his hand and place it over my right breast then lean down and kiss him again, he doesn't resist.

I close my eyes and before I know it I am lost, lost in the moment and the feeling of his hands making smooth, soft movements across my breasts, my shoulders, down my back, his lips kissing me all over. It's exquisite and heady and warming and sexy, I instantly moisten down below. I hear his moans of pleasure as he lifts me and squeezes my backside, moving us so that I'm lying down and he is on top of me.

I moan out loud to the sensation of his lips kissing every part of me and his warm breathe against my skin, especially my breasts. His lips and tongue gently tease my nipples, they harden and elongate with his touch, his hands slide down my body and smoothly remove my lacy shorts, then he spreads my legs apart
– Holy crap, I've never had oral before!

"You are so beautiful baby, such soft skin," he murmurs.

I'm panting and quivering for him, I want him so badly. Then his hot breath is on me, between my legs, his tongue gently lapping against my clitoris.

"Tristan," I moan and buck my body, my head craned back. I can feel I'm building…so quickly. How, how is that possible, is this how it's supposed to be?

"Oh god…" I groan, just as I'm about to climax he stops and gently blows on me. And that's all it takes – The most mind-blowing orgasm rips through me, I completely lose who I am, and it doesn't stop, it just keeps going on and on.

My eyes roll into the back of my head....I shake and shudder as I slowly come back down to earth. *Whoa! What was that?* I've never felt like that before, that was…..amazing! *Oh Tristan, the power you yield over me…*

Then it hits me, I just had non-penetrative sex, and I didn't freak out. Unwelcome tears start to flow against my cheeks. I think it's relief, letting go…*oh, Tristan…* I bring my hands up and hide my face, I feel so stupid for crying.

"Baby!" Tristan gasps, I am up and into his arms in a heartbeat.

"Sorry," I sniff, cradling my head under his chin.

"Don't be," he whispers.

I look up into his deep eyes. "Don't stop," I choke. "I want you inside me, I want to feel you," I sniff.

Tristan kisses me from the corner of my eye, down my cheek until he reaches my mouth, my tears quickly subside as my lips part for his tongue, his taste, he moans as he kisses me more ardently. I can feel his erection between my legs, straining against his sweats, teasing me. I slowly rub up and down against him, he moans with pleasure, then pulls back from kissing me, panting hard.

We stare at each other for a moment, some unspoken truth passing between us. Then he stands, reaches into his bag, throws a condom on the bed and swiftly removes his sweats. My chin almost hits the floor; seeing him in all his naked glory is something to behold.

Damn, he's sexy!

Kneeling on the bed, he rips the packet open and carefully places the condom on his mighty fine manhood. "Are you sure about this?" he questions.

I nod silently to him, feeling nervous again.

He pulls me onto his lap. "Say it," he orders.

"Yes, I want this, I want you," I say, but my voice is shaking, giving me away.

He closes his eyes and tenses his jaw. I reach up and caress his cheek.

"Please…" I whisper. "Before I get too nervous…" I add.

His eyes flash open. "Hold on to me," he says.

I wrap my arms around his muscular shoulders, we stare at

each other, our lips inches apart. I feel the tip of his erection at the opening of my sex. I gasp and try to grind against him.

He instantly stills me. "Slowly baby," he softly scolds.

I nod once keeping my eyes locked on his. Then, slowly, very slowly, he eases himself into me, scrutinising my face as he does. He keeps going until his full length is buried deep inside me, filling me completely. *I was right he does fit me like a glove.*

He feels amazing. This feels amazing. I'm on cloud nine.

"Ok?" He questions.

"Yes," I pant.

"More?" He asks.

"Yes…please," I whimper, urging him to move. He starts up a steady, slow rhythm. I reach down and kiss him, teasing his tongue with mine. My hips start to sway to their own beat, moving in time against him, causing more friction…*oh shit!*

I can feel it building within me…again…so quickly. Tristan slowly picks up the pace. The feeling is beyond anything I could have imagined. *Is this what it's supposed to feel like?* I throw my head back in ecstasy and keep up the relentless rhythm. *Oh, baby, you can do this to me all night long.*

"Oh, baby…" Tristan moans, I look down and watch him moving in and out of me, it's so sexy, so hot. His cheeks start to flush, our eyes catch again, and I can tell he's close. I feel myself tighten, then tighten some more.

"Oh god…" I grip his shoulders with my hands. There are no more words. I'm just sensation and feeling. I feel like every cell in my body is about to explode, and I climax loudly, screaming out his name.

"Sorry," I pant, feeling guilty, yet still moving.

"Don't be," he grunts as he moves slightly, and picks up the pace. "Oh Coral…" He moans, moving in and out of me. "You feel so good, baby." I feel myself building again, and cry out as we both climax together and fall down onto the bed. *Oh my god!*

CHAPTER THREE

WE LIE FACE TO FACE, both panting and coming down from our lovemaking. Tristan pulls me closer to him, studying my face, and gently running his knuckle across my cheek.

"Are you ok?" he asks in a deep, worried voice.

I grin from ear to ear.

Tristan chuckles slightly and kisses me. "Are you sure?" he asks, losing the grin.

"Tristan you should know me by now. Do you think I would hold back if I weren't ok?" I say stroking his cheek, my eyes pleading with his. He looks mollified, but I can't be totally sure. "What's going on in that head of yours?" I ask.

"Loads," he blurts.

I frown back at him.

He gently kisses the tip of my nose, slides off the bed and walks into the bathroom, when he returns his condom has disappeared, but his erection hasn't.

I grin up at him.

"Can't," he says, answering my unspoken question. "No more condoms," he adds pulling the quilt back and slipping inside. "Come on," he says tapping my backside lightly. "Get under the covers, you'll get cold."

I have to agree, I will, so I get inside.

Tristan lies on his back and holds his arm out waiting for me, as I place my head on his shoulder, he puts his arm around me and starts stroking my back and across my shoulders. I place my hand on his chest and softly stroke his smooth, marbled, perfectly defined pectorals. Then I panic. What if that was as good for him as it was for me?

Oh god, I hope he says yes!

I look up at him and instantly lose my train of thought. Tristan is staring up at the ceiling, deep in thought.

"I'm fine," I tell him firmly.

He looks down at me and stares back for a couple of seconds, I can see he still looks a little nervous, apprehensive, then he stares up at the ceiling again.

"More than fine actually, I've never had it so good…" I stop and think about it, nope not even after climaxing with Justin, I never felt this good. "I didn't know it *could* feel this good," I add, pleading for him to understand.

"Why didn't you tell me earlier?" he asks, his tone sharp.

"Tell you what?" He pulls his arm from underneath me and leans up onto his elbow, so he's hovering over me, then he cocks one eyebrow up at me – *Oh that!*

"Do you think it's something I'm proud of?" I gripe. "I made a mistake, a stupid mistake and it cost me." I bite. *Why is he asking about this now?*

Tristan sighs deeply and closes his eyes for a moment.

"Besides," I grin, feeling ecstatic. "I didn't freak out!"

"Freak out?" he says darkly. *Ok, so how do I put this?*

"I talked to George about you, from the very moment we met, I knew I wanted you, but I wasn't sure how I could even begin to…to have something, to be with you sexually. Sometimes I have nightmares about what happened," I quietly admit.

"Fuck!" He hisses and squeezes his eyes shut. When he opens them, I can see they are full of turmoil. He leans down and presses his lips hard against mine; it's just not painful.

"I guess it's not something that's easy to say," he murmurs against my lips.

"No, it wasn't. I was afraid…afraid that if we were going well and I told you, I'd lose you," I admit.

"That's not going to happen Coral," he softly scolds.

"Why did you react the way you did? You scared me."

"I know, and I'm sorry about that, I just…if I could find him…" Tristan drifts off again.

"Don't," I say pressing my finger to his lips.

"Did you go to the police?" he asks, taking my fingers in his. "Report it?" *Here we go!*

"No." I gaze down at his bare chest.

He gasps in shock. "Why the hell not Coral?" he snaps, lifting my chin, so I have to look at him.

"I told you, I tried to find him but…I think everything he said to me was a lie," I whisper.

Tristan grits his teeth. "So I'll never find him," he hisses.

"I don't think so," I answer. "But like I said, even if I did know who he was, you know how the system works, it would have been my word against his…" I sigh heavily. "I know that sounds bad, he could be doing the exact same thing to some other girl right now, but it's who I am and how I handle things. I'm very good at blocking out bad things that happen, repressing them."

Tristan closes his eyes and pinches his nose, then he sighs heavily, and gazes down at me. "Did you tell anyone?" I shake my head. "You went through it alone?" he gasps in horror.

"I had no choice," I tell him.

"What do you mean? You have Gladys, your sister!" he barks. I can see he's angry again.

"Tristan don't…please, I…I think to be fair, I was in shock," I whisper.

He shakes his head in exasperation at me. How do I make him understand that what happened then, was nothing compared to what happened to me as a child?

"I find it hard to….to open up to people. I'm very private," I say sheepishly.

"You didn't trust your mother or sister?" he snaps questioningly.

"Adopted mother and sister," I clarify sarcastically.

"Don't be a smart arse," he scolds. "And stop trying to change the subject!" he barks.

I shake my head in exasperation. "Fine! I tried to handle it on my own for a few weeks, it happened just before I got the studio. I figured I could handle it, then I realised I wasn't coping so well, so that's when I found George." I blurt out.

"And he knows?" He questions.

I nod my head. "I couldn't tell him straight away, I was too…ashamed," I whisper.

"Well if you didn't talk about that right away, what did you talk about?"

Shit! Me and my big mouth! – I suddenly feel trapped. I don't want Tristan to know about that part of my past. I don't want him to know how much of a freak I am, or at least, that I feel like it.

"Other things," I whisper, staring out into space.

"Like what?" I try to struggle out of his arms. "Why do I get the feeling that there's more?" he asks sharply.

"Tristan don't, ok!" I snap. "You know more about me than anyone else ever has. Can't you just be satisfied with that?"

Tristan glares back at me.

I pull him close to me again. "Please Tristan, I don't want to fight. I know that must have been a shock to hear, and you probably feel really angry about it' – "More like helpless," he interrupts, his voice acerbic, his eyes staring back at me with a look I've never seen before. I can't quite put my finger on it. Is it pity, remorse, hate?

"I just…I want to make you safe," he tells me in a softer tone.

"You do!" I try to reason with him, but I can see a veil creeping over his face. "Please don't pull away from me," I whisper. "Don't shut down on me."

"What do you expect?" he answers sharply. "You won't let me in, it's very frustrating."

"There's nothing you can do anyway, except to keep loving me and being with me the way you have been. I feel like the luckiest girl in the world, don't spoil it."

"Spoil it?" he spits. *That's it, I'm done. I want to go home!*

Pulling out of his arms, I get out of bed, pick up my clothes and head towards the bathroom, but Tristan stops me by wrapping his arms around me.

"I'm sorry," he whispers, squeezing me tight. "Don't go." He turns me around and stares down at me, then softly strokes my cheek. "Stay," he whispers, gently running his knuckle down my cheek.

"No, you need some time to process this and' – "I'm sorry, stay… please," he interrupts.

Leaning down he presses his lips hard against mine - it's almost painful again. "Please, don't leave me again," he murmurs against my lips, the tremble in his voice makes my resolve instantly falter.

"Ok," I whisper, feeling exhaustion wash over me.

I guess no sleep, and no food over the past couple of days is finally catching up with me. I feel like I could sleep through the whole weekend. I walk around the bed, dropping my clothes on the floor, and climb under the quilt.

We both lie on our sides gazing at each other, not touching.

"I wish I could take it away," he whispers.

"You do, you just don't know you do."

"How?"

"By being you, by loving me the way you do. It makes all the bad things kind of disappear."

His mouth pops open in shock. "*All* the bad things?" *Damn it!*

"Tristan," I grumble. He's getting closer to figuring it out, and I don't want him to. "Can we talk about something else," I say frustratingly.

"Like what?" He says, slightly bemused.

"How about how good that was?" I say grinning cheekily at him. His dimples deepen, and his lips twitch fighting back a smile, but his eyes are still dark and brooding. "And we've only just begun," I say, closing my eyes.

Then I remember my original question. *Shit, what if it wasn't that good for him?*

My eyes flash open meeting his. "It...it was good for you too, right?" I question.

"Coral." Tristan closes his eyes in frustration and runs his hand through his hair. When he opens his eyes, he leans closer to me, takes my face in his hands and gently kisses me. "Better than I've ever known it with anyone else," he admits. I scan his face trying to detect the lie, but I can't see anything that would make me think otherwise. I close my eyes and let that answer sink in.

Tristan squeezes me harder, pulling me closer to his solid muscled body. "So you love me," he whispers into my ear.

I smile, keeping my eyes closed. *This is a far better conversation.*

"Yeah, god knows why?" I joke.

"I don't know why either," he exhales. *What?*

"What?" My eyes flash open. "Tristan that was a joke," I admonish.

"You could have any man you want, and you pick me?" He says in astonishment.

"I don't want anyone else but you," I whisper, trying to convince him of how I feel, his arms tighten around me. "Sounds like I'm not the only one with issues," I say observantly.

God knows why he would have issues. He's loving, caring, sweet, clever, handsome, has a body to die for, plus he's got a thriving business that's made him very wealthy. I just don't get it. What exactly does he think he's lacking? It's not love. So what is it?

I decide to mull it over in the morning when I'm more straight headed. I can think more clearly and get it out of him, somehow. *Whoa!* – I suddenly understand Tristan's perspective of me. How frustrating it is, to not know something about that person, to have them hold a secret that they won't tell you? I sigh heavily, maybe someday....someday I'll tell him.

I sleepily open my eyes and stare up at him. "See you in the morning," I say, yawning involuntarily.

Tristan smiles, but I can see he's still deep in thought. I find myself drifting off, I've never felt so relaxed, so safe and protected; it's a beautiful feeling.

"Tristan…" I murmur.

"Yeah baby," he answers huskily, stroking my hair, my shoulders.

"We need to get a really big pack of condoms tomorrow," I drawl, sleep taking me before I can hear his reply…

I WAKE UP TO A flood of sunshine filling the room. My first thought is of Tristan, turning over I reach out to him, only to find he is not there. I lunge forward searching the room for him, listening intently for any sound, any movement, the room is silent except for my shallow breathing. My heart sinks, then I notice a piece of paper lying on his side of the bed, reaching over I pick it up...

Gone to get breakfast, be back soon.
Stay where you are beautiful. Tristan Xxx

I'm instantly flooded with a warm, homely feeling. How sweet of him, but I wish he'd have woken me before he left, that scared me for a second. Stepping out of bed, I wonder idly what time it is.

As I look out through the ceiling height window, I see the sun is high up in the sky, so I know it can't be too early.

I pad along the bedroom, into the bathroom, and clean myself up after last night's sex. Once I'm done, I walk over to the double sinks and wash my hands, yawning widely as I do, then I look up at myself – *Holy crap!*

I have panda eyes from my mascara smudging, and my hair is standing up all over the place, what a sight! – I'm really glad Tristan *hasn't* seen me like this, it's really not attractive! – I wash my face twice, removing all traces of make-up, clean my teeth and brush the knots out of my hair. Staring back at myself, I feel satisfied that I look half decent, and make my way back to bed.

As I lie on the bed waiting for Tristan's return, I re-run the events of last night through my mind. I remember him showing me the photos of his folks, the idea I had springs to mind again and I wonder if it's something I can get done one of the days next week, maybe on my lunch hour? Then I sigh heavily, I have to deal with Susannah next week, Tristan said she is nice, but I know what I'm like, it's not going to be easy.

Then I think about the fact that for the first time in two years, I had sex, and I didn't freak out – well I kind of did the first time – but either way, I didn't the second time. A slight shudder runs through me as I recall walking out on him – I quickly banish the thought.

I close my eyes and think about us making love, Tristan was warm and soft and gentle and a million miles away. I sigh again knowing that is the truth of it. Well, we're going to do far more practising this weekend, so hopefully, he'll see that I'm ok. In fact, I think he did do some good as far as replacing the memories go, the feelings and the emotions, but I'm still not sure if Tristan is going to be the same with me as before, he seemed so distant after I told him that I'd been...I can't even bring myself to say the word – I can't believe I told him.

I shudder remembering his reaction, and how I felt when I thought he didn't want me anymore, that was scary and has made me realise some home truths, what I've been denying admitting to myself.

I know now, that no matter what I simply cannot lose him. I cannot be without him. He is my life now. And I know that only a few days ago, that level of commitment, of being intimate with someone, scared me half to death, but it's been overtaken by the feeling of losing him, so for me, that is now more scary than committing to this, to us.

I sit up and gaze out at the sparkling blue ocean. It's another beautiful day. I sigh blissfully. *Who'd have thought I'd be feeling like this?*

I think about synchronicity, how everything seemed to fall into place at exactly the right time so that Tristan could make his way into my life. Joyce leaving, Rob disappearing, colliding with Lily, if it weren't for all those things happening, I'd be sat in my studio right now, bored and lonely, denying to myself that I wanted someone in my life, constantly convincing myself that I was better off on my own, when the truth is, I'm not, at all.

I shake my head in wonder. Then I get a flashback of Tristan gazing up at me as he moved inside me. Desire explodes within me, I want him again, now. I hear movement downstairs.

He's back!–*Such good timing!*

"Coral," Tristan calls out. He sounds like he's running up the stairs.

"Morning baby," I shout back. I hear Tristan chuckle. Then he walks in with a bag and two take-out cups.

"Good morning sleepyhead." He smiles his deep dimpled smile at me.

I can't help swooning at him. He's wearing his sweats from last night, a pair of trainers and a white t-shirt that moulds to his broad shoulders and strong muscled arms, but most of all, what hits me more than anything, is his just shagged, dishevelled looking hairdo – *God he looks good!*

"Hey sexy," I reply flirtatiously.

Tristan chuckles kicks off his trainers and joins me on the bed. I instantly feel very naked as he sits there fully dressed, he leans towards me and kisses me softly on the lips.

"Hi," he says croakily.

"Hi," I say feeling shy.

He chuckles. "A cappuccino for the lady," he says handing one to me.

"Thanks," I squeak.

I take it from him, lean over to place it on the floor, and that's when I spy my lacy shorts and vest top, I pick them up and shove them under the quilt. Tristan stops what he's doing, and cocks his head to the side, his lips quirking up at the corners. "What are you doing?" he chuckles.

"Um...." I feel like I'm blushing as he sits there appraising me. "Nothing," I say pulling my vest top on and scrambling under the quilt to get my shorts on.

Then I kick the quilt off me, crawl along the bed to him and kiss him hard. All I want to do is have him over, and over again. I am not interested in food –at all.

"Hey," he chuckles, running his hand down my cheek. "Can we eat first?"

"You're hungry?" I grumble.

"Yes." He answers pulling out a large Styrofoam box and handing it to me with a pair of plastic knives and forks, then he does the same for himself. I watch him open his box, which reveals a full English breakfast. Tristan dives into the bag and pulls out two white bags and hands one to me. "Toast," he says in explanation.

Opening his bag up, he takes a bite of his toast and starts digging into his breakfast. That's when I know we need to fit food shopping in at some point today. I have to get back to my healthy eating.

"Please eat Coral," he tells me between mouthfuls. "I can tell you've already lost a couple of pounds, I don't want you wasting away or getting ill." *Damn it, how could he tell?*

"Oh, I can tell," he says, spookily reading me.

I look up at him and see that he's stopped eating, and has one eyebrow cocked up, just like me. I stifle a giggle and open my box, expecting to have the same, but yet again, Tristan has thought of what I like, and it definitely isn't a full breakfast. Instead, I have an omelette.

I smile broadly at him. "Thank you," I lean forward and kiss his cheek. Then start digging in, feeling ravenous. Mmm mushroom and spinach omelette, it is delicious, and just what I need after not eating much over the past few days.

"Breakfast in bed," I smile, thinking how nice this is. "No-one's ever done that for me," I add, my voice sounding unintentionally sad.

Tristan looks astonished. "Seriously?" he says his eyes wide.

I shrug. "What about you?" I ask between mouthfuls. Tristan instantly looks uncomfortable, his cheeks flushing slightly. "Ah, you have," I say guessing right.

"Yes." He reluctantly answers.

"And who was the lucky lady?" I ask teasingly. He raises one eyebrow at me. "You don't want to tell me?" I scowl.

"Not really," he answers darkly, still frowning.

"Why not?" I whisper. *Do I really want to know?*

"Because it turned out she was..." Tristan breaks off, his cheeks flushing red. I'm starting to notice he does that when he gets mad about something, but I think we've been through enough since last night, so I decide to drop it.

"Tristan, don't worry about it, please." He looks across at me, I smile tentatively at him. "This is an awesome omelette," I say in appreciation, trying to change the subject.

"I'm glad you like it," he muffles between forkfuls.

I look across at Tristan's box and I'm astonished to see he's almost finished – I wish he wouldn't do that – I feel like I should stop too.

"What?" he asks, putting his empty box in the take-out bag.

"You eat really fast," I say taking another bite.

"I do when I'm hungry," he admits.

"It's not good for you, you know."

"I know."

"I hate eating on my own," I say hoping he'll take this on board.

"Then I shall endeavour to slow down," he says, smiling his cheeky grin, his dimples deepening.

I shake my head at him and chuckle. As I take the final mouthful of my omelette, Tristan whips the box from underneath me and stuffs it into the bag. Then he holds his hand out for my knife and fork, I silently give them to him, he seems in a hurry, and I don't know why.

"You seem in a rush," I say taking a sip of my drink.

"That's because they'll be here in an hour," he tells me.

"Who will?" I ask, wondering what he means.

Tristan cocks one eyebrow up, grinning from ear to ear. "The delivery guys," he says.

Shit - I forgot all about them, I go to fling myself out of bed.

"Relax Coral," he says launching himself on top of me. "I had other plans before they arrive," he adds sexily, his eyes glinting wickedly. He kisses me hard on the lips. It takes a couple of seconds for my brain to register what he means.

Pulling back from me, Tristan reaches over to the other side of the bed and launches his hand up in the air, smiling down at me with his most sexy, panty-combusting smile.

I look up and see he has a very large box of condoms in his hand. "You remembered," I giggle, wriggling underneath him.

"It was the first thing on my mind this morning, having you again, you sexy, brave girl."

My heart hammers against my chest. "I'm not brave Tristan," I whisper.

"Oh yes you are," he argues.

I roll my eyes at him and smile. "So you want to have me again?" I tease.

"Yes." His eyes dilate as we gaze at one another.

"So take me," I challenge.

"I want you to tell me something first." He softly says. My smile instantly fades. *What does he want to know now?*

I bite my bottom lip, nervously. "Ok," I whisper.

"If I do anything…anything that makes you feel uncomfortable' – I press my finger to his lips, feeling relieved. "I know what you're asking, and yes, I will tell you," I tell him firmly.

"Give me your word," he adds.

"Tristan," I moan. He's lying on top of me, his erection pressing into my belly, it's turning me on, big time – I just want him, less talk, more action.

"Say it," he snaps.

"Ok!" I breathe my hands held up. "I give you my word."

"Good." His mouth swoops down on mine, pushing my lips apart, claiming me, possessing me. *Whoa! This is different to last night. He's definitely not holding back!*

He pulls my vest over my head, I yank his t-shirt off and try to kiss his chest, his shoulders, but he shakes his head at me and pushes me down. Then his mouth is on my nipples, sucking them slowly, making them hard and elongated again – *Jesus, I didn't know you could feel it down there when*…He tugs a little harder on my right nipple, it feels exquisite.

"Tristan," I gasp aloud, almost climaxing.

"Oh Coral, you're so beautiful." He breathes.

He gently caresses my breasts in his soft hands, then starts kissing down my torso, his hands softly following, caressing every part of me. Then taking me by surprise he flips me over, gently moves my hair out of the way and starts kissing the back of my neck, sending shivers all the way down my spine.

"You have such beautiful skin, so soft." He says.

I can feel his erection digging against my backside. I close my eyes and moan aloud, this is exquisite, Justin was never like this with me – *Shut up Coral!* – I push that thought away and concentrate.

"I'm going to kiss every inch of you," he adds, making me swoon.

Tristan moves again, kissing across my shoulders, down my back. He works his way down, kissing and nipping along my backside, and moves all the way down my legs, running his hands up and down, leaving soft, wet kisses as he does.

My whole body is on fire.

When he reaches my feet, he kisses along the arch of each foot, then he works his way back up, he moves up to my hips and flips me over again. Then slowly and seductively, keeping his eyes on mine, he peels off my shorts. *Oh wow, he's so sexy…*

Pushing my legs apart, he starts kissing the inner thigh of my right leg. Just as he reaches my sex, he gently blows up and down my clitoris, then smiles his most devilish smile at me. I practically convulse, then he starts on my left leg, and I know when he reaches *there*, it'll be over, I won't be able to take it.

As he reaches my sex, he closes his eyes and plants a soft kiss, right there on my clitoris.

"Tristan!" I hiss and breathe out, trying to stop the trembling.

"You are so sexy," he whispers, his eyes boring into mine. Oh, I'll never forget this image, his face between my legs, his deep hypnotic eyes staring up at me.

Then his mouth is on me, in me – *Oh my god!*

His tongue is there, inside me. Then he pulls out and licks up and down my clitoris. Then he changes, and he's going round and round in soft circles, then he gently sucks, then stops and gently blows again, and that's my undoing.

I come loudly, calling out his name. I feel like I've just come apart at the seams. That was amazing. I can still feel it flooding through me, to every bone and muscle in my body. My heart is hammering against my chest, my breath coming in sharp gusts. *Whoa!* – As I start to come down, I start to drift. I feel like I'm floating in the air, I'm so light…

"Baby?" Tristan chuckles lightly.

I force my eyes open. *Where have I been?*

"Sorry," I pant, blinking several times. I feel like I've just left the planet for a while.

"You're very responsive," he murmurs, leaning down to kiss me.

"That's because it's you…" I murmur against his lips.

"What are you saying Coral? You've never…?" Tristan stops, he's half smiling, slightly bemused.

"Tristan, I've only ever slept with one other guy…and.' I swallow hard 'It was never like this, let's put it that way." I tell him, feeling shy.

His mouth pops open, and his eyes widen in shock. "One guy?" He says incredulously.

I don't think he believes me. "Yes." I gaze up at him.

"One guy?" He murmurs again, slowly shaking his head in disbelief. Then he starts to smile, a very sexy, lazy smile, I smile back at him. He leans forward, gives me a quick, chaste kiss, then starts his slow, sexy decent down my body, kissing me all over.

Oh no! I don't think I can take it again.

He gets to his feet, and still shaking his head in amazement, he pulls his sweats off and stands there completely naked. *Oh boy!*

He looks even better in the daylight, the sun beating down on his body. I can see every tiny muscle that's been perfectly defined, his body is simply glorious, so god damn glorious, and so are all his moves. Kneeling on the bed, he opens the condoms, rips a packet open and places it on his erection.

Taking him by surprise, I sit up, push him down onto his back and straddle him, my hands resting on his chest as he softly strokes my hips with his hands.

"I was never any good at this position," I whisper, my hair falling around my face.

"I very much doubt that," he says, gazing up at me. I smile down and him, then I sit up and take hold of his hot, heavy erection in my hand, he hisses at my touch. I position him and slowly ease myself onto him until I have taken all of him.

"Tristan," I close my eyes and moan, I feel so full.

"Ah, baby…" He murmurs.

I open my eyes and see Tristan has his closed. His mouth is slack, his hands digging into my hips. Then his eyes flash open, his look hot and heated. He moves his right hand across my abdomen, softly tracing the skin, then his thumb skims down and starts to gently rub my clitoris, round and round. I throw my head back and begin to move…*oh fuck*…up and down, slowly grinding into him.

"Jesus Coral…you're so tight," he gasps between gritted teeth –I'm so close again.

Tristan suddenly sits up, his hands caressing my breasts, his mouth sucking my nipples. I place my hands on his shoulders and ride him harder, desperate for the release, but Tristan suddenly lifts me, pulling me off him…*No!*

He lays me down, lifts up my legs and wraps them around his neck. Then he's in me again, pushing, faster, in and out… *Whoa! I've never done it like this!*

"Oh baby," he croons, his eyes melting me.

"Oh god…" I moan, my eyes closing.

I'm so close…He stops again…*No!*

He takes my legs and wraps them around his waist, then he encircles his arms around my waist and in one swift movement, he's kneeling, and I'm sitting on him. *Oh!*

He feels so big inside me this way.

"Tristan!" I wrap my arms around his neck and grind into him.

He takes hold of my face and kisses me hard, just as he starts to move again. He pumps himself up and into me, quickly developing a synchronised rhythm…*Wow, we just seem so in tune with one another…*

I feel myself quicken, everything starts to tighten up…*Oh god!*

"Ah…Coral!" He growls, pumping faster.

I come again, screaming a garbled noise of his name. He crushes me to him, still pumping into me, still kissing me hard until he finds his release.

"Oh, baby…" He whispers against my lips, and we both collapse onto the bed.

CHAPTER FOUR

I LAY IN POST-COITAL bliss, across Tristan's chest. He's running his fingertips up and down my back, soothing me somehow; it feels amazing. Neither of us says anything as we slowly catch our breath, but there's one thing I do know through my dreamy haze of happiness, Tristan turns me on big time, I don't think I'll ever get my fill of him.

What a way to start the day! I can't help chuckling at that thought. Tristan starts to chuckle too, my head moving up and down against his chest as he does.

"What are you laughing at?" he titters.

I look up to his face. "I was just thinking, what a way to start the day," I giggle.

"You got that right baby." He flips me over and lies on top of me. "Every day," he whispers his face serious as he leans down and softly kisses me.

"I hope so," I whisper. He runs his hands through my hair, and stares down at me like he can see straight through me again – It's unnerving.

"I love you," he whispers and kisses me hard, his erection digging into my belly – *Again?*

"I love you too Tristan," I whisper, kissing him back with everything I've got, and before I know it, I am lost in his touch, only this time it's different because Tristan takes his time and makes sweet, slow love to me...

I LAY STARING UP at the ceiling in a dreamy haze. I feel so loose, my muscles feel so light. I'm floating in the clouds again. Is this what it's supposed to feel like?

"Well, that was different!" I giggle.

"What was?" Tristan asks. He's lying flat on his back with his forearm draped across his forehead.

"Twice Tristan…really?" I cock one eyebrow up at him. He opens his eyes and smiles his sexy smile at me. "You…you know a lot of moves," I add, smiling shyly.

He turns on his side and gazes at me. "I love that shy smile of yours," he says, his thumb tracing my bottom lip. "I wanted to make up for last night," he adds.

"I think we can safely say you did that," I chuckle, turning on my side to gaze back at him and admire his hair free chest. "Do you shave?" I ask running my fingers across his chest. "You know your chest?"

"No. Why?" He asks cocking his head to the side.

"You're dark-haired, dark-haired men are normally more hairy than light-haired," I say, hoping he won't probe any deeper, well not with questions anyway. *Coral!*

"Guess I'm just lucky then," he titters smugly.

I smile weakly at him. "I'm glad," I whisper, making circles around his nipples.

"Why?" He chuckles. *Damn it!*

"I just…I don't like hairy men. It turns me off I guess," I say, purposely smiling up at him.

"Turns you off huh?" He says. I nod shyly again. "Hey," Tristan reaches out and strokes my cheek. "I want to tell you something," he adds.

"Ok," I squeak, hoping I'll like it.

"You have an amazing body Coral," he says, making me feel self-conscious. "So sexy, and your curves…" He blows out a deep breath. I can't help smiling shyly at him. "And these babies," he adds, squeezing both my breasts. "I've never seen a better pair. You really are the full package Coral, I don't think I'm ever going to get my fill of you."

"Huh! Who'd have thought it, Tristan the sex maniac," I blurt.

"Maniac for you," he admits, his eyes dilating as he leans forward like a predator stalking its prey.

"Do we have time?" I ask feeling quite astonished he can go again.

He moves us so that the full length of his body is pressed against mine, my back to the mattress. I can feel his erection digging into my belly, then his look changes to the same one he had last night – the broody look.

"What is it?" I whisper.

Tristan closes his eyes and presses his forehead against mine. After a moment, he opens his eyes and gently kisses the tip of my nose. "You're so beautiful, so brave…" He whispers, his voice all husky and sexy again.

"Why did you say that last night?" I question.

"Say what?" He asks, his eyebrows knitting together.

"That you don't know why I love you? You made it sound as though you don't think you deserve me?"

"I don't," he answers smartly.

I frown deeply at him. "Yes, yes you do," I say, feeling totally bewildered that he would think that.

"Can I make you happy?" he questions aloud.

"You do," I bark. "Tristan, what's this really about? You said you had breakfast in bed before then you broke off like you didn't want to talk about it. Did she hurt you or something?"

He looks horrified like I've really caught him out.

"Tristan talk to me," I whisper, trying to coax him into telling me.

"It's…it's, very difficult when you're a man in my position." Tristan sits up with me in his arms, so I'm sat in his lap again, but I know he's not finished, so I keep quiet.

He reaches up and softly strokes my cheek. "Having money isn't all it's cracked up to be. I mean yeah, it is great being able to buy whatever you want, whenever you want it, but…" He takes a deep breath and exhales, running his hand through his hair.

"Finding someone who genuinely likes you for who you are, and not your money is…difficult. I met a woman, eight years ago now, we dated for three years. I thought we had something special. I thought I loved her, but it turned out…" He takes another deep breath.

"I feel so fucking lucky to have met you and that you feel the same for me as I do for you, that it's genuine. You don't know how often I've wondered if I'd ever find that girl, who would be with someone so different like me, she was like you at first, she said that she liked the fact that I was different. Then one day I was told by a confidant that she'd been seen out with her ex, on the very night she told me she was out with her girlfriends, I was gutted. When I confronted her about it, she told me that she was comforting him, that his father had died suddenly.

"She told me that they had stayed in contact as friends and that there was nothing more there, but I knew she was lying, the confidant told me that she kissed him at the end of the evening. When I asked her about it, she flat out denied it, she said that she loved me, wanted to marry me, spend the rest of her life with me. But I couldn't look her in the eye and see…" He closes his eyes for a moment.

"I lost the trust, and a relationship without trust just doesn't work, so I ended it. She begged me not to, cried a lot, swore to me that nothing had happened between them, but for me, it was over." He stares out at the window for a moment, then looks back at me and slightly shakes his head.

"After that happened, I kind of resigned myself to being on my own, or meeting someone who had their own money. Which I did, if you're in the right circles you generally do, but none of them held any interest for me…then I met you." Tristan gazes down at me and strokes my cheek. "I'm just as scared as you are, of being hurt, of you leaving me. But I trust that you're here right now because of me, not my money." He frowns deeply, searching my face.

"Tristan," I breathe, I need to make him understand. "I can't do anything about the fact that you have money, but I'm telling you now if you somehow lost it all, I'd be standing right by your side through it all, and from then onwards. Or if I'd have met you and you didn't have money, I'd still be here with you right now. It's you I want not your money."

He smiles down at me and gently kisses my lips, but I want to tell him more, how I really feel, what I've been holding back from him.

"You rocked my world when I first saw you, turned it upside down. I was completely beside myself, no man has ever affected me the way you have. So I'm really glad that you've met me, someone, who loves you for who you are and I'll tell you something else. No-one in the world will ever love you as much as I do, and will for the rest of my life." Tristan looks shocked and kind of awed, I try to ignore his heart melting look and continue.

"I know we have only known each other for a short amount of time, but I know it, I feel it, I couldn't imagine being with anybody else. And to think of what it would be like to not have you in my life is just....un-imaginable." I shudder as a recall leaving him again.

Tristan's arms snake around my waist, and he gazes at me in awe. Now I get it, now I understand why he's so happy that he's met me. It makes perfect sense, and I agree, it must be really tough to meet someone who genuinely wants you, not your millions. It also explains why he hasn't had a relationship for such a long time.

Tristan smiles bashfully at me as I lean down and kiss his lips again. "Forever," I whisper.

"And ever," he adds running his fingers through my hair, softly kissing my lips.

And I know it's going to happen again...

IN A DREAM LIKE STATE, I wobble to the bathroom. Tristan has gone downstairs to warm up the cappuccinos in the microwave. I'm supposed to be getting ready, but I don't seem to have much concentration. I feel like I'm floating on air, I don't even feel like I'm in my own body. Is this what being in love, and having hot, body-rocking sex is like? If it is, then I've been a fool, a very big fool to be thinking I wasn't missing out on anything.

Dropping my towel to the floor, I step under the overlarge square shower head and turn it on. I lean my head back, close my eyes and let the water cascade across my face, and soak my hair. Picking up my body wash, I go to squirt some into my hands, but I'm suddenly aware I'm not alone, I spin around.

Tristan is casually leaning against the shower door. He's got his arms crossed, and he's gazing at me with a hot, heated look. I swallow hard. All he's wearing are his sweats; his glorious upper body is all on show for me.

I want him again – *Coral you just did it, three times!*

Tristan is smiling at me with such a seductive look in his eyes, I think I may climax without him even touching me.

"Mind if I join you?" He asks.

Join me? Is he kidding? I'm in the shower!

"I..." I suddenly feel very, very shy. "Really?" I squeak in astonishment.

"If you don't mind," he says, his sexy smile appearing.

"Um...I...I guess so," I say, thinking I probably look like a drowned rat at the moment.

Tristan strips his sweats off and opens the door. I instantly notice his penis is standing to attention, yet another erection. *What's this guy on?*

"Are you on drugs?" I giggle through the spray.

"Drugs?" He cocks his head to the side. I grin widely and look down at his erection with one eyebrow cocked up. "Yes," he growls, grabbing hold of me, pressing the length of his solid body against mine. "You're my drug, and I'm very, very addicted."

"I better give you a hit then," I giggle, placing my hands on his backside and pressing him harder against me.

"Stay there," he whispers and dashes out the shower, seconds later he is back with a condom on his erection. *Boy, he doesn't waste time!*

As he reaches me, he pulls me to him and kisses me hard. Then he takes a couple of steps forward and pushes me against the tiled wall, his hands all over my body, his kiss heated, wanting, so full of love and passion – *This is so hot!*

"Wrap your legs around me, baby." I gasp and do as he asks.

"I've never done this before," I whisper shyly.

"Done what?" He asks, kissing me hard again.

"Showered with someone," I whisper.

He frowns down at me. "And shower sex?"

I smile shyly and shake my head at him.

He smiles enigmatically at me. "Keep your legs gripped," he says as his hands lift me up further, then he reaches down to his erection and slowly sinks himself into me, filling me right up. God, I want him, so badly, he turns me on so much. I don't think I'll ever get enough of him.

Then surprising me, he really starts to move, fast. He makes a low, sexy noise in the back of his throat, then he grasps my wet hair between his hands and kisses me, passionately, pulling my lips harder against his, his tongue invading my mouth... *Holy crap!*

Picking up the pace we move faster together, Tristan is pounding up into me. I'm bouncing up and down, my breasts jiggling as I try to hold onto the sensation without climaxing too quickly. I open my eyes and watch as Tristan takes hold of my left breast, he squeezes and caresses it, then sucks the erect nipple.

"Oh god!" I come un-done, climaxing loudly, watching him do that was so fucking sexy. I grip my arms around his neck, my leg muscles tensing while my orgasm overtakes me, each wave making me feel weaker, light headed…I think I'm going to pass out.

Tristan is still pounding up into me, then suddenly he stills, his mouth open, his tongue tracing my bottom lip, his eyes wide and dilated.

"Fuck…" He hisses as he finds his release, gently biting my bottom lip.

We sink down to the shower floor, and for some odd reason I begin to giggle, then I really start to laugh – I think it's because I'm so elated, so happy and I've just had…I've lost count how many orgasms I've had so far this morning.

Hysterical laughing now ensues – *Maybe it's because I feel good about sex again?*

"What are you laughing at?" Tristan asks, laughing too.

"I don't know," I cry out, rolling onto the floor, laughing so hard that my belly is truly starting to ache. Tristan can't help but join in with me, laughter is too infectious like that…

WHEN WE FINALLY compose ourselves, and the laughter has ceased, Tristan helps me to my feet, then pulls the condom off and throws it on the shower floor. We kiss each other ardently, caressing, squeezing and appreciating each other's body.

"Can I wash you?" Tristan asks.

I find it strange he would want to do that, then I feel his erection grow against my belly.

"Maybe another time," I whisper against his lips. "If you do, I don't think we'll get out of here." Tristan grins cheekily at me, and kisses me sweetly, then checks the time on his watch.

"I think you're right." He suddenly looks serious. "We have ten minutes," he adds.

"What?" I gasp in horror. "I'll never be ready on time!"

Tristan strokes my cheek, it instantly calms me. "You don't need to be ready baby. We know where everything is going. I can sort it, take your time." I take a deep breath, feeling calmer. *How does he do that to me?*

"May I?" Tristan says, pointing to the shower.

"Be my guest," I say, gesturing for him to go first.

Leaning back against the tiles, I watch him shampoo his hair. I watch the bubbles ripple across his shoulders, down his mighty fine pectorals, swimming into a v as they reach his slim abdomen, then down to his impressive manly parts – *Boy I'm a lucky woman*.

Tristan winks at me as he sees me watching him. "Enjoying yourself?" he chuckles.

"You have no idea," I answer dryly, biting my bottom lip. The urge to get down on my knees and taste him is...overwhelming.

"Later," he admonishes, his eyes darkening. I pout like a teenager. Tristan finishes up and pulls me under the shower. "Don't be too long," he tells me sternly, then kisses me briefly before he leaves, leaving me spent and sated.

Something deep within me blossoms. I can't explain what it is, all I know is how it makes me feel, and I feel like I'm on drugs. I'm as high as a kite. I sigh blissfully. I intended to take a long lazy shower, but now all I want to do is be as quick as possible and be next to Tristan again. I'm really starting to feel kind of lost and empty when he's isn't next to me.

I wonder to myself if that is a good thing. If this ends, goes wrong, I don't think it's something I will ever recover from – I push the mournful thought away and try to keep my mind focused, as George has taught me, on the now and what Tristan and I will be getting up to today...

TEN MINUTES LATER and I'm done. Hair washed, body shaved in all the right places and buffed with my shower cream and exfoliating sponge – now I feel refreshed. I have dressed in my white skinny, three quarter length jeans, my mint camisole and my green wedges to match. I stare at myself in the bathroom mirror, my cheeks look flushed – guess that's all the sexing!

Smiling broadly at myself, I pick up my makeup bag and

start putting on my face. I go through the motions on autopilot, because I can't stop thinking about what Tristan revealed to me this morning. Quite frankly, I'm shocked that he's been on his own for so long, longer than me in-fact, and I can't help wondering about this girl and whether she did, in fact, cheat on him. Then I wonder who the confidant was. Who told him that they were seen together? Must have been someone he really trusted.

I brush the stupid thought away. If Tristan had stayed with her, he wouldn't be here with me now, so I have to be thankful to the confidant, whoever it was. Then I think about his broodiness last night, that strange look he had. I have to wonder what was going through his mind. I hope it doesn't return, it gave me such a sinking feeling in the pit of my stomach – *Stop Coral, don't think like that!*

I shake my head at myself, look up at my reflection and finish off my make-up, trying my best to quiet the crazy talk going on in my head.

With my make-up done and my hair drying naturally with a lovely wave, I walk back into the bedroom and pick up my handbag. Finding my mobile, I quickly check my messages and see I have none from Rob or Carlos - *I wonder if they're ok?*

I try to tell myself they've gone away on holiday to try and renew their relationship or something, make amends, at least I hope that's what's going on; and if it is, I hope they are having a good time. Then I think of Bob – *Shit!*

I've just realised I won't be there tomorrow to cook him his Roast Dinner. I better call Gladys, see if she will take one over to him, at least it will ease the guilt I'm feeling for not being there for him.

"Hello?" A deep male voice answers the home line.

"Malcolm?" I say, feeling surprised he's answered the line.

"Yes?" He says.

"It's Coral."

"Ah, hello darling." He sounds genuinely pleased to hear from me.

"Hi, is'" – "I'll go and get her for you. How are you feeling, is your nose better?"

"Yes thanks, much better."

"Good, glad to hear it. Darling, Coral's on the phone for you…" I can hear Gladys in the background, she sounds busy.

"Be quick darling, I've got bacon and eggs on the go," she says a little frantically

"Can you take Bob a dinner tomorrow?"

"Oh goodness, poor Bob, I won't be here darling." *Damn it!*

"It's ok, I'll sort it," I gripe. "You'd better go before your eggs burst," I add.

"Bye darling." She slams the phone down.

"Bye," I mumble sarcastically to my mobile and hang up. I guess I better talk to Tristan, I've got to get some decent food in Bob somehow, throwing my mobile in my bag, I skip down the stairs to find him.

Reaching the kitchen, I spy Tristan sat on one of the breakfast stools, going through some paperwork. He hasn't seen me, so I take a moment to appreciate him. He's dressed in a fitted black t-shirt, dark blue jeans, and a pair of trainers; he really does look too good to be true.

Just as I think, that he runs a hand through his messed up hair, making my stomach flutter madly. I don't know why he hasn't combed it into place, as is his usual style, but I don't care, he looks really hot – really hot and sexy, and I like it, I like it a lot.

I'M SAT ON ONE of the breakfast stools with my arms and legs wrapped around Tristan, as he kisses me over, and over. He seems to like kissing as much as I do, and he seems different today like he's gotten over his broodiness about what I told him. I hope so, this Tristan I like, he's playful and sexy, and I can't get over how much he seems to like me, love me even.

"What are you thinking about?" he asks kissing me again, his tongue softly lapping against mine, making my legs feel wobbly even though I'm not standing.

"You," I answer honestly.

"Me?" He says, surprised.

"Yeah," I try to hide the sigh.

"What about me?" he enquires, kissing the corner of my lips.

"Nothing…" I decide in that second not to say anything, it may spoil his mood.

"Tell me," he urges.

"I just thought ...you're different today," I say looking tentatively up at him, my mouth running away with me again.

His eyes darken. "Different how?"

"In a good way," I explain.

"You're not going to tell me." He guesses.

I shake my head at him.

"I wish you would, I want you to be open Coral and really tell me what's going on in that head of yours. The more I know, the better my chances are of understanding you."

Ok, that sounded like George!

"Oh!" I whisper.

"Yeah oh, so are you going to spill?" He asks his eyes lightning as his mood elevates.

I think about it for a few seconds. "It's just, you seemed kind of…distant last night," I say looking at the floor, shrugging slightly.

Tristan sighs and gently lifts my head, running a soft finger down my cheek, I see his jaw clench then release. "I was mad, really, really fucking mad. To be honest, I don't think I've ever felt that mad like I could annihilate an entire village. When you told me…I just saw red. Of all the people for that to happen to, you're so sweet and beautiful, so kind, so strong and courageous." Tristan shakes his head in disgust. "I'll never understand it, men who rape, abuse, do all that kind of shit!" He snarls, his nostrils flaring, his cheeks flaming.

"I thought I would wake up to..." I trail off. "I'm glad you're back to being *you*," I tell him, taking his face in my hands and kissing his full lips.

"You know I'll probably be...well, I'll try not to be..." He says, shaking his head again.

"What?" I whisper.

"Overprotective." He replies grudgingly.

A part of me feels really good about that, as long as Tristan doesn't take it too far and become a complete ogre. *No way, I won't let that happen, I'll tell him before it gets that far.*

"What are you thinking?" He asks examining my face.

"That I love that you want to protect me so much," I whisper, leaning my forehead against his.

Tristan seems relieved. "You'll tell me won't you, if I start to smother you, you know…get a little' – "Yes," I say, finishing his sentence for him. "I know what you're trying to say, and no, I won't put up with it if you go too far, which I'm sure you won't," I say lifting my head and gazing up into his warm, chocolate eyes.

"Somehow I get the feeling you will definitely put me in my place if I go too far," he says. "You have far too much spark and fire in you to be that kind of woman," he adds.

"Damn right," I say, punching him playfully. "I'll kick your ass," I add, chuckling hard.

"Oh really?" He says, his eyes glinting wickedly. I don't have time to react. Tristan launches me over his shoulder and playfully slaps my backside. I yelp in surprise and slap his ass back. He throws me onto the beanbag, landing on top of me as he does, then he decides to tickle me – Launching one of my worst triggers!

"Stop!" I scream in panic, my heart beating a frantic tattoo against my chest. *Holy fuck!*

Tristan leans back, his hands held up showing me he won't touch me. "What did I do wrong?" He questions.

I stagger to my feet, my breathing erratic and wipe at the sheen of cold sweat that has formed on my brow. "I'm sorry," I pant, bending down to put my hands on my knees, trying to ease the spinning head.

"Me too," he says. I look down at Tristan, he's frozen in place, carefully watching me –*Shit!*

"Tristan you can get up…I'm sorry, I'm sorry…" I say clutching my throat, swallowing hard against the bile that's risen.

Tristan slowly stands and walks with gentle, soft steps until he reaches me. "You don't like tickling?" he surmises. I shake my head, unable to answer him, and stare down at the floor, praying he doesn't ask me about why I just freaked out – *Fuck!*

"Why?" He softly asks. The front door is knocked, guess the delivery is here, and I'm thankful, it's saved me from his question.

"I need some fresh air," I say.

Tristan looks torn like doesn't want to leave me, then he nods at me and reluctantly, he turns and stalks towards the front door. I step outside where I know I won't be seen by the delivery guys and lean my head against the wall. I take a deep breath and close my eyes. I feel the panic subside, only to be overtaken by anger – *Fuckers!*

If they hadn't done what they did to me when I was a child, that moment wouldn't have been ruined. It would have been a normal playful thing that couples do, not' – "Coral?" I flick my eyes open. Tristan is in front of me with his hand held out, giving me a choice to take it or not, as I look up into his eyes, I can see the confusion, the frustration; there's nothing he can do; I take hold of his hand and still myself. Closing my eyes, I take a moment to bask in the glorious feeling of his hand grasping mine.

"Open your eyes beautiful," he tells me.

I gaze up at his warm eyes.

"Are you ok?" He asks, watching carefully for my response.

"Yeah," I sigh, wondering what Tristan's really thinking – *She's a nutball, and I'm running for the trees, surely?*

"What are you thinking?" He asks, echoing my thoughts.

I laugh sarcastically at that one, then frown. "That I'm just waiting for the moment when you say you've had enough, and you leave," I whisper softly, my stomach rolling at the very thought of it.

"You'll be waiting a long time," he tells me, caressing my cheek. "Are you sure you're ok?" he adds.

I nod silently at him, although I'm not sure I am.

"Want to talk about it?" he asks.

I shake my head again.

Tristan looks irritated for a moment, then adjusts himself so that his facial features form a panting combusting smile. "As you wish," he says.

I gaze up at him in awe. There is no way I would let that go, I'd be too intrigued as to why the person reacted that way. But I can't help grinning back at him, it's almost as though it happens all by itself. Like my face has nothing to do with it.

"May I?" He asks, leaning into me.

I nod once.

His soft lips brush gently against mine. I feel the anger

dissipate, the fog lifting just as my heart picks up and my breath catches in my throat...*Will I ever get used to this feeling?*

"Let's go back inside," he whispers. I look up at him gazing down at me. *What is this magic that he yields over me?*

"What?" He whispers.

"Nothing," I laugh inwardly at myself, take his outstretched hand, and walk in a dreamlike state back into the house.

CHAPTER FIVE

THE FIRST DELIVERY to arrive is the gym equipment. Tristan has, in my humble opinion, gone overboard. Though he assures me, he has the same amount of equipment in his other homes. So including a swimming pool, we now have a treadmill, a stepper, a cross trainer, a rowing machine, an exercise bike, a full weights machine free weights with several benches and a fitness ball.

Tristan has also ordered a vibration plate. Which admittedly, I've never tried before, but Tristan says they are awesome and make you feel really good, so I'm looking forward to trying that later. But as I stand in the gym, with my arms crossed, I can help thinking it's really is too much.

"Really?" I say sarcastically to Tristan, as he reaches me. "Is it all really necessary?" I question.

"Absolutely!" He tells me ushering me out of the gym.

We leave the three men to it that have brought all the equipment in, and are busy building the weight machine – *Good luck there!*

"Why?" I ask as we head back up the stairs.

"It's good to keep your body guessing." I smile back at Tristan. I'm not really sure what he means.

"I don't understand?" I say.

"You keep swapping what exercise you do, so your body never knows what's coming. Basically, you're tricking your brain." I frown at that one.

Tristan rolls his eyes at me and smirks. "Ok take average Joe, he goes running for half an hour, three times a week, it's the same thing he's done for years, but he's not as fit as he used to be and he can't keep the love handles at bay. Basically, the brain tricks the body, it tells you you're having a great workout, when in fact it's become a very easy one; which means you don't burn the calories, work the muscle groups or the heart and lungs."

Whoa! – This is definitely food for thought. Maybe I shouldn't be swimming every morning? I should be rotating it with something else? Then I think if I keep staying with Tristan, I won't need the gym anymore, not with all his sexing – I stop that thought in its tracks!

"What?" Tristan stops and gazes down at me, a slight smile playing across his lips.

"No wonder you have the body of a twenty-year-old," I say dryly.

"Jealous?" he smirks.

"No!" I banter, punching him lightly on the shoulder. "But you've definitely given me something to think about," I add, walking up the stairs to the kitchen.

"Coral, you have a beautiful body, you don't need to worry," he assures me, but I choose not to get into that one.

"How do you know all that anyway?" I ask.

"I'm interested in health and fitness, and I read a lot," he answers smugly.

"Hmm," I cock an eyebrow at him.

"We have ten minutes," he says leaning down to kiss me. "Until the next delivery," he adds caressing my body, deepening the kiss. I lose all thoughts and try hard to concentrate on keeping my heart from bursting out of my chest...

THREE HOURS LATER and all the furniture we had chosen has been delivered. The house is ours again. In the living-room, we now have a very large white u-shaped sofa, so at least we have something to chill out on tonight, a flat screen (ridiculously big) T.V with surround sound, although Tristan seems to be very frisky, so I doubt we'll get to watch a movie.

The Bose stereo system has arrived and been strategically placed for optimal sound – so Tristan says, he seems to take his music seriously. The dining room now has a very long table and chairs, and the smaller beech table and chairs are nestled neatly in front of the floor to ceiling windows in the kitchen.

Tristan didn't agree with the colour at first, but now it's there, he's changed his mind.

His office is now fully kitted out, and the other beds and bedroom furniture arrived for the spare rooms. Although, I can't see when they'll ever get used, and the rest of the bedroom furniture for the master suite has been put in place, finally, I can unpack my weekend bag.

I place my girly stuff in the top drawer of the bedside cabinet, and I'm about to stuff my underwear into the next drawer when I remember about the walk-in closets. Picking up my bag, I open the door and head inside – *So much room!* – I'm just hanging up my clothes when Tristan walks in, smiling sexily at me.

"I like those," he says, pointing to my skinny black jeans.

"You do?" I smile.

"Yeah, I bet they'll look really, really good on you," he says darkly, prowling towards me.

"Don't," I chuckle hanging up the jeans. "Or we'll never get out of here."

Tristan reaches me, and pulls me into his arms, kissing me passionately. "Is that so bad?" he mumbles against my lips, his hands squeezing my backside.

"No," I whisper. "But I wanted to cook for you tonight. How am I supposed to do that with no kitchen equipment?" I sound whiney.

"Well, we could always get a takeaway, and we could shop tomorrow," he says pulling my camisole up, his fingertips running up and down my lower back, sending sparks all over my body.

"Please," I beg. "I really want to cook for you," I grumble.

I've always been like that though, once I get an idea into my head I have to follow through with it. Besides, I want to thank him for looking after me and feeding me after my little coming together with Lily, but it looks like my body has other ideas. Tristan has not stopped kissing and caressing me, making me want him all over again.

Wrapping my legs around him and gripping his hair at the nape, I willingly let him take me over to the bed – *I am not going to be able to walk properly tomorrow!*

WE LIE ON OUR BACKS, both panting hard. Turning to look at each other at the same time, Tristan chuckles and runs his hand through his damp hair.

"Jesus woman!" he grins, turning on his side to caress my hardened nipples.

"What?" I pant, swallowing hard. *I'm so thirsty, that was a workout!*

"Nothing," he chuckles, sitting up.

"No, tell me," I retort. "Did I do something wrong?" I ask shyly.

Tristan whips his head round, dives on top of me and kisses me softly, his fingers moving my hair out of my face. "The complete opposite actually," he says gazing at me intensely. "You're surprising me at every turn," he adds.

"I don't understand?" I say, trying not to frown.

"I've never had it that good Coral. You're blowing me away, in everything you do. Especially the sex..." He smiles his mischievous smile at me.

"Hmm," I close my eyes and smile.

I really feel like I can be myself with Tristan, I can let down some barriers, and I know he won't push me to do anything I wouldn't want to do. I cringe inwardly at the triggers I know I have and hope that they never get bought up. I hope Tristan doesn't want to do any of *those* things.

"Do you think this is normal? Or is it that we have very strong chemistry?" I question.

"Couldn't say if it's normal, but I think we can safely say we are very, very compatible in that area, big chemistry," he grins, his eyes widening playfully, his dimples deepening.

"So I guess you got it pretty bad for me," I say playfully.

"Bet your damn ass I have," he retorts, kissing me all over, making me chuckle again...

WE ARE IN THE CAR, heading home from shopping, and what an experience that was! Tristan didn't take his touch away from me for a moment. If he wasn't holding my hand, he was touching my waist, if he weren't doing that, his hand would be resting on my upper arm squeezing gently every now and then. I feel so good about us that I feel like singing it from the rooftops.

"Still want to take that bath?" Tristan asks, gently squeezing my knee, his look screaming sex.

"Yes," I giggle and slap his hand away – *He's so frisky!*

He pulls the car into the driveway, switches off the engine and presses the button for the gates. They start to close behind us, then he turns in his seat to gaze at me.

"What?" I ask feeling shy.

Tristan smiles deeply at me then frowns. "Am I pushing too much?"

"What?"

"Wanting sex?"

"What? No, Tristan, you're not!" I admonish. "I was only teasing you," I add.

"Ok," he smiles his sexy smile at me, my stomach flutters wildly in response. Then he slowly leans forward, making his intention clear. *Are we about to have car sex?*

My throat instantly dries, my heart starts manically beating, and my breath kicks up a few notches. His lips reach mine and begin their slow torture, his tongue teasing, taunting me. I moan and close my eyes, then wrap my hand around his neck and pull on his hair. He groans with pleasure and pushes his lips harder against mine.

"Oh what you do to me," he growls against my lips.

"I could say the same," I whisper breathlessly.

I look down and see his erection straining to be released from his jeans. I reach down and start to caress him. He closes his eyes, his breathing getting harder. I kiss him softly, teasing him with my tongue. Then I tightly squeeze his erection and bite down on his full bottom lip.

"You'd better get me inside," he hisses, "before I explode in the car." *Damn it!*

"No car sex then?" I say pouting at him.

He shakes his head at me. "Another time," he replies, his face dead serious.

Tristan jumps out of the car, comes round to my side, hauls me out, slams the car door and carries me in his arms to the front door. Placing me down he unlocks the door, wraps his arm around my waist and swings me inside, I giggle aloud again. Then he punches in the code for the alarm and turns to stare at me with a hot, heated look.

I walk back towards the kitchen, beckoning him with my forefinger. He stalks towards me; his look making my legs tremble. I bump up against the breakfast bar and gasp, Tristan reaches me and snakes his hand around my waist.

"Take me," I whisper. "Here, now…" I pant.

Without a word, he spins me around, so my back is against his front and pulls off my camisole. He caresses my breasts, making my nipples strain against the strapless bra that I'm wearing. My head falls back against his shoulder, my mouth slack from his touch, then his hand slides down and undoes the button on my jeans.

"Tristan," I whisper. He pulls the zipper down, skims his hand underneath the stretchy material and slowly pulls them down to my knees.

"You have such a sexy body," he says all deep and husky.

Standing up, he gently squeezes my backside with his one hand as his other moves my hair to the left, then he leans down and plants soft kisses across my neck, then a gentle blow, then another kiss, I can feel it all the way down there. He continues to kiss me across my right shoulder then my left, my whole body feels so sensitive, I shudder at his touch.

I move my hands round to his erection and continue rubbing him. Then I feel him unclipping my bra, he throws it on the floor, revealing my full pert nipples, that are just aching for his touch. His one hand moves across my breasts teasing, softly pulling my nipples, his other hand heads south, slowly, across my belly, underneath my knickers and between my legs. I gasp as his fingers reach my clitoris. He fingers circle me gently a couple of times, then he sinks a finger inside me.

"Ahh…" I cry out at the contact.

He pulls his finger back out and continues to tease my clitoris, slowly going round in circles, making me tremble inside.

"You're so ready," he whispers in my ear.

I close my eyes to his touch. "Yes," I moan.

"I want you!" He suddenly stops teasing my clitoris and slowly pulls my pants down to my knees, then I hear the sound of his belt being unclipped, his jeans being pulled down, and the tell-tale sound of foil ripping.

He pulls me sharply against his body. I can feel his erection digging into me. "Look at me baby," he softly says. I twist my head around, bow my back and stare up into his wide dark eyes. "You're so sexy," he whispers, then leans down and claims my mouth, kissing me hard.

I squeak aloud as pleasure spikes through my whole body, I want him now –*God this is so fucking hot!*

"Bend over baby," his soft husky voice requests. *Oh, doggy position!*

I lean forward, my torso resting on the cool breakfast bar, just aching to feel him inside me. Instead, he bends down and starts trailing soft kisses across my backside, his fingers finding my clitoris again, then he bites each butt cheek softly, making me gasp aloud.

"Oh baby, you have such beautiful skin, so soft," he murmurs sending kisses down the back of my legs, his fingers still caressing my clitoris.

I can't take it anymore. "Tristan!" I gasp. *I'm going to come.*

"What do you want?" he questions.

"You, in me," I garble. He stands up, his fingers still teasing me and then he slowly, positions himself at the opening of my sex, teasing me. "Please…" I whimper and ever so gently, he pushes himself inside me. Then he pulls back and does the same thing again, then again…

"Yes," I cry out.

"More?" He asks.

"Yes, faster…" I beg. He picks up the pace, my muscles instantly clenching. Everything starts to quicken, tighten… *Really…now…already?*

"Christ… you're so tight," he groans.

"Faster Tristan, I'm going to…" I can't finish my sentence, I have to concentrate, or I'll come and fall to the floor.

He picks up his pace, moving in and out of me, my insides clenching with this delicious torture. I want to come, but I don't want him to stop. I would quite happily spend the rest of my life with Tristan buried deep inside me. The room starts to fill with the smell of sexy lovemaking, our sweaty bodies and Tristan… *Oh, his scent drives me wild!*

"Oh god…" I squeeze my eyes shut, trying to control the building, but it's no use, it's going to happen now!

"Tristan!" I call out as we reach our high together.

"Christ Coral…" he cries out, collapsing on top of me…

AS I LAY THERE IN some sort of post-coital glow, Tristan starts to kiss my back. He slowly works his way up across my shoulders, until he reaches my neck. I turn my head to the side and smile up at him.

"How about that bath?" he chuckles.

"I think I need it now," I titter back.

He kisses me briefly, then slowly pulls out of me, making we wince.

"Sore?" he asks.

"Yes," I scold. "No more of your sexing Mr Freeman." I tease, turning round to face him.

He smiles sweetly at me, then his face turns serious, brooding, as he gently runs a finger down my cheek. "My beautiful, sweet girl," he whispers and softly kisses me.

I close my eyes and lean my head against his chest. "My gorgeous, gentle man that makes me feel so safe and protected," I whisper back. "I don't think I'm ever going to get enough of you."

"Or I you," he adds. *Oh, Tristan, I love you so…*

"I'd better get up there," I say leaning back to gaze up at him. "If you want to be fed that is?" He smiles enigmatically at me then sinks to his knees. *Oh no! Not more sex?*

"Tristan, what are you doing?" I ask wearily.

"Lift up your leg." He says.

I frown and give him my right ankle. He slowly undoes the strap and takes off my wedge, then does the same with my other wedge. Then he slowly pulls down my knickers and jeans, so I'm just stood there, completely naked, while he's still fully dressed, well, apart from his impressive manly bits poking out from his jeans.

He looks up at me through his long lashes, his eyes all wide like a puppy. "Do you have any idea how beautiful you are, how sexy?" he says standing to his feet and taking a step back to admire me.

"Tristan!" I squeak, trying to cover the essential bits. "You're making me feel self-conscious."

"You should be proud of your body Coral," he lightly scolds.

Shaking my head at him, I lean down to pick up my clothes, but he stops me by swinging me up into his arms and kissing me swiftly. "Leave them," he whispers. "I'll bring them up when I've unpacked the car."

"Let me help you," I argue.

"No."

"Yes."

He laughs lightly at me. "Do you think you'll ever just agree to one of my suggestions?" he questions.

"No," I chortle. "Except…maybe…" I break off.

"Maybe what?" he asks, pecking me on the lips.

"Maybe in the bedroom," I say, grinning widely.

I like Tristan taking control, moving my body how he wants. I like his moves. Plus, I don't have any of my own, and I certainly don't have any confidence to perform them, even if I did have.

"Hmm, so I can dominate you in the bedroom, but that's it?" He says. *Holy Fuck!*

I frown deeply, my breath kicking up a few notches. *That's not what I meant!*

"Who said anything about domination?" I say, swallowing hard. "Is…is that what you want to do, dominate me?" I squeak breathlessly. *No fucking way! That's weird kinky shit, he better not be into all that!*

Tristan stops walking, his frown mirroring mine. "No, I don't," he whispers, looking confused.

I swallow hard and try to keep my breathing normal, but I feel like I'm losing it, and this is the last thing I wanted Tristan to see. He's bound to pick up on it, then question me about it.

He narrows his eyes at me. "What's wrong?" he softly asks.

"Please let me go," I beg.

"Permanently?" He questions, his voice low, his jaw clenching.

"No!" I scold. "Just…please put me down, I'd really like my bath now," I say trying to change the subject. He releases me, so I slide down his body. "Thank you," I say lightly and kiss his lips.

He's frowning quizzically at me again.

I shake my head at myself and bite my bottom lip. "Sorry," I whisper then I reach up and softly stroke his cheek, holding his worried gaze for a moment. I smile weakly at him, then silently turn and walk towards the stairs, glad to be away from *that* conversation happening.

I AM SAT ON THE edge of the bath waiting for it to fill up. I have my towel wrapped around me, and I have Tristan's electronic candles going, making the room feel like a relaxing spa. I have my favourite Enigma album on – The Screen Behind The Mirror – The slow, heavy beat is filling the room, relaxing and soothing me.

I hear a soft tap on the door. "Tristan, you don't need to knock," I chuckle.

He pops his head through the door and smiles at me. "May I come in?"

"Yes." I can't help rolling my eyes at him.

He walks over to me, kneels down and looks up at me with those puppy dog eyes again. "I'm sorry about earlier," he says.

"Don't worry about," I retort, trying to change the subject.

"Coral, it's important…very important. I don't want to fuck up in the bedroom and lose you because of it," he says.

"You're not going to lose me, Tristan, so it's irrelevant," I argue.

His lips set into a hard line, then he slowly nods his head. "I have something for you," he tells me. "Give me a moment." Tristan walks out the bathroom, when he returns, he's holding a large, gift-wrapped box in his hand. "Here, for you," he says handing it to me.

I cock one eyebrow up and accept the gift. *More presents?*

The first thing I notice is that it's heavy, which has my curiosity peaked. Pulling at the bow, then lifting the lid off, my heart melts when I see what's inside. Earlier today as we strolled through the shops, I spied an Aromatherapy shop and popped in to pick up some oil for my bath tonight.

The shop assistant had taken me over to the samples to help me chose, leaving Tristan at the counter, talking to the other member of staff. What I evidently hadn't noticed, was the gift he swiftly purchased for me, we both had so many bags in our hands at the time, it would have been easy to disguise; come to think of it, it was the only time he wasn't touching me.

I run my hand over the lid that says Aromatherapy Essentials.

"How did you' – "I have my ways," he beams interrupting me.

"Brilliant, but sneaky," I smile.

"Do you like it?" He tentatively asks.

"Yes, I love it," I say pushing back tears of appreciation. *When did I turn into a blubberer?* "Thank you," I whisper, leaning down to kiss him.

"Open it," he says excitedly.

I place the box on my lap and lift the lid. Inside, I can see there are so many bottles of oils that I could be here all night going through them. As I delve further, I see there's a guide to Aromatherapy book and an oil burner with tea-lights.

"Do you have any idea how sweet and romantic it is that you bought this for me?"

Tristan shrugs. "I just want to buy you things I know you'll like...and use," he says, his cheeky grin appearing.

"You have been listening," I say dryly.

"Attention to detail," he says tapping his head.

"Well, you've got both presents right so far," I say jingling my bracelet at him.

He smiles shyly at me, gets to his feet, and kisses my forehead. "I'll be unpacking the car," he tells me and slowly saunters out of the room.

Picking up the small bottle of Sandalwood oil that I purchased for myself, much to Tristan's dislike, I shake it, so several drops fall into the bath water. Apparently, it's one that's used for relaxation. I know I definitely need to do more of that! *I'm trying, I'm getting there.*

As I'm pinning my hair up, I get a flashback of Tristan in the store, arguing with me about who was going to pay for a tiny little bottle of oil. No wonder he got so agitated when I purchased it, he'd already bought this gift for me.

I shake my head, it must have cost a fortune!

With the bath filled, I switch off the water, let my towel fall to the floor and step into the humungous egg-shaped bath. I sink down slowly into the warm water, it feels wonderful, and the scent of Sandalwood in the air is actually making me feel a little drowsy...

"Hey," I hear his voice whisper.

My eyes dart open, I must have drifted off for a second, Tristan is leaning his arms on the edge of the bath, his chin propped on top.

"Hi," I whisper back.

"May I join you?" He asks very politely – *God I love that about him, he's so gentlemanly.*

"Yes." I smile and watch him strip his clothes off in no time at all.

Leaning forward so he can sit behind me, I suddenly wonder why I haven't felt hot. It's been another sweltering day, yet I haven't felt uncomfortable in the house at all. Tristan pulls me gently towards him, so I'm lying against his chest.

"Has this house got some special coating on the walls or something?" I say.

"Why do you ask?" He questions.

"Because I didn't know it was so hot outside until we went out, this house is well, cool," I say by way of an answer.

"That's because it has an Air-Con system," he answers.

"A what?" I balk.

Tristan chuckles. "It's like an air-conditioning unit, but better."

"That's a bit extravagant, isn't it? I mean it's not like we normally get summers like this," I say.

"True, but it's been useful so far." His hands start wandering across my body.

"Oh no, you don't mister!" I playfully slap his hand that almost reached my breast.

"Sorry...you're kind of hard to resist," he says, kissing my cheek.

"Well resist until I have fed you, sir, that's an order!" I try for a scolding tone, but it just comes out as playful.

"Yes, ma'am." Tristan starts massaging my shoulders, just like in my daydream. I surrender to it, it feels magical. I had no idea that being with someone could really feel this good. I thought it was just in books and movies, definitely not in real life. How wrong I have been...

"Nice?" He questions.

"Wonderful," I breathe.

"Coral, are you afraid of being dominated? It's something I need to know baby." *Shit!*

I instantly tense up, his hands pause on my shoulders. My heart has picked up, so much so that I think he can hear it banging against my chest – *Please say you don't want this!*

"Why? Do you want to dominate me?" I manage to squeak out.

"Don't change the subject," he scolds.

I stay silent, racking my brains for something to say, so he doesn't get suspicious. Tristan continues massaging me, and I have to wonder if he's doing this on purpose.

"I think what we have is hot, off the charts hot. But everyone's different and like's different things…" He says, but I detect a hint of nerves.

"I suppose," I whisper, scowling at the water.

"This guy that you were with, how long were you two together?" He asks lightly.

"You really want to know?" I sigh.

"Yes." His answer is immediate. *Great!*

"Why?" *Where's he going with this?*

"I just do," he says nonchalantly.

"Fine!" I huff. "Two years."

"Really?" Tristan sounds surprised.

"Yes."

"Hmm, I didn't think it would have been that long," he muses.

"Why?"

"I don't know really, gut feeling maybe."

"It was on and off, he wanted more…I…I didn't."

"When did it end?"

"Why are you asking?"

"Curious." I don't believe him, he has an ulterior motive, I'm sure he has.

I sigh heavily. "Five years ago."

"So, he never dominated you?" *So much for a relaxing bath!*

"No."

"So back to my original question. Are you afraid of being dominated?"

"No." I snap. *Liar!*

"You're not?" He questions.

"No." My answer is clipped.

"So why didn't it work out with this other guy?"

"Tristan," I sit up and turn in the bath, so I'm facing him. "Why are you so interested? It was in the past, it didn't work out," I say feeling frustrated.

"Just trying to get to know you, baby, like I said, I don't want to fuck it up."

"You won't."

"But unless you' – "Tristan," I close my eyes in exasperation. "Seriously, where are you going with this? I came in here to have a nice relaxing bath, and I have to say, so far it isn't working out for me."

He looks wounded.

"Ah, Christ Tristan! What?" I say, my hand splashing into the water.

"I guess I'm trying to work out what kind of sexual experiences you've had, you know…what you did with him that you liked, so…" He breaks off reading my expression. "You don't want to say, do you?"

"Not particularly," I grumble.

"I'd still like to know' – "Christ!" I take a deep breath. "We didn't do much of anything, just plain sex Tristan, no oral, pretty boring stuff. I was young, scared, I had no confidence, and no idea of what I really liked, what turned me on. Satisfied?" I snap.

"Did he hurt you?" His voice is suddenly low and ominous, his expression frozen as he waits for my answer.

"No, not in the way you're thinking," I say, staring down at the bath water.

Tristan seems to relax a little. "How did he hurt you baby?" he asks, his voice soft.

I close my eyes. "He cheated on me with my best friend, Harriet."

"She can't have been much of a friend," he muses.

"No, I guess not." I snap. It still stings when I think about it.

"And he can't have realised what he had," he says.

"Oh, …he did," I retort.

Tristan frowns. "If he did then why did he cheat on you?" He asks with his head cocked to the side.

I take another deep breath and slowly blow it out. He's just going to keep questioning me, I know he is, so I may as well just get this over with.

"Because he wanted me to commit to him, move in together, and he wanted to do more in the bedroom and I wouldn't, and…" I grit my teeth. "It's like I said to you, I'm not sure...I still don't know if I'm doing this right. I don't know what intimacy is, or how to be close to someone..." I drift off for a second, knowing that is true, then continue.

"Harriet was a lot of fun, she was very pretty and very confident, she knew who she was and what she wanted." I close my eyes trying to push the memory away of me catching them at it. "So I guess they were perfectly matched for one another," I bite.

"How did you find out?" He whispers reading my mind.

"I caught them shagging!" I hiss.

"Do you miss him Coral?" I look up at him staring down at the water, waiting again for my answer.

"No Tristan! I don't miss him at all," I bark. He doesn't look convinced – *Great!*

"Look, he was my boyfriend, and she was my best friend. I thought they both cared for me, like I did them, so to find them..." I close my eyes and take a deep breath. "I don't care that it ended with Justin, it wasn't going anywhere anyway, and I don't think it would have bothered me that much if I'd have caught him with someone I didn't know...but my best friend? If he had come to me and said he wanted to end it, respectfully, and then started seeing Harriet, I wouldn't have minded at all. I'd have been happy for him, for both of them, but they didn't.'

I shake my head, feeling stupid. "I know most people don't think like this, but to me, your best friend should be the person that's most loyal to you, not the one that does the dirty behind your back with your boyfriend. It made me feel like neither of them gave a shit about me, and that's what hurts the most. It had been going on for months, and when I caught them, they both disappeared out of my life. I didn't even get an apology. In one day I lost my boyfriend, my best friend, and my social life."

"Your social life?" He questions.

"I'd known Harriet since school, we were drinking buddies. I didn't have anyone else, Tristan."

"Oh, I see," he says frowning back at me. "You didn't go out with your sister?"

"No, Debs has always been more of a homely girl, and they were trying to conceive, so she wasn't drinking. She told me she was pregnant the same day I'd caught them two at it!"

"Hmm..." Tristan looks deep in thought, then he gazes at

me again, his eyes all deep and mysterious. "Do you know what turns you on now?"

"Yes, you!" I say, hoping to change the subject.

He smiles wryly at me. "That wasn't what I was asking, and you know it," he says.

I close my eyes again. "What Tristan, what do you want to know?"

"I don't…" I open my eyes and see him run his hand through his hair. "I guess I'm just trying to work you out, and I know a little bit more now."

"Yeah…enlighten me," I say sarcastically.

"You have issues with sex." *Oh crap!*

"No, I don't," I argue petulantly.

"Yes…you do, you were with this guy before you got the studio, before…" he breaks off. *Before I was raped!* "I think you know where I'm going with this," he adds.

"Do I really come across to you as someone who has issues with sex?" I say with one eyebrow cocked up.

"You seem very relaxed with *me*…" He says frowning deeply. "But you freaked out again today because I tickled you. I swear it's linked, sex, touch, men. I know there's something you're not telling me…" He adds. *Fuck!*

"No Tristan, there's not," I whisper, trying to get him off the subject, I cross my arms and pout at him, feeling really annoyed. Tristan picks up my right foot and starts massaging it, it should feel really good, but I'm too worked up to appreciate it.

"Are you done questioning me?" I bark.

"Yes," he frowns.

"Good. My turn," I say, surprising him.

"Oh?" he cocks his head to the side and smiles wryly at me. "I'm all ears."

"Yesterday, when I came back, you said 'I'm not sorry I pushed, it made you leave, and it's made me realise a few things' when I asked you what you meant, you said 'later' well, it's later, so spill," I bark.

He stops massaging my foot for a moment as he scrutinises me, then he shrugs and continues, his thumbs digging deeper into my feet – *Oh, that's starting to feel really good.*

"Ok, well firstly, it made me realise that you have issues, very deep and disturbing issues that you really don't want to share with me," he softly says. *Holy crap, he knows…he knows I have secrets, shit!*

Tristan continues. "Secondly, I realised that it's ok, you know…if you don't want to tell me, then that's fine." I stop breathing and just stare at him with wide eyes.

"And thirdly, you walking out the door and leaving me, has made me understand the depth of my feelings for you. I knew the moment you left that it doesn't matter how many times you run because you're scared, I'll always come after you. I'll always fight for you and bring you back home." Tristan stares down at me with dark, brooding eyes.

"Oh," I breathe, trying to take it all in.

"Satisfied?" he asks, throwing my words back at me.

I decide not to answer him. Instead, I lean back, rest my head on the edge of the bath and close my eyes, my shoulders slowly start to work their way down from my ears.

"Come back over here baby," Tristan says, I open my eyes and stare hesitantly at him. He has his hand stretched out towards me.

"No." I pout.

"Please, let me massage you, you're shoulders are almost up to your ears." He gives me his sad, puppy dog look.

I roll my eyes at him. "Fine!" I grumble. I turn around, so I'm leaning against his chest once more. His hands start massaging my shoulders again…*oh that feels so good!*

"I'm sorry," he whispers in my ear then kisses my cheek.

I say nothing, if I open my mouth, it may lead to more dialogue, more questioning. Or, he might want me to comment on what he just told me, and I don't want that, I can't take it.

"Who are we listening to?" He asks chirpily.

"Enigma."

"They're good."

"Yeah…they are," I say, my voice sounding unintentionally sad.

"Hey," Tristan takes hold of my chin and turns me to face him. "I really am sorry. How can I make it up to you?"

"By not questioning me anymore," I whimper, feeling vulnerable.

"Done, anything else?" He says.

"Yes, by making *non-dominating* love to me when we finish this bath," I answer dryly.

His eyebrows rise. "Miss Stevens, you shock me. You want it again?" he teases, then sighs blissfully. "Oh it's a dirty job, but somebody's got to do it," he chuckles, running his hands across my breasts.

"Well, I would have said I'm glad it's you, but after that interrogation, I'm not so sure!" I scoff.

"Interrogation?" he says, chuckling to himself.

"Glad you find it amusing," I bite, but a stupid grin is already appearing on my face, giving me away.

"Ah, baby..." He soothes wrapping his arms around me, squeezing me tight and chuckling in my ear. I shake my head and laugh along with him, not really understanding what I'm laughing at. How can I go from feeling vulnerable and angry one minute, to lighthearted and playful the next?

Oh Tristan, what you do to me...

CHAPTER SIX

TRISTAN HAS STAYED upstairs after our gentle, sweet lovemaking, citing he has some work to do. So there I left him, on the bed, laptop sitting on his legs, looking as gorgeous as ever – *Wish I was sitting on his lap right now*!

I grit my teeth at myself – *Coral!* - Jeez, I'm turning into a sex maniac too!

Shaking my head at myself, I head down the stairs feeling much calmer than I did in the bath. I shudder slightly, all that questioning...I hope Tristan's just guessing about my past, I really don't want him to know that side of me.

As I reach the kitchen, I take a moment to assess how I really feel. I am definitely feeling more relaxed now, I guess that's all the sex, and I'm feeling very excited to be cooking in Tristan's awesome kitchen.

Right! Time for some music to cook by!

Switching on my MP3 player, I plug it into the new player Tristan bought for the kitchen and scroll through my albums. I decide on Barry White's Greatest Hits, his songs are about love, and that's exactly how I'm feeling right now – very, very loved up!

Can't Get Enough Of Your Love Babe starts playing, Barry doing his little speech at the beginning, then the beat comes in, and he starts singing. I can't help moving my body, dancing and singing along to the tune as I try and find where Tristan has hidden all the kitchen equipment we bought today. Finally finding what I need, I take all the food out the fridge and start doing my thing.

Five minutes later, I have the fish poaching in the oven, so

I start on cutting up the potatoes to parboil them. I stop for a moment and take a look at my surroundings. I absolutely love this kitchen, this house and Tristan...*oh Tristan...*

Laughing at myself, I turn back to preparing the potatoes. As I put them on the boil, Barry starts singing You See The Trouble With Me. I sing away, knowing all the words, thinking of Tristan the whole time, how he makes me feel, how crazy I am about him.

Preparing the vegetables, I put them in the steamer ready to be done for a few minutes before the meal is ready, then I prepare the crusty topping for the fish. Knowing I have some time before I make the sauce for the fish, I pour myself a glass of wine and have a little dance around the kitchen.

The track changes again, Never Going to Give You Up starts playing, I get lost in it and slow my body down, moving in time to the beat, singing along, slowly swaying my hips from side to side…I love dancing, I miss dancing…*Maybe we should all go out when Rob's back?*

I open my eyes to take a sip of wine only to find Tristan standing five feet away from me, his jaw nearly hitting the floor, a look of shock and awe spread across his face. I stop dancing and smile shyly, feeling a little embarrassed he caught me – Boy he looks good, he's back in his black sweats and another white vest – *I want him again right now!*

Tristan's eyes darken, then taking me by complete surprise, he smiles his most sexy, panty combusting smile and starts dancing towards me. My mouth pops open in shock as he closes the distance between us – *Oh my God, Tristan can really dance, who knew? He looks so fucking sexy!*

Placing my wine down, I join in with him. His wraps his arms around my waist, crushes me to him, and we grind, sexily in the middle of the kitchen…*Holy fuck!*

Then Tristan leans down, singing in time with Barry…"I'm never, never gonna give you up," his voice is really quite good. "Whatever you want, girl you got, and whatever you need, I don't want to see you without it." Tristan carries on like that, singing to me.

Is there anything he isn't good at?

The timer beeping on the cooker makes us both stop and turn around. I smile up at Tristan, reading my thoughts he lets me go. I walk over to the music and turn it down a little, opening the oven door I check the fish, it's ready for its crusty topping.

Ok, I need to get rid of Tristan. I don't want him in the kitchen while I cook, I won't be able to concentrate, and I want to surprise him. Opening the fridge, I pour him some wine and hand it to him.

"Thank you for the dance sexy, but you need to go," I say.

Tristan takes the wine and gazes down at me. "Do you have any idea how sexy you look when you dance like that? It should be illegal," he says. "Especially in those little shorts."

I look down at myself. I'm wearing my dark blue P.J cotton shorts that I normally sleep in. Ok, they fit really snugly, and I know they show off a bit of my butt too, but I knew I'd probably get hot cooking in my sweats. I did not think Tristan would think I look sexy in them– at all.

"You're looking pretty hot too baby. Now go!" I chuckle.

Tristan doesn't move. He just stands there staring down at me, teasing me with his sexy smile. I try and push him out of the kitchen, giggling as I do. Tristan starts chuckling at me because I'm not making him move very much, it's like he's made out of iron or something.

Putting his wine down he grabs me by the waist and crushes me against his body, then he leans down and kisses me, passionately, his tongue battling with mine. His moans of pleasure are making my blood pressure feel like it's spiked, I lose all thoughts.

Pulling back from me as quickly as he grabbed hold of me, he steps back panting as heavily as I am. *Whoa!*

I gaze up at him, trying to think what I was doing before he kissed me like that. Tristan looks a little bewildered too. I shake my head, trying to clear my thoughts…what was I doing? *Dinner, yes, that's what I was doing, cooking a meal!*

Moving closer to him, I pass him his wine peck him on the lips, then walk away, trying to get my head together so I can finish off this meal.

THE MEAL IS READY. So I call Tristan through to the kitchen, he's been searching for a film for us to watch later, not that I think we'll watch it, I think we'll be screwing like rabbits. My stomach fills with butterflies, just thinking about having sex with him is enough to stop my heart beating for a second or two.

I decided to set up the new kitchen table, rather than eat at the breakfast bar; it looks nice now it's ready for a meal. Alicia Keys starts singing If I Ain't Got You, just as Tristan makes his way over to me. I swoon at him for a second then quickly snap myself out of it – *He's going to think I'm a complete lunatic!*

"Here." I place Tristan's plate of food in front of him, trying to ignore how sexy he is and how gorgeous he smells.

"Wow!" Tristan looks shocked.

"What?" I chuckle sitting down next to him with my plate.

"This looks amazing Coral." I smile shyly and pick up my knife and fork. "I'm serious this looks like Michelin star food." I frown at him, but I can see he really means it.

I look down at the meal I have cooked, a meal I've done I don't know how many times, thinking it doesn't look that special, but to me it's easy, cooking seems to come naturally to me.

"Now you're being silly," I choke.

"No Coral I'm not. Care to tell me how many Michelin star restaurants you've eaten at?"

I take a sip of the cool, crisp white Chardonnay that Tristan has poured and shrug.

"I thought so. I'm telling you, this looks Michelin."

I place my wine down and look at the meal again. I've made Seabass, which I lightly poached then roasted with a crusty herb topping and placed on a bed of wilted Spinach, which I have served with diced and roasted salt and pepper potatoes, steamed asparagus, long stem broccoli, and garlic and lemon butter sauce –*Simple!*

"Ok then, it looks Michelin," I retort, scrutinising the meal.

"Damn right it does," he croons then leans towards me, "thank you, baby." He puckers his lips for a kiss.

I giggle, lean forward and peck him on the lips. Then I watch as he carefully fills his fork up with a little of everything, finally dipping it in the sauce, and then placing it in his mouth. His eyes widen as he slowly chews, then he starts to shake his head – *Oh No! I'm sure the fish was cooked right through?*

"What's wrong?" I say my voice a little wobbly as I try to hide the panic.

Tristan swallows then gazes at me, his eyes going all soft and warm and crinkling at the corners, he leans in to kiss me again, his dimples on full wattage.

"That tastes amazing," he tells me, brushing his lips against mine. "Almost as good as you," he adds, his eyes darkening.

I almost choke on my own spit – *Did he really just say that?* I am speechless.

Tristan grins deeply at my shocked expression and turns back to his food. "Wow!" he says taking another bite.

"You're making me feel self-conscious," I say as I fill up my fork with fish and sauce.

"Sorry," Tristan looks guilty for like a split second. "But this really is good, yet again you surprise and amaze me. Where did you learn to cook like this?"

"I didn't. I'm self-taught." Tristan gapes at me. "What? You don't believe me?" I scowl.

"No no, that's not it. You really taught yourself?" He says, slightly bewildered.

"Well Gladys taught me the basics, and her meals have always been pretty much the same, you know meat, potatoes and veg. It's all I ever ate growing up, so I guess it kind of went from there." Tristan still looks astonished as he continues to eat and drink his wine.

"That's fair enough Coral but how did you get from that to this?" He questions pointing at his plate.

"When you've got a lot of time on your hands…" I sigh heavily remembering how I felt back then. "I guess it all started when I got the studio. I was bored…a lot of the time, so I kind of got into cookery shows, you know, Master Chef, Hairy Bikers, that kind of thing. I liked watching them, they were the only thing I could watch that took my mind off things, gave me something to focus on. I guess I just…if I really liked the look of a certain dish, I'd buy the ingredients and attempt to cook it, only I kept finding that it would always work out fine first time around. Bob was my taster, I thought he was biased, but now you've said that…maybe not." I ponder.

"So you're a natural," he says his eyes sparkling.

"Yeah…I…I g-guess," I stutter feeling quite astonished that he likes it that much.

"What a lucky bastard I am," he chortles.

"Yes, you are," I say shocking myself. *That was confident for me.*

"Yes, I am," he croons, leaning in for a kiss. I peck him on the lips and smile. "Did you study cookery at school?"

"No. I couldn't concentrate for very long on one subject, not unless I was fascinated by it."

"What were you fascinated by?"

"Science, Physics, Art. I had a lot of energy too, so I played a lot of sports, only…" I break off remembering how bad I was, how many fights I started and ended.

"Only what?" he questions.

I sigh inwardly. "I was in the Netball team, and we used to have matches against other schools, and well, if they cheated or tried to get one of our players sent off…I'd kind of lose it…" I say, cringing inside.

"Lose it how?" he asks evidently intrigued.

"Fighting Tristan. I was a very angry, highly volatile, scared young girl ok. Now, can we change the subject?" Tristan has frozen like a statue, his fork halfway up to his mouth, a deep frown etched across his forehead – *Great, I better say something, get him off the subject.*

"So what fascinated you at school?" I ask.

He places the food in his mouth, still lost in thought, then after a couple of minutes, he comes back to me and shrugs. "I wouldn't say I was fascinated by any of it really. I just knew that I wanted to make money, somehow?" he says.

"Why? I mean why money?" I ask.

"Because I hated not having what I wanted when I wanted it. Don't get me wrong, my folks were awesome, they showered me with love and affection and that you can't buy. But it gets a bit much when you have to keep walking past all the shops with the new clothes, the cool clothes, only to be taken into charity shop after charity shop…" Tristan trails off, lost in thought.

"They tried their best, I know they did, but I couldn't stand having to have second-hand clothes. The second-hand shoes and trainers, however, were much, much worse. God, they would stink to high heaven. I remember asking for a new pair of trainers for Christmas one year. Gran actually said ok, but I couldn't have anything else as they were so expensive, which I was happy with, just that one present. But come to Christmas

Day, I find I have new trainers, only there the really geeky ones that you just know you'll have the crap beaten out of you for wearing. I didn't get my Nike's, I was gutted." He stares out the window, he looks like he remembers something painful, then he turns back and smiles at me, and eats more of his food.

I smile hesitantly back at him, wondering what that must have felt like.

Tristan continues. "I guess it kind of went on like that you know, Gran constantly saying no to me. Like if I asked for something nice to eat in the supermarket, like a packet of liquorice or a chocolate bar, I would never get it," he says, his cheeks flushing red.

"So that's what pushed you to want to make money?" I guess.

"Yes, and wanting to take care of my folks in their old age." Tristan stares down at his meal for a moment.

"Which you did," I say proudly.

"Yeah, they were pretty healthy, happy, and well taken care of. So yeah, I guess I did achieve that goal, but what about you baby, what was your dream?" I shake my head in response.

"I didn't have a dream," I answer my voice low.

Tristan gazes down at me. "No dream?" He asks quite astonished.

"No. Why? Should I have had one?" I say, frowning back at him.

Tristan chuckles at me. "You're having me on," he says. "Come on Coral, we all dream about being something when we're young. Fireman, policeman, nurse... you know all that kind of stuff." I shake my head at him and shrug my shoulders *– I honestly don't see what the big deal is.*

"What was yours?" I ask, taking a sip of my wine.

"Well, when I was about four I said Postman Pat because he had a car, which I thought was really cool." I raise my eyebrows at him. "My folks never had a car," he clarifies.

"Really?" I say, astonished.

Tristan shakes his head, frowning deeply. "Always the bus," he says, a slight edge to his tone.

"I liked Postman Pat too," I say trying to pull him out of his reverie.

"When I got a little older, and the teachers asked again, I said 'a man in a suit'." He adds.

I chuckle at Tristan. "Why did you say that?"

"Because when Gran used to take me into town, *on the bus*, I would watch all these men in suits with nice cars, going about their business. They had shiny shoes, shiny suits and shiny cars. Whatever they were doing, I wanted to do it too," he says firmly.

Wow, he was so determined from such a young age!

"Guess that kind of makes sense, and you certainly reached your goal," I take a deep breath. "I know we haven't known each other that long Tristan, but I'm really proud of you, of what you've achieved. I imagine it takes a lot of guts and sheer determination to get where you are today. I hope you feel proud too?"

"I do," he smiles, then leans forward and kisses me again. "And thank you, it's nice to know you feel like that," he says, tenderly stroking my cheek. "But you haven't answered my question?" he adds.

I go for a change of subject. It's something I've been thinking about since this morning.

"Can I drive your car tomorrow?" I ask.

Tristan gazes at me in disbelief. "My car?" he asks swallowing hard. I don't think he likes the idea.

"Uh-huh," I take another forkful of food.

"Yes...yes, of course, you can. I didn't know you wanted to drive it...I..." Tristan narrows his eyes at me. "Nice change of subject," he scolds –*Crap!*

"I tell you what, you answer my question and you can drive it anytime you want. In fact, if you like it I can buy' – "Stop!" I take a sip of my wine. "You were going to say buy me one, weren't you?"

"Yes." Tristan beams, his eyes sparkling.

I shake my head at him. *Not that conversation again!*

"So why no dream Coral?" he repeats.

"I did have a dream," I answer quietly, gulping back the rest of my wine. Tristan is watching me, waiting for his answer – *Crap! I want to drive that car, so I guess I better tell him.* I sigh heavily, close my eyes and pinch the bridge of my nose.

"My dream was to have a loving, caring family," I whisper so quietly I wonder if he actually heard me. Opening my eyes I see him staring back at me, his expression torn, he looks nauseous, but now he's got me going on the subject, so I feel like I should explain it to him.

"They were always arguing, fighting, there was always something breaking or being smashed. I lost count of the number of times I hid under my bed because I was never quite sure if my Dad would lose it one day and hit me, or Kelly would find me. I'd hide under the duvet with the pillow over my head to try and drown out the noise, the constant shouting..." I look down and see I'm mimicking my actions, pulling the duvet over my head.

"That was before it got really bad. So when the teacher asked me, I would always say I wanted to be a roller skater, because it was the only thing I had that got me out of the house, away from the noise – you finished?" Tristan nods.

In a huff, I pick up our plates and storm over to the kitchen sink – I hate remembering the past – and blast the water over the empty plates.

"I'm sorry." He says. I turn and see Tristan leaning against the breakfast bar, giving me some distance. He looks awful like he's riddled with guilt for bringing it up.

"Fuck!" I let the cutlery clatter to the bottom of the sink, walk over to him and wrap my arms around his torso, resting my head on his chest. "I hate talking about the past," I croak.

"Yeah, I've kind of gathered that," he says, his arms enveloping me.

"Then why do you keep bringing it up?" I choke.

"I'm sorry baby, I had no idea you were going to say that, *at all!* I thought you would say you wanted to be a princess or a nurse, you know stuff kids say. Really, baby, I was not expecting that." Tristan rocks me gently, soothing the pain away.

"Christ!" I squeeze my eyes shut trying to push the demons away that are lurking in the forefront of my mind, just waiting to come and get me again.

I can't wait for more Hypnotherapy!

"You're scared?" Tristan guesses.

"Yes," I whisper.

"What of?" he asks, his voice low and husky.

"Let's just call him the boogie man," I say by way of explanation.

"The boogie man?" he says, his voice deep.

"Yeah…nightmares." I twist my head and lean my chin against his firm, muscular chest. "Did you really just say I can drive your car tomorrow?" I ask, beaming up at him.

"You really do jump ship don't you?" I frown back at him. "What I mean is you can go from one emotion to another, instantly; it's quite fascinating," he says matter-of-factly.

"Oh well, I'm glad I…fascinate you," I answer sulkily.

"Hey now, that's not how I meant it." He says, his tone is soft.

I pull out of his arms. "I know you didn't," I say, but I still don't like the fact that he said it. I frown at myself as I place the plates and cutlery in the dishwasher and switch it on. "Incidentally how did you get this place so quickly?" I add, trying to change the subject.

"I gave them an offer they couldn't refuse," he answers smugly.

"Which was?" I question.

"Six months worth of rent, so they could look for another place."

"You're kidding?" I choke.

"No." He looks so proud of himself.

"Do you always get what you want? When you want it?"

"Yes, well most of the time," he says, shrugging his shoulders at me.

"Except me," I retort.

Tristan's face falls. "I thought' - "No one ever really owns anyone Tristan, not really." I stare back at him feeling pissed and moody, and I know exactly why.

I shake my head at myself, feeling guilty I just said that. "Tristan, please just ignore what I just said, I'm feeling a little… off," I tell him bluntly.

"So the car?" he says a little unwillingly.

"Yeah…the car," I sigh and walk over to the kitchen table. "More?" I ask.

"Please." I pour more wine into both our glasses and hand one to Tristan. I know I need to make amends. I don't like hurting him, and I don't like feeling like this. I want it to go back to how it was half an hour ago.

"I am so sorry, that was out of line. When I get upset or scared about something, I blurt things out I don't really mean, it's something I'm working on with George. So yes, I would love to drive your car tomorrow, if you don't mind me taking it for a spin, and no, I didn't have a dream like all the other boys and girls."

"Apology accepted, not that you need to apologise," he says, leaning down to kiss me.

"Yes I do," I murmur against his lips. "I'm not blind Tristan, I could see you were hurt," I add, swallowing hard.

"Coral, you didn't hurt *me*, what upset me was that I knew you were upset. So don't beat yourself up so much, everybody says things they don't mean when they're scared."

I nod once. *How can he be so...so forgiving?*

"If I put the fire on will you curl up on the sofa with me?" he asks, stroking my cheek.

"Yes," I whisper, gazing up at him.

He pecks my lips once more. "Thank you for the meal, it really was delicious," he adds, licking his lips.

"You're welcome." I smile back at him, then picking up our wine glasses, I walk into the living room, and as I get myself comfortable on the over-large, very squidgy sofa, I watch Tristan turn on the fire. "Hey sexy," I say handing his wine to him, as he sits next to me.

"Hey yourself," he says taking a sip and gazing adoringly at me. "Your bruises have almost gone," he says, tracing his forefinger under my right eye.

"I know, at least I won't have to cake my face in tons of make-up on Monday," I chuckle, thinking back to how dreadful I must have looked.

"Coral, I want to ask you something?" *Oh boy here goes!*

"Ok," I sigh.

"If you could go away tomorrow, anywhere in the world, where would you go?" *That's easy!*

"The Hawaiian Islands," I answer a little too eagerly.

"Why?" Tristan asks, his head cocked to the side.

"Are you kidding me, the scenery, the amazing beaches, need I say more?" I squeak.

Tristan chuckles at me. "Ok, I'll give you that, it is beautiful," he nods in agreement. "But?" he adds. *How does he know there's more?*

I glance shyly at him. "Tell me," he croons.

I take a deep breath. "Ok, I picked Hawaii because ever since I was about eight years old, I've wanted to go watch the big surfing competition they hold there each winter."

"Why?" I can see Tristan is finding this quite amusing.

"Ok, don't laugh at me, but I kind of find the big waves fascinating, and the mad surfers who ride them even more fascinating. I mean, who does that? Who risks their life for the ultimate wave? I know it's kind of stupid, but it doesn't mean I'm not in awe when I watch them on T.V."

I take a deep breath, feeling stupid for sharing. "I've always wanted to see it in real life, you know, hear the roar of those gigantic waves, the wind in my face." I shrug my shoulders and stare at my glass of wine, Tristan thinks it's stupid I know he does. "Plus, they have a really amazing cuisine over there, I'd love to try the food and wine," I add. *Maybe that can be our first holiday together?*

"They do, do they?" he grins.

"Yes, they do," I answer smartly, trying not to laugh.

"I should have known you'd pick a place with great food," he chortles.

"Why would you say that?" I question.

"Because you have a passion for food and cooking," he simply says.

"Yeah, I guess I have a thing for it, but it's just a hobby."

"Hmm…I'm curious Coral. If you could do or be anything you wanted, wake up tomorrow and you're living that life, what would it be?"

"Jesus Tristan I don't know!" I say, feeling exasperated. *How did this change from places to visit to life-affirming questions?*

"Haven't you ever thought about it?" He asks, his voice low.

"Well…no I haven't," I answer, wondering where all this is going.

"Ok, well I want to set you a challenge," he tells me.

I shake my head at him. "No, I have enough of those," I answer darkly.

"You do?" He says, his head cocked to the side in amusement.

"Yes, George is forever setting me new challenges," I say, rolling my eyes.

"Like what?" He asks, evidently intrigued.

"Trust me. You don't want to know the answer to that one."

Tristan frowns and is quiet and contemplative for a moment, then continues. "Ok, well not a challenge, but something I'd like you to think about."

"What do you want?" I ask gloomily.

"It's not bad Coral, relax." He soothes.

I'm tense, worried already about what he wants. I feel my shoulders start to work their way up to my ears. *Be brave Coral!*

I take a deep breath. "Ok, shoot," I blurt.

Tristan chortles. "Ok, I'd like you to think about the question I asked. What would you do if you could, no questions asked and no excuses either. Money doesn't matter so don't think about that part of it."

"Um, ok, that sounds easy enough," I answer, but I'm curious as to why he wants to know, then I realise – *Crap! This has something to do with my job.*

"Why do you want to know that?" I ask, my voice wobbling slightly.

"This has nothing to do with your job Coral!" he admonishes in a deep and powerful voice, freakily reading my mind again. "And I'm not going to keep repeating myself on that one, it's a given. But I suppose the question I'm asking is to do with it, and whether you would choose to stay, or go for a different career?" He looks a little pissed at me.

"Why are you so interested in what I do for a living?" I ask questioningly.

"Because I think you're wasting your talents." He states.

"You do?" I frown, then snort sarcastically. "And what talent is that, may I ask?"

"You're a chef, a cook, a natural. I'm surprised you've hung onto your job for so long, and you haven't left out of sheer boredom." He says sarcastically.

"What?" I scrutinise his face.

"Most people who are creative, have creative talents like chefs, artists, writers, actors, dancers and so on. They are all artistic, creative personalities that are living their lives as they are meant to. You, on the other hand, are definitely creative, yet you sit at a desk everyday typing out what must seem like very mundane letters," he says, gazing down at me.

"I don't just type letters," I spit back at him.

Tristan narrows his eyes at me. "I know you don't," he barks and runs a hand through his hair. "Look, I want the best for you, which means I want you to be really happy with what you do. I want you to wake up every morning with a big smile on your face knowing that what you're doing day in day out is what you truly love to do." He says, sounding frustrated.

"Oh!" I hadn't thought of it like that - *Too quick to jump the gun Coral!*

"Oh!" Tristan repeats my words back to me, when I look up, I see he's smiling at me. "So you think you can do that?" He adds dryly.

"Think about what I want to do?" I squeak.

"Yes." He states firmly.

I frown back at him. I'm trying to work out if he's right? I thought I would always be at Chester House right until I retired, but now Tristan's said that I don't know what to think. Maybe that kind of stuff just isn't for me?

"I don't know Tristan," I say biting my lip, feeling the nerves creeping in.

"What don't you know?" He says, with a slight sigh.

"I just...I just think some things are best left alone," I answer begrudgingly.

"Like what?" he asks.

I sigh inwardly. "Like...look, I never..." I look away from Tristan for a moment trying to gauge it right, what I'm trying to say, it's very difficult to have any kind of coherent thought when he's gazing at me like that.

"Ok, so I'm in school, and I'm a nightmare. My grades are terrible and none of the teachers like me. I have no future, no prospects and no dream. I have no goal of going into further education like college or University because as far as I'm concerned school sucks, big time. Like you're supposed to know what you want to do with your life at fourteen years of age," I blurt out as dryly as I can, then I continue.

"So I finish school at home, my exam results were just...well tragic, I was so nervous about letting Gladys down if I didn't get high scores that I built myself up into a frenzy, and failed most of them. I knew there was no way I was going to do it all over again. I guess I just figured I'd go out into the world and just get a job, just like everyone else does.

I sigh heavily. "I suppose, if I'm truthful, I was more

concerned with keeping myself on the straight and narrow. I didn't want to go down the same path as my mother. So for me, staying straight and holding down a job was, and still is a big achievement for me. I'm not walking her path." I take a deep breath, then a big glug of wine.

Tristan's eyes darken. "When you say straight and narrow?"

"Tristan I swear to god if you mention a word of this to anyone, especially Gladys' – "Coral," Tristan barks in frustration, interrupting me. "You should already know you have my complete trust, whatever you tell me stays with me, I give you my word for god's sake!"

"Fine!" I huff back. "I was drinking alcohol and smoking pot at school, I was heading down the same path," I say, turning away from him.

"Ah, I see," Tristan turns away from me and stares out the window.

"Running for the hills yet?" I ask observing his reaction out the corner of my eye.

"No, just thinking how bad you must have been feeling to resort to those measures."

"Anything to block out the pain," I bite my brain to mouth filter failing on me again. I notice Tristan's demeanour change to shock and squeeze my eyes shut for a moment – *Coral you idiot, keep it zipped or he's going to find out!*

His mobile beeps at him, Tristan takes it out his pocket and stabs his code in with his forefinger. "Damn it!" He hisses, as he gets to his feet.

"What's wrong?" I whisper.

He doesn't answer me, he just marches into the kitchen and disappears from view. For a split second, I feel like that's it, he's ending it all, and I don't blame him. I'm jumping from one emotion to the other, it's tiring, and I'm constantly feeling on edge in case I blurt something out that I don't want him to know, then it gets all uncomfortable, well it does for me, and I'm left hanging…just like now – *God damn it, where is he?*

"Tristan?" I call out for him, but there's no reply. I go to stand, but see him re-appear with his mobile to his ear. "What are you doing?" I question.

He holds his forefinger up to me. He's speaking rapidly at whoever is on the line. As I look up at the new clock on the wall,

I see it's ten past ten in the evening. I can't help wondering who he's speaking to at this time on a Saturday night.

"Sorry about that," he says, joining me on the sofa again.

"Late night bootie call?" I chuckle, but really I'm checking on him.

"No, a meeting I'd forgotten to move, so I left a message for Susannah."

I grit my teeth, *her*.

"Oh Susannah," I say trying not to sound jealous. Although why I should when I have the gorgeous Tristan Freeman sitting next to me I don't know.

"Problem?" *Damn, he's razor sharp today!*

"Nope," I answer dryly.

He narrows his eyes at me. I stare blankly ahead.

"Want to watch a film?" he asks.

I think that's a good idea, my mouth can't run away with me then.

"Sure, yeah...that sounds nice," I answer glumly.

Tristan flicks on the T.V, which instantly illuminates the large room.

"Just for the record," he says staring ahead. "It doesn't matter what road your parents travelled down Coral, we all have choice and free will. So please, try to free your mind and expand it to the possibility that there is a more enjoyable career out there for you. That's all I'm saying on the matter." Tristan dashes a scornful look at me then starts scrolling through the selection of films. *Hmph!*

My mouth sets into a hard line, I guess that told me!

CHAPTER SEVEN

I AM DREAMING I AM in a busy, bustling place. Steam keeps rising around me, and someone is shouting my name. When I turn to see who it is, he shouts at me again.

"Coral, I need two beef wellies, three salmon, and one pork loin. Pronto."

I turn around again and realise I'm in a kitchen, a big professional kitchen. Everything is stainless steel, and there are lots of chefs all wearing white uniforms. When I look down at myself, I see I'm in a white uniform too, why am I...?

"Coral?" I blink my eyes open and see Tristan gazing down at me. "Good morning sleepyhead."

"Hi," I croak, blinking around the room. Tristan is sitting on the bed fully dressed, and he smells divine. I lean up on my elbows. "You're up already?" I grumble.

"Yes, we have a big day today," he tells me. It takes me a moment to ascertain what he means. Then it comes to me – *The Car!*

"Yes!" I beam, almost jumping out of bed.

"Stay where you are," he tells me and hands me a big glass of what looks like my vegetable juice.

"How did you' – "Guessed. Try it. Tell me if I got it right." I take a tentative sip – *Perfect!*

"Delicious," I answer. "You should have one too, it's good for you," I add.

"Already have." I narrow my eyes at him and drink the remaining juice. "Oh…I had a really weird dream?" I say staring blankly ahead, trying to remember it.

"And?" He chuckles.

"I was in a chef's uniform. I think I was running a restaurant?" I say

"Hmm, sounds like you've been thinking about what I said," he says, his face looks smug.

"Well forget it! It's very long hours, working weekends, I'd never get to see you," I say sullenly.

"Hmm…" Tristan is not convinced. "Come on, get up baby, take a shower and meet me downstairs. I have a surprise for you."

"Tristan," I groan. "How am I supposed to keep up when you keep being the wonderful one who bears gifts all the time?"

He smirks at me, then leans down and pecks me on the tip of my nose. "It's not a gift, now come on, out of bed. The sun is shining, and it's our last day together, I want to make the most of it," he tells me firmly.

"I have a good idea how to make the most of it," I say seductively, pulling the quilt down to reveal my pert, toned breasts.

"Oh no you don't, there's plenty of time for that later, come on, up!"

I groan and fall back down onto the pillows.

"Definitely not a morning person," I hear him chortle as he walks away.

I stare up at the ceiling and try not to think too hard about the fact that Tristan will be gone all week, that this is our last day together. My heart sinks to the pit of my stomach, I have no idea how I'm going to handle it – *Stop it Coral!*

I nod in agreement and push the thought to the back of my mind…

GETTING OUT OF bed was fine, walking, however, was not! Muscles I didn't even know I had are aching so badly, it's hard work trying to walk in a straight line. *Damn, I thought I was fitter than this!* – Tristan looked fine when he walked away, which is quite frankly, rather annoying. Maybe my body will get used to it, and the muscles will repair quickly? I hope so, I don't want him thinking I'm a total flake!

Walking into the bathroom, I feel as though Tristan is in the room with me, his smell is everywhere, that delicious mind-boggling scent of his, his shower gel and his aftershave, mixing into one and wafting around everywhere is making it hard to concentrate. *Ok, Coral get a grip!*

Walking over to the sink, I pick up my toothbrush, squirt some toothpaste and start cleaning, but I can't help thinking back to the dream and what Tristan asked. Do I really want to try out a different career? Is that something I really want to do, cooking, be a chef? I always thought of it as a kind of hobby, not a career, but maybe Tristan's right? Admittedly, there have been times when I've been bored out of my head at work, but that's normally when it's quiet, and Joyce has gone home early, and I've got no work to do.

Hmm, definitely something to keep thinking about...

AS I'M SHOWERING and getting nervous about driving Tristan's Eighty Grand worth of sports car, I have a sudden thought – we haven't discussed children. If Tristan and I really are the ones for each other (I think setting up home together, albeit Tristan's home is a pretty big step) then surely things like marriage and kids should be discussed?

I mean, I know we've kind of brushed over marriage – Just as I think that I get an image flash up in my mind's eye. I'm in a long, ivory wedding dress and I'm walking towards Tristan, he looks so smart and handsome, and he's smiling his deep dimpled smile at me – *Stop!*

I freeze mid-wash. Hold the phone, did that just happen? *Whoa! That was weird!*

I'm suddenly catapulted back in time to the dream that I had, and Tristan calling me Mrs Freeman – *Ridiculous!*

I shake my head, involuntarily getting shampoo in my eyes – *Damn it!* – I decide to leave the big thinking until I'm out the shower…

TWENTY MINUTES LATER, I am dressed. My hair has dried into mellow waves, I'm spritzed with perfume, and I'm putting my make-up on at the bathroom mirror. I spot Tristan's aftershave and pick it up to see which one it is – Millionaire by Paco Robane – *Figures!*

I put the bottle back down, and concentrate on the task at hand. *Ok, so where was I?*

The dream, the dress, marriage! *Am I denying it to myself?* George said that I should believe it's possible for me.

I stare back at my reflection. "Is that what you want Coral, to marry Tristan?" I question aloud. A resounding yes echoes around my head – *Holy Crap!*

I shake my head at that thought, it really is quite absurd, we have only known each other a couple of weeks, and I'm thinking marriage! *You need to slow yourself down girl and get a grip!*

I suddenly feel deflated about it all, like I've taken the excitement out of the prospect that it could actually happen for me.

I glare back at myself. "You know what, you wanna marry Tristan you go right ahead." *There, that told me!* – I shake my head at myself. *What am I talking about?*

Putting down my eyeliner and reaching for my mascara, I decide to tackle the next big question – Kids. My heart slowly sinks. How do I tell him I can't have them, that I'm unable to conceive? I feel sick just thinking about it. Closing my eyes, and pulling my hand up to cover my mouth, I take a deep breath and try to stop the nauseous feeling. Opening my eyes, I gaze back at myself. If it's something Tristan really wants, then he should be with someone who can give him that, surely?

My stomach rolls…I hate the thought of him being with anyone else, but if I can't give him what he wants…I blow a deep breath out…this could be the end of us – *Stop Coral, you're worrying about the future again, just go downstairs and ask Tristan the question. Do you want kids?*

I stare back at my bright wide, sparkling because of Tristan, coral blue eyes, and take a deep breath. "You can do this!" I nod at myself and make my way out of the bathroom.

Picking up my shoulder bag from the bedroom, I wander down the first flight of stairs. I decided to dress in my jeans, t-shirt and my Nike Air-Max trainers (just to see if he says anything) and because I want flats on to drive the car – I'm buzzing with an excited, nervous feeling!

Walking hesitantly into the kitchen, the first thing I notice is the overpowering smell of Croissants and Chocolate – I feel myself light up inside, I really like those. The second thing is that Bruno Mars is singing in the background, Locked out of

Heaven is playing, my head starts to bob as I sing along to the words.

Then I see Tristan sitting on one of the breakfast stools reading a newspaper.

He's dressed in his dark blue jeans, a light blue t-shirt which clings to him in all the right places and – *Oh my God!* As I look down I see he's wearing the same trainers as me, except his are dark blue and mine are gunmetal grey.

"Hey," I skip over to him and kiss him on the lips, surprising him.

"Good morning. Mmm…you smell heavenly," he says, pulling me closer and kissing my neck.

My pelvic muscles clench in the most delicious way, I instantly feel hot and moist down below.

"What perfume are you wearing?" he asks, nibbling my earlobe.

I almost climax there and then. "Absolutely Irresistible," I groan, my head falling back, my eyes closing involuntarily, my heart spiking, my breathing erratic.

"That you are," Tristan murmurs against my neck, softly kissing and grazing his teeth down towards my shoulder.

"Um, Tristan…you shouldn't really be doing that if you want to get out of here," I murmur, trying to sound as though I'm capable of a conversation.

"Really?" he questions, still kissing my neck, my jaw.

I grip his hair at the nape and pull his head back, then kiss him with all the pent up sexual energy I have felt since he denied me this morning.

"That," I growl against his lips. "Is not fair, you deny me then tease me?"

"I was just kissing you," he says all innocently with puppy dog eyes.

"Do you have any idea how that makes me feel?" I say sitting on the bar stool next to him.

"I think I have a pretty good idea," he smirks.

"Oh really?" I challenge.

"Yes." He replies smugly.

"Then how does it make me feel?" I question.

Tristan looks bashful for a moment then he turns his intense gaze on me. "Exactly the way I feel when you kiss me."

"And how do I make you feel when I kiss you?" I ask, arms crossed.

"Like I want you, instantly," he says his face intense, his eyes dark. *Oh wow!*

"Ditto," I breathe, uncrossing my arms. "So what'll it be Mr Mogul, sex or car?"

"Both," he says grinning cheekily at me. I shake my head at him and laugh. "Mr Mogul?" He questions – *Crap! I can't believe I just said that out loud.*

"Have you?" I ask trying to change the subject.

"Have I what?" he smiles.

"Had car sex?"

"Yes."

"When?"

"I was a teenager."

"Oh," I feel myself deflate a little.

"You?"

"No," I whisper, feeling shy again.

He leans towards me, so he's almost touching my lips, taking my breath away again, then he moves and brushes his lips across my ear.

"Maybe," he whispers in a low husky voice, my body shudders all over. "We can do that today," he adds. My heart is pounding. *Car sex?*

I swallow hard. "Yes," I whisper.

He moves again, so he's right in front of me, and runs a cool soft finger down my cheek.

"Whatever you want baby," he says, seeing straight through me again.

I stare down at my fingers. *Why do I suddenly feel hot and flushed?*

"Hey?" Tristan slowly lifts my chin up, so I have to look at him, I don't know why I say it, but I do.

"I love you," I whisper. "So much…" I frown at myself. "Too much…" I add.

Taking hold of his face, I kiss him, hard.

"Coral," he mumbles, pulling away from me, and placing my hands on my lap. "You need to eat, and so do I, can we do that first?" he asks, smiling down at me.

I stare at the floor feeling utterly rejected. Then I think back to our conversations that have involved sex, and it hits me, he doesn't want me like that. I think back to last night, we had sex on the sofa, halfway through the film just as I thought we would – but we didn't when we went to bed, or this morning.

"You…you don't want me like that?" I whisper, frowning deeply, keeping my eyes on the floor.

"Hey," he tips my head up. "Yes, I do, always."

"I don't believe you," I whisper, avoiding eye contact.

"Well, I do," he retorts.

"Prove it," I breathe.

In the next breath, Tristan is up on his feet, has swung my bar stool around and pulled me into his arms. His mouth claims mine as his one hand tugs on my hair, and his other hand slides up my leg, gripping my thigh and my backside.

I kiss him back with all the passion I feel burning inside me, I grip his hair with my hands then wrap my legs around him. His erection is firm and hard between my legs, making me want him all over again. Then taking me by surprise, he lifts me into his arms and carries me over to the sofa– *Ok, got that wrong, he does want me!*

Placing me down, so my back is lying on the sofa he sinks to his knees. He unties my trainers, throws them off, undoes the belt on my jeans, the button, and the zipper and pulls them off me. Then he takes hold of my knickers and yanks them to the side.

"You think I don't want you?" he questions as his thumb starts circling my clitoris, his look full of hunger and want for me. "Do you?" He questions.

I can't concentrate, I can only *feel* as his thumb continues circling, fulfilling a need I feel deep within me. Then with his other hand, he deftly undoes his belt, his zipper and pulls down his jeans and boxers, freeing his erection – *Holy fuck!*

I moan in approval. Then he stops, pulls a condom out of his pocket, rips it open and puts it on. "Lift up your legs," he orders.

I instantly do so, he grabs me by the hips and pulls me towards him, so I'm right on the edge of the sofa, his tip teasing my clitoris, his thumb still making circles.

"You want this?" He growls.

"Yes," I gasp.

He slams into me. *Whoa!*

"Ahh..." I feel so full, the feeling is exquisite.

Then he really starts to move, pumping hard and fast, in and out. I watch with wide eyes as his erection pumps in and out of me, it's so fucking hot, so sexy, god I love him!

"Tristan!" I gasp. I can already feel I'm building.

"You think I don't want you?" he pants, pumping harder, faster. It's all going so fast!

"No!" I shout.

"Because I do," he grunts. "I'll always want you. Can you feel me, baby? Can you feel how much I want you?" he croaks, his cheeks flushing, his eyes dark chocolate – *Holy fuck!*

"Yes," I cry out, my back arching, my head craning back. *Jesus, I'm so close!*

"Give it to me," he shouts. "Come with me, baby." I manage to look up at him, he's right on the edge. "Now Coral!" he shouts, and I let go, just as he does, my head spinning, my whole body tensing as my orgasm pulses through me, through every cell in my body.

Tristan collapses on top of me, his head on my chest, and I float away to a far distant place. I feel so content, so happy. It's pure ecstasy, a sea of sexual bliss...

"I'm sorry," he croaks.

I open my eyes and see Tristan has his chin propped up on my chest. He's staring at me with wide, guilty eyes.

I frown back at him and take his face in my hands. "What for?" I whisper.

"That was...I'm sorry," he repeats and rests his forehead on my chest. I run my hands through his hair and chuckle, his head whips back up, his look is one of confusion.

"Tristan, that was hot," I say, still breathing hard.

"Hot?" He questions.

"Yes," I giggle. "Don't you think so?"

"I just..." He trails off again, closes his eyes and places his forehead back on my chest.

"Tristan," I pull his face up to look at me. "What's wrong?"

He clenches his jaw and stares at me, his eyes still wide. "You don't think I was rough with you?"

"What?" I choke. "No, Tristan, not rough, that was..." I

stop, trying to think of the right word to say. "Mind-blowing," I add staring back at him. *Why is he acting like this?*

I think about our lovemaking yesterday, after our bath and on the sofa, he was so sweet, so gentle with me. I don't think he's ever been like this, so…so *rough?*

My face falls as it dawns on me why he's acting like this; he doesn't want to be rough with me because he thinks it will trigger what it felt like being raped, how I felt then.

"I knew I shouldn't have told you," I choke out, trying to fight back the tears. He lifts his head again but doesn't say anything. "I'm right, aren't I? You don't want to be like that with me because you think it will remind me of being raped?"

Horror dawns on his face, he knows I've worked it out. "Coral'– "No, don't Coral me," I choke. "Tristan, that was nothing like…" I squeeze my eyes shut and grit my teeth, trying to reign in my temper. "Tristan," I whisper and open my eyes. "That was nothing…nothing like that, you and I, we have passion and love on our side. Don't you understand that?"

He still doesn't look convinced. I sigh inwardly. *How can I make him understand?*

"You can do that again, anytime you want, I thought it was really, really hot." I pant.

"You did?" He questions quizzically. "I…I didn't hurt you?"

"No!" I bawl running my hand through my hair. "Baby, isn't sex supposed to be varied?"

He closes his eyes and puts his head back on my chest.

"Tristan, I love that you're so sweet and gentle when you make love to me, you get right in there when you do, right into my soul. But that doesn't mean I don't enjoy a quick hard fuck too," I say hoping to shock him. It has the desired effect. His head snaps up and a very coy smile appears on his face.

"Coral Stevens, what language," he softly scolds.

"Well, if you don't cheer up, I'm going to flip you over, straddle you and fuck you all over again!" I say, teasing him.

His sexy grin appears as he softly shakes his head at me. "My, my, surprising me again," he says, his eyes going all warm and gooey.

I take his face in my hands again. "Tristan, I love you, and I trust you. I know absolutely, without a shadow of a doubt, that you will never, ever hurt me, ok? Now stop moping, and help me up. All that fucking has made me hungry." I chuckle.

He finally laughs along with me, then leans forward, takes my face in his hands, and kisses me softly. "You are one surprising, challenging woman," he says, his thumbs skimming my cheeks.

I stare back at his beautiful face. "And you are one challenging man," I retort.

He smiles shyly at me, kisses me briefly, then leans up onto his hands and gently pulls out of me. "I'll just get rid of this," he says, winking at me.

I watch him walk along the hallway towards the downstairs bathroom, when he steps inside I sit up and pick up my discarded jeans. I'm just buckling my belt when he walks back in the room. Bending down in front of me, he picks up my trainer and holds out his hand for my foot.

"Left or right?" I tease, even though it's obvious which one he wants.

He cocks an eyebrow up at me. "Right." He answers sternly.

I give him my right foot, he pushes my foot in the trainer and ties up the lace, then he does the same with the left.

"Why thank you," I say sweetly.

"My pleasure," he laughs, shaking his head at me.

"So what now?" I ask.

He cocks his head to the side. "If I remember rightly, you informed me that 'all that fucking has made you hungry'?" he says.

"Ah, but I didn't say what kind of hungry?" I tease.

His mouth pops open. "Again?" he gasps.

I shake my head, laughing at him. "No," I chuckle. "Definitely food, although I like the idea of car sex," I say kissing him on the cheek.

He rises to his feet, pulls me up by my hands and crushes me against the length of his body, then kisses me so softly I literally melt in his hands.

"I have a favour to ask," I say, remembering Bob.

"Anything you want, it is yours," he tells me softly.

"I need to get dinner to Bob today, a roast. They do takeaways at The Sportsman."

"Of course, at lunchtime or' – "No, we normally have them early evening," I interrupt.

"Ok, consider it done." He kisses my forehead and takes hold of my hand, steering me back towards the kitchen. Well, that's that then, I don't have to feel guilty about Bob anymore.

"Take a seat," Tristan says when we reach the breakfast stools.

I prop myself up, place my chin in my hand and watch him move around the kitchen. How can it be that even the way he moves is hot and sexy? I could watch him all day long. *Jeez Coral, get a grip!*

I blink several times trying to snap myself out of it. I've got it so bad for him, shaking my head at myself, I take a deep breath in trying to reign in my overactive imagination, and I'm hit with one of the best smells in the world –Tristan and Chocolate Croissants – *What more could a girl ask for?*

"Yummy," I beam at him.

"I guess you know what my surprise is," he says, smiling widely at me.

"Wouldn't be Chocolate Croissants by any chance?" I say, smirking at him.

Tristan shakes his head at me as he brings the plate out of the warmer, and places it in front of us. There are already two small plates set up, with forks and napkins and two glasses of orange juice. "Coffee?" He asks.

"Yes please." Tristan brings the jug over and fills up both our cups.

I am loving that this feels so normal, so easy going. It's as though we've been together for years, not days.

"When did you get all of this?" I ask picking up a warm croissant and ripping it open, the smell is divine.

"Yesterday." He says, smirking slightly.

"But I didn't see you pick them up in the supermarket?" I say.

"I guess you're not very observant," he chortles. *I know he's winding me up!*

"No, you're sneaky," I bite narrowing my eyes at him as he sits next to me. "Snap." Tristan looks bemused. I kick his foot, which makes him look down.

"Ah Nike's..." he exhales, a look of appreciation on his face.

"Indeed," I say, smiling broadly.

Bruno starts singing Just The Way You Are, I hadn't even noticed the music was still playing, I guess I was preoccupied. I can't help humming along as I eat and drink.

"You like Bruno Mars?" Tristan asks.

"Yeah, he's really good," I say smiling shyly at him.

Tristan leans down and sings a little of it to me, just like last night, then kisses my hair and returns to his food.

I smile nervously at him. "So I wanted to ask you something," I say, my heart instantly hammering against my chest and my throat going as dry as a bone, I pick up my orange juice and take a long drink.

"I'm all ears." Tristan smiles and caresses my cheek.

I clear my throat. "So...I think, stop me if I get this wrong, that you and I are kind of like...well for life?" I say a little breathlessly.

"Yes, we are." Tristan is gazing at me that way again, I have to look away, or I'll never get this out. I stare ahead, out through the windows, the sunshine making me squint. My leg is jigging up and down with nerves.

"Ok, so...I was just thinking about...well kids." I take a bite of croissant which I shouldn't have done as I can no longer swallow, a lump has formed in my throat that I can't get rid of.

"Kids?" Tristan's voice sounds off, so I turn to look at him.

He's gone as pale as a ghost. *Oh no!*

I swallow hard. "Hey, are you alright?" I ask touching his arm.

"You want kids?" he asks, his eyes wide.

"Well I...actually, I was asking you that question. I just think it's important to get it straight what both partners want. I mean, I don't see the point in two people being together especially if one wants kids and the other doesn't...." I trail off, and look outside again, hoping and praying Tristan will say he doesn't want them – *Then I'm off the hook!*

"It is an important question." Tristan's voice pulls me from my musing. "A very important one and I completely agree, no point two people being together if they want opposite things."

I stare back at Tristan with wide eyes, my stomach sinking.

"Honestly, I've never really thought about it. No partner, no need to think about it I guess," he adds, shrugging nonchalantly.

I frown back at him. "Ok, but what do you see when you look to the future? Do you see yourself as a father?" Just as I say that the strangest thing happens, I instantly picture Tristan throwing a little two-year-old boy in the air and catching him as the kid screams in delight. He would make a really great Dad.

"I don't know Coral. Like I said I've never really thought about it before." I nod and look out at the window again. "What's brought all this on?" he adds.

"I don't know. The question just popped up while I was in the shower, and I thought I don't know the answer to whether you do, and it's an important one, so I thought I'd ask." I stop there, my voice sounding far too high pitched for my liking.

Tristan narrows his eyes at me as he assesses what I've just told him. "And if my answer had been yes?" *Damn it, he's too shrewd!*

I shrug nonchalantly at him, his cocks his head to the side scrutinising me even further.

"And no?" I shrug again not wanting to give anything away, although the question has not been answered.

"And you Coral?" *Damn it to hell!*

I gaze straight ahead trying to think of an answer, then I decide to lie, I can't do it. I can't tell him the truth, it's too scary. I turn and look at him, trying to make my eyes look all melty and warm like he does with me, leaning forward I brush my lips against his.

"I don't know," I whisper.

Tristan frowns then takes my face in his hands. "You don't know?" he repeats.

"Uh-huh," I murmur against his lips again.

"Well that's odd," he chortles. "But then there's nothing that's traditional about you Coral," he says kissing the tip of my nose.

I pull back from him, sniggering to myself. "Fuck up," I say tapping my head.

"Confused more like, and I'd say lack of home life and a sense of feeling grounded. Maybe with time, the answer will become clearer." Tristan says.

I exhale loudly. "How do you do that?" I instantly feel relieved and take another bite of croissant.

"Do what?" he asks sipping his coffee.

"Make all my worries feel like they disappear," I breathe. "Oh and sound so wise, older than your years, like you have all the answers," I add, keeping my eyes on my croissant.

"Guess I'm just lucky," he says, his voice all husky and deep. My heart booms and the butterflies return. My appetite has gone again.

"You've gone pale," he says frowning at me. "Are you feeling unwell?" he asks, placing his hand on my forehead.

"No, you make me feel a bit woozy sometimes," I answer honestly.

He visibly relaxes and smiles shyly at me. "I do?" he says, removing his hand from my forehead. Tristan sounds proud of himself and a little smug.

"You want me to lose two stone?" I gripe.

"No – I absolutely do not – I love your curves." He tells me firmly.

"Then stop being so...so perfect and sexy and brilliant and nice." I stop talking and force the rest of the croissant into my mouth – it's not attractive, really it isn't– then take several gulps of coffee to help me swallow.

Tristan is really chuckling to himself now, evidently finding my squirming and suffering amusing. I finish my coffee and turn in my seat, so I'm facing him.

"Ok, George is always telling me I worry too much about the future, well about everything but' – "He's got you nailed down to a tee," Tristan interrupts, still chortling.

I glare at him, he instantly stops laughing, so I continue.

"So the whole kid's thing isn't something to worry about? Or is it? I'm trying not to, but what if you decide you do and I don't, or vice-versa? People change their minds with stuff like that all the time, and I can't...I just...I don't want to lose you, Tristan. But at the same time, I'd rather cut the cord now, so to speak, than get totally and utterly wrapped up in each other's worlds, only for it to come crashing down." *Jeez, I feel like I'm having a session with George!*

I burst out laughing at myself, it kind of helps, a little.

Tristan turns and takes my hand in his. "Ok, first things first. You are over worrying about things that may or may not happen that you can't change. Secondly, if in the future you decided you want kids, your wish, my darling is my command'

–"But' – "Oh no you don't. No interruptions," he says shaking his head at me.

I purse my lips and stare back at him.

"If I decide I want kids and you don't, I would not leave you Coral. I would accept that I already have everything I want in the palm of my hands, as in you. If I did want kids and you do too, they would be…an added bonus. The difference between being a couple to being a family, so whichever way either of us goes, we will still be together. Does that help you feel more relaxed?" He softly asks.

"Yes...and no!" I reply.

Tristan smiles down at me. "Ok, what's the no part?" He's so patient with me.

"Resentment," I answer clearly.

"Resentment?" he questions frowning at me, trying to understand.

"Yes, you'll totally resent me if I say no and you want them, surely?" I squeak out.

"No, I won't Coral. Don't you understand? You're the cake, the amazingly rich, sweet chocolate cake. Kids would be the icing on the top." He tells me firmly.

I chuckle at that one. "I like your analogy of it."

Tristan smiles his sexy smile. "Yeah me too, that kind of worked," he says surprising himself.

I chuckle even harder. "Yeah, it did."

"Ok now?" He asks, stroking my cheek again.

"Yes." I swallow hard. Tristan sighs in relief, picks up another croissant and rips it open, and I die a little inside. I have to find the courage to tell him the truth, something else to talk over with George.

CHAPTER EIGHT

I AM SAT IN THE driver's side of Tristan's F-Type, and I'm buzzing with excitement. Tristan has driven us to a quiet country road so I can get a good feel for it. The sun is blasting down making the roads nice and sticky – although the car is as cool as a cucumber as Tristan wanted the roof up – and the sky is a perfect blue, not a cloud in sight.

"Comfortable?" he asks, looking a little worried.

I beam at Tristan. He looks so good, sitting there, looking fresh, clean, and sexy as hell with those aviators on.

"Love these bucket seats," I say looking around at the rest of the interior. It has that new car smell, and I'm surprised Tristan has chosen black leather interior; I feel like I'm in the kit car from Knight Rider.

"Concentrate Coral!" Tristan admonishes. I hear him speak, but I'm drawn to the song playing in the car.

"Who's this?" I ask innocently.

"Coral!" Tristan balks.

"I want to know!" I moan.

"Fine! It's Aqualung, Strange and Beautiful." I raise my eyebrows at him.

"Is that what you think of me?" Tristan instantly looks uncomfortable – *Great he thinks I'm strange!*

"Before drawing any conclusions, I think you should listen to the words," he drawls sarcastically.

"Oh!" I frown back at him.

"Coral!" Tristan is getting really annoyed with me.

"Right, sorry." I look straight ahead.

"Now remember, it's a rear wheel drive car, you get it wrong, the back flips out we' –"I know we go for a spin," I interrupt.

"Which we don't want," Tristan adds, shaking his head.

"Definitely not," I scoff, agreeing wholeheartedly.

"Ok, I'm going to put it into Auto, keep your foot on the brake."

"Can't we have Sports mode?" I whine, Tristan look says it all. "Ok, ok Auto," I stifle a giggle as he's taking this all very seriously.

"Now release the brake and gently push down on the gas." I lift my foot and touch the gas, but a little too much and we lunge forward, I panic and hit the brake.

"Try again, but really gently this time." Tristan encourages.

I do so, and this time it works, and we gently pull away. The feeling is amazing, the car sounds awesome, and I feel totally cocooned. I keep my speed down, getting a feel for the car, I don't want to get it wrong and go skidding out of control, plus, I haven't driven a car in ages. I see a bend coming up, I know the handling on this car is meant to be awesome, so I don't brake, I just let the car glide around.

"Nice Coral, not bad at all," Tristan says, nodding his head in approval.

"Thanks," I squeak with excitement, glancing across at him.

"Eyes forward!" He barks. I panic and stare straight ahead. Maybe this wasn't such a good idea with Tristan *in* the car, when I look at him, I find it hard to look away. "Want to go faster?" He asks.

"Hell yeah!" I giggle, glancing across at him again.

"Well go on then," he says, gesturing with his hand, smiling widely at me. I grin a Cheshire cat grin and push my foot down on the gas. The car growls as it picks up speed, making me smile even wider – *Ok maybe Tristan can buy me one of these!*

As we whoosh around the country roads, the car effortlessly eating up the miles, I realise I'm having the time of my life. Not only am I in a very sexy car, but I have a very sexy man beside me to boot. I take the next bend with a little more enthusiasm than Tristan likes, but the car makes it, effortlessly.

"Careful baby," Tristan says his voice low.

"Ok," I answer mulishly, but I don't slow down.

He puts his hand on my knee and squeezes tight, which

does not help my concentration at all. "This is the first time you've driven her, take it easy ok?" *Her?*

"Your hand on my knee is not helping me concentrate," I retort. Tristan instantly lifts his hand from my knee, which makes me smile.

As I continue to drive, my confidence grows, and I really feel as though I'm getting to know the car, so I push harder. As we hit a straight, I see Tristan in my peripheral vision, he looks as though he's getting more and more nervous by the minute. I fight the laughter that wants to burst out of me, my lips twitching into a smile.

"Happy?" Tristan asks.

"This is amazing!" I screech, whacking it into another bend.

"Ok baby, let's not wrap us around a tree," he says, gripping his hands together. *Jeez, he really is nervous!*

"Ok," I titter. In the distance I see a lay-by and start to slow down, finally pulling in so Tristan can take over. Tristan puts the car into park and puts the handbrake on, leaving the engine purring beneath us.

"Fun?" he asks, his eyes wide with excitement.

"Amazing," I reiterate.

"Want one?" he chuckles which makes me roll my eyes at him. "I'll take that as a yes."

Tristan leans in and kisses me forcefully, his lips moulding perfectly to mine. It's like his lips were made just for my lips. Whenever we kiss and make love, it feels as though it's always in such synchronised symmetry, which makes me wonder if Gladys is actually right and there is a Soul-Mate out there for each of us. A car pulling in behind us stops us from our little bit of fun - *There goes our car sex, maybe later?*

We giggle at nearly being caught, then Tristan steps out, and walks around to the driver's side. With wobbly legs, I step out of the car using Tristan's hands for support. Then he walks me round to the passenger side and helps me slide into the low seat and shuts the door. I watch him jog around the car, open the driver's door, lean down and press a button, the seat starts to move back, so he has enough room for his long legs, then he slips inside. *Damn, he looks sexy today, and even sexier behind the wheel of this baby!*

He starts driving again. He really is very good at it, and very fast – which again I'm surprised at. My control freak tendencies don't make for a very good passenger, but with Tristan, I feel safe, I trust he won't fuck it up.

Which makes me go back to this morning, and thinking about the whole wedding thing, I mean, it's too early, of course, it is, but I can't help thinking that Tristan should know that he's changed my view of it all. So I decide that tonight, I'll talk to him, tell him how I feel.

Deep in thought, I hadn't noticed that we are heading east out of Brighton.

"Going somewhere?" I ask.

"Indeed we are." Tristan beams at me and clutches my hand.

"Will you tell me where?" I ask, feeling a little apprehensive.

"Hastings." Tristan turns to see my reaction. "Ever been?" he asks.

"No, I haven't actually, you?" I say, staring at his profile.

"Just once for the day, I was a kid I don't remember it much." He tells me.

"Did you plan this?" I ask, narrowing my eyes at him.

"Yes." He smiles widely at me. *I knew it!*

"When?" I ask, smiling back.

"Last night while you were preparing dinner," he says smiling coyly. *I didn't think he was working!*

"Why Hastings?" I ask.

Tristan smiles warmly at me. "Because it's got culture, history, and great beaches."

"What, and Brighton hasn't?" I say dryly.

Tristan chuckles at that one. "What are you thinking? Do you want to go, or turn back?" he looks worried.

"No way, I've never been. I'd really like to see it," I tell him.

"Good. It's meant to have some really quaint little shops. I thought we might find something for the house." Tristan looks across at me and smiles sweetly.

"Good idea batman," I banter.

"Thanks, Robin," he chuckles.

I lean back into my plush bucket seat and enjoy the scenery.

Leaving Brighton behind actually feels quite invigorating, refreshing; but more than anything, I'm just in awe to be spending the day with Mr Moneybags; he really is quite something…

IT HAS TAKEN US an hour to reach Hastings. Tristan has spent the whole time throwing questions at me, all random stuff that comes up in everyday conversations like favourite colour, clothing, music, films, books and food. He's been very careful not to ask questions about my past, which I really appreciate, I really want to enjoy today.

I sigh inwardly. I am doing my very best to block out the fact that we'll both be back to work tomorrow, and Tristan will be gone all week. I can't even begin to think about how I'm going to feel when he's gone. A shiver runs down my spine making me shudder – I stamp on that line on thinking, I want to enjoy today!

Then I remember I have legs-that-go-on-forever Susannah to deal with. I tried to convince Tristan as we got into bed last night that I was sure to work out the new programmes by myself, that Blondie didn't need to come and train me, but he disagreed –*Stupid Millionaire Mogul!*

"I have one more question," Tristan says, pulling into a car park right on the seafront.

"No!" I pout – I told him no more questions until I get a drink of some sort; my throat is so dry from talking so much.

We find a parking space away from all other vehicles, right at the far end. I notice two security men patrolling the car park. I have to wonder if Tristan purposely found this one because of that. Then I wonder if you can search car parks on Google. I bet you can, I shake my head at my over-active imagination.

"Why are you parking so far away?" I ask.

"I don't want any fucker scratching my car," he growls.

"Oh!" That's understandable, it's not cheap.

Tristan gets out the car and walks around to my side, opening the door for me.

"Please, just one more," he asks, as he takes my hand and helps me out of the car, it's so low it's not exactly easy to get in and out of.

"Fine!" I huff.

Tristan takes my hand, and we start walking. "When we first met, you looked like you knew who you were meeting. It could have been Craig or Pete, but you knew who I was. How?"

Holy crap! Of all the questions to ask me – I decide to lie.

"Joyce showed me a picture of you," I squeak, looking anywhere but at Tristan's face.

We stop walking as we've reached the pay meter, Tristan puts the money in, and the ticket pops out. Another security guard I hadn't noticed appears out of nowhere making me jump as he greets Tristan.

"Gorgeous car mate," he says slapping him on the back. They start talking cars and engines. I'm glad of the interruption. Maybe Tristan will forget what he's asked me. I turn around just in time to see him hand a twenty to the guard.

"Keep an eye on her for me?" I have to stop myself from laughing. *Boys and their toys!*

"No problem mate." The security guard shakes Tristan's hand, I can't help rolling my eyes.

We walk back over to the car, and I wait patiently while Tristan puts the ticket in the window. Then he walks over to me, takes hold of my hand, and taking me by surprise, he pulls me up against him and kisses me like we haven't kissed in days, finally dipping me down low, so my hair touches the floor, I feel dizzy by the time he stops.

We start walking again, my hand in his, neither of us saying anything. I'm trying really hard to keep the stupid loved up grin off my face. Tristan glances at me, smiles deeply, shakes his head at me then chuckles too.

"Did you plan to park here?" I ask.

"I sure did." He says.

"Why?" I chuckle.

"Because it's the only car park with security, and I figured if I tipped them, they'd look after the car." He says, shrugging slightly.

"Seriously?" I choke.

"Yes," Tristan says firmly. "I really like my car!"

"Yeah, I've noticed," I add dryly.

"So where to my darling, the beach or a walk in town?" he asks animatedly. He looks excited, like a young schoolboy; it's cute.

"Town, I'm thirsty!" I reiterate.

"Town it is!" Tristan squeezes my hand, and we head in the direction of The Old Town…

WE LOCATE A QUAINT little café in town, and we have ordered some coffees and a bottle of water for me that I instantly glug back. Tristan has also ordered a Toasted Sandwich citing he is hungry again. I guess a couple of croissants aren't enough to keep him going.

I don't know how he stays so slim with the amount he eats. I guess it must be swapping his workouts around like he told me.

"So, am I going to get the answer to my question?" He asks again, a slight smirk stretched across his face.

"I told you," I say, looking out the window at the shoppers melting in the heat.

"Don't believe you!" He scoffs.

"Tough!" I retort.

"Tell me, please...." He leans forward, places his hand on my cheek and turns my head around to face him.

"It's embarrassing," I moan. I also don't want him to know how badly I didn't want a male boss.

"I won't laugh." He assures me.

"Yes, you will!" I snort.

"No, I won't." He argues back, his voice firm.

"Fine!" I close my eyes and say it. "I Googled you," I whisper, opening my eyes to stare out the window again. "This place is so nice, I bet it looks lovely in the winter with all the shop windows lit up," I add, trying to get off the subject.

"It certainly does." I look up, and the lady who took our order is placing our coffees down.

"Thank you." Tristan and I both thank her at the same time.

She smiles warmly at us both. "You're welcome, toasty won't be long love," she says to Tristan.

"Ok, thank you." Tristan smiles up at her, stopping her in her tracks. *Jesus H Christ!* She's got be in her sixties, and she's blushing.

"No...no problem dear," she says looking all flustered as she walks away.

I want to roll my eyes, but I don't. Tristan takes a sip of his coffee then places his cup down. He doesn't say anything about the Google thing, which I'm glad of. *That was a close one!*

"And what about Mogul?" Tristan says pulling me from reverie. *Shit!* – I decide to act like I didn't hear him. "Coral?" I glance across at him. Tristan is smirking at me, his head cocked to the side. "Earlier today, you called me Mogul," he repeats.

"Uh-huh," I take a sip of coffee and stare out the window.

He lifts his chair and shuffles closer to me. When he reaches me, he pulls on my chin, so I have to look at him; we are almost nose to nose.

"Why did you Google me?" *Christ, I thought he'd dropped this one!*

I decide on the truth, he doesn't need to know I was staring at him for hours after I found him. "I was scared," I whisper.

"Scared?" He repeats, his brows pulled together.

"Yes," I hiss, feeling annoyed we are having this conversation in public.

His eyes bore into me. "Of me?" He softly asks.

"No, of who you *could* have been..." I sigh in frustration and run my hand through my hair. "I never wanted a male boss' –
"Most men are creepy to you," Tristan interrupts.

I stare back at him with wide-eyed worry. "You really do listen," I whisper, glancing at the couple sitting near us.

"Yes I do, and I'm sorry for interrupting you. I won't again, please continue." *God damn it!* It's so hard to be mad at him when he's so bloody polite like that!

"Basically that's why I like where I work, Joyce is– sorry *was* my boss. Everything was comfortable, controlled." I take another sip of coffee.

"And then I come along," he says smiling boyishly at me again.

"Yeah…" I roll my eyes and smile at him, then frown remembering how I felt only two short weeks ago. "I had to see you weren't some creepy fat cat in a suit," I tell him.

"What would you have done if I was?" He asks, drinking more coffee.

"Left," I answer immediately.

"You wouldn't have given it a go anyway?" He asks, surprised.

"Tristan I..." I run my hand through my hair then start blurting it all out. "It's like…like I have a built-in radar for creepy, slimy, bad men. I can tell them a mile away, almost as though I can smell the creepiness oozing out of them." I take a deep breath, clear my throat and carry on drinking my coffee.

"Why?" I ignore that one. "And Mogul?" He asks jumping to the next question, but it's not a better one.

I decide on the truth. "I was mad at you for putting the idea in Joyce's head about selling. It was a nickname I made up for you. I hated you before I'd even met you, hated you for taking Joyce away, of making my controlled, comfortable life turn on its head." I bob my tongue out at him, then smile.

Tristan's eyes widen and darken as he stares back at me, then he swallows hard and takes my hand in his. "Coral, I didn't put the idea in her head, Joyce asked me," he tells me, his cheeks flaming too.

"What!?" I hiss. I feel all the blood drain out of my face. *I don't believe this! Why is everyone lying to me?*

Tristan entwines our fingertips and softly squeezes, making me feel calmer, then continues. "Joyce asked me if I knew about anyone wanting to buy at the moment, I asked her why and she told me all about her plans' – "What! What do you mean, her plans?" I interrupt.

"Here's your ham and cheese toasty love." The lady places Tristan's food in front of him.

"Thank you," he glances up at her then his eyes flash back to me. "Coral," he whispers, I think he thinks I'm about to have a full-scale meltdown.

"She lied to me," I hiss.

"How?" he asks, with wide eyes.

"She told me that you'd heard about John and made *her* an offer, but you didn't?" I squeak.

"No, I didn't," he answers firmly – I absolutely believe him.

"What the fuck is going on? Why would Joyce lie to me?" I say, feeling incensed.

"I don't know baby." His thumb starts making small circular movements across my knuckles, trying to calm me, ease me.

"Everyone's lying to me," I hiss, fighting back the tears.

He leans forward, softly kisses my cheek then whispers in my ear. "I'm not."

I gasp and choke back the tears, gripping his hand more firmly. "I know," I whisper back, then lean forward and stroke his cheek. "That's how I know I can depend on you, rely on you. I know you value honesty." I croak.

"Yes, I do baby," he says.

Freed By Him

For once in my life, I actually feel like letting something go, instead of it pissing me off all day. Tristan will be gone tomorrow, we have so little time, and I don't want to spend today feeling pissed. I want to enjoy Tristan for as long as I can, I want to make the most of the time we have together.

"Fuck it," I hiss. "I'm not letting anything spoil this day, what's done is done, right?"

Tristan looks amazed. "Yeah…can't change the past baby."

"Or people lying either," I add.

"Nope, can't change that." He adds.

I feel satisfied I can handle it. I mean, it seems everyone bar Tristan is keeping something from me nowadays. I take a deep breath, and another sip of coffee feeling satisfied that I have my emotions in check.

"Eat your Toasty babes, it'll go cold." I tell him.

Tristan smiles and leans in for a kiss. I lean forward, kiss his lips then get up and order two more coffees…

HASTINGS IS BEAUTIFUL. We have walked through the Old Town, strolled down George Street, the High Street and All Saints, which are full to the brim of historical things to see and do; and all the quirky tiny passageways to walk around are just delightful. There is history everywhere you turn, old houses with the history of the smugglers, the Museum and the Smugglers Caves.

It has great cafés and restaurants, and the pubs look really oldy-worldy too, I want to come back in the winter. Tristan agreed it's a must, and that we should stay at the oldest place we can find, a weekend here would be so much fun. And to make our day even more magical, we've bought two really lovely boat paintings for the house by a local artist, the way he captured the light is what made us both gravitate towards his work, and we both agreed they would look lovely in the bedroom.

"Have you ever had a photo-shoot done, professionally?" Tristan asks me as we stroll hand in hand through the streets.

"No," I chuckle. "Why would I want to do that?" I balk.

"Because one day when you're wrinkly, you might want to look back on how utterly breathtaking you really are." He says his eyes all warm and sincere.

I shake my head at him. "I think you're biased!"

"Really?" He counteracts, his head cocked to the side.

"Yes." I scoff.

"Look behind you." I turn around and see the reason for his question. I am stood looking at the shop front of a photography studio.

I turn back around and shake my head at him. "No, no way!" I'm too late.

Tristan picks me up by the waist, chuckling to himself as he does, takes the couple of steps needed to reach the door, swings it open, steps inside and puts me down.

"I won't do it," I pout, crossing my arms.

He completely ignores me and turns to the man behind the counter, who looks a little shocked at us bursting into his store. "Good afternoon, any chance of a couple of photos to take away?" Tristan asks in his persuasive way.

"Yes, of course." The man ushers us into a back room. It has white walls and a white floor. He places a stool in the centre of the room and starts to set up his camera. Tristan starts dragging me towards the stool.

"Tristan!" I moan.

"Don't argue it's happening," he growls.

"Only if you're with me," I say and pull him along with me.

"Ok. Are you ready?" The cameraman asks.

Tristan sits on the stool and pulls me down, so I'm sitting on his left leg, at an angle.

"This was supposed to be just you," he scolds mulishly.

I place my arm around his shoulders and shake my head at him. "Believe me, these photos will look so much better with you in them." He frowns at me and shakes his head.

For some reason, our earlier conversation starts running through my head. I decide to be truthful with him, and hopefully shock him, so I lean down, so I'm right next to his ear.

"Oh, and by the way," I whisper. "When I Googled you I hadn't even met you, yet I spent ages staring at all your pictures, I thought you were the most handsome man I had ever seen."

I hear his breath catch. I sit back up and stare down at him; it's definitely had the desired effect. His cheeks have flushed, his lips are parted, and his eyes are wide, deepening, growing darker as the second's tick by - *Ha it worked!*

"Eyes to the camera please, say cheese." I turn and smile at the camera, the flash blinding me then turn to see Tristan still staring up at me, he's totally speechless. *Ha!* – That means I'll have that photo, and I'll always remember what I said to him, right then, the look on his face is priceless.

Finally, he speaks. "Oh you did, did you?" he whispers all seductively.

I gaze down at him, feeling brave. "Yes, I did."

He places his hand on my cheek and pulls my head down, so his lips are at my ear. "I knew I was right, you even loved me back then," he whispers.

My mouth gapes open, I guess it's my turn to look shocked. The photographer keeps snapping away, as Tristan smiles up at me with that sexy grin of his, I can't help but smile back. Suddenly the atmosphere between us changes, charges; filling the room with an invisible force of electricity. Tristan is looking up at me in that hypnotic way of his, my breathing alters as my heart begins to pound against my chest. *Whoa!*

Tristan takes my hand and places it against his heart; it's beating just as fast as mine. I can feel the pull from him, his eyes darkening, pulling me into his hypnotic gaze, I'm aware that there's still a flash going off, but I don't take any notice of it.

"See the effect you have on me," he whispers, his eyes dark and dilated.

I nod once. "It's the same effect you have on me." I manage to whisper.

"Is it?" He questions – *How could he be unsure of that?*

"Kiss me," I whisper.

Tristan entwines his hands in my hair and pulls my head down, so our lips connect, and it's like he's kissing me for the first time, I'm instantly transported to another world. His kiss consumes me, caresses me, it's so powerful and strong, his tongue expertly lapping against mine – I think I'm going to faint, I feel dizzy.

"Coral..." He moans against my lips. It heats my body, boils my blood and makes everything south of my belly clench with delicious anticipation. I moan in response and kiss him back, revelling in his skill, how he tastes – *Fuck, I'll never get enough.*

Unfortunately, we start to get a bit heated, forgetting all

about the cameraman. Until he clears his throat bringing our attention back to him, we both look up surprised and a little embarrassed.

"All done," he says, looking embarrassed and starts to take the card out of his camera.

I bite my lip feeling guilty. Tristan lifts me off his lap, and we walk shamefaced to the front of the shop. Tristan pays the photographer, and we waltz out of there with twenty A4 shots that the photographer printed off for us. Tristan also bantered with him to send the photos in a zip file so we can blow up any particular ones that we like and frame them. *Great! I really don't want pictures of me all over the house!*

The moment we are out the shop, Tristan pulls me against his body. "Any other secrets to do with me that you want to share?"

"No," I answer playfully, he leans down and kisses me, hard. We hear someone shout 'get a room' and quickly pull apart. *Ok, that was uncomfortable!*

"So where to now?" He chuckles.

"The beach," I say, grinning widely.

"The beach it is," he says, his answering grin reflecting mine…

CHAPTER NINE

WE LOCATE A BEACH called Camber Sands. It's truly breathtaking, there's miles of white sandy beach with lots of sand dunes. My mind instantly pictures Tristan and I up to no good behind one of the sand dunes, my body quivers just thinking about it. *Definitely got sex on the brain!*

As we stroll along the beach, enjoying the sunshine and the nice breeze that's kicked up, I can't help wondering what Gladys and Debs are up to and why Gladys didn't tell me about Malcolm. I hatch a plan that I intend to execute next week.

Then I start thinking about telling Tristan about my dream of him, and the image I had of marrying him, but I chicken out. I just feel like it's too soon and I might blow it.

"You're quiet. What are you thinking about?" Tristan wraps his arm around my shoulders and kisses my temple. I panic for a second then try to think of something random to say.

"Dancing." *Weird!*

"Dancing? Yes, you can certainly do that," he offers.

"I was half expecting to have to wipe the drool from your mouth," I banter.

"Oh, ha, ha, I can't help it if you totally blow my mind. You really are a very sexy dancer."

"You're not so bad yourself Mr Freeman, got some sexy moves going on there."

"Thanks." Tristan looks very pleased with himself, but in fairness, not many men can look that good on a dance-floor. Tristan absolutely, without a doubt, does!

"Maybe that should be my new career, lap dancer," I retort.

Tristan stops walking, halting me too. As I look up, I see his mouth has popped open, his brows are pulled together, and he's staring, wide-eyed at me.

"J-Joke," I stutter.

He blinks several times, his face still contorted. *Jeez, chill out!*

"Not a funny one!" he barks back.

I giggle and snuggle against his chest. "As if I would do that," I say.

"Do you do that often, dancing?" He says.

"Used to be out every Friday and Saturday night with Harriet, then it all stopped, well everything stopped." Tristan tightens his grip on me. "But I think I would have stopped anyway, I was partying too hard, and the hangovers were becoming a little bit much to take, and I was desperate to have my own place, so I saved the money I would normally spend on a night out. I knew it would bulk up my deposit and get me there quicker. Then when I got the studio, I joined the gym, met Rob and got a social life again."

"And you haven't been out dancing since?" he asks.

"Sometimes with Rob, but only if it was a gay bar and Carlos was with us."

"Carlos?" Tristan stops us again. "Who's Carlos?"

I look up at him and smile. "Are you jealous Mr Freeman?" I ask, smiling broadly.

"Yes." He answers honestly, taking me by surprise. "I'm jealous of any man that gets to spend time with you."

I giggle at that one. "Carlos is Rob's husband."

"Oh." His frown disappears, and we start walking again. "So, you were saying…about dancing?"

"Well, Carlos is a big beefy guy so I knew if anyone gave me a hard time, he'd sort it for me. Do you go out dancing?" I add, instantly picturing him in a dark nightclub, doing his thing - *Man he can move!*

Tristan shakes his head with a mock laugh. "No, not really, a little bit through University."

"Too busy building an empire," I answer dryly.

"Yeah, I guess." I look up at him, he looks a little sad. "Can I ask you something, it's just an observation," he states.

"Shoot," I say without thinking about it.

"I've never seen you in a dress or skirt for that matter, not at work or' – "I prefer jeans," I interrupt wanting to get off the subject.

"And at work?" *Bollocks!* – I decide not to answer and just shrug my shoulders. "Alright, I get it, subject closed." He says, his soulful eyes capturing me.

I lean up and kiss his cheek. "Thank you," I whisper.

Tristan stops walking and gazes down at me, he's got that strange look again. He leans down, his hands holding my face and kisses me so tenderly, I almost faint.

"Gotcha!" He grabs me by the waist as I hang onto his strong arms. He pulls me closer to his chest. "You need food," he says sternly.

"No, it's you," I answer breathlessly.

"Me?" He retorts, his voice high.

"Yes, you just..." I can't find the words, it's so hard to describe how amazing and heady he makes me feel. "I told you, you take my breath away," I whisper, keeping my eyes closed while the blood rushes back to my head.

"Ditto," he whispers in my ear.

I squeeze him tighter and bury my head under his chin. "Tristan," I mumble. "You're changing my mind," I whisper.

"Changing your mind about what?" he whispers back.

I take a deep breath. "About...well, us...you know, moving in together...getting married."

"I am?" he says, sounding surprised.

I swallow hard. "Yeah...I think I want to marry you." *What? Coral, what are you doing!*

"You do?" I look up and see Tristan's face break into his most breathtaking smile.

"Yeah," I sigh. "Someday..." I rest my head against his chest, closing my eyes as I do. Tristan doesn't say anything, he just wraps his arms around my shoulders and holds me, for which I'm truly grateful. I can't believe I just said that out loud, so much for waiting.

WHEN WE ARRIVE back in Brighton, Tristan drives us straight to The Sportsman so I can purchase Bob's dinner.

"What are you doing?" I question as I take off my seatbelt.

"Coming in with you," he says.

"Tristan, you don't need to hold my hand," I scold. "Besides, someone might scratch your car," I warn teasingly, as the car park is pretty packed.

He suddenly stops and looks around the car park. "You're right, I'll wait here." I smile sweetly at him, step out the car and head into the restaurant.

Five minutes later, I am back with Bob's dinner. Tristan steps out the car, takes the bag from me, helps me into the seat then places the bag on my lap. "Don't spill it," he warns, I can't help giggling at him. I actually consider winding him up by pretending to almost drop the bag, but he might try and save it, then crash the car, so I decide against that plan.

Five minutes later, I am knocking on Bob's door.

"Coral," he says, looking surprised.

"Hey Bob, I've got your dinner here," I say brightly.

"Coral, you didn't need to do that," he says. "Come on in." I step inside, walk over to the kitchenette, grab a plate and dish up his dinner. Then I fold out his little table and place his meal down.

"Come on Bob, don't let it get cold," I say.

Bob walks over to me and squeezes my shoulders. "You spoil me Coral," he says sweetly.

"I like looking after you," I tell him. "Besides, you need a decent meal inside you. You can't keep eating all that canned crap," I remind him.

"Thank you, darling, you really are the sweetest," he says and starts tucking into his food. *Jeez, he sounds like Tristan!*

"Need anything else before I go?" I ask looking around his studio. Everything looks good, it smells and looks clean, and there's no sign that Bob is struggling with anything.

"No darling, you've done enough." He tells me.

"Ok, but you have my number if you need me right?" I remind him.

"Yes, stop fussing," he scolds. I smile down at him, kiss his cheek and head out the door; feeling desperate to be back in Tristan's presence, I miss him already. I wave to Bob as I shut the door behind me.

As I pass my studio, I stop and take a quick peek inside and see that all is well, as I carry on walking towards the gym, I have the strangest feeling like I'm leaving a part of me behind. I shrug it off and carry on walking along the concourse, back to Tristan waiting for me at the gym car park.

AS WE DRIVE BACK towards Tristan's mega pad, the atmosphere in the car charges, getting heavier and denser the closer we get to it. We keep stealing silent glances at one another, and I have a very strong feeling we are both thinking the same thing. Parking the car, Tristan jumps out with lightning speed and opens my door for me. Pulling me out a little vigorously; he crushes me to him, and kisses me with a renewed passion I've not felt from him before – something's different, but whatever it is, I don't care – I want him, right here, right now.

He suddenly stops and gazes down at me.

"Do that again," I challenge.

He leans down and kisses me, hard. I jump up and wrap my legs around him, kissing him back with as much passion as I can muster, everything south of my navel tenses and tingles in anticipation. Tristan marches over to the front door, and still kissing me, he unlocks it, pushes it open, steps inside and kicks it closed with his foot. In our heated passion, we slam against the wall, right next to the alarm that's started bleeping.

"Oh Coral," he pulls back, panting breathlessly, then he lets me go, leaving *me* breathless, and punches the code into the alarm.

I stay frozen up against the wall, watching him, then he's back in front of me, not touching me, but staring at me with a dark, solicitous look in his eyes. He places his hands against the wall, either side of my face and leans into me, his lips inches from mine.

"What do you want Coral?" he asks, in his husky, sexy voice.

Every muscle in my body clenches in delicious anticipation.

"You," I whisper. His mouth swoops down on mine, pushing, pulling…wanting. *No!* – I had other ideas. I push him forward then yank him by the arm, swing him around and slam him up against the wall.

"What the' – I place my finger on his lips to silence him. Then sink to my knees – I want to taste him.

"Coral' – "Don't say anything," I warn and unbuckle his belt. Then I open the button on his jeans, pull down the zip, and pull his boxers down with his jeans so his erection springs free. I take hold of him with my right hand and gently squeeze, running my hand up and down his shaft, I stare up at him, then lean forward, place my left hand on his thigh and take him in my mouth.

"Jesus," he hisses. He tastes so good! *This is so hot!*

I lick, suck, and tease his tip with my tongue, then cover my teeth and take him deeper into my mouth. I'm not sure how far I want to go with this, but I suck hard. I'm not really sure what I'm doing as I haven't had any practice, but I try my best.

"Ahh…Coral!" I hear his moans of desire, it feels so good to hear, it feels so good to know I can do this and he's enjoying it.

I suck him several times, his erection getting harder and heavier in my mouth. I decide I want him like this. I want him to come like this. I've never done that before.

"Coral stop," he grunts. "Or I will come," he states. "And I don't want to." He adds.

I look up at him, his head is arched back, his eyes squeezed shut. I think he's trying to control his orgasm, so I suck harder, flicking my tongue back and forth across his tip, taking him deeper into my throat. *Whoa! This is really turning me on too!*

I look up at him, he's completely at my mercy. Desire swims so strongly inside me that I feel myself climax a little too; he's just so damn sexy.

"Coral I…" Tristan shudders once. I feel his leg tense beneath my hand. He bends forward, I look up at him, he's almost stopped breathing, his mouth is slack, his eyes dark. I suck harder, he tenses again, squeezing his eyes shut for a moment, then they flash open.

Our eyes lock right at the moment I feel him ejaculate in my mouth.

I keep sucking and swallow quickly, not sure about whether I like it or not, then I swallow again as Tristan shudders once, twice, three times, I feel his legs shake a little.

I can't help but feel triumphant. As I look up at him, I kiss his tip, smack my lips together then smile shyly at him. That was so hot! I didn't know doing that would turn me on so much. *I'll definitely be doing that again.*

Surprising me, he leans down, grasps me by the shoulders, pulls me up against him, turns me around and crushes me against the wall, kissing me hard, pressing the length of his body against mine. I can still taste him in my mouth.

"Jesus Coral…" he hisses against my slack mouth. "Have you done that before?"

"No," I squeak. I can see the surprise in his eyes, it makes me feel even more triumphant.

He leans down and kisses me, slowly, softly, his tongue doing a slow salsa with mine, then he pulls back and gazes at me like I'm the air that he breathes – again.

"My beautiful, sexy woman," he whispers. *Whoa!*

"My sexy man," I whisper back.

Tristan swoops down, crushing his lips against mine, moaning with want as his tongue pushes into my mouth, probing hard. I kiss him back as desire, thick and heavy pulses through me, he suddenly pulls back and gazes down at me again.

"Arms up," he orders, so I do.

He pulls my t-shirt off me, then he unhooks my bra and throws it to the floor, he crouches down, his hands on my hips and sucks hard on my right nipple. My legs start to shake uncontrollably.

"Tristan," I gasp. "I can't stand."

He picks me up into his arms. "Wrap your legs around me," he pants.

I wrap my legs around him, and with my arms around his neck, he walks us over to the sofa, kissing and caressing me the whole time. Throwing me down onto the sofa, he rips off his t-shirt, kicks off his trainers, then slides his jeans and boxers down in one fell swoop and steps out of them. I have never seen him undress so quickly.

He's stood above me, completely naked, his erection hard and ready for more. Boy, he's a sight for sore eyes, just look at all those muscles ripple – my body reacts by sending another wave of shivers between my legs, I feel my underwear moisten even more and my clitoris throb with anticipation.

I lick my lips and stare up at him. He leans down and swiftly removes my trainers, socks and jeans, then he slowly makes his way up my body, starting with my feet, kissing, sucking, and squeezing with his hands, moving all the way up my legs. I tremble and shiver, I know I'm going to climax the moment his lips or tongue touch my sex, I'm so close.

Peeling my knickers off slowly and seductively, Tristan throws them aside, and opens my legs so wide it's almost too painful, using his soft fingers to open me up, he licks his lips and stares down at me, his eyes full of deep and delicious thoughts –*Fuck!*

I moan and throw my head back urging him to taste me, lick me – I look up again, locking eyes with him as his fingers start to make slow circular movements, his eyes not leaving mine, making my body convulse and my hips push upwards.

"Taste me!" I cry out, unable to take the pressure, I need to come.

He leans down, keeping eye contact with me the whole time, his look full of devilish delights, then his tongue flips out and teases my nub, over and over, round and round. I feel the build-up taking over me, every cell in my body awakening and exploding.

"Oh god…" I cry out as I feel my pelvic muscles contract.

"Come for me Coral," Tristan demands, right at the moment I reach the precipice. I come hard, my body bucking and bowing, all thoughts are gone. I'm just sensation…

I feel Tristan leave me, opening my eyes in confusion I see him crouched next to his jeans. Two seconds later, he's stood over me, placing a condom over his erection. He stops and gazes down at me for a second. Then he slowly crawls up the sofa, so he's hovering above me, his elbows supporting his weight. He kisses me so gently it brings a tear to my eye.

"Beautiful," he whispers and slowly eases himself into me. I close my eyes and throw my head back. *Oh, he's so perfect for me…I feel so full…*

Tristan leans up, his back straight, and grabs hold of my thighs then he really starts to move, like he did earlier.

I gasp and moan as he picks up the pace. "Tristan," I whisper.

I pull my legs up and open them wide, just as he leans down and caresses my breasts, squeezing and rubbing my already pert nipples, then he really starts to move, pumping harder into me. The feeling is exquisite, all sensation and touch then he moves his position, hitting the absolute right spot inside me.

"Ahh, faster," I gasp, as I feel myself tighten around him.

"Christ…" Tristan complies and starts pounding into me, I feel his balls slapping against my backside. I feel everything quicken and tighten inside me and I climax again, shattering into a million pieces. I feel like I'm going to pass out, the orgasm just goes on and on and on...

"Ah, Christ..." I hear Tristan shout, I try to open my eyes to watch him, but I can't, I can't control the waves of ecstasy that has taken over me. "Fuck!" Tristan slams into me once more then stills, his hands gripping my thighs so tightly.

I am finally able to open my eyes. I watch him shudder several times, his head is craned back, his eyes closed and his mouth slack as his orgasm ripples through him. He keeps his eyes closed as he comes down from his high, his hands still gripping my thighs.

Then he takes a deep breath and gazes down at me, coral blue eyes meet dreamy chocolate brown, we both start smiling at the same time, then start giggling. Tristan leans down on his elbows and strokes my forehead, kissing my lips between chuckles.

"Wait right there," he tells me, as he gently pulls out of me. *Like I can go anywhere!*

I can't move. I still feel like I'm floating somehow. I turn onto my side and watch in appreciation as his naked body walks down the hallway to the bathroom. Damn that body of his is to die for; he really has the cutest butt. I shudder slightly, feeling cold for some reason, I need Tristan's warm body next to me.

Walking back into the room, he sees me shiver again. "Cold?"

"Yes, I need your warm body here," I say pulling him on top of me.

He grabs one of the fleece throws we bought and drapes it over us. I huddle closer to him, inhaling his intoxicating scent. As I look up at him, I see his features change, taking on a more serious note. He's got that brooding look about him again.

"What is it? What's wrong?" I run my fingers through his hair and stroke his cheek.

Tristan takes a deep breath in then exhales slowly, he seems nervous.

"Coral, I wanted to ask you something," he says, staring down at my lips. He's dead serious that I can tell. I frown up at him wondering what this is all about.

"Ok," I whisper.

He takes another deep breath. "Coral Stevens, will you do me the honour of being my wife, will you marry me?"

My breath catches in my throat – *Fuck!*

IT'S MONDAY MORNING, and I'm sat at my desk eating my muesli in a trance-like state. I am engaged; engaged to be married! - My stomach rolls with the very thought of it. Why the hell did I say yes? I feel myself start spiralling down into a major panic attack. *Ok, calm down, deep breaths, deep breaths!*

Married! Married!– I can't even bring myself to believe that it's real, I feel like I'm in some sort of twilight zone and any minute I'll wake up. *Two weeks, two weeks!*

How can you get married after being together for a few short days out of two weeks? I must be off my rocker! Maybe it's a top-secret government experiment, and I'm secretly being drugged? I push that stupid thought away then I get into even more of a panic.

He wants me to move in with him – Crap that means selling my studio, but I don't want to sell my studio! *Shit. I hadn't thought of that!*

My throat instantly tightens, and my stomach twists with anxiety. *You really should have discussed all these things with Tristan last night Coral!*

I nod in agreement with myself. I guess I would have if we weren't busy christening rooms, floors and walls. But in all honesty, I don't want him to know I'm having a meltdown. I don't want him to know that I feel sick whenever I think about walking down an aisle, or trying on a dress, or having so many faces staring at me as I say I do – *Oh fuck, do I?*

With shaking hands, I put down my bowl of muesli, unable to eat anymore, and hold my head in my hands, hoping this will help give me some sort of guidance. *Inner voice?*

Yes, yes, George is always telling me to listen, to let the inner voice guide me. I squeeze my eyes shut and ask the question – Should I be marrying Tristan, is it too soon? Am I doing it because I really do love him that deeply, or that I'm afraid to lose him? – *Damn it that's too many questions!*

Giving up on trying to work it all out, I decide to just let it go for now and calm myself down, I've got all this week on my own. I'm back at my studio and my routine. I'm sure the answer will become clearer. Then I panic again. *What if I change my mind?*

Tristan will hate me, I know he will – *Fuckety fuck, fuck!*

Stupid ass Coral, *'I wanna marry you Tristan',* Why the fuck did you say that? I feel like screaming at myself, slapping myself around the face. I mean, I love Tristan, of that much I am sure – but marriage. Isn't that just, like, way too soon?

To attempt to take my mind off it all, I try to concentrate on what I have going on this week. Tristan is going to be away until Friday night. I try not to think too hard about the fact that he won't be here, that I have five whole days and four nights without him, the thought is very sobering, painful - swallowing hard, I try to clear my head and get back to this coming week.

I'm going to be busy which is good, less time for panicking about – *Stop*!

Ok, so I got the photos of Tristan's folks, which I sneaked out of his wallet this morning. So that's the first thing to sort, next buy a cocktail dress for Friday night and some decent Lingerie – that's a must!

Thirdly, I need to call Gladys and Debs. I need to speak to them both. I could go for lunchtime or see them Wednesday night when I'm free. Then I think that I'd rather have the evening to myself, some time to really think through everything, like who I am and what I want.

Time alone – I swallow hard. I'm never going to get time alone again. *Yeah, but isn't that the whole point of being in a relationship, getting married, you don't have to be alone anymore?*

I frown at my own thoughts – I actually like alone time, well some of the time, not all the time, I place my head in my hands again –*Fuck, I'm so confused!*

I take a deep breath and try to get back to what I have going on. Training with Will tonight, George and Cindy tomorrow, I want her to work on the dresses again, seems the sex thing has worked itself out. I instantly picture Tristan's hot, naked body.

I take several deep breaths attempting to clear my mind of him and pick my muesli back up, but it's no good. My mind keeps drifting back to last night, to Tristan proposing to me, and the conversation that followed…

TRISTAN TAKES A deep breath in then exhales slowly, he seems nervous.

"Coral, I wanted to ask you something," he says, staring down at my lips. He's dead serious that I can tell. I frown up at him wondering what this is all about.

"Ok," I whisper.

He takes another deep breath. "Coral Stevens, will you do me the honour of being my wife, will you marry me?"

I stare back at Tristan with wide eyes. "Tristan...I," I'm lost for words.

"Say yes," he urges, his eyes still brooding. I can't quite believe he's just asked me, I think I'm in shock.

"Don't people move in with each other first? You know.... see how it goes before committing?" I squeak.

"So move in with me," he says, shrugging slightly.

I close my eyes. This is way too heavy, and deep. "Don't you think it's a bit soon, I mean we've only known each other' – "I know," he admits, his eyes pleading with me. "Marry me," he asks again, his voice all husky, sending shivers right down there –*Again!*

I gaze back at his big brown eyes. I try to think logically, rationally, but deep down – way deep down inside of me – I already know I want to spend the rest of my life with him, I couldn't imagine being with anyone else.

"You said earlier that you wanted that," he says.

"I know," I admit. "And I did mean it, but I just didn't expect you to ask, not yet anyway." I balk, trying to think of the right thing to do here.

Tristan closes his eyes and leans his forehead against mine. "Marry me," he whispers. "Be my wife, I want you. I love you Coral. I have from the very first moment I met you." Tristan opens his eyes and kisses the tip of my nose, then continues.

"Last week when I walked out of your studio, I felt like I was leaving myself behind. Like there was a part of me missing, I didn't understand it at all, until I was next to you again at Lily's party, because you had already become the missing piece, the love that lights me up inside. I want you, so badly baby. I really want you to give me a chance to show you how much I want you, to take care of you. I want to give you the world Coral, please, let me do that. Let me take care of you. Marry me?" *Who can say no to that?*

The words are out of my mouth before I can stop them.

"Yes." *What? Coral what are you doing?* "Yes, I'll marry you," I whisper.

Tristan's face almost splits in two, his smile is so wide. Pulling me into him, he kisses me with such a powerful, loving force, that I feel like crying – *again!*

"I love you," he croaks, his cheeks blushing as his eyes glisten with unshed tears.

Oh my God!

I take his face in my hands and kiss him tenderly.

"I love you too, so much." *This is crazy!*

SOMEONE WALKING INTO the office pulls me out of my reverie. I spin in my chair and see Joyce looking oddly at me.

"Coral, what are you doing, do you have a bad stomach?" She asks me.

I frown back at her in confusion, then look down and see my arms are gripping my waist. *I did not know I was doing that! Did I put my muesli down?* I stare blankly at her while I wait for my heart to get back to its regular beat, and the butterflies in my stomach to stop swirling. Finally, I take a ragged breath, I try to talk, but nothing comes out, so I clear my throat and attempt a fake smile.

"Sorry Joyce, I'm absolutely fine, really I just...." I drift off again. I don't seem to have much concentration at the moment.

"Come into my office please," she asks firmly. I swallow hard and follow her in. "Shut the door." I close it behind me then turn to face the music, only when I see Joyce, her face is full of elation, not condemnation.

"Darling, did you have a good weekend?" she titters.

"Um...I, well yes," I murmur.

"I'm glad, but you seem a little pre-occupied. Try to keep your head together while you're at work please." I gaze blankly back at Joyce. "Coral?" Her loud voice quickly snaps me out of it.

"S-Sorry," I whisper then frown at myself – *Get a grip!* "Yeah, no, I will," I say, nodding at Joyce; she's still frowning at me.

"Very well, back to your desk," Joyce tells me firmly.

I nod, then quickly scurry out of her office.

Back at my desk, I pick up my muesli in a vain attempt to try eating. I put the spoon in the bowl, fill it with muesli and lift it to my lips, but I drift off again, thinking about how much more I revealed to Tristan last night…

CHAPTER TEN

WE ARE IN THE living room, on the sofa. Tristan has me wrapped up in his arms, after making love again, well hot sexy sex, but maybe it's still making love? Either way, I am happy. I am happier than I have ever been. Although, I still have no idea why Tristan wants me, I drive myself crazy sometimes, so god knows how it feels to him; when he's with me I mean.

"What do you want baby?" Tristan asks, pulling me from my thoughts.

"A bath," I murmur.

Tristan chuckles at me. "No, I mean what kind of wedding?"

Seriously, he wants me to answer that now?

"I…I don't know. I don't have a clue," I whisper.

"You've never thought about it?" He asks lightly.

I shake my head at him. "No, never…" I whisper. I briefly look down at his chest, my forefinger making small circles across his pecks.

"Never?" Tristan repeats, sounding astonished, I look up at him. "You really are one of a kind," he says his eyes crinkling at the corners as he smiles down at me.

"I know," I admit. "I'm a weird fuck up remember?" I add lightly.

Tristan chuckles as he leans down to kiss me. "You never imagined yourself married?" he asks stroking my hair. I shake my head at him. He chuckles lightly again. "Most women have that planned from childhood."

"I know," I say, feeling as though it's just confirming how weird I am.

"Hey!" Tristan tugs on my chin, so I have to look up at him. "There's nothing wrong with that baby." He tells me firmly.

I swallow hard. "I guess…" I say, feeling like a freak again.

"Coral don't do that," Tristan scolds.

"Do what?" I ask, feigning innocence.

"Think that you're weird because you haven't thought about it." Tristan leans up on his elbow. "I bet you, if you got all the women in the world and asked them if they dreamed about their wedding day, a good third of them would say no." He adds, softly stroking my cheek.

"Maybe…" I retort. "Tristan, I couldn't even see myself in a relationship so…" I trail off, trying hard not to think about what this really means.

"I guess it's time to think about it then," he says. "What you want." He adds.

I swallow hard again. "When exactly were you thinking about this going ahead?" I ask my voice shaking, giving me away.

"The sooner, the better," he answers his eyes brooding again. "You're nervous," he quickly assesses.

"Very, aren't you?" I balk.

Tristan's eyes bore into mine as he silently shakes his head. "I know what I want," he softly says, his thumb running lightly over my bottom lip, making me lose my train of thought. "Do you really want this Coral?"

I look down at his chest. I find it so hard to think straight when I look at his face. "Yes, I do but…what's the rush?" I ask.

"I just want my life to start with you Coral. I want to build it with you. I want you as my wife, not my girlfriend. Girlfriend just sounds so…so fickle, like it's not permanent," he says waving his hand in the air, but as I gaze up at him, I can tell he's hiding something from me. I just don't know what it is.

"You're lying," I reply. "So why don't you tell me what you're really thinking?"

Tristan smiles his enigmatic smile at me. "There's no fooling you is there?" he says.

"No, but isn't that one of the reasons you want to marry me?" I say sweetly.

Tristan leans down and kisses me again. "It sure is," he smiles.

"So...?" I take a breath and gaze up at him. He's gone broody again.

"I just...I don't want to lose you," he says all wounded and wide-eyed.

I frown at him. "That doesn't make sense. Just because people get married, doesn't mean they can't leave one another, people get divorced all the time," I retort.

"I don't mean that," he says, his eyes finally meeting mine.

"Then what do you mean?" I ask. He shakes his head slowly, frowning deeply as he does, staring down at my swollen lips. He's definitely hiding something - It suddenly it dawns on me.

"Oh, I get it!" I sit up a little more so we're nose to nose. "You're afraid I'll meet someone else, right, choose them instead of you?" I say, searching his face.

Tristan sinks back down onto the sofa, so he's lying on his back and throws his forearm over his eyes. *Jeez, I thought I was the one with issues.*

"You deserve better," he mumbles.

"Hey!" I shout, tugging at his arm, so he has to look at me. "Will you please stop that, if anyone deserves better it's you, so please stop saying that."

"How can you think that?" He moans.

"Tristan," I groan. "I come with a load of crappy baggage, stuff I'm still trying to sort out in my head. I'm surprised you're interested in me at all. Men are supposed to want confident, outgoing, sure of themselves women, not someone like me. And as for you, well just look at you." I say waving at all of him.

He shakes his head at me not understanding. "Tristan, you're a real catch, the kind they talk about in books. Tall, handsome, sexy alpha male, who's confident, sexy and successful….did I mention sexy?" His mouth twitches as he tries to hide his smile.

"Shall I tell you the names of the women who I know are attracted to you? Shall I tell you what it's like to be out in public with you? How it makes me feel when I see so many women craning their heads round to get a second look at you?" I balk.

"That's just not true," he argues.

I roll my eyes at him and continue. "Yes, it is. And just to add insult to injury, you're a smart, funny, captivating, sweet, soulful, well mannered, big-hearted man, that doesn't come with a load of baggage like me. At least you've got your shit together!" I bite feeling a little irritated at him – He has no idea what it feels like to be me. I'd love to have his confidence, his laid-back attitude, his patience, his forgiving nature.

"I still think you deserve better." He says, closing his eyes. *Ok, I'm starting to feel a little pissed at him.*

"Ok then, tell me, Tristan. What kind of guy would you rather I am with?" His eyes dart open, his broodiness is gone. His jaw is set, his eyes wide.

"I don't want you to be with anyone else," he states firmly.

"Well that's settled then, you must deserve me," I say pouting at him. "Do you want to know why? – "No, I don't' – "Because you put up with my bad behaviour, and you're so patient and forgiving with me it's unnerving, and despite all of that, well more than that, you bring out the best in me. I never, ever thought any man would be able to do that. I haven't laughed so much…" I stop and think about what I'm saying.

"Actually, I've never laughed so much, I've never had this much fun with a fellow human being before. I know that sounds weird, but…well, I've never felt this happy before, sometimes I feel like it's a dream and I'm going to wake up and feel devastated. You make me feel safe, wanted, cherished loved." I frown deeply remembering how badly I used to feel about all those emotions.

"Tristan, I've lived my whole life thinking I'm not worthy and I don't deserve love, I've never let anyone get close to me, not even my family. I always felt safer just with me, no one could hurt me that way, but it's so lonely it's hard to describe."

"Try," he whispers. "I want to know what you think baby, how you think."

I swallow hard and frown, trying to think of an analogy. *How can I explain this?*

"Ok, it's like living your life inside a steel cage, you want to let people in, but you don't have the key to unlock the cage, but you also don't want the cage to open because you know it's there to protect you from any further pain. *You* changed all that for me from the very moment I met you. You unlocked the cage, leaving me feeling totally and utterly vulnerable, completely at your mercy, and that really scared me, I didn't even know you." I smile shyly. I can't believe I just told him that.

"So that's why you were so dead against us?" Tristan softly says.

"Yes," I whisper, tears springing to my eyes. "You see, because of you, the cage is gone. You've set me free."

Tristan gasps. "Oh, baby!" He pulls me into his arms, so my back is on the sofa, his strong masculine body pressed against mine. "That's how you always felt?" He asks, softly stroking my cheek.

"Yes, all the time, and you've changed all of that," I whisper.

Tristan slowly closes his eyes and presses his forehead against mine. "I don't understand how you can change, just like that?" he asks, leaning up to look at me.

"I don't either. I'm not saying my issues have disappeared because I know they haven't. It's just…I guess I don't feel alone anymore." I softly say, realising how true that is.

"You've always felt alone?" he gasps again.

I nod silently.

"Oh, baby!" Tristan crushes me against his chest and starts kissing me all over. On my lips, my cheeks, my nose, my forehead – *Could he shower me with any more love?*

"Don't feel sorry for me," I beg.

He lifts his head and gazes at me with wide eyes. "I don't understand baby, you have Rob and Carlos, Gladys, Debbie *and* Joyce. Don't you talk to them?"

"I know I do, but no, I don't talk Tristan, only to George. You see, the damage was already done before I met my new family." *Shut up Coral!*

"I don't understand?" he says. "What damage?" *Shit!*

I look away from Tristan trying to think of something to say, something that will sidetrack him, something far away from the real truth of the matter.

George comes to mind. *Yes, use his analogy!*

"Ok, so George told me that all our belief systems get built from a very early age. So for me, it became that people are bad, that they can't be trusted and that I'm better off on my own. No emotional ties, that way I couldn't get hurt again. I mean, I'm not going to hurt myself, am I? I'm not going to let myself down. But all the adults in my life, pre-Gladys, let me down and treated me badly Tristan. So as much as I love my family and friends, I couldn't take the risk of letting them in. What if

Gladys was pretending to be nice and turned out to secretly be just like my Mom? Or Deb's was like my sister? I couldn't take that risk, so I guess it just carried on like that, I just felt safer on my own, until I met you." I end with a whisper.

"I wish I'd have met you sooner," he croaks.

"I wouldn't have been ready for you," I tell him.

"How do you know that?" He argues.

"Because it's only been over the past year that I started to feel like I actually wanted someone in my life, I just didn't know how to go about it. I guess reaching my 30th made me take a step back and take a good hard long look at myself. I tried to imagine myself still feeling the same when I hit my 40th, you know doing the same thing, no change, and I realised I did want change, but I was too scared, too stuck in my ways to do anything about it." I take a deep breath – *Boy this is getting intimate!*

"So, it was meant to happen now?" he says, smiling down at me.

"Yeah," I smile. "I think so. Tristan that day when we met, and I walked into reception, and you turned and looked at me, the only way I can describe how it made me feel was…well, I felt like I was home, I was finally home."

"Oh Cora, me too babyl!" He gasps, crushing me against his chest again. Then taking me by complete surprise, I hear him sniff loudly. *Oh my god!*

"Are you crying?" I squeak in astonishment.

"No," he croaks into my hair.

"You are!?" I gasp trying to get him to show me his face, but he's not having any of it. So I wrap my arms around him and hold him tighter against me. "Baby, don't cry for me, please."

"Kind of hard not to," he sniffs. "Your pain is my pain, or haven't you figured that out yet?"

I squeeze my eyes shut. "Tristan, it really scares me how much I love you."

"Scares me to baby," he croaks.

"Well, at least we're in the scared boat together," I whisper, holding him tighter to me.

He chuckles at that one. "Do you think I'm a wuss now?" he mumbles.

"Sorry?" I say, bemused.

"For crying, am I less of a man to you?" He asks.

"Tristan, look at me," I demand.

Reluctantly, he lifts his head. His eyes are slightly red, and he has a few stray tears on his cheeks. I lift up my hands to his flushed cheeks and wipe away his tears, then kiss his soft lips.

"No baby, I don't think that at all," I solemnly tell him. "You're all man to me, I couldn't feel safer in anyone else's arms, and everyone cries baby, even the toughest of men." I smile up at him and stroke his cheeks with my thumbs.

He sniffs again then leans down and kisses me; his lips are so soft from his tears. "Still wanna marry me?" he croaks against my lips.

"Yes," I answer, smiling up at him, wondering what I did to deserve this angel, this magnificent man in my life.

He gazes down at me, his face haunted with some unnamed emotion.

"Good," he whispers. "But I have a condition." He adds…

THE PHONE RINGS pulling me from my musing. I pick up the handset in a daze. "Garland and Associates, Coral speaking." My voice doesn't sound like me. I frown deeply at the handset. The line is free. There's no one there. Realization dawns that it's my mobile buzzing in my bag, not the landline – *Not a good sign!*

Replacing the handset and taking my mobile out of my bag, I look at the screen, but it doesn't say who it is. I hate answering anonymous calls.

"Hello?" I say, my voice low, unfriendly.

"Darling it's Gladys." She shrieks.

"Oh hi, I didn't recognise the number?" I softly say.

"I'm on Malcolm's mobile." She tells me.

I roll my eyes. "Gladys, where's your mobile?" I ask, already knowing the answer.

"Lost it." *How many is that now?* It's a good job she only has a cheap pay as you go mobile. "Can you talk darling? Are you at work?" She asks.

"Of course I'm at work!" I snipe. I'm trying not to get mad at her, even though I know she's hiding something.

"Well, I'll be quick. What are your plans for this Wednesday?" *Great, there goes my evening to myself.*

"Well'– "Marvellous darling," she interrupts, then continues excitedly. "Malcolm and I have something for you, so we'll see you for tea. It will be just you darling?" she questions.

I frown deeply. "Why?" I question suspiciously.

"Because, well…what we have for you…Oh, I can't tell you over the phone. Malcolm made me promise," she says, sounding giddy.

"Yes," I sigh. "It will be just me." I sound sad.

"Oh good," I hear Malcolm shout something in the background. "Oh yes, Saturday darling are you free?" Hmm… let me think – I'll more than likely be shagging Tristan's brains out.

"I'm not sure, why?" *Why do I feel nervous?*

"Well now you have plans," she chuckles.

"I do?" I balk.

"Yes, Malcolm and I are getting everybody together for a barbeque to meet before the wedding." She tells me.

"Everybody?" I squeak.

"Yes dear, let's see…there will be you, Debbie, Scott & Lily. Malcolm's daughters Ellie and Erin and their families, Joyce and…oh you'll never guess' – "Gladys," I interrupt, she sounds excited which is great, but I know what she gets like when she's got her jabbery head on, she'll talk me to death. "Count me in," I tell her a little sombrely.

What about Tristan? Hmm, I don't want to go on my own, but I'm not ready for everyone to meet him yet. I'm not ready for the third-degree treatment that I know we'll get – *Fuck, what do I do?*

"Oh lovely darling, we'll see you lunchtime, at the house." She says.

"Ok," I mumble. *Great a day without Tristan while he's here in Brighton!*

"Darling are you alright?" Gladys asks, sounding concerned.

No, I'm not! *Fuck it, he has to come!*

"Yeah sure…I can bring a friend right?"

Gladys sniggers down the phone. "That wouldn't be Tristan by any chance?" She says.

I cringe at the gleeful tone her voice has taken on. "Gladys, please don't make a big deal out of it, we're just friends. I don't want him being made to feel uncomfortable' – "Oh hush, he'll be fine!"

"Gladys!" I scold. "You and Debs are terrible when you get together. Please, I don't want Tristan to be embarrassed, or me," I add.

"I embarrass you?" she asks, her voice a little high pitched.

"Yes, no, I mean...just..." Gladys is sniggering again. I sigh inwardly. "Never mind, see you Wednesday," I say hanging up to even more laughter.

So now we have a day full of Gladys and Debs and happy families, meeting more new people – *Great! God help me!* – God help Tristan, I hope he can handle it. Shaking my head, I stare blankly at my half-eaten bowl of muesli. Picking up my spoon, I take a mouthful and start chewing. It tastes like cardboard – *Yuck!*

I put the bowl down and try to work out what they have planned for me on Wednesday, but nothing comes to mind. I'm still mad at Gladys, *and* Debs. I know they are both keeping something from me, but maybe I can use this opportunity to talk to them about it, that *was* my plan for this weekend gone, I guess I kind of got sidetracked.

I get an image flash up of Tristan going down on me – everything south of my waistline contracts. My soul feels as though it's trying to leave me to go find him, my heart feels like it's going to burst out my chest – I squeeze my eyes shut, but it doesn't help, I can't breathe!

Ok. Coral deep breaths, yes you have the sexiest man on the face of the planet, but come on, get a grip. You're at work for god's sake!

Once my breathing calms down, I take another mouthful of muesli. I must make sure I eat, if I lose more weight Tristan's going to know I've not been eating, and he won't be best pleased, just like the comment he made last night about not eating all my evening meal!

Not that I should worry about what Tristan thinks. It's not like I can help it, I'm in love, I've lost my appetite – if I don't eat, I don't eat, if I lose weight it's just tough, there's not much I can do about it.

Wiggling the mouse on my desk, I take a look at my inbox, there are some letters with a red flag next to them which means Joyce needs them urgently, I go to open the first one up, but no matter how hard I try, I cannot stop thinking about Tristan's condition…

I LOOK UP AT Tristan with wide, worried eyes. "What's the condition?" I whisper, not really wanting to know the answer.

"I want to know what happened to you." He gazes down at me, his eyes deep and intense. I frown back at him, I have a sinking feeling I know what he means – *Being raped, he wants all the gory details!* – I wish he would drop it!

"Tristan," I try to move, to pull away from him.

"Don't run," he whispers, gently holding me against him.

"I'm not running I just..." I stare up at the ceiling. "Why? Why do you want to know?"

He leans down and kisses my cheek. "I just do."

I sigh heavily. "Fine!" I grumble. I decide the best way to go about it is to let Tristan ask the questions. "Ask away," I gripe, waving my hand.

Tristan shakes his head in frustration. "I'm just trying to get my head around it Coral, why you're the way you are."

I stare back at him. I don't think we are actually talking about the same thing here.

"What do you mean?" I ask, my voice trembling slightly.

"All men make me nervous. All men are creepy. You've always felt alone, you don't like to be tickled, you find it really hard to let people in, you don't trust anyone. Shall I go on?" *Fuck – He's not talking about what I thought he was.*

"You know about my past," I bite.

"Not all of it," he says, shaking his head. *Shit!*

My heart starts pounding against my chest, my breathing erratic.

"Tristan...please," I breathe.

"Does George know?" I ignore that one. "Why can't you just answer the question?" He adds I can tell he's getting annoyed with me.

"Tristan," I squeeze my eyes shut. "Please don't do this," I whisper, my mouth dry, my throat getting tighter.

"Baby, look at me," he demands. I open my eyes and gaze up at him. "I'm right here baby, nothing and no-one is going to hurt you," he tells me, softly stroking my cheek, but I feel frozen. "Why do you look so scared?" he adds.

"Because I feel trapped!" I shout.

"Trapped?" He says, his voice low.

"Yes, now move Tristan, get off me...please," I whimper,

choking back unwelcome tears. I don't want him to know about that part of my life! *Christ, he's just got enough out of me!*

His eyes narrow, but he rolls onto his side, freeing me. I stand up and pull my knickers on, then yank Tristan's t-shirt over my head. Then I stomp into the kitchen – I need a drink.

I hear Tristan footsteps following me.

"Why can't you answer the question?" He repeats in a soft tone, moving around the breakfast bar to reach me. I glance across at him and see he's put his boxers on. My heart starts pounding even harder, just looking at his body makes it happen.

I turn away from him and pour myself a Brandy. I gulp it back in one go, wincing slightly as it burns my lungs and hits my empty stomach.

"Baby…" I see Tristan in my peripheral vision taking a step towards me.

I turn to him and put my hand up to stop him. "You're not my god damn therapist Tristan!" I snipe. Turning away from him, I start to pour another large Brandy.

"That's not the answer," he softly says, his long fingers enclosing around mine. He takes the brandy off me and places it on the side, takes my other hand away from the glass and turns me gently to face him. "I want to know Coral, all the good and the bad. I want to start my life with you, and I want everything laid out on the table," he softly says, gazing down at me with those big, loving, soulful eyes.

I begin to feel very nauseous and lightheaded. "Tristan," I whisper and squeeze my eyes shut. "Believe me when I say there are some things you'd rather not know."

"I very much doubt that, please tell me," he softly says.

"Tristan," I mumble. It's a warning; a plea for him to stop.

"Come on baby, it can't be that bad, surely?"

"Tristan," I choke and bring my hands to my face, trying to hide the tears that are cascading down my cheeks. "Please, I'm begging you…" I sniff.

"Please tell me, baby, open your heart to me," he breathes.

I look up at him through blurry eyes. "Why, it's not like you can do anything about it? It happened, that's it. It's the past!" I shout running my hand through my hair. I feel like I've got thousands of ants crawling under my skin.

"Please baby," Tristan holds his hand out to me. "Talk to me, let me in," he begs.

"No!" I scream in outrage, my hands clenched into fists at my sides. "Why can't you just let this fucking go!" I storm out of the kitchen.

Reaching the stairs, I run up them two at a time, desperate to get away from him, from his questioning – I feel like screaming I'm so fucking angry. When I reach the master suite, I slam the door behind me in a rage and come to a stop in front of the king size bed. It's happening again, just like it did with Justin, they get too close, start to mean too much to me, and I pull away, start to self-destruct it. I pace the floor, my hands gripping my hair in frustration, I hate being like this! Why can't I be like other people? Why for just one fucking second can't I feel normal, whole?

Sometime later, I hear Tristan call me from the bottom of the stairs. I don't want him here right now, I'm too full of rage to have any kind of coherent conversation. I just need some space, some time to think things through.

"Tristan, don't come up here," I shout, warning him. "I need to calm down ok, just give me some time."

"Ok," he answers, but he doesn't sound too happy.

I fall to the floor, the rage finally turning back to tears. I curl myself into a ball and rock myself. Why can't he understand that I can't talk about the past? It's too horrifying to remember, and I don't want to remember, I don't want to go back, I just want to get better.

I squeeze my eyes shut and rest my head on my knees, trying my best to push the horror of my past away, but what seems like moments later, I hear Tristan again.

"May I come up?" *God damn his good manners* – I just can't say no!

"Ok," I croak, then heave myself up off the floor and sit on the edge of the bed. Tristan walks in, I keep my eyes to the floor, so all I can see are his naked feet, crouching down in front of me, he hands me another Brandy, then takes a sip of his own.

"Baby, I'm so sorry I pushed, I didn't mean to upset you. But you've kind of answered my question, whatever it was that happened to you…must have been really bad," he whispers.

I finally look at him. "Do you like seeing me like this?" He solemnly shakes his head. "Then stop asking," I whisper.

"I can't do that baby. You don't have to tell me now, I know it scares you." Reaching up he swipes a tear from my cheek with his thumb. "But we can't start a life together with the past hanging over our heads baby."

I sniff loudly and stare out the window, I know he's right, of course, he's right. My leg starts jigging up and down, he places his hand on my knee to calm me, the jigging stops.

Tristan continues. "I want you, and no matter what *you* think, whatever you tell me won't change my mind about you, I'm in this for life," he says, squeezing my knee.

I sniff again and sip my Brandy. "But it will Tristan, look at how different you were with me after I told you about ...." I look up at the ceiling and take a deep breath. I don't want to keep crying.

"Yes, it did make a difference, but a good one I think. It's just made me want to protect you even more. Maybe in time, you'll learn to trust that no matter what you say to me, I won't leave you Coral. I'm not your Dad, or haven't you worked that part out yet?"

My breath catches in my throat, he's right again. I've never had a stable male in my life. Gladys has always been on her own. How was I ever supposed to come to trust that not all men are like that, without a positive role model to look up to?

"Tristan, this has nothing to do with you leaving me, I know you're not my Dad, you're nothing like him." I snap.

"Then what is it?" He asks.

As I stare back at him, I silently wonder if I should just let George tell him everything, I'm not sure if I can, and I hate reliving it.

"I hate talking about the past," I whisper. "And you want to know, and that's making me nervous. You want to get married sooner rather than later but then you've put a condition on it, and that's not fair. Why can't you accept me the way I am?"

"I do accept you the way you are, I just want to know all there is to know about you like you do about me."

"Have you considered the possibility that I may freely open up to you once we're married because I'll feel even more secure?

I'm not saying that's what's going to happen, I may never tell you, but have you considered that?"

"No, actually I haven't. That's a good point," he muses.

"And have you considered that the more you push for answers, the more you push me away from you?"

"No, I hadn't' – "And have you considered that by dropping it altogether, that you have more chance of me actually telling you one day?"

"Ok, very good points Miss Stevens, every one of them taken on board. And I agree, wholeheartedly, no condition, let's get married."

My mouth pops open in shock. *He agrees with me?*

"But you just said'– "Coral, I don't want to make this any harder for you, you've been through enough. Just give me your word you'll tell me...one day," he says, with his hand on my cheek.

Reluctantly, I nod my head, but it will probably be George that tells him.

"Well that's good enough for me," he smiles his enigmatic smile.

I sniff again. "I told you the week we met when you took me to lunch...I told you I'm not like other people. I don't run right. You want to change your mind about it all, now's the time," I offer.

Tristan grins, drains the last of his Brandy, kisses me briefly and stands up holding his hand out to me. "I'm not going anywhere. Now, how about that bath?"

I look up at him in awe and wonder – S*eriously what the fuck is he doing with me?*

SOMEONE IS CLEARING their throat, trying to gain my attention. I look up in surprise to see Susannah stood at the side of me. She's impeccably dressed in a dark blue skirt suit. I think she's wearing that very same pencil skirt I first saw her in.

"Hi Coral," she smiles down at me.

"Hi," I mumble, hoping she'll leave me to my thoughts and my breakfast. "You're early," I add despondently.

"Yes, I always am," she states, pulling a chair up next to me.

My appetite vanishes. "I'll just get rid of this," I say, taking my bowl into the kitchen with me. Great, I don't do well with new people, and she's going to be here all week. *Marvellous!*

Once I've washed my bowl and spoon, I decide to visit the ladies, purely so I can avoid Blondie a little more. Checking my bun is still in place, I stare back at myself in the mirror. Maybe it's the lighting in here, but I notice I've got grey circles appearing under my eyes. *Lack of sleep, too much shagging!* – And that my cheeks look sallower – *Not eating enough!* – Ok, smart arse enough!

I take a step back and check myself in the full mirror, straightening my white blouse and running my hands down my dark blue suit trousers, my thoughts go to little miss perfect, who's sat at my desk, who's…..I think back to last night, to how sweet Tristan was when we took a bath together. Then I sigh inwardly, remembering the conversation that happened during dinner…

CHAPTER ELEVEN

I PICK UP THE bottle of Casillero Del Diablo, it's my favourite Cabernet Sauvignon, and place it on the kitchen table. The lights are off, I have the electronic candles on, and my favourite artist is softly playing in the background. It's my own mix of Bryan Adams; all his love songs. Where Angels Fear to Tread is playing, the words reflecting how I feel about Tristan, how easily he seems to have got into my head.

I take a step back and admire my handy work. Yes, this looks very romantic. I call Tristan again. He's been holed up in his office while I cooked dinner. Finally, he comes strolling out of his office. When he reaches me, he takes me in his arms and kisses me hard, tipping me back, so my hair skims the floor. *Whoa!*

When he's finished this little romantic display of affection, he looks down at the table. "Very romantic," he says, smiling down at me.

I smile shyly at him. "Take a seat," I say and walk over to the kitchen to collect our meals. As I walk back to Tristan, he picks up the wine and pours a little in each of our glasses. I place our meals down and take a seat next to him.

"Wow!" He beams at me.

"Don't start that again," I warn.

He leans down and takes a big whiff. "Smells delicious."

I roll my eyes at him and laugh. I have made Beef Wellington with a red wine jus, creamy mashed potatoes, and served them with roasted asparagus and carrots.

"How long has Susannah worked for you?" I ask as I tuck into my meal.

"This is delicious," Tristan beams. I roll my eyes. "Another signature dish," he adds.

"Tristan!" I scold.

"I've already told you, six years," he says. I calculated it correctly, Tristan split with that woman when Susannah had been working for him for a year.

"Did she know?" I ask.

"Know what?" he asks taking a large gulp of red wine, he looks frustrated.

"Why are you getting frustrated?" I question.

"I'm not," he argues petulantly, then frowns taking another forkful.

"Yes, you are," I laugh.

Tristan places his knife and fork at the side of his plate, puts his elbows on the table and folds his hands in front of him. "What do you want to know?"

"Did she know you split with that woman?" I repeat.

"No. I've told you I'm very private. I don't mix business with pleasure." I cock one eyebrow up and smile wryly at him.

"Except for me," I whisper.

Tristan smirks. "Yes, except for you."

"So...did you...?" I don't know how to ask without him thinking I'm getting weird about her.

"Did I what?" He asks.

"You know...well did you ever consider Susannah as' –

"No," he interrupts. "She is definitely not my type."

"Why do you say that?"

"I like brunettes."

"The other woman was dark-haired?" I squeak.

"The other woman?" he asks, his head cocked to the side.

"Um...yeah the one who...you know...cheated on you," I end in a whisper.

Tristan sighs and picks up his cutlery and tucks into his meal. "Yes, she was," he finally says. *Hmph! I pictured a blonde.*

"Susannah is pretty, stunning even. She's smart, sophisticated..." I want to say she wears skirts that are so tight you can see her stocking belt, but I refrain myself.

"And?" his cheeks start to flush giving him away.

"I just thought..." I trail off. Maybe I'm barking up the wrong tree here?

Tristan sighs. "I agree Coral, she's is pretty and smart, but not for me."

"Why not?" I question.

"What's with the twenty questions about Susannah?" I shrug nonchalantly. "Oh come on! There has to be a reason?" Tristan argues.

"I just want to get a better idea of her that's all. I'm going to be working with her all week," I answer artlessly. I take a large gulp of wine, then top up both our glasses.

"She's not that bad," Tristan frowns, taking a drink of wine.

Hmm…There's something there, I know there is–*Maybe a drunken Christmas Party?*

I think back to the first time I met her, how she touched Tristan's arm, the way she smiled at him. I wonder…And before I can stop the words from falling out of my mouth, I say it.

"Have you slept with her?" I whisper, my heart in my mouth.

Tristan turns his gaze on me, he looks pissed –*Uh-oh!*

"No. I have not," he scolds, his voice deep and husky.

"So there's never been anything there?" I confirm. Tristan stops eating, stealing a glance at me he picks up his wine, then leans back in his chair and appraises me. "What?" I murmur, wondering if he's about to tell me off.

"A few years ago, before she was married, Susannah admitted to...*liking* me." I frown at the way he hesitated and said *liking*.

"You mean loved you," I say, sounding like a sulky teenager.

Tristan's eyes dart up to meet mine. "Coral, you have to believe me'– "So what happened?" I interrupt. Tristan sighs heavily and takes a drink of wine. "I told her the truth, which was I didn't feel the same, she took it gracefully, and that was that."

"Weird," I mumble.

"Sorry?" *Shit, I didn't think he'd hear that.*

"I just think it's weird that she carried on working for you that's all. I mean it can't have been easy, falling in love with the boss only for him to say 'no sorry not interested' that would've been enough to make me want to leave." I take a forkful of food.

Tristan shrugs. "She assured me it was no problem, and so far it hasn't been," he says, scrutinising my expression. I try to

Freed By Him

put on my mask on, but it doesn't work. "Don't go dragging up the past with her Coral," he warns.

"Wasn't planning on it," I say, laughing sarcastically. Then I drink some more wine, it's making me brave.

"I mean it. She's a valued employee. I don't want to lose her," Tristan adds in a firm voice.

I glare back at Tristan. "Fine," I whine, holding my hands up in surrender.

So I was right all along, I thought there was something subliminally nagging away at me about her. I still think it's weird that she stayed. I decide that maybe Blondie and I should go out to lunch together, maybe if I word it right I can get it out of her, I'm sure there's more there. Inspiration hits, I could act like I'm infatuated with Tristan and ask Susannah about his dating history, whether he's single, blah, blah, blah – *Yeah that ought to do it.*

"I was thinking about getting back into my routine," I say, changing the subject.

"Routine?" He still looks a little pissed.

"Yeah, swimming every morning," I explain.

"Mix it up baby," he reminds me.

"Oh yeah, I will. Thanks for reminding me, but I still want to start my day with a swim tomorrow. Can we check out the pool after dinner?"

"Of course we can. Another room we haven't christened." Tristan grins at me with dark, heated eyes, everything south of my waist contracts. If that's what we are doing, then we have tons more rooms to do. A big grin spreads across my face. *When I think of the possibilities!*

Tristan finishes his meal in double quick time. I'm eating slowly again – *What is wrong with my appetite?*

"Are you finished?" he asks disapprovingly, eyeing my half eaten plate of food.

"Uh-huh." Tristan picks up our plates. I watch him take them into the kitchen, clean them off and put them in the dishwasher – *He cleans up too, he really is too good to be true!*

I turn back to the window and stare out at the glowing sunset, red, orange, blue and purple all mingled together – It's so beautiful.

"So," Tristan whispers his arms snaking around my waist,

his lips grazing my ear, making me catch my breath. "You want to go swimming?" he asks, his voice all husky, sending shivers all over my body.

I shake my head, my mind completely changed. I twist my head to face his, take one of his hands and place it over my right breast. "No, right now I have other ideas." Grasping his hair by the nape, I pull his lips to mine and kiss him passionately...

I LEAN AGAINST the sink in the ladies in a vain attempt to stretch out my legs. I'm having to work very hard on not walking funny today. *Damn Tristan and his acrobatics in bed!*

As I go into another yoga move, my mind wanders to the conversation that followed after dinner...

WE ARE ON THE floor in the cinema room. I am spread out across Tristan's torso, my chin resting on his chest as we both catch our breath. Tristan has his eyes closed as his fingertips continue to make smooth circles on my back. He seems very happy and sated.

"I was thinking about what you said the other day, about going out for dinner." He doesn't answer me. "Shall we go out on Friday, when you get back?" I ask.

Pulling me up by the shoulders, so we are almost nose to nose, Tristan leans towards me and kisses my cheek. "I'd love to take you out." I smile like a love-struck teenager.

"So where to?" I ask, hoping he doesn't take me to some really posh place. I'm much more comfortable in places like Las Iguanas.

"Oh no you don't, it will be a surprise." *Crap! What am I meant to wear?* "What are you worrying about?" he asks, reading me easily.

"If I don't know where we're going, how am I supposed to know what to wear?" Tristan gazes at me for a moment.

"That's easy, I'll be in a suit so...." He says, grinning sexily at me.

My heart stutters, picturing Tristan in a suit and dining out with him. It's going to be very hard not to jump over the table and rip it off him, then make mad, passionate love to him.

"What are you thinking?" Tristan leans into me and kisses

my neck, right below my ear. "Your breathing's hitched up, your eyes are dilated. I'm intrigued, what are you thinking?"

I clear my throat in an attempt to speak. "How sexy you look in a suit," I whisper.

"Sexy eh?" He's still trailing soft kisses up and down my neck. I clamp my legs together in some sort of effort to stay in control.

"Very," I whisper.

"I'll have to remember that," he chuckles kissing me once more, then he leans his head back and closes his eyes.

"Why?" I ask, my voice sounding all floaty.

"So I can tease you at work," he says, his deep dimpled smile dazzling me.

"You wouldn't!" I admonish.

Tristan chuckles hard, the vibration of it spreading through me, making me smile along with him. I shake my head at his teasing ways...

IN A COMPLETE DAZE, I head out of the restroom. I'm halfway down the long hallway when I swear I hear Tristan's voice - I instantly freeze. Ok, now I think I can hear him, and I know for a fact he's on his way to London, I'm losing it! Taking another couple of steps forward my desk comes into view, I instantly stop walking – Tristan *is* stood there, and he's talking to Susannah.

At first, I think I'm actually hallucinating and squeeze my eyes shut then open them – *Nope he's still there!* –Then I pinch myself, thinking I might actually be dreaming and I haven't woken up for work yet – *Nope he's still there!*

What is he doing here? He told me he was leaving not long after me, I wanted to walk from his place this morning, but after having sex for the third time; I knew I wouldn't make it on foot, so he got Stuart to drop me off.

I sigh heavily, so he really is here. I wish he wasn't. All I want to do is take him upstairs to the boardroom, lock the door, close the blinds, rip that damn sexy suit off him and shag him senseless. I try to close my eyes so I can get my head together, get some rational thinking going on, but I'm captured by Tristan. I could watch him all day, the way he moves, walks, talks, laughs, but then something else catches my eye.

Tristan has made a joke, Susannah's head falls back as she laughs along with him, and for a tiny second, I can see how good they would be together. They haven't noticed me yet, so I lean against the wall, cross my arms and continue watching them. Tristan is laughing freely with Susannah, he looks so relaxed, so much so that I wonder whether I've actually seen him that relaxed with me. And as for Susannah, married or not, I can see straight through her pretences, she still likes Tristan – a lot.

In fact, I would go as far as to say she's still in love with him. *How is Tristan not seeing this?*

Oh! She's got it bad, she's hiding it well though, but not well enough for me not to notice, and unfortunately for her, that rears up the ugly green-eyed monster within me. I have to fight the urge to stomp over to them and tell them both to get a room. Shaking my head at myself and taking several deep breaths, I square my shoulders and walk over to my desk.

"Good morning Coral." Tristan winks at me. I hope Susannah didn't see him do that. *Besides, he shouldn't have, we are at work!*

"Good morning Mr Freeman," I answer politely, keeping my face deadpan.

Susannah looks from me to Tristan, her eyes narrowing.

"Did you have a nice weekend?" he questions sweetly. *Bastard!*

He knows exactly what we did this weekend – Sex lots of it, exploring each other's bodies! My heart starts hammering, and my sex starts throbbing frantically, so I decide to wind him up.

"Very quiet, a little boring actually," I say raising my eyebrows at him, then I take a breath, and his scent reaches me, knocking me for six – *Oh, he smells so good*.

I take a deep calming breath and pull my chair out before my legs give way and sit down.

"Oh?" Tristan cocks his head to the side, his lips twitching as he tries to hide his smile. *Jesus Christ, he looks good!*

"Can I get you anything, Mr Freeman?" I say, trying not to sound too stern.

Tristan smiles his dimpled, sexy smile. "No thank you Coral. Is Joyce free?"

I pick up the handset and dial her. "Mr Freeman would like

to see you," Joyce tells me to let him come through. I put the handset down, walk over to the door and open it for Tristan.

"Thank you Coral." His eyes scream sex as he walks past me into Joyce's office. I grit my teeth at him and quickly pull the door shut before my knees buckle on me. *God, he smells divine.* As I turn and walk over to my desk, I notice Susannah is eyeing me suspiciously.

Crap, I hope she didn't pick up on anything!

"So how do you feel about the change Coral?" *She's probing!*

"Let get to work," I say ignoring her question completely. Susannah pulls a face but doesn't say anything. "You'll need to give me half hour to get these urgent letters done for Joyce, and then we can start the training," I add, opening up the first document.

"Have I done something wrong?" She asks all innocently.

What! Besides eye fucking my man? No not at all!

"No," I answer smartly, trying to concentrate.

"I think I'll go get a coffee, would you like one?" She asks.

"No thanks, I'm good." Susannah stands and walks away.

The moment she's gone I release my breath, not realising I'd been holding it, and stare blankly at my screen – *This week is going to be hellish!*

Right at that moment Tristan comes sauntering out of Joyce's office, closing the door behind him.

"You!" I hiss. Tristan's eyes widen with apprehension.

"Me?" He asks all innocently, pointing to his lovely strong chest.

"Yes, you!" I squeak, rising from my seat to a standing position.

"What?" He chuckles, obviously amused by my apparent hissy fit.

"Don't do that!" I scold.

"Do what?" He smiles, his dimples deepening.

"Wink at me and tease me in front of Blondie." *Oops!*

"Blondie?" He repeats, his voice low and definitely not amused. He frowns down at me, all traces of humour gone – *Crap!*

"Yes, she still likes you, Tristan!" I cross my arms in an attempt to be mad at him. "You seemed very comfortable with her, laughing away together." I couldn't drip more sarcasm into my voice if I tried. "Do you like her Tristan?" I question my voice squeaking a little too much.

Tristan crosses his arms and glares back at me. "Do I really need to answer that question?" He says his voice full of disapproval.

"Yes!" I squeak.

He rolls his eyes at me and shakes his head. "Did I, or did I not ask you to marry me?" he questions.

"Yes, but that's not the point!" I argue.

"Not the point?" He chokes. "I think it makes it blatantly clear it's only you I want."

"You're still missing the point!" I squeak.

"Am I?" He questions, frowning at me.

"Yes! Look at it from my perspective, firstly you've worked together a long time and you've told me she admitted to you that she likes you." I close my eyes and pinch my nose. "Secondly, you must have blinkers on or something to not see how much she's still attracted to you. What if she finds out? What am I meant to say to her? It could get very ugly."

Tristan puts his hands in his pockets, rocking back and forth on his heels, looking every inch the millionaire mogul. He stares at the floor for a moment. "I see your point, I'll go talk to her," he says, walking past my desk.

"No!" I shriek in a half whisper, stopping him by touching his chest. It sends an electric shock through my system.

"Susannah won't say anything, even if she did find out," he says trying to assure me, by subtly entwining his fingertips with mine.

I sigh heavily, closing my eyes to the feel of his fingers wrapped around mine.

"Give her a chance Coral, she's a nice girl. I think you two will really get on with each other." I narrow my eyes at him. "She's happily married," he states.

How do I tell him I know she's got it really, really bad for him?

"She's not!" I retort. "She'd dump her husband in a heartbeat if she knew she could have you," I manage to whisper.

Tristan sighs and runs his hand through his hair. "So maybe she still holds a torch for me, I don't know, and quite frankly I don't care. It's her problem, not mine," he snaps.

Freed By Him

"But she wants you," I quiver. The very thought of him with another woman is unbearable.

"But she's not going to get me, is she?" he softly says, his eyes going all warm.

"Damn right she's not!" I say, crossing my arms.

Tristan chuckles at me. "Am I detecting a little jealousy?"

"No!" My voice does not hide anything my feelings at all.

"Relax Coral, she holds nothing for me, there's no interest there at all."

I look up into his eyes, I see no contradiction, but it's still not going to be very comfortable though. I decide to implement my plan today, shopping can wait until tomorrow. I will bombard her with questions until she admits it, then I can warn her to stay away from my man, and stop eye-fucking him.

"Ok?" Tristan asks in that sexy, husky voice of his.

I look up into those deep, chocolate eyes of his. "Yes," I whisper incoherently. "What are you doing here anyway?" I add.

"Meeting got delayed, I'm leaving now though." He softly says.

I look down at my desk, my heart constricting – A whole day without him, I feel sick. I close my eyes and try to push the nauseous feeling away. I feel his fingertip start to trace a line from my temple, across my cheek and down to my lips.

I exhale loudly and look up meeting his deep brown eyes. We've been saying our goodbyes since five o'clock this morning, neither of us able to sleep. So why does this feel so hard, why do I feel like my soul is cracking in two?

"I feel the same," he whispers, leaning down he gently kisses the edge of my lips.

I place my hand on his cheek, savouring the feel of his skin. I take a mental picture of his face, trying to imprint every curve, every line. I run my thumb across his bottom lip, trying to get the feel of it etched into my brain so I can call upon it whenever I want him.

I gaze up into his eyes, memorising the deep chocolate colour, the hazel flecks, the perfect large round shape, and his thick eyelashes, remembering how they rest on his lower lids as he sleeps.

Tristan suddenly pulls back and stands upright, hearing someone coming down the stairs. I take a step back, and turn to see it's one of the other secretaries, she half smiles at me as she reaches the bottom of the stairs, then stops and dashes a full-blown smile at Tristan.

"Good morning," she says all breathless and pink-cheeked.

Tristan nods to her with a stony face. "Good morning."

She blinks several times, her smile fading, then turns and walks down the hallway, turning back twice to ogle at Tristan.

"See," I whisper, crossing my arms.

"I couldn't give a fuck!" He snarls, surprising me. "I don't care what any other woman thinks about me. It's only you." He adds.

My mouth pops open – *Oh Tristan!*

"I know," I whisper. "Me too, only you baby."

He leans down once more and caresses my cheek. "I have to go. See you soon baby," he whispers.

I swallow hard and fight the urge to cry, I must be strong. I know Tristan can see that I'm upset. A whole week, a whole week without his lovely face, his strong body, his loving words – *Don't crumble Coral!*

I take a deep, steadying breath and smile up at him.

"See you soon," I whisper back.

He hesitates for a moment, just as reluctant to leave as I am to see him leaving. I square my shoulders purposely, so he can see I'm ok. I'm handling it, well sort of.

"Tristan go…I don't want you racing in your car and…" The thought of him having an accident because he's late grips me – *Stop!*

"I won't, I'll be careful," he assures me.

"Ok. Call me when you get there?" I whisper.

"I will. Bye baby," he whispers.

"Bye…" I croak back, unable to say anymore.

Tristan gazes down at me looking totally lost. Then he takes a step back and stares at the floor a moment, before marching off without looking back at me – *Ouch that hurt!*

I stare at his retreating figure for a moment, then stepping around my desk, I run down the hallway so I can see him one last time. I watch his tall, manly figure cross reception, and walk through the glass doors.

"Bye Tristan," I whisper, trying to tell him telepathically that I love him.

A strange melancholy washes over me. I wince at the feeling and hug myself tightly, I feel like I'm breaking in two. I squeeze even tighter, almost as though I'm trying to hold myself together. The very thought of having to wait so long to see him again is unbearable. I'm sure that's not normal behaviour, I'm sure you're supposed to feel elated, and all dreamy and loved up when you're not together. So why am I suddenly feeling so low?

See, this is the very reason why you didn't want to get involved with someone, cause they just get you feeling all fucked up inside!

I find myself nodding in agreement, this is too much, it's too scary. Maybe I should talk to Tristan when he's back, face to face, tell him the whole marriage thing has got me all twisted up inside?

I hear my mobile buzz in my bag. I dash over to my desk, pick up my bag and yank my mobile out. I'm about to switch it to silent when I notice I have a message, I haven't actually started work yet, so I allow myself to check it out, I close my eyes for a second hoping it's Rob with some sort of news.

Be Good Wife. I Miss You Already - Tristan Xxx

I cover my mouth with my hand to stop the sob that wants to escape me and fall into my chair. I sit, staring blankly at the message, feeling totally lost and withdrawn. *Fuck!*

One minute I feel like it's too much and I want to run a million miles away, then I'm instantly pulled back, not wanting to be apart from him for a single second. So my ego is telling me to run, and my soul is whispering to stay. Can I be that brave, can I take a huge step like this? I already know the answer to that question.

It's simple, I love him. I adore him.

My stomach turns, I clutch it tight, and I have to question - Is it really possible to feel this much love for another person, to have it run so deep it feels as though they reside in every cell of your being? I fight the urge to run after him and kiss him just one last time, feel his arms around me, his breath on my cheek.

I decide to text him back, tell him how I feel.

*Nearly ran after you for one last kiss. This is crazy, scary. I

love you so deeply it hurts, this day is going to suck big time! I miss you too. Hurry home Hubby Xxx*

I press send and check the clock on the wall, it's nine o'clock, time for work. I put my mobile onto silent, place it in the top drawer of my desk and get on with the letters that Joyce has sent across to me. At least if I can concentrate on that, I don't have to think about the hollow feeling in my chest…

CHAPTER TWELVE

THANKFULLY, THE morning flies by. I thought it would drag like crazy, but there are a lot of new programmes I need to learn. In all fairness Susannah has been pretty good, friendly, a little over-friendly if anything. As elevenses roll around, we both go for a coffee in the chill out room.

"Mr Freeman's a fantastic boss Coral, I'm sure you're going to get along just fine, everybody likes him. He really is one of the nicest people I have ever met." Susannah says.

Jeez, she's simply gushing about him.

"Yeah, …he seems like he really looks after his staff. Joyce said he really cares, which is pretty unusual," I reply. *Play it cool Coral!*

"Of course, you wouldn't know why?" She says with a smug smile on her face. *Grrrrr!*

"Sorry?" I act bewildered.

"It's not common knowledge." She says flicking her long blonde, perfectly straightened, shiny hair.

"What isn't?" I ask.

Susannah looks around her to make sure no one is within hearing distance. *So she's a gossip too, I hate gossipers!*

"The suicide?" She whispers, her eyes sparkling. *That's weird? Why would someone's eyes sparkle about that?*

"Suicide?" I whisper, frowning at her.

Susannah nods once and moves closer to me, I don't like it.

"Ten years ago, an employee killed himself. The cleaners found him, he'd…well you don't need to know the gory details. The point is after that happened Tristan changed. I think he felt guilty that he didn't know that the guy was having so many problems. Anyway, after that he pulled everyone in individually, some people left, some stayed. Rumours flew around that he was helping some people out financially, but no names were ever mentioned."

"Why did the guy kill himself? Did they find out?" I whisper.

Susannah's eyes sparkle. "Apparently he was a secret gambler. Had a wife and kids, but he was buried up to his ass in debt." She really seems to be enjoying herself. Who thinks that giving news out like that is fun? Ok, the guy had an addiction, but that's no reason to think it's cool to gossip about his death. The guy died for goodness sake, left a wife and kids.

"Do you think Tr – Mr Freeman would have paid off the debt?" I ask, thinking back to what Tristan told me about his other P.A, what was her name?

"Probably, want another?" She asks, pointing to my cup.

"No, no thanks," I say, trying not to frown.

Susannah walks away which gives me a moment to take in what she's said. Now it all makes sense, Tristan did feel guilty about what happened, that's why he helps others out so much, he doesn't want the same thing happening again, which of course is understandable. But I don't understand why he thinks it's his responsibility to be like that, he runs a business, not a charity.

Ok, maybe I'm just too cold hearted about people, and Tristan is the opposite. Maybe it comes from his folks, caring about others, helping them out. Either way, I feel sick to my stomach. Why didn't he tell me? I hate that Susannah knows and I didn't - *Boy we've got some talking to do!* I feel a little dazed as we head back to my desk, but I'm soon pre-occupied with these stupid ass new programmes.

Grrrr, I hate this, I hate change!

There's no way I'm going to remember all of this, not with Tristan buzzing around my head and little miss prissy sitting next to me. I decide to ditch my plans for lunching with her, I really feel like I need a break from her. There's something I can't quite put my finger on, something strange and unnerving about her, she's too friendly, and I don't like the way I can feel her watching me. I shrug it off, deciding it's probably my own petty jealousy and the fact that she's another new person I have to deal with, either way, I'm lunching on my own.

When I look up at the clock for the fifth time since our break, it finally says 12.30pm.

"Well, I'm off for lunch," I say to Susannah.

"Oh, ok." She seems surprised.

I smile weakly at her, and head for the ladies, thinking about last night and what Tristan said to me about dresses, he can be so sweet and romantic. *Oh, Tristan!*

WE ARE SAT ON the sofa in the cinema room. I'm trying to concentrate on what Tristan's telling me, but I just keep going back to eating out and what the hell I'm going to wear. I decide at that moment to be brave, get my arse out there tomorrow on lunch and buy a god damn cocktail dress *–Be confident Coral, you can do this!–* I have to agree with myself, but before I attempt to do this, I have to ask the question.

"So hopefully, once that plan is put into action, I should only have to go up to Leeds once a month. You can come with me if you like and meet Karen." Tristan has thrown me off my question.

"Um...sure, that would be nice," I say picking at the blanket Tristan draped over us.

"What? You've gone serious?" He says.

"Tristan are you...do you like dresses? You know cocktail dresses, and heels and all that kind of stuff?" I exhale loudly, glad I got it all out in one go.

"Why do you ask?" His face falls as he frowns back at me.

"Just curious," I say trying to act casual, I take a big glug of my wine hoping it will give me some Dutch Courage – *I think I need it!*

Tristan is watching me, his eyes narrowing suspiciously.

"Coral as far as I'm concerned you would look sexy in a bin-bag. Wear what you want darling, what you feel comfortable in." *Damn it! How does he do that?*

"So you don't like' –"I'm not saying that," he interrupts, staring at his wine glass.

"Then please answer the question," I plead.

Tristan sighs then looks across at me. "Yes, yes I do."

"And stocking and suspenders and all that lingerie kind of thing?" I squeak.

Tristan's eyes dilate. "How did we go from dresses to'– "I just want to know," I interrupt, batting my lashes at him for optimal effect.

Tristan shakes his head slightly as though he's been stunned, picks up my hand and kisses the back of it, then leaning forward, he moves in, so we are almost nose to nose.

"Baby you are the sexiest woman I have ever met... the most attractive woman I have ever seen in my life. I really meant it when I said you could make a bin bag look good. So please, if you want to wear that kind of thing then do it for yourself, not for me. Ok?" *Wow, he sure knows how to melt my heart with words.*

"Ok," I squeak in reply, but it still hasn't answered my question. So I'm going for a yes, I mean, what man doesn't right? So tomorrow, I'll be lingerie shopping too...

THE DOOR TO THE ladies swings open. I look up and see it's one of the other secretaries, she smiles awkwardly at me and goes into one of the stalls. I look down and see I still have soapy hand-wash dripping between my fingers. *Good God Coral, get a grip!*

Frantically washing and drying my hands, so I don't have to make conversation, I quickly exit the ladies. Returning to my desk, I see Susannah is sitting in *my* seat, and she's already on the internet.

"Well, I'm off," I say, picking up my handbag and my mobile from my desk drawer. Knocking on Joyce's door, I walk in and check if she needs anything.

"No darling you go on ahead," Joyce tells me. As I'm stood in her office I think about the dress I'm about to purchase, and the fact that I don't have Rob or Carlos to call on to help me choose the right one. So maybe Joyce is my best bet?

"Um...Joyce," I look up at her.

"Hmm?" She's concentrating hard on whatever she's reading.

"Where..." I sound croaky, so I clear my throat. "Where would I go to get a cocktail dress?"

Joyce cocks her head to the side, looks over the rim of her glasses and smiles at me.

"Shopping on your lunch?" I nod vigorously, hoping and praying she won't ask me what it's all about. "No time then, I'd say Coast. It's down on East Street." *God, I'm going to miss her.* "They have some lovely dresses, and their sizing is good, none of this 'it's half the size it says it is' nonsense." I chuckle knowing exactly what she means.

"Thank you, Joyce." I walk over to her desk and kiss her lightly on the cheek. "You're a lifesaver." She beams up at me.

"Don't worry if you run over a little bit, I'll keep Susannah busy," Joyce adds.

"Oh, ok thanks." I walk out of her office with renewed enthusiasm. *I am going to buy a dress!*

"Hey Coral," I stop just as I'm walking past my desk, and look down at Susannah.

"Yes?" *Maybe she wants me to pick something up for her?*

"Are you free tonight? I thought it might be nice for us to get to know each other a little more." She smiles sweetly at me, but her eyes are hiding something. *There really is something weird there!*

"Actually, I have a gym class Mondays and Thursdays, so I can't, sorry." I go to walk off, but she stops me again.

"And tomorrow?" she shouts.

I turn back and stare at her, she has her legs crossed, her eyes narrowed, and she's tapping her pen on the paper pad. Is she trying to work out where I go and what I do?

"I have a regular spa appointment." I lie and go to walk off again.

"And Wednesday?" She shouts.

I turn around *again* and see she's trying to hide the fact that she's gritting her teeth. I feel a strange warning sensation start at the back of my neck and trickle down the length of my spine – She knows! I swear to god she knows about Tristan and me! *Shit!*

"My mother invited me this morning to have tea with her Wednesday," I answer. Trying to work out what it is about her that I recognise, something that I've seen before?

"Well as you're *so* busy in the week, how about Friday?" she bites.

I glare back at her. Why do I get the feeling the answer to this question is pivotal?

"Can't, out with friends," I answer artlessly.

She glares at me for another moment then turns back to the screen. I frown deeply at the very odd conversation that just ensued and scuttle out of the office, down the stairs, through reception and into the bright sunlit day. *That was weird, she's weird!*

Finding my sunglasses out my bag, I pop them on. Mobile in hand, I go to call Tristan when I notice I have another message, please be Rob.

I have arrived safely gorgeous, and I love you that deeply too darling. Keep your chin up, don't think the worst. I'll try and reschedule some meetings, and see if I can get back to you sooner, but I can't say for sure. I like the sound of Hubby, Wifey – Stay safe, I'll call you tonight. Tx

I close my eyes and hug my mobile. The melancholy feeling from this morning seems to have dissipated – *Thank God!* I don't want to walk around feeling like that all week. I hear several voices and open my eyes, the other receptionists are out for lunch. I hear one of them make a snide comment about me, the other women laugh along with her joke – So they do think I'm weird. *Figures I am!*

I try calling Tristan, but it goes straight to voicemail, hanging up I decide to try him again once I've finished my shopping spree.

BACK AT WORK, I march straight past my desk, ignoring Susannah completely, and head into Joyce's office, hoping she'll give me her honest opinion on the dress of choice. If she hates it, I'm taking it back. Locking the door, I strip out of my blouse, then my trousers, take the dress out of the bag and carefully slip it over my head.

"So what do you think?" I ask a little hesitantly. At £135, I think it's a little over-priced, but it seems the more you pay, the better the fit. Besides, Tristan paid for this and the lingerie with the card he gave me, I hope he likes it all.

"Coral, you look lovely darling. It really suits you." Joyce says.

I have chosen a stunning halter-neck dress in Royal Blue. It has a pleated bodice with vertical pleats heading down to the knees, and a wide waistband for a flattering, draping fit. I liked the red one too but I thought it was a little Christmassy, but I may go back and get that colour if Tristan likes this one. But most of all, I liked this dress because it's called The Goddess Short Dress, I giggled out loud when I read the label.

"You really think so?" I ask ignoring my trembling legs, my shaking hands.

"Yes, any special occasion?" Joyce asks patting her hair in place.

"Tristan's taking me out Friday night," I whisper, not wanting Blondie to hear.

"Why are you whispering?" Joyce asks.

I glance at her office door defiantly, then grit my teeth, my nostrils flaring.

"Ok, let's have a chat. Come on sit down, actually don't, out of that dress first."

Joyce helps me out of the dress and hangs it on the back of her door, while I get back into my blouse and trousers. When I'm done, I sit opposite Joyce, her big mahogany desk between us, and stare out of the window.

"Come on then, out with it." Joyce prompts.

"Tristan's away all week, and *she's* being weird with me. I think she knows we're um...dating. Tristan doesn't want anyone knowing yet, and I agree. It's just... – I lean forward, Joyce mirrors me – 'I know *she's* in love with him." I whisper.

"With who?" Joyce frowns.

"Tristan," I hiss.

"Susannah's in love with Tristan?" Joyce gapes back at me.

"Yes, he told me last night, that told him she liked him, it was years ago. He said he wasn't interested." I clench my teeth and stare down at the desk.

"Well that sounds reasonable," Joyce argues. I shake my head in disagreement. "Coral don't let this come between the two of you. You do have a tendency to blow things out of proportion." Joyce tells me with one eyebrow raised.

"I do?" I frown.

"Yes," Joyce titters. "It's who you are darling," she adds waving a hand in the air.

"Oh!" I sigh heavily. Maybe I am over-reacting to Susannah because of what I know?

"Now, if that's everything I have some calls to make," Joyce tells me.

I stand from the chair and walk over to my shopping bags. For some strange reason, I don't want Susannah seeing these.

"Can I leave these in here?" I ask.

"Of course darling put them in the bottom of the cupboards over there." Joyce points to where I need to go.

"Ok." Carefully stowing my bags away, I walk over to her door and unlock it, just as I'm about to open it, I hear Tristan's voice – '*I didn't put the idea of selling into her head, she asked me*' – I turn around slowly. Even if it hurts Joyce to know that Tristan told me the truth, I have to know why she lied to me, why she didn't just tell me.

"Um...Joyce," I squeak.

"Quickly Coral." *Ok, maybe now isn't the time.*

Joyce sighs in resignation. "Coral, really I'– "Why did you tell me that it was Tristan's offer that made you think about leaving? He told me...he told me that *you* approached him, and asked if anyone was looking..." I trail off, my voice wobbling.

Joyce doesn't answer me, she just sits there, looking shocked.

"I'm not mad at you. I just don't understand why you weren't honest with me." I say.

I stare down at the floor, too afraid to look up.

"But maybe it's the same reason that Gladys didn't tell me about Malcolm, and Debs didn't tell me about their house being up for sale. Apparently, I'm...difficult." I stare up at the ceiling in a vain attempt to look anywhere but at Joyce, after all, it's the first time I've ever confronted my boss, my aunty, for lying to me, and she's way scarier than Gladys or Debs.

"Sit down please Coral." Joyce puts the handset back in its cradle and watches me walk over to her, sitting down I fidget several times until I feel comfortable enough to sit still.

"Firstly, I'm sorry I lied to you. Secondly, I'm extremely annoyed that Tristan shared that with you. Thirdly, I was trying to protect you. I didn't want you thinking I didn't care about you or your future here in the company. I know how much this job means to you, and *I* have loved working with you all these years. Watching you grow from a shy, temperamental young girl, to a headstrong, very capable woman. It's almost been like... like having my own daughter.

"I knew how much this would hurt you by my leaving and selling up. I wanted you to think that…well, I don't know what I thought. I just didn't want to hurt you. Flipping the truth on its back seemed the most ideal way to go. Evidently, I was wrong!" Her lips twitch to smile, but her eyes look so sad.

"It's ok," I gush. "I understand you care about me, I know that, and you feel like another mother to me too. Besides, Gladys told me about John's letter, about how he wanted you to move on. I understand that it makes sense. I just wish you had been honest that's all, I feel like everyone's hiding something from me lately." I end in a whisper.

Joyce sniffs, clears her throat and smiles warmly at me.

"I am sorry darling…it's just everything has seemed so… so difficult lately' – "Joyce you don't have to explain anything to me, I think you're doing exceptionally well…considering the circumstances." I feel mortified for upsetting Joyce. *I should have kept my mouth shut!*

"How about you and Tristan? Is it going well darling, does he make you happy?" Joyce asks.

I nod vigorously and try to hide the love-struck smile that's taking over.

"Ah, can't stop smiling, that's a sure sign." Joyce smiles warmly at me. I can't help the giggle that bursts from within me. "It's about time," Joyce adds. I roll my eyes and go to argue, but Joyce stops me. "That will be all Coral. Come on, back to work." I nod silently and stand.

"Are you going to Gladys' on Saturday?" I ask, hoping she'll say yes. I don't think I'll get much time with her before she leaves.

"Yes, I spoke with Gladys last night." I smile deeply at her. "Well, off you go." She waves her hand at me, I know she's busy. Smiling broadly, I scuttle out of her office and back to my desk. Susannah moves out of my seat and into her own; which reminds me, three times I tried to get hold of Tristan today. He's a very busy man, I know that, but I need to talk to him about her.

"Do you always take this long for lunch?" Susannah snipes.

I look up at the clock – *Shit! I've been gone an hour and forty minutes.*

"No. I do not," I bark back, enunciating each word. "I was

shopping for the boss!" I hiss at her, she wisely shuts the hell up...

TWO HOURS INTO the afternoon, Little Miss Prissy goes off for her afternoon coffee, and I'm left to take a breather. God, she's been like a bear with a sore head since I got back. *I wonder what's eating her?* I still think she's worked out Tristan and I are seeing each other, but according to Tristan, it shouldn't bother her. After all, she was just sooo cool with Tristan turning her down – *Yeah right!*

Just as I think that I wonder what she's been up to on my computer. I start checking all my files, they seem normal, where I left them. Then I check Google history to see what she's been searching, nothing comes up. *That's odd!*

I click it again and find the history is empty. I suddenly remember I have a Google image page saved to favourites from when I looked Tristan up! *Shit! How embarrassing!*

I should have deleted it. I hope she hasn't seen it. I click on favourites and scroll down the small list of sites I have saved, mostly for Joyce, and find that the page I saved of Tristan is gone. I look up and down the list again, just to make sure I'm not going completely bonkers – *Nope it's gone, definitely gone!*

Ok, that really is weird. If she saw it there; why the hell would she delete it? Then I think maybe I deleted it, and I don't remember doing it? I nod my head in agreement. It sounds more logical, and I'm all for logic and reason, just like Spock – *Yes, yes I must have deleted it at some point!*

Strange though...I don't remember doing that.

AS THE DAY DRAWS to a close, I start to feel a little panicky about going back to my studio. I contemplate staying at Tristan's, but I soon realise that I need to be back at my place. I need distance from his things, and his smell and his...well he's just all over that house now. And it's bursting with memories of the two of us. I think being there will make me feel even more melancholy. With my mind made up, and the workday over, I wait until Susannah has left before I go into Joyce's office to get my bags and say goodnight.

"How's it going?" Joyce asks as I pull my bags out of the cupboard.

"Ok," I answer keeping my eyes on the floor.

"Coral, I'm here if you need me, you know that don't you?" Joyce softly says.

I sigh heavily, walk over to her desk and slump into the chair.

"I have some concerns," I huff. "But I'm not really sure you can help Joyce. I think it's Tristan I need to speak to," I add.

"Is it about Susannah?" I nod in agreement. "Yes… well, she certainly comes across as nice and polite but…." Joyce trails off.

My eyes flick up to meet hers. "But?" I question.

"Something…" Joyce says her eyes narrowing.

"That's what I think. I mean, I know I'm not easy to get on with, but she just seems…" I wave my hand in the air unable to put my finger on it.

"Like she's hiding something?" Joyce implies.

"Yes!" I squeak in relief. That's it. It's like there's something there, something I'm not seeing.

"Well, you just keep your head down young lady and don't get involved. Do your work and don't tell Tristan." *What?*

"Why?" I frown in confusion.

"Because if she's playing some sort of game, do you really want to come across as the one who is whining, the one who's being difficult? No, you don't. Any further concerns bring them to me, I'll start a log. She said something odd to me today," Joyce says drifting off for a moment. "Anyway, forget about her. Go home, enjoy your evening, that's an order, I don't want you sitting at home fretting about it, ok?"

"What did she say?" I ask with wide eyes.

"That is none of your concern Coral, what's important is that you have me as a back-up. Now go home," she admonishes.

I sigh heavily. I wish she would tell me what she said. "Ok, well goodnight Joyce, see you tomorrow." I stand and pick up my bags.

"Goodnight darling." I wave goodbye as I head out of her office.

Switching off my computer, I put my overnight bag from staying at Tristan's over my shoulder – I really need to get a second set of toiletries and make-up to leave at his place – pick up my handbag, my shopping bags, and head down the stairs into reception.

"Cori," I hear a voice whisper. It's got to be Joe. I whip my head around, but I can't see her behind the desk at reception.

"Joe?" I call out. I see her head peek up from behind the counter. "Joe, what are you doing? Why are you hiding?" I titter.

"Has she gone?" She whispers.

"Who?" I ask, but I have a pretty good idea.

"That woman who's working with you. Why is she here anyway?" She questions.

"Um..." Going against everything Tristan told me about keeping the take-over quiet, I decide to let Joe know. I want her to keep her job. I want her to get her kids back. "She's gone, Joe. Want to walk out with me?"

Joe sags with relief. "Thank god!" she exclaims. I watch her pick up her handbag and walk around the desk to join me. We both wave to Tom as we head out the building. Once we're at least ten feet away from the office, I stop walking and turn to Joe.

"Want to tell me why you're hiding from Susannah?" Joe looks nervous and simply shakes her head at me. "Joe," I whisper. "You have to tell me," I add scrutinising her.

"I just got a call muddled up earlier, she came down to reception, she..." Joe stares out at the road.

"Tell me, Joe!" I scold.

"She made me cry..." Joe whimpers, her voice trembling with unshed tears.

"What!" My temper immediately fires up. "Why? What did she say?" She shakes her head at me. "Joe!" I stamp my foot in annoyance, she has to tell me!

"She called me...I don't know the word. I think she said icompit, inco' – "Incompetent?" I interrupt, Joe nods. *What a bitch! How dare she!*

"She said she didn't understand how I even got the job, that I'm useless. But it wasn't so much what she said, it was how she looked at me when she said it... she scared me." Joe starts to cry silent tears – Blondie has really ruffled her feathers.

Letting my bags drop to the floor, I pull her into me and let her cry it out, trying my best to comfort her. What the hell is this woman up to? Who the hell does she think she is going round upsetting everybody? Joe has to tell Joyce, so she can log it all.

"Joe we have to go back inside. You have to tell Joyce' – "No!" she barks and jumps back out of my arms.

"Why not?" I ask a little shocked.

Joe shakes her head and sniffs loudly. "Because she said she'll deny it, she said it's my word against hers, so I better keep my mouth shut," she says, her bottom lip wobbling.

"Oh she did, did she! Listen, Joe, I'm going to tell you something. It's top secret, no-one knows, so if I tell you, you have to give me your word that you'll keep it to yourself. If anyone finds out, we both lose our jobs." I stare back at her with wide eyes, I want her to see I really mean it.

"Ok," she squeaks. "I will."

I take a deep breath – *I really hope you don't make me regret this Joe!*

"Joyce is leaving, she's selling the company. The news will be announced in two weeks time."

Joe's eyes widen in shock. "Oh no! I'm going to lose my job," she squeaks.

"No you're not," I tell her firmly, she looks up at me in wide-eyed wonder. "You remember Mr Freeman?"

Joe nods and smiles, her cheeks blushing red –*Yeah he can do that to a girl.*

"Well he's the one that's taking over, he knows about your situation, Joe. Your job is safe, I give you my word." Joe swallows hard and breathes a sigh of relief. "Susannah is his P.A in London, she's only going to be here this week then she's gone, for good." Joe sags with relief again, and we smile at each other. "Look I don't like her either, she's really odd. But that doesn't mean you need to take her shit lying down Joe, you really need to tell Joyce." I reiterate.

"But' – "Want me to come in with you?" I ask. I know Joyce makes her nervous.

"Yes please," she whimpers.

I pick up my bags, and we silently walk back in the building and up to Joyce's office, knocking on the door I wait for Joyce to answer.

"Remember," I whisper to Joe. "You don't know anything

about the take-over ok?" Joe nods earnestly. "I'll go in first, tell Joyce you want to talk to her, you tell her the rest." Joe nods again and starts twiddling her fingers, looking a little nervous.

"Come." I hear Joyce shout.

Opening her door, I see her look of surprise as Joe, and I enter her office. "Joe has something she'd like to tell you, Joyce, do you have five minutes?"

Joyce frowns as she looks from me to Joe. "Goodness Joe, why are you crying?"

Joe looks at me, for some help, I think?

"It's ok Joe, just tell Joyce what you told me. Everything will be fine." I squeeze her shoulder and lead her to sit in the chair opposite Joyce. "I have to get going, I'll see you both tomorrow."

As I turn to leave, Joe calls out to me.

"Cori," I roll my eyes, *Coral, it's really not that hard*.

"Joe," I sigh. "My name is Coral, as in the coral blue sea."

She blushes and smiles sweetly at me. "Sorry Coral, I just want to say thanks. You're a really good friend." *Ah sweet*. My heart melts for her.

"You're welcome, just be honest ok?" Joe nods at me and turns in her seat to Joyce, I nod to Joyce as I close the door behind me.

Then I look up at the clock, it's 5.30pm – *Shit! I'm going to be late for Will!*

I better get a taxi home, then I remember the £150 pounds in cash that Tristan stuffed into my hands this morning to cover taxies to and from work. I argued with him of course, and I certainly don't intend using it all, but to be fair my legs are really aching from all the sex we've been having, so right now I am truly grateful for it. Dashing through the building and out into the bright summer evening, I locate the nearest taxi and head back to the Marina.

CHAPTER THIRTEEN

BOY THAT WAS A work-out! As I walk out the gym and head down the concourse towards my studio, I can't help wondering what game Susannah is playing. I mean she's not just weird with me, she's obviously got Joyce's suspicions going, and she's really upset Joe. Gritting my teeth, I wonder aimlessly where she's staying and debate for a split second of whether I should go pay her a visit, have a little chat, threaten her even to stay away from Joe. Then I hear Joyce's voice – *'keep your head down, do your work and don't tell Tristan'*– shaking my head I decide to take Joyce's advice and try to forget about her.

As I reach my studio, I stare blankly at the patio door. It seems like a lifetime ago I was back here, yet it was only last Friday gone, just a few short days. Taking a deep breath, I say a silent prayer that the melancholy doesn't return. Putting my key in the door, I unlock it and walk inside.

AN HOUR LATER I have showered. A long, hot relaxing shower, to try and ease my aching muscles, although I bashed my elbows several times, I think I've got used to Tristan's huge shower, I must remember to be more careful. The air-con is on the room a perfect temperature, and. I have made a large salad for tea. Cajun Chicken for me and plain Chicken for Bob. I've already learned that for Bob, anything spicy is foreign crap, he likes everything plain.

As I'm sitting at my tiny table attempting to woo my appetite back, and staring blankly at the T.V screen, which is playing a recording of The Hairy Bikers cookery programme, my mind wonders to Tristan. I wonder where he is, what he's doing, and if he's ok. Quite honestly, it's driving me mad. I was never like this with Justin, I never missed him, or ached for him, not like this.

From the moment I left work, I have not stopped thinking about Tristan, his smile, his smell, his laugh, even the way he walks. I miss him, and I want his sexy body in my bed. I don't feel as though I can think clearly anymore, I feel like I'm drugged up on him, it's unnerving. I feel like I'm losing control of my own emotions.

Pushing my salad to the side, unable to eat anymore, I'm momentarily racked with guilt. I hate wasting food, so I decide to keep it for tea tomorrow. Maybe I'll be so hungry that I'll gobble it all up? Once I've stored it in a container and placed it in the fridge, I shuffle over to the sofa and attempt to clear my mind of all things Tristan and watch the show.

"WHO?" I MUMBLE. I dart upwards, blinking my eyes open. I am on the sofa. It's gone dark outside, the show has ended, the T.V has gone onto standby, and the studio is pitch black. I must have fallen asleep. Then it happens again, a strange noise, whatever it was must have woken me up. I frown deeply and strain my hearing as I try to locate the odd sound. Then I see it, a shadow, a human shadow illuminated across the flooring from the lights outside. *Holy crap!*

I snap my head around. It's coming from the front door, which I never use, and whoever it is, is just stood there, not moving at all and not knocking the door either. I swallow hard.

Who the fuck is that?

The hairs on the back of my neck stand on end, just as a cold shiver runs down the length of my spine. I glance across at the clock on the wall, it's 2.45am – *Fuck, who is outside my door at this time in the morning?*

I feel the panic try to take over, my hands are trembling, my breathing erratic. I stay firmly seated on the sofa staring at the figure by the door. I can't work out if it's male or female. *This is freaking me out!*

Then I think, maybe I should say something…I quickly change my mind, I'm not that brave. I look across the room, my bag is on my tiny fold-out table – *Damn it!* I need my mobile, but I don't want to make any noise, and these floors creak when you walk across them. The door handle starts to move, it instantly stops my train of thought; whoever it is, is trying to get in – *Holy Fuck!*

I swallow hard and try to keep my heart steady and my breathing calm, just like Will has taught me. *I wish he were here now!*

As I keep staring at the door, the shadow suddenly disappears, I sag with relief - *Thank God I always keep that door locked!* – Part of me wants to leap up, unlock the door and see who it was. I'll get a good view of them walking away, surely. But I can't move, I am frozen to the sofa, with my eyes firmly fixed on the door, I think I'm in shock.

Then I start to think a little more clearly. *I wonder if I should I call the police?* Then I think, what do I tell them? It could have been anyone! It could have been someone who lives in one of the studios and was a little drunk, got the wrong place? I shake my head at myself, knowing full well I'm making excuses up, trying to convince myself that it was nothing, so I don't have a full-scale meltdown.

Maybe I should go and stay at Tristan's tonight? At least his place has an alarm system. As the fear starts to subside, anger takes over. *Fuck that, I'm not being forced out of my own place!* Marching over to my handbag and finding my mobile, I call the police. I figure whoever it was might have left some fingerprints, something the police can use.

HALF AN HOUR after calling them, I'm told there's no immediate danger so they won't send anyone to me until tomorrow morning. I tell them to forget it and just log the call. Slamming my mobile down on the table, I pace the room wondering if I should stay here after what's just happened. Picking my mobile back up, I decide to call Gladys, maybe I can go stay there for tonight. As I go to call her, I notice I have five missed calls and three text messages. *Shit, Tristan!*

I hadn't taken my mobile off silent when I left work. I open the call logs, the first one starts at 8.50pm the rest are in ten-minute increments, I open up the first message.

Coral, I can't get hold of you. Are you alright? Please let me know baby. I love you. I miss you. Tristan Xxx

Then I open the second.

Coral. Seriously starting to get worried now, I've called Joyce, and she said you left work on time. As soon as you get this call me, it doesn't matter what time. Tristan.

Then the third.

Fuck's sake Coral. Are you mad at me about something? Because not answering calls or replying to messages is very childish of you, I await your reply. Tristan.

Oh dear! Tristan is not a happy bunny, and in fairness neither would I be. I decide to text him if I call I might wake him.

Hey, I'm really, really sorry. I forgot to take my mobile off silent after work. I fell asleep on the sofa, just looked at my mobile. Tristan, I'm so sorry I didn't mean to worry you. Call me if you want to, if not sweet dreams. I love you. Cx

Literally, two seconds after sending it, Tristan is calling me. "Hey," I walk over to the kitchenette and pour a big glass of water, eyeing the front door as I do.

"Coral!" Tristan sounds relieved.

"I'm ok," I whisper.

"Thank god, you have no idea the things I was imagining." I roll my eyes then frown at myself. I may feel like he's over-reacting, but maybe he has a point. Somebody just tried to get into my place. A shiver runs down my spine again, just thinking of what might have happened.

"I'm really sorry, I wish you were here," I tell him, and boy do I mean it.

"Next time!" He admonishes in his deep, husky voice.

"I know, mobile off silent. I get it," I sigh and take a long drink of water.

"What's wrong, you sound worried?" He quickly surmises.

"Do I?" I squeak.

"Yes," he states firmly.

I contemplate telling him what just happened, but he'll tell me to go stay at his, and I don't want to do that. Or worse still, he'll drop everything and drive down here.

Oh, what to do?

Inspiration hits. "I just had a bad dream, that's all." *Jeez, I'm doing a lot of lying lately.*

"Oh, baby! Want to talk about it?" he asks softly.

"No, I'm good. Just the usual," I say hoping to placate him.

"Want to share with me what the usual is?" he softly says.

I try to think of one of the many dreams I can tell him about, to try and ease his worry. I definitely don't want to tell him about the really bad ones.

"Just....I'm always running, running away from the really tall men in black cloaks. I can't see their faces, but I know they are bad, like aliens or something and I'm running and jumping, sometimes I jump over rooftops like in the matrix, sometimes I jump over mountains. I fly through the air. I have to keep moving so they can't catch me, it's the fear that's the frightening part…" I end in a whisper.

Tristan is silent. After all, he can't save me from the bogeyman.

"Have they ever caught you?" he asks hesitantly.

I giggle at that one. "No, I'm too fast!"

Tristan is silent again. I instantly picture his face staring broodingly at me.

"Tristan I'm ok. You don't have to worry about me. I had a kick-ass session with Will tonight. I can take care of myself. So please, don't worry ok?" I wonder who I'm trying to convince - Tristan or Me - I eye the front door again.

Tristan sighs heavily, then yawns. "I know you can baby, but that doesn't stop me from wanting to protect you, take care of you and keep you safe."

I smile deeply at his beautiful words, Tristan yawns again. "Go back to sleep baby. Shall I call you in the morning as I *walk* to work?" I say dryly.

He chuckles at me. "You're not getting a taxi?"

"Nope," I answer cheekily.

"Ok," he laughs. "What time?"

"I leave the house at 8am." I tell him.

"Yes, call me, and I'll call you back, save your bill." I roll my eyes at that one.

"Tristan I get a ridiculous amount of minutes for free, don't be daft!"

"Alright, have it your way. In five hours time I better get that call," he admonishes.

"You will," I giggle.

"Ok, sweet dreams my gorgeous girl." My heart thumps slowly and deeply three times, stops, then starts beating rapidly against my chest.

"You too, speak tomorrow," I say breathlessly. Trying to get the words out with no oxygen in my lungs is a trying feat.

"Dream of me," he whispers.

"I will, you too," I say closing my eyes, really wishing he were here.

"No doubt about that," he whispers back. *Oh, Tristan!*

Tristan sighs then starts humming Some Enchanting Evening to me.

"Hey," I scold softly. "Go to sleep!"

"Yes Ma'am," Tristan titters.

"Love you," I whisper.

"Love you too baby, Goodnight."

"Night." I can still hear him, he hasn't hung up.

"Hang up Tristan!" I whisper.

"Can't, don't want to say goodbye." I slump onto the sofa. "Me neither. But we both need some sleep, and I need a clear head tomorrow, I've got such a manic day ahead," I say.

"So have I," he adds sarcastically. Yes, I'm sure his day is going to be more hectic than mine.

"That's it then. We hang up together, ok?" I say smiling widely.

"Ok," he chuckles.

"One, two, three…" My thumb hovers over the end call button. I can hear Tristan humming again. "Tristan!" I half scold, giggling as I do.

"What?" he chuckles, feigning innocence.

"It's late baby. I don't want to be tired and cranky at work tomorrow." And right now I'm freaking out, I can't concentrate – I dash a look at the door again.

"No, I don't want you to be either. How's it going with Susannah?" *Shit!*

"Fine," I mumble.

"That bad huh?" he says.

"No…I just…" I stop unable to articulate anything positive about her, so I pretend to yawn instead.

"Ok, sleepy I'm going. Miss, you like crazy," he says, sighing heavily.

"Miss you too baby," I whimper.

"Love you. Bye." Tristan whispers.

"Bye…" I whisper back, I hear Tristan chuckle then the line goes dead. My heart stops beating again. I take a ragged breathe in and slowly exhale. Picking up my water, I take one last look at the door, then walk over to it and check it's definitely locked. Then turning around I do the same with the patio door. *This place is secure.* I tell myself over, and over as I make my way up the stairs and into bed.

I AM DREAMING I'm on the boat again. Tristan is calling me, but I don't feel the same warm, blissful feeling as I did before. I feel on edge like all my senses are on hyper-alert like I can sense there's danger. Tristan calls my name again, only it sounds slightly twisted, like…like he can't breathe – I immediately know something's really wrong.

I silently head up the stairs. Tristan's calls are becoming more frantic like he's trying to find me, but he can't. I want to call out to him, but a voice inside my head tells me not to, that I shouldn't alert anyone to my presence.

As I reach the top of the stairs I scan the deck, I can't see Tristan anywhere. As I look up above me, I notice the sun isn't shining like before, dark, ominous black clouds have covered it, pushing the blue sky away. The wind starts to howl, whipping my hair around my face.

I can hear thunder in the distance. I look out to the horizon, forks of lighting are lighting it all up, giving me a glimpse of the coming storm, the swelling sea, I feel scared, and I don't know why.

I hear Tristan's strangled sob as he calls my name again. It's like he's got no strength left in him, I have to find him. I launch myself onto the deck staying as low to the ground as I can, my eyes darting left to right, trying to work out where his voice is coming from, then I finally locate him. *No! Tristan!*

He's tied to the mainsail, his arms are bound and bleeding, he can't move at all, and his head is lolling from side to side, blood oozing down the left side. I want to run towards him, so I can untie his arms, stop the bleeding, but I'm scared. I feel like a child again, too frightened to do anything.

"Tristan," I whisper trying to get his attention. I call to him three times, then finally, he groggily opens his eyes and when he sees me; they widen with fear.

"Run!" He growls so menacingly I shudder inside.

"What?" I frown back at him and take a step forward, holding my hand out to him.

"I said run!" He barks so loudly at me; it makes me jump.

"Tristan," I whisper. "What's wrong?"

His eyes suddenly move from focusing directly on me to behind me.

"Behind you! Move!" He bellows.

I whip my head around just as Susannah hits me hard across the head with something, it really fucking hurts. I howl in pain, and as I fall onto the hard wooden deck, she launches herself on top of me. She looks shabby, her hair is all over the place, and her lips are pulled back over her teeth. I can feel her hands crushing my throat –*Oh fuck! I can't breathe!*

"He's mine!" She screams psychotically. "Mine!"

Her hands grip my throat even tighter. I can feel I'm losing consciousness. I look up into her black eyes, she looks totally deranged. I go for a couple of gut punches, but each time I hit her, she squeezes even harder.

I can feel myself slipping under, and right before I do, my very last thought is of Tristan, of his safety, and my love for him. I look up at him, and from my strange position on the deck, I see him upside down, trying to free himself; he looks totally enraged – *Tristan!*

And then the blackness envelopes me...

I WAKE UP COUGHING choking and gasping for air, gripping my throat instinctively. *What the fuck was that all about?* - Sitting up, I grab my water and take several long gulps, trying to clear my throat of the constricting feeling that's still there. Then I take several deep breaths and squeeze my eyes shut, trying my best to push the nightmare away. I'm soaked in sweat, my heart is hammering against my chest, and I feel thoroughly shaken.

God, that was freaky!

I try to laugh it off, make light off it, but something about that nightmare has got me feeling on edge. Like my instincts are trying to warn me I should be wary of Susannah, and that I should be careful. I lie down and stare up at the ceiling. *That's ludicrous! Why should I be worried about Susannah?*

I figure it must be the fact that somebody was outside my place last night and tried to get in, that's got me all worked up and on edge. Add that to the fact that Susannah hasn't exactly made a good impression on her first day, and the fact that I'm missing Tristan like crazy, put them all together, and yeah, that'll make a freaky dream. I should know, I have enough of them. Checking the time, I see it's 6.10am, my alarm goes off at 6.30am anyway so I decide to get up, get ready for my morning swim, and forget about that haunting nightmare.

AS I HEAD BACK to my studio after my morning swim, I can't help wondering where Tristan is right now. Is he still sleeping? I picture his face, his soft breathing as he sleeps, then I think he's probably awake and already at work; the man has so much drive and ambition. Which makes me think about my career choice and whether Tristan is right? Should I be doing something different?

I push the thought away, I can't think about that right now, I have to get back to my studio, get ready for work and face another day with Susannah. The thought makes me feel a little uneasy, especially after that awful dream. She really does come across as a nice person, but she's already done some damage, and she's only been with us a day.

As I reach my studio, I stand at the patio door and stare through to the front door, checking it's still closed. Unlocking the patio door, I step through cautiously, I hate that whoever was here last night has made me feel like this, uneasy about coming back to my own place. So I decide to put on some music while I get ready, it's always guaranteed to pick me up.

ARETHA FRANKLIN'S, YOU Make Me Feel Like A Natural Woman is playing as I wonder out of the bathroom after showering. I start singing along to it, thinking how Tristan makes me feel like that, natural, playful, womanly. With my hair wrapped in a towel and my robe on, I walk over to the fridge and pour myself a large glass of vegetable juice.

My appetite has vanished again, just like Tristan, so I figure if I drink lots of juice, at least I'm getting my vitamins and minerals. Just as I'm heading back into the bathroom, the track changes to Lonestar's Amazed. I dash back into the living room and press next. That song, those words…far too heavy for this time in the morning. The next song starts, it's The Corrs, Runaway – *Yes! This is how I feel about Tristan!*

I start singing along as I walk back into the bathroom. Then I take the towel off my head and start slowly brushing my hair in the mirror, thinking how poignant this song is, and how I would, given half the chance, run away with Tristan.

My player flips to the next song, Whitney Houston's I Have Nothing starts playing –Hmm, maybe not such a good idea. This song is making me realise that I really don't have anything if I don't have Tristan – I've never felt like that before, about anyone, or anything. I quickly push that thought aside. The song continues. Whitney is easily hitting the high notes, I stop singing, I can't reach that high.

Tittering to myself, I grab my Coconut Oil and massage a little into my hair, flip my head up, twist my hair and pin it into a bun. Then I start with my makeup. As I'm putting on my mascara, I think about seeing George tonight and telling him about Tristan's proposal. My stomach does a backward flip, and then swarms with butterflies –*Whoa will I ever get used to that feeling?*

I hope not, it's very heady and exciting. Then I think of Cindy and the second Hypnotherapy session. I really hope it works again and I'm able to wear the dress. I really want to look nice for Tristan, but more than that, I want to feel good about myself. I want to feel feminine and girly, I snort with laughter at myself – If there's one thing I've never been is girly. As a kid I was always running around the garden like a tomboy, even my favourite T.V shows were tomboyish – Knight Rider, Black Beauty, Dr Who and Star Trek, not exactly girly programming.

With my make-up and hair done, I wonder over to my handbag so I can find my lip gloss, and as I do, I notice my mobile is flashing at me. Dropping the lip-gloss and picking it up, I punch in the unlock code, and it shows a new message. Flicking it open, I'm shocked to see I have a message from Tristan.

Morning Sweet Pea, hope you slept well. I can't wait to hear your voice. Don't forget to call me ;-) Love Tristan Xxx

I chuckle at his candour and his wink. Then I check what time he sent it – 6.35am – just as I was heading out the door to go swimming. I have never taken my mobile with me before, for some reason I don't trust leaving it in a locker, but maybe I should from now on. I go to press reply, checking the time as I do, and see it's already 7.45am, I still have to get dressed, and I'll be speaking to him shortly, so I decide to wait and head up the stairs.

Thankfully, I picked up my dry cleaning yesterday, which I had completely forgotten about over the weekend – I'm not surprised though, being with Tristan makes me forget most things – so at least I have something decent to wear today.

Rummaging through the plastic bags, I find my light blue trousers and my short-sleeved, cream blouse. Once I'm dressed, I slip my feet into my wedges and head down the stairs. Picking up my handbag and my keys, I spray a little perfume and put on some lip gloss, which I didn't do earlier. That's Tristan again, making me forget what I was doing.

I suddenly remember I need to ask him about the suicide. I forgot all about it after what happened last night, I must remember to ask him today. I don't like that Susannah knew and I didn't – *That pissed me right off!*

I switch off the air-conditioner, smiling as I recall the memory of Tristan buying it for me. Then I turn off my amp and unplug my MP3 player, just as Beyonce's Halo starts playing, pausing the track, I attach my headphones and walk over to the patio door.

I go to pull it open and nearly fall over – *I locked it?* I've never done that before! Feeling a little miffed that I'm being extra cautious, I unlock it and pull the door open. Stepping outside into another bright, blue-skied, sunshiny day, I pull the door shut and lock it, then check again that it's definitely locked.

"Morning." I jump a mile in the air.

"Oh hey Bob," I say breathlessly.

"Blimey! You're jumpy today?" He says, staring at me quizzically.

I nod and stare out at the boats bobbing on the water. "Hey Bob, you didn't see or hear anything strange last night did you?" I casually ask.

He looks up from his morning paper and frowns at me. "No, why?" I walk over to his tiny table and sit in the chair opposite him.

"I fell asleep on the sofa last night, and I was woken up early this morning, someone was outside my front door. They tried the handle…they tried to get in…" I sound frantic, and my leg is jigging up and down. I'd better calm down. I don't want to worry Bob.

"What!" Throwing his morning paper down on the table, he grabs hold of my free hand. "Why didn't you tell me? Why didn't you wake me up?" I shake my head at him and stare out at the boats. *Like a doddery old man could save me!*

"Did you call the police?" he asks.

"Yeah, but whoever it was had already gone, so they said there was no danger and that they would come by today, I told them not to bother," I say, sounding glum.

"Why?" Bob questions.

"Well there's not much they can do today is there? I needed them last night!" I squawk in annoyance.

Bob rolls his eyes at me. "If they turn up today, you want me to let them in?" he asks.

"Sure, why not," I shrug.

"Anything ever happens like that again young lady you come straight round to me, I'll sort them out," he says, showing me his fist. I try not to chuckle. I really don't think Bob would do very well against a burglar if that's what it was.

"I will," I tell him sweetly. Because he is sweet and kind, he's like the Granddad I never had. Standing up I lean down and kiss him on the cheek. "Thanks, Bob, see you tonight," I say.

"You're not staying with that fella of yours?" He asks looking up at me.

"No…he's away all week." I sound sad. Bob nods once and goes back to his paper. "Well, I'll see you later," I say knowing the conversation is over.

"Have a good day," he says propping his legs up on the spare chair.

I muster a smile, turn around, take a deep breath, squaring my shoulders as I do, and put on my sunglasses. I take my mobile out of my bag to call Tristan and begin walking along the concourse. It rings three times then it's answered - *By a woman!*

"Hello, Coral. I'm Karen." *Karen?*

"Um…Hi Karen." I try to think of the name, where have I heard it before?

"I'm Mr Freeman's P.A in Leeds," she tells me –*Ah of course!*

"Your accent is awesome," I tell her because it is.

She chuckles lightly. "Mr Freeman's meeting's run over, he told me you would be calling him with an update and to say sorry if he wasn't back in time. He said to let you know he'll call you at work." *Work! He can't do that, Blondie will be there.*

"Yes, of course, Karen, it's no problem at all. Say thank you to Mr Freeman for me." It feels really weird calling him that.

"Of course I will. It was nice speaking to you Coral, maybe we'll meet someday?" She sounds so friendly, so normal and nice. *I wish she were the one training me, not Susannah!*

"I hope so, I'd really like that," I smile easily.

"Me too, well I'd better get on." *Inspiration hits, maybe she can help me?*

"Karen, can I ask you something?" I ask cautiously.

"Sure, fire away." *Ok here goes!*

"Have you met Susannah?" The line is silent for a long time.

"Yes, yes I have." She finally says, but her tone has changed, she doesn't sound so happy and light anymore.

"Oh, ok." I stare out to sea, maybe I'm not going to get anything out of her, but I push anyway. "It's ok, you don't have to say anything. It's just that she's upset one of the girls in the office, and she's not great with me either. I just wondered if it was because she was away from home, you know…a little pissed to be training me, missing her husband maybe?"

"Well…I…" She seems hesitant to say anything. "I don't like to gossip' – "Neither do I," I interrupt, then continue. "It's just… I think she's a little odd, I just wanted to make sure it wasn't me I guess."

"It's not you," she says, her voice low and quiet.

"Oh?" *Now I'm intrigued.*

"Coral, I really don't want to talk about this at work, especially on Mr Freeman's mobile," she says sounding a little worried.

"Of course, I understand." *Damn it!*

"I take lunch at one. Want me to call you?" She offers.

"Really, you would? I don't want to take up your lunch hour." *Please say yes!*

"No it's fine, I'll call you later." *Bingo!*

"Great thanks. Bye Karen," I say cheerfully.

"See ya." Karen hangs up.

I stare out at the sparkling blue ocean, feeling a little pissed I couldn't talk to Tristan, but also wondering what *that* conversation's going to be like. Shrugging it off, I decide to pop into the gym and see if Will is in yet, I need to ask him something. When I ask at reception they tell me he's not in yet, so I leave my mobile number, telling them it's urgent and can get Will to contact me, ASAP. I'm sure he will, he hasn't let me down before, and maybe he can give me some advice how to deal with the situation if it happens again. Plus, I need to let him know that I panicked last night, so maybe we need to work on some other type of training, some other technique?

Feeling satisfied that I've got control of my emotions and the whole *'someone tried to get into my studio'* situation, I pop my headphones in and hit play. Halo continues where it left off, and I stop myself from singing aloud. I really can't hit those high notes, and I don't want to upset the commuters going to work. I'm sure the last thing they want to hear is a squawking bird as they head into the office.

As I make my way into work, listening to the song, it suddenly becomes so clear. This is me, and the guy in the song is Tristan, he is my Halo. He is just like a ray of sunshine brightening up my days, making me feel safe, and I am one hundred percent addicted to his light, his warmth, his embrace, and I pray he will never fade away.

The moment I walk into work, I go straight into Joyce's office so I can tell her about my strange incident last night, only to find she isn't in yet. *Damn it!*

Heading back to my desk, I find a post-it note on my screen
– **Be in at 11am, Joyce x**
Well, that's just great!

CHAPTER FOURTEEN

SUSANNAH IS BEING strangely nice to me today. Very chatty, and I can't work out why. As our mid-morning break comes around, she follows me into the kitchen for a coffee. Unfortunately, I feel a headache coming on because Susannah has not stopped talking today. I cannot for the life of me, work out what she's up to. Yesterday she was weird with me, and today I'm her best friend. *It's very odd!*

"So are you with anyone Coral, do you have a boyfriend?" She asks.

I decide not to lie. I'm smiling too much lately. I don't think I can hide it.

"Yes," I answer. "And you're married I see," I say, gesturing to her wedding and engagement rings.

"Kind of obvious isn't it." She laughs, but it's off.

"How long have you been married?" I ask smiling as I do.

"Two years." She answers; humourlessly this time.

"How did you meet?" I want to keep her talking, keep control of the conversation.

"We'd known each other a long time." She answers gravely. It peaks my interest.

"Are you ok?" I can't work out if she's genuine.

Her lips twitch with a smile, but it doesn't reach her eyes. "We're having…difficulties," she says. *I can't tell if she's playing it up?*

"Oh!" I look away from her. I don't know her well enough for her to be sharing that kind of information with me. Then I hear Tristan's voice in my head *'she's happily married'* – I frown in confusion trying to make sense of what she's saying.

"I'm sorry," I mumble as I pour two mugs of coffee.

She shrugs nonchalantly. "Sometimes it works, sometimes it doesn't." *What? What does that mean?* I stop what I'm doing and look up at her. "We're getting divorced," she whispers, her eyes glistening over - *Fuck!*

"Oh! Susannah, I'm sorry, that can't be easy," I offer by way of condolences.

"Thanks, but I guess when it's over, it's over," she says, as though she doesn't give a fuck.

I nod in agreement, then I think about where she lives – London – she'll meet someone new. Then I wonder whether she actually wants to, and then I wonder if Tristan knows about this.

"There's no way of working it out?" I ask tentatively. Susannah shakes her head at me. "So what are your plans?" I ask. "I take it you live together?" I add.

"No, well, yes. Sam kept his house, rented it out and moved in with me. I guess he'll go back there. We haven't really worked stuff like that out yet. We only made our decision this Sunday gone."

Ah, maybe she's not herself because of what's going on in her love life? Then I think about Karen's odd reaction this morning. None of it is making sense, in-fact I'm starting to feel very confused. Plus, it isn't helping that every time I look at her, I keep seeing the crazy, deranged Susannah from my dream.

Susannah continues. "Although, I am thinking about getting out of London altogether, make a fresh start," she says wistfully. *What!?*

My throat instantly goes dry, why do I get the feeling I know where this is going?

"I don't blame you, got anywhere in mind?" I ask brightly as I reach for the milk out of the fridge.

"Actually, funny you should say that..." My heart sinks to the pit of my stomach. "Being here, down by the coast has made me realise how much I need a change, I think it would do me good, you know fresh air, walks on the beach…" I reluctantly hand her coffee to her, avoiding eye contact.

"I guess so," I answer artlessly. *Come on Coral, be brave!*

Meeting her eyes, I smile purposely. "So you might move here?" I ask brightly, taking a sip of coffee. She instantly blushes – *Gotcha!*

"Maybe, I don't know yet," she says, smiling down at the floor.

Liar! You know full well what you're doing!

Susannah looks up at me and smiles wearily. I make myself smile sympathetically at her, then I nod and walk out the kitchen, heading back to my desk, unfortunately, with Susannah following me. *Ugh! I feel like throwing up!*

She's moving here because Tristan is, I know she is. Then I think about her job, she'll have to get a new one...unless...unless she's after my job? Or maybe she'll convince Tristan we should work together. I don't know, but either way, I don't like it, I don't like it at all. I feel all the blood drain out of my face. *Damn it!*

Of all the weeks for Tristan to be away, why did it have to be this one? I need to talk to him, and I need to talk to him now!

"Coral are you ok, you've gone very pale?" I put my coffee cup down, and rub my stomach as though I'm in pain.

"Yeah, just not feeling too great, must be the curry I had last night." Lie, lie, lie that's all I seem to do nowadays. "I'm going to the ladies," I say.

Turning swiftly on my heel I march away from her.

FUCKETY, FUCK, FUCK! I have not stopped looking at the clock on the wall, I want lunchtime to come around, and I want it now. My leg keeps trying to jig up and down with nerves – I don't want Blondie to see that. And I wish she would stop smiling at me like that like I'm her new best friend. Finally, after concentrating on the new emailing system she is showing me, 12.30pm comes around. Leaping up from my chair, I say goodbye to Blondie, grab my bag and head out the building. Just as I reach the end of the road, I realise I haven't asked Joyce if she wants anything, which I always do if I'm heading out, so I call her mobile.

"Coral?" Joyce answers sounding concerned.

"Joyce, I'm outside the building. Did you want anything picking up?" I ask sweetly.

"Actually darling, if you have the time and you don't mind. I really fancy one of those Frappuccino's from Starbucks." I smile to myself. Joyce is rarely naughty.

"Yep, that's no problem," I answer. "Oh Joyce, while I've got you, can I have five minutes when I get back?"

"Of course you can. I'll call you through when I'm free."

"Thank you," I answer and hang up.

Walking into town, I make my way over to St James's Street. I go straight to the place I need for Tristan's present and get that organised. I'm surprised it only takes a few minutes to do, then I head over to Starbucks. As I do, I can't help checking my mobile for a call from Tristan or Karen –*Nothing!* – I hope Tristan's ok.

As I step into the coffee house, I see there's a queue, so I stand next in line. I'm about to try Tristan again, but the conversation going on in front of me has got my attention. They are evidently a couple of gay guys, and the one is telling the other about his friend finding out that the guy he had been dating for five years had, in fact, been secretly married for ten years to a woman and had three kids.

"How did he not know that?" the one says to the other.

"I don't know, but Kevin is well and truly cut up about it. I'm just glad he found out now, and it didn't drag on any longer."

"That's awful! How did he find out?"

"Well, he thought he was seeing someone else, but he didn't want to start going through his phone or following him, he thought that was a bit desperate and stalkerish." *Yes, it is!*

"So what did he do?" the other asks.

"Got a P.I on it." He says. *My ears prick up!*

"You're kidding?" The other chokes.

"No, she's the one that found it all out for him." He says.

"Never would have thought to do that," he says shaking his head. "Bet that cost a fortune," he adds.

The other shakes his head. "She didn't cost that much actually, which I was surprised at, and they were really quick apparently. He made the call, and within a couple of days he got the answer he needed."

"Well, I suppose it's better than snooping around yourself," he says.

"Yeah, I guess," says the other, nodding in agreement.

"Hello, Miss?" I look up and see I'm next in line, moving forward I stare blankly at the menu. My stomach is rumbling at me, but I really don't feel that hungry. Then I spy the Sticky Chocolate Brownie Swirl in the pastry section.

"Miss, can I take your order?" The staff member looks a little annoyed. I guess I'm holding the queue up.

"I'll take Mocha Light Frappuccino, a regular Cappuccino and a Chocolate Brownie Swirl to take out." She nods in response, and I pay for my order. The two chaps who were talking have gone to sit down, but the conversation they had has got me thinking...

"Miss, heellooo?" I turn and look up. *Oops! She's talking to me.* "Your order?" she says a little sarcastically.

"Thanks." I take it from her and walk out the coffee house. Just at that moment, my mobile starts ringing. *Damn it!*

Stuffing my swirl into my bag, so I have a free hand, I answer the call.

"Hello?"

"Hi Coral, it's Karen."

"Hey, thanks for calling me back."

"It's no problem."

"Are you sure you want to talk about this?" I don't want her to feel like I'm pressuring her.

"No, really it's fine. So who's she upset?"

"The receptionist Joe, don't get me wrong she is a little bit 'nice but dim' at times, but she wouldn't hurt a fly, she certainly didn't deserve to be belittled like that."

"No, well that's Susannah for you."

"What do you mean?"

"Look, between you and me, I can't stand her, and Claire in Birmingham doesn't like her either."

"Why, what's she done?"

"It's not really what she's done, it's how she is. She can be very coarse, and sometimes, she's very argumentative with other people, for no apparent reason. Personally, I think she's a vindictive bitch!" Karen states.

"You do?" I squeak. "Have you told Mr Freeman?" I question, wondering if she has.

"No. You see, we all keep it zipped when it comes to her, because for some reason Mr Freeman – with all due respect to him, he's a brilliant boss– for some reason he seems to think she's amazing. I've seen it first hand, she is so different with everyone when he's around, then the moment he leaves she goes back to being...I don't know....just weird." Karen adds.

"Yeah, weird seems to be the right word." I have a thought. I decide to put it out there, question it, see what Karen's reaction is. "You know, the way she talks about Mr Freeman, you'd think she's in love with him, not her husband," I say artlessly.

"Coral *everyone* knows she's is in love with him, it's written all over her. It's a little bit freaky to be fair, but it doesn't seem to bother Mr Freeman so...did you say, husband?" *Oh My God! I'm right, and I'm not the only one who's thinking it either!*

I swallow hard. "Yeah...why?" I say, trying to sound casual.

"You know, none of the girls believes she's actually married."

"What?" I chuckle. *That's a little odd.*

"No, seriously they don't. Everyone thinks she's made him up. Ask her about it, she instantly clams up. She doesn't talk about him at all," she says.

"But she's got rings on?" I blurt.

"Coral," Karen chuckles. "Anyone can wear a ring and pose that they are married."

"Well...yeah, I guess, but why would she do that?" I mumble trying to get my head around it all. *That's weird?*

"No idea," she says. "When she *supposedly* got married all the girls in the London office were waiting for her to bring in her wedding photos, but she never did. The last person that asked about them, she snapped their head off, and it all got dropped, which we all thought was odd. Most women can't wait to show off their wedding photos, so why didn't she?"

That's true, I remember when one of the secretaries at Chester House got married last year, she went on about it for months, and she did bring photos in, in-fact I think she brought a video too. *Ok, this is getting weirder by the minute.*

"Ok, so you're saying most people think her husband is fictitious?" I ask, hardly able to believe my own words.

"Yes." Karen firmly answers.

"But why would she do that? It doesn't make any sense?" I ask, frowning deeply.

"No idea, like I said she's weird." I get the feeling Karen and Susannah have had a run in at some point.

"She told me this morning that she's getting divorced. And that she wants to relocate," I say quietly.

"Careful there Coral, she'll be after your job," she says.

I try not to panic. "You think so?" I ask squeakily.

"Look, I know Mr Freeman is relocating down there, he told me this morning. It doesn't make any difference to me. I've still got my job, which I love. Claire's cool about it too, but I can't imagine Susannah being satisfied with only seeing him once a month if that!"

"No, I don't suppose she would be, not if she's in love with him," I whisper.

I drift off for a second, racking my brains for a logical answer to all this. Ok, so married women are women of value. They must be a good catch if a guy has snapped them up, so maybe she is playing that card, to make Tristan jealous. I shake my head at myself, that doesn't make sense! – Ok, so she pretends to be married so she can fake a divorce and....and Tristan will comfort her in her time of need, console her...*No!*

My mouth suddenly goes dry, and my throat constricts.

"You there Coral?" Karen says.

"Yeah...sorry, just trying to work it all out," I whisper, my mind already elsewhere.

"Don't waste your time on her. You're best to steer clear." I nod in agreement.

"Has she ever been funny with you?" I ask.

"Loads of times, but I just ignore her, she's not worth it. Besides, I don't have to see her too often, and I'm not going to leave a job I love because of her."

"Don't blame you." As I look up, I see I have reached work. "Karen I have to go, I'm back at work, she might overhear us."

"Yeah no problem, call me if you need anything," Karen says.

"You're calling on your mobile?" I ask.

"Yeah," Karen says.

"Ok, I'll programme you in, and ditto, ever need anything just holler," I say.

Karen chuckles. "Good luck for the rest of the week." She says.

"Thanks, I think I'm going to need it," I say brightly, trying to make light of a bad situation.

"Oh Coral, just for the record, if I knew there was training going on, I would have volunteered. I've never been to Brighton," she says enthusiastically.

"Well, you're welcome anytime. If you want a break for a weekend or something, just come on down. You can stay at mine, I think we'll have a good time," I offer, knowing somehow that we will, I can tell. *Probably because she reminds me of Harriett* – I quickly quash those thoughts.

"Really?" she says excitedly. "Coral, that's really nice of you. I'll take you up on that offer."

"Great." I giggle, feeling lighter for the friendly chat.

"I'll see you soon then," Karen chuckles.

"Definitely. And thanks for talking to me."

"You're welcome," she says. "See ya."

"Bye Karen." I hang up. Wow, she was so nice, like normal nice, not weird nice like Susannah. *Why the hell didn't Tristan send Karen to me?*

I instantly feel miserable that he didn't, this week could have been so much fun, and Karen would have taken my mind off the fact that Tristan is not here. I look solemnly behind me, hoping that Tristan will appear out of thin air and start walking towards me, that deep dimpled smile on his face and his eyes shining brightly for me. Shaking my head at myself, I walk the few steps needed and push through the glass door.

I KNOCK ON JOYCE'S door. I hear her call me, so I go through and pass the Frappuccino to her. She's on the phone, but gestures for me to sit down. I pull my swirl out of my handbag and pull a piece off, placing it my mouth I start chewing. This does not taste like cardboard, it tastes absolutely delicious! Maybe I can just survive on these until Tristan's back? I'd have no problem doing that.

Picking up my Cappuccino, I take a long drink and continue to devour the Chocolate Swirl. By the time Joyce has finished her call, I have finished my swirl and my Cappuccino.

"I have to be quick sweetheart," Joyce says sipping her drink.

"Ok. Firstly, someone tried to get into my studio last night." Joyce spits her Frappuccino out in shock. I quickly move out of the way just in time, so it sprays the table and not me – *Oops!*

"Coral!" She scolds. "You can't just say something like that without warning me!"

"Sorry," I say apologetically. Then as I'm helping her clean up the mess, I tell her what happened, the full story. Then I tell her what Karen has told me about Susannah, she looks just as puzzled as I feel, but she logs it all on the file.

Just as I'm leaving her office, Joyce insists I stay with her tonight. I decline gracefully, explaining that I have George tonight and I've got Bob to look after me.

"If you change your mind, even if it's in the middle of the night. Just come over ok?" Joyce tells me worriedly.

"Ok." I half smile at her. If I'm truthful, I don't want anyone but Tristan. Only he can take away the fear of someone getting in, no one else can do that.

"Promise?" Joyce asks. *Grrrr, I hate that word* – I nod silently and head out of her office.

As I walk down the corridor towards the ladies, I get another call on my mobile, as I check it I see it's the gym. Answering the call I find it is Will, and I go through the details of last night's events.

"You need some magnetic door sensors, the moment the handle is moved the alarm will trigger, and they'll go running," he tells me. *Thank you, Will!*

"Where will I get those from?" I ask.

"Argos, Amazon, B&Q. Depends how quickly you want them?"

"Tonight," I answer. *If they make me feel more secure why wait?*

"Well you won't get it from Amazon until tomorrow' –"I know," I interrupt. "I'll take a look online, probably Argos. I can pick them up on my way home."

"As for panicking, most people do Coral. You have to be the one that beats the fear, control *it* don't let *it* control you." I nod vigorously as I listen to Will. "Stay focused. Think of the weapons you have at your disposal." *Huh?*

"Weapons, what weapons?" I question.

Will sighs then rushes his words out at lightning speed. "Coral come on, haven't I taught you anything? Hands are for?" *Oh, ok now I get what he means!*

"Pushing the nose up into the brain," I answer triumphantly.

"Good. Fingers?" Will prompts.

"Pushing the eyes into the socket, or ripping the throat out," I answer, squirming slightly at that one, I hope I never have to use it – *That's Rambo shit!*

"Body weight?" He questions.

"Use my weight like you taught me, throw them down," I answer.

"Good, legs and arms?"

"Again, use them to take down the assailant, throw them over my shoulder or take their legs out from underneath them," I breathe.

"Yes. You see, you know what to do, you've just got to stay focused and not panic."

"Easier said than done!" I snap.

"Coral, use what I've taught you, even if you get it slightly wrong it doesn't matter. You don't need to stay and fight. Just remember to protect yourself from getting hurt with a calm focused mind, then once you have them down, run. It's simple." *No, you make it sound simple!*

"Ok, thanks, Will. I'd better go, my lunch is nearly over," I tell him.

"Ok, see you Thursday."

"Yep, see you then."

"Oh Coral, I'm on till 9pm tonight you need any help fitting the alarms, just let me know. I'll pop over when I'm finished."

"Will, I could give you a big kiss right now, you know that?"

"Eh, less of that I'm a happily married man." He teases.

I roll my eyes and chuckle. "I didn't mean it like that," I smile.

"I know you didn't. I'm just pulling your leg," he laughs.

"Will!" I scold laughing as I do. "I'll call you if I need you," I chortle.

"Be safe," he tells me then the line goes dead.

I use my mobile to find Argos, locating the Brighton branch I start my search. I find a Yale easy fit door and window contact at £22.99. Adding two to my cart, I think about what Will has said to me about weapons – *Right, I know what's a good weapon!*

Searching Baseball Bats, I quickly add one of those to my cart too, then I use the check and reserve system, thankfully they have them in stock at the Brighton Branch, so all I've got to do is pick them up and pay for them tonight.

As I come out of the ladies and head back to my desk, I decide to text Tristan. He hasn't tried to call me today, and I haven't had another text from him either, which I find strange.

Tristan, I haven't heard from you today. I guess you're really busy. I just wanted to let you know I miss you, badly, and I can't wait till you're home. Be good baby Xxx I love you Coral xx

Putting my mobile back on silent, I place it in my bag and go to open my inbox when I see a note from Susannah –**Gone to Lunch back at 2pm** – Just as I read it, I hear really loud laughter coming from down in Reception.

Picking up the handset, I dial Joe. "Hey, Joe."

"Hi Coral," she whispers. *Yay! She got my name right!*

"What's with all the laughter?" I ask.

"*She's* going out to lunch with *them*," Joe murmurs. *Ah, the other secretaries.*

"Really?" I squeak in surprise.

"Yeah, she's the one with the cackling laugh," she giggles.

"So much for heartbreak…" I mumble.

"What?" Joe asks, intrigued.

"Nothing Joe, I'd better go. See you later."

"Bye." We both hang up.

I shake my head in wonder. How can anyone with an actual husband, who is supposedly getting divorced, be laughing and joking as though they haven't got a care in the world? *You know why* – I snarl at myself. Brushing the thought away I open my inbox and start on the letters Joyce has sent across. Just as I'm finishing off the second letter, the line starts ringing.

"Garland and Associates, Coral speaking," I say, as I continue typing.

"Hello, beautiful." *Tristan!* I almost drop the phone. Hearing his voice is like hearing an angel come to comfort me.

"Tristan," I whisper, feeling all the stresses and strains fall away.

"I've got to be quick baby, I'm about to go to another meeting. I just got your text, and I just wanted you to know I've been thinking about you all day." I close my eyes and sink back into my chair.

"You have?" I smile.

"Of course I have," he chuckles.

"It's so good to hear your voice," I tell him, feeling tears bubbling up – *Damn it!*

"Same here baby. You ok?" He asks in his low, sexy voice.

"I am now." I sniff. Tristan chuckles, he sounds in high spirits. "You?" I ask.

"I have a beautiful fiancé to come home to. I'm on top of the world." I smile like a love-struck teenager. "Baby, I have to go, call you tonight?" he asks.

"Ok," I whisper. Then I remember about Saturday. "Oh Tristan, don't make any plans for Saturday." I groan.

"Why's that?" he questions.

"We're going to Gladys's," I grumble. "That's if you want to go."

"Yes, I do. What's the occasion?"

"She's getting all the family together for some pre-wedding dinner thing. Malcolm's family will be there too." I add.

"Introducing me to your family already must be serious," he says.

I can't help laughing at that one. "Tristan, it's not funny," I chuckle. "It's going to be such hard work," I grumble.

"It'll be fine baby. You'll have me with you." *Yes, yes I will.*

"You really want to go?" I squeak.

"Of course," he scoffs. "Try keeping me away."

"I miss you," I whisper, feeling the gaping hole in my chest re-open.

"Ah baby, you have no idea. But I have to go, call you tonight?"

"Ok," I sigh heavily.

"Love you," he whispers.

"Hurry home," I whisper back.

Tristan chuckles and hangs up. I lean forward, replace the handset and sit staring at the screen. Then I hear my mobile vibrate. Checking no-one is around, I take it out my bag and see I have a message. Opening it up, I see it's from Tristan.

*No matter how far away, no matter the distance, remember

we are under the same stars, the same moon. I'm always with you, even if I'm not there physically. Believe me, baby, I'm right there with you. I love you, and I can't wait to see you again. Your beloved Tristan Xxx*

Oh, Tristan! – I burst into tears. His beautiful words have made me cry. I put my mobile away, and scuttle off to the ladies so I can clean up my face. Coming back to my desk, I actually feel like I'm in physical pain, the dull ache that started when he left has blossomed into a full-blown crater, a big empty crater. I feel empty and lost, and I hate it, I can't handle it. I want him home and in my arms...

CHAPTER FIFTEEN

I BLINK MY EYES open and look up at Cindy. Her short, black bobbed hair is very shiny today, her skin as white as snow, and she's wearing a deep cherry red lipstick; she reminds me of Snow White.

"How are you feeling?" she asks.

"Good," I answer getting up from the sofa and moving over to the chair.

"It's good to hear that you had some positive results from our last session. Hopefully, if we keep it up, we should have you feeling really good in no time at all." I nod in agreement and smile at George. "Well, I'll leave you to it." Cindy picks up her handbag and throws it over her shoulder.

"Thank you, Cindy, I really do appreciate it," I tell her.

"You're very welcome Coral, good luck. See you next week." I smile tentatively at her.

"George." Cindy takes his hand and shakes it.

"Thank you, Cindy, good to see you," George says.

"You too." She smiles at us both, then heads out of his office.

Sitting in his chair, George turns to me and picks up his pad and pen. "So Coral, where would you like to begin today?"

"Tristan asked me to marry him," I blurt without thinking.

George's eyebrows rise in surprise. "He did?" he asks, astonished.

"Yes." I frown and fidget in the chair.

"And what did you say?" he asks softly.

My jaw clenches. "I said yes," I whimper. *Christ! One minute I'm mad, then the next...*

"You did?" He says, looking even more surprised. "Well... well that's wonderful Coral, congratulations."

I shake my head and stare at the floor.

He instantly stops smiling. "Oh dear," he says quietly. "Let's discuss."

"George I think...I know I'm not ready. It's too soon," I interrupt. "I mean I know I love him, it feels like he's the one for me, but...." I stare out the window.

"Go on," he urges.

"Right now, I have a bigger issue," I snap, clenching my jaw.

"Bigger than marriage?" He asks, his one eyebrow cocking up.

"Yes," I tell George all about Susannah, about the strange dream, the advice Joyce gave me; and what Karen told me.

"It does sound strange," George confirms.

"What do I do?" I ask.

"I would follow Joyce's advice. If there's any chance she's unstable, you need to keep your distance."

"But that's just it George, I'm afraid for Tristan. She's evidently still in love with him, I just have this horrible feeling she'll flip when she finds out about us. I don't care what she says to me, I can look after myself. It's Tristan I'm worried about, he's too trusting. What if she hurts him?"

"Worrying about the future again," George admonishes.

I sigh heavily and run my hands through my hair that I took out the bun before seeing Cindy. "So what, I say nothing? I don't warn Tristan?" I bite back.

"It is a tricky situation to be in with you both working for him, and he has known Susannah a lot longer than you," he muses.

"Exactly!" I screech. "This is the whole reason I didn't want to get involved with him in the first place." I bellow feeling angry and frustrated. "Maybe I should just quit!" I hiss.

"And what good will that do?" George questions.

"I don't know," I sulk wrapping my arms around myself. George shakes his head at me. "She's dangerous," I add, keeping my eyes on the floor.

"You don't know that," George warns.

"Someone tried to get into my studio while I was there George, nothing like that has ever happened before. Don't you think it's a bit of a coincidence? She turns up, and I have that happen?"

"What!" he bellows. "Did you call the police?" he asks with wide eyes.

"Yes." I hiss in frustration.

"And what did they say?"

"Nothing, they didn't come over. Whoever it was tried the handle and couldn't get in, so they left."

George purses his lips. "So you didn't see who it was?" he questions.

"No!" I whine.

"It could have been anyone," George admonishes. I huff in my seat. "Let's get back to Tristan and his proposal. Why did you say yes?" I shrug noncommittally. "Coral, I can't help you if you don't talk to me," he peers down at me over his glasses.

I stare out the window for a moment, trying to think of the right words.

"Well, at the time the answer was yes. I had no reservations…I don't know, maybe I just got carried away in the moment you know…we made love, he proposed. I felt safe, warm, protected… in love…" I shake my head at myself. *Am I evil?* – Sometimes I feel like I am, if I turn around and tell Tristan it's off, he's going to be crushed. I know he is…*why did I say yes?*

"What's changed your mind?" George asks.

"It's too soon, people don't…" I break off – *I'm so fucking confused!*

I want to be with Tristan, I know I'm in love with him, but at the same time I don't, because it scares the fuck out of me!

"Actually they do," George says, pulling me from my musing. "I presume you were about to say people don't fall in love that quickly?" he questions.

I nod in reply.

"Coral, there are millions of people across the world that have met and married very quickly, and it has lasted." *Oh, well I didn't know that!*

"He wants to know…everything," I shudder. "He doesn't want anything from the past hanging between us, he wants me to lay it all out for him, but I can't." I whimper.

"Why not?" George asks.

"He'll reject me, I know he will," I retort.

"No, you're presuming he will," George counteracts. "Coral, just because he has asked, and you have said yes, it doesn't mean it has to happen straight away," George says softly.

"He wants it to happen soon," I mumble.

"Ah, I see," George shifts in his chair. "What are you most nervous about? Commitment, intimacy, relying on another person besides yourself?" he questions.

"All of those, but mostly…I guess…I just keep thinking that Tristan deserves better. Someone who can make him really happy," I answer.

"You think you are undeserving of him?"

"Yes." I reluctantly answer.

"Well, he obviously doesn't think that," George replies. "Coral look at me."

I look up from staring at the floor.

"Coral, he has asked you to be his wife. I'm sure he wouldn't have asked you if he didn't think you were worthy of him. You must make him very happy. Otherwise, he wouldn't have asked, surely?" I think back to what Tristan said earlier *'I have a beautiful fiancé to come home to, I'm on top of the world.'*

"Ok, ok. Maybe I do make him happy, but I don't know if he wants a family though, and you know I can't have kids," I argue.

"Coral, why do I get the feeling you're self-destructing? It's like you're doing it without even realising it, like your trying to find all these reasons why you shouldn't be together?"

"It's not that," I snap. "I just don't…if he wants kids and I can't, what's the point?"

"That's ridiculous there's always adoption," George scolds.

I sigh heavily. Maybe he's right, maybe I am self-destructing? I dig deep to try and find the reason why I know I'm scared. Scared of getting hurt, scared that Tristan might leave me, scared of really opening my heart and letting someone love me, completely, warts and all. Ok, I'm scared, but like George says a life without risk isn't a life worth living.

"I'm scared," I whisper.

"I'm sure you are it's a big step Coral, but I have every faith that you'll see that you are stronger than you think you are, strong enough for the both of you."

I close my eyes and swallow hard. "You think so?"

"Yes, I do," George tells me firmly.

I look up at George. "I'm scared I'll let him down, and he'll hate me for it."

George takes off his glasses and leans forward in his chair. "Coral, we all make mistakes in relationships, married or not, but that's where being in love comes in, we love, and we forgive, and we move on. The successful couples that I know who are together and are still very happy, live by that motto. Remember no-one is perfect, not you, not Tristan, not anyone. He's going to make mistakes too you know, you'll probably be hurt, upset, but you have to ask yourself, would you rather a life with that, as in being love with all its ups and downs, or would you prefer a life of solitude?"

"Love," I whisper.

"I thought you would say that," he says. "You just have to be brave Coral, find the courage and the strength within, and you will see over time, that it all starts to feel very natural, you won't be worrying about this or that anymore, you'll just be happy." George smiles fondly at me. "Remember Coral, you over analyse everything, and you worry far too much, try giving yourself a break from it all, a few days off…maybe try just going with the flow?"

"Ok," I breathe. "I will, I'll try," I add. I know he's right, I do freak out about stuff. I worry and over analyse, but I've been like this for so long, I don't know any other way.

"Now any other concerns?" George asks.

I shake my head. I feel all over the place at the moment, and I know the only cure is Tristan, I want him home.

"Alright then, until Friday?" he asks.

"Actually George, can I skip this week?" I ask politely.

"Of course, any particular reason?" he asks.

I tell George about my date with Tristan and the dress that I've got. *Hopefully, I'll feel ok to wear it* – George wishes me luck, I hug and kiss him and leave his house feeling just as frustrated as I did when I walked in…

THAT NIGHT AFTER picking up the alarms and fitting them to the front door and the patio, I take the baseball bat upstairs and place it next to my bed. Then I do some Yoga to try and relax.

I remembered to take my mobile off silent, so I actually got to speak to Tristan for a while, but it felt strained on my part.

I don't want to tell him someone tried to get in, he'll worry and drop everything, and that doesn't help, he'd only have to go back again next week. And I can't tell him about Susannah because I know that Joyce is right, it will come across as though I'm being difficult, and I still didn't ask him about the member of staff that died. I couldn't pluck up the courage, for some reason, I get the feeling it won't be something he'll want to talk about.

And I'm panicking about hurting him, I know myself, I can feel it creeping up on me like I'll just end it because it get's to be too much. I've already done that once, and the last person in the world I want to hurt is Tristan. He means so much to me. I just feel like everything is fucked up at the moment like it's all gone wrong since he left.

With a heavy heart, I reluctantly get ready for bed. Curling up under the duvet, I try to clear my mind of all things, including Tristan…

I'M DREAMING I'M walking down a long corridor with white walls and doors that swing open. The fluorescent lights above me are bright, I think I've been here before, I think it's a hospital. I'm aware that someone is holding my hand. I turn to see who it is and realise I have to look up – I'm a child again. I'm with a lady in a long white jacket, I don't recognise her face, but she turns and smiles warmly at me.

"Ok Coral. Your mommy is just through this door." She pushes the door open, and I walk with her. Mommy is sat at a table in orange pyjamas, she looks poorly.

"Is mommy sick again?" I ask her. She kneels down and puts her hands on my arms. I wish she wouldn't do that, I don't like strangers touching me.

"Yes, sweetheart. Mommy isn't very well. Would you like to say hello?" I shake my head at her. "No?" she questions.

Mommy looks up and see's me, her eyes are all red and puffy. She stands up and opens her arms wide.

"Coral," she croaks then she starts to cry.

I look back at the lady.

"It's ok, you can say hello." She tells me.

I shake my head again. I don't like this place, it smells funny. I don't like the people they look at me funny too. I put my thumb in my mouth and suck, it makes me feel better.

The lady turns around, so I hide behind her legs and peek at Mommy. Her face has gone really red, and she's showing her teeth. She is angry, just like before. I hide even more.

"Annie calm down!" The lady is talking to Mommy, her hands are held out. Mommy is shaking her head and puffing her cheeks in and out, then she sits down in her chair and looks down at the table, rocking back and forth.

"Come on Coral, come and say hello." The lady takes my hand and goes to walk towards Mommy.

"No!" I cry out and pull my hand out of hers. I am scared.

The lady picks me up into her arms. *No! Let me go!*

"I won't let her hurt you," she says; she doesn't seem bad, not like Mommy.

"Ok." I cling to her and hide my face on her shoulder. The lady sits down in the chair, I am on her lap – I don't like it. I peek at Mommy from behind my hand. Mommy is mad, her eyes are black and strange. She pulls her hand back and jumps forward to smack me, just like she used to.

"You little bitch! It's all your fault' – I cover my ears. I don't want to hear it.

The lady carries me away. I look over her shoulder, two men are holding Mommy down, she is screaming at them…

I SCRAMBLE UP from my sleeping position feeling totally disorientated. *Fuck!* – My heart is hammering, my throat dry, I sound like I've been running uphill. *Why the hell did I just dream that?* - I squeeze my eyes shut trying to blank it out. I don't understand why I dreamt that, why it's come back and what's triggered it? It's an old memory, a very old memory. I shiver internally. I hated that place, I can still smell the disinfectant, hear the cries of other patients. I shake my head in wonder and question it again – *Why did I just dream that memory?* I lie back down and try to figure out the answer, I wonder for a moment if there's something wrong with her. Maybe she's got sick in that Psychiatric Hospital?

I shake my head at myself – *Who cares!*

Turning on my side, I try to go back to sleep, but all I can see is a pair of black, hate-filled eyes staring back at me...

I WAKE THE following morning with a banging headache, I know it's because I've hardly slept. After the dream about my mother, all I kept getting every time I fell back to sleep were more nightmares. Each one becoming more strange and unpredictable, mostly Susannah and my Mother, several times they morphed into the same person, black eyes, lips pulled back, teeth exposed, looking totally deranged and psychotic.

As I lie in bed trying to understand it all, I decide to ditch my morning swim. I really don't feel too good at all, my stomach twists with anxiety confirming my thinking – *Great!*

In fact, I'm starting to feel really freaked out about it all. I still can't work out why that memory of my Mother came back. And I definitely can't get my head around the fact that she kept turning into Susannah, or the other way around – Pulling my quilt off me, I stagger to my robe, wrap it around me and try to forget about last night. As I wander down the stairs in a zombie-like state, I check both doors. All is well.

Heading to the fridge, I pour myself a veggie juice. As I lean against the kitchen sink, slowly drinking it down, I have a sudden thought – *What if my subconscious is trying to tell me something? Am I getting another premonition?*

I frown deeply, trying to work it out. I think that question through, but nothing comes to the surface. I wonder for a moment if I should go and talk to Gladys, she has always understood my weird psychic ways. It used to be stronger when I was in my teens, but it rarely happens now. I used to freak Gladys out when I would hear the phone ring and tell her who it was before she picked it up, and she was really freaked out when she was due to travel with her bowling club.

I woke up that morning, and this voice kept telling me she shouldn't go. I begged her not to, and she finally agreed. That night, the coach lost control on the ice and crashed. One woman died, several others were injured, and from that moment on Gladys told me she would always listen to me if I ever asked her to do something like that again.

I contemplate going over to see Gladys before work, then I decide that I'm being silly. I'm going to see her tonight anyway. Finishing my drink and washing up my glass, I shuffle into the bathroom, telling myself to forget all about the nightmares and concentrate on today – I think I need a very long shower to help wake me up...

HEADING INTO WORK, I push through the glass doors, look up and see Joe is at her desk.

"Hey, Joe. You ok?" I ask.

She smiles warmly at me. "Yeah, I'm good thanks."

"Good." I try to smile back at her.

"Oh Coral! She's already in," she whispers to me. *Ugh! Susannah!*

I smile and roll my eyes in annoyance, making Joe giggle and walk up the stairs, but I'm actually feeling really nervous, and I can't work out why. Walking across the hallway towards my desk, I see it's surrounded by all the other secretaries, and they're all laughing. I can guess who they are laughing about, and who's initiating it all.

Squaring my shoulders, I march straight over to them all.

"Morning ladies," I say loud and clear.

They all turn in one and stare at me. I sigh inwardly – It's just like being back at school. I spy Susannah sitting in my chair, flicking her long blonde hair. Some of the secretaries leave, a couple of them start tittering between themselves, and the other's go back to whispering with Susannah.

I decide to leave them all to it and march off to the ladies. It's the only way I'm going to keep my cool. If I have to wait for her to get out of my god damn chair, I swear I'll yank her out of it by her perfect hair. It's long enough to get a good hold of – *Stop it Coral!*

As I stand washing my hands, I can't help thinking back to the dream and my Mother. My stomach rolls just thinking about it, I fight back the bile that has risen – *Oh God, not today, please not today!*

As I work on calming myself down, the sickening feeling slowly subsides, thank god! Then, stalling for more time, because

I don't want to go back to my desk until they have all gone, I check my make-up and my bun. *Jeez, I look really tired!*

Taking a deep breath, I reluctantly make my way back to my desk. With my coffee in my hand, and my chair vacated, I sit down at my desk and open my inbox, nothing! – *Great!*

I smile hesitantly at Susannah, as I watch her walk along the hallway back towards me. I guess she went down to the communal area, where all the other secretaries are. I wonder what she's up to? She grimaces at me as she takes the seat next to me, and opens her laptop. I frown at my computer screen. *What is she's doing?*

"So," she says turning to smile at me. "What's his name?"

"Who?" I ask, reluctantly turning to face her.

"Your boyfriend," she nips. "Who else?" She adds sarcastically. *Fuck!* Quick Coral any name, top of your head.

"Justin!" I blurt. *Why did I just use my ex's name?*

Susannah nods then crosses her arms. "So what do you think of Tristan?" She asks. That's the second time she's used his first name – *I hate her using it!*

"I can't really say," I answer, she cocks her head to the side. "I don't really know him," I add, feeling all the blood drain from my face.

"Oh, I didn't mean as a boss. I meant as a man. He's sexy don't you think?" she questions.

I turn in my seat and frown at her. "I hadn't really noticed," I say being careful to keep my voice steady. I turn back around and keep my eyes fixed on the computer screen.

"Funny, I thought I saw him wink at you on Monday." I feel my eyes widen with fear – *Fuck! What do I say?*

"Did he, I hadn't noticed," I calmly reply. *Eyes straight ahead Stevens!*

"Is it right you live at the Marina?" she asks. *How does she know that?*

"How do you' – "Janice told me," she interrupts. *Who the fuck is Janice?*

"Y-yes," I stutter, wondering if I've done the right thing.

"Coral, I don't want to get you into trouble, but' – "Trouble about what?" I snap, my head whipping round to her.

"Well, I know about the Google page you see. I don't think Tristan will be very impressed if he finds out, and what with your behaviour this week and your inability to take in any new information throughout your training, I'm pretty sure he'll have no choice but to let you go," she says vindictively.

I feel a shiver run down my spine. *Shit! She did delete it!* – And what the hell is she talking about? Ok, yeah I've struggled a little this week taking new information in, but that's because I can't concentrate. And what behaviour?

Susannah continues. "Besides, do you really think he would be interested in someone like you?" She adds icily. *What! How dare she say that!*

I glare back at her. She's got that weird look in her eyes again. I decide at that very moment, I'm better off keeping my mouth shut and reporting all this back to Joyce, even though I want to punch her in the face for saying that.

I turn back to my screen. "I think we should get on with the training, don't you?" I say glancing across at her, she's smiling an evil, wicked smile at me.

"Yes let's," she says sweetly. I can't help shaking my head, as a sarcastic snigger falls out of my mouth – *She's unbelievable!*

"Something funny?" she asks sweetly again. I turn and give her my arctic, ice cold, no-nonsense glare – *I know your game lady!*

"No, nothing at all," I snap and grit my teeth as I glare at my screen. I swear to god, if she lays one finger on me, I will break her nose…

I AM HAVING A terrible morning, and Susannah knows it. All of the work I have done over the past two days seems to have filtered out of my brain like it was never there. I can't remember how to do anything that she showed me, and if I'm correct, it was all pretty simple. Of course, I know it's because I can't concentrate, there's just too much going on right now. And I have a sinking feeling she's going to go back to Tristan and tell him I'm crap, and that he needs to get someone else – *Well Bollocks!* –If that's what he wants to do then so be it, there's not much I can really do about it.

"Coral, will you please concentrate. I don't want to have to show you this again," she spits at me. I turn in my seat and glare at her. *Keep your cool Coral!*

"You know… if I remember correctly. *You* are here to train me, and in doing so, you will show me what I need to learn, even if it means showing me over, and over again until I get it right. That's what training is, right?" I smile sarcastically at her.

She flicks a piece of fluff off her skirt as though she hasn't heard a word I have said.

My anger turns to full-scale rage. I can feel the adrenalin pumping through my veins, I'm ready to smack the shit out of her. I haven't felt this angry, this explosive, since I was at school. I'm not sure how much more I can take, I feel like screaming at the top of my lungs.

I look up at the clock, it's 12.15 – I'm lunching early, if I stay I swear I'm going to split her nose open, I pick up my bag, and stand.

"Where are you going?" She snaps.

I completely ignore her and walk over to Joyce's door. I knock the door and see if she wants anything, she's on the phone but shakes her head at me. I nod, shut her door, and head back past my desk.

"Coral, I asked you a question. Where are you going?" Susannah snaps.

"To lunch," I growl carrying on down the hallway, glad to be getting away from her.

I feel her yank my arm, I snap it out of her grasp.

"Don't touch me!" I threaten my hands bunching into fists. She crosses her arms and stares down at me – I hate that she's taller than me!

"Nice little place you've got," she tells me.

I frown at her in confusion. "What?" I snap.

"That little studio," she says. My eyes widen, and my heart triples its beats. *Stay cool, keep focused!*

"How do you' – "I've seen it," she whispers leaning closer to my face, her eyes darkening. *Holy crap, she knows where I live?* My suspicions to who was outside my place Monday night come rushing to the surface – *It was Susannah, I know it was!*

"Stay away from him," she hisses. *What the fuck is this about?*

"Who?" I snap, trying to feign innocence because I'm sure she means Tristan.

"Tristan!" she hisses, glaring quizzically at me, almost as though I should know this, then Susannah starts to laugh, leaning her head back as she does. It's a strange, crazy kind of laugh. My instincts kick in again, warning me she's dangerous.

I carefully take two steps back. "You and Tristan are together?" I question.

Her face falls, and that crazy look appears in her eyes. "Yes, but we're keeping it a secret, at least until the take-over happens. You see Coral, we're engaged, we just couldn't help ourselves, he actually has taste, he knows what's good for him' –"Let me guess," I snap. "You're what's good for him?" I say gritting my teeth.

She nods her head several times, her lips curling up into a strange smile.

"So much for your husband," I hiss.

"He's mine." She states firmly, flatly, almost threateningly. Then she starts twisting her hair around her finger in a childlike manner as she stares down at the floor. "He loves me' –her eyes dart up to meet mine– 'I know he does." She starts twisting her body to and fro, rocking herself.

This woman is crazy!

"Right," I say as sarcastically as I can. *Coral, be careful!*

I realise I am right to warn myself, this is not normal behaviour, even for a crush, this is strange, totally losing it behaviour. In a flash, she moves towards me, and now she's closer, I can see how her eyes have changed. Her pupils are so dilated it's making her eyes look like black coal – The dream, that's what it was all about, my subconscious trying to warn me! Her eyes look exactly like my Mother's used to, and at that moment I know, I can feel it. She really *is* dangerous! *Shit!*

"I wouldn't mention this to anyone," she hisses. "After all, who will they believe? Me, or a freak like you that needs constant therapy," she adds. *Fuck! She knows I'm in therapy?*

Moving closer to me, she tries to run her forefinger down my cheek, but I slap it away and take a step to the side.

"Don't touch me!" I hiss.

"You just broke my nail," she growls menacingly, her lip twisting up over her top teeth. She looks just like the crazy Susannah from my dream –*Ok that's it!*

Stepping forward, so I'm right in her face, I take a deep breath and try to keep my voice steady. "You better get something straight lady. You don't scare me, and you'd better not even think about threatening me again, or you'll wish you hadn't you crazy fucker." Susannah takes a step back in surprise. "That's more like it. Oh and I see you anywhere near Joe, I'll rip your fucking head off, got it?" She starts smiling at me – *Fucking Crazy Bitch!*

I shake my head at her and stomp out of the building with the force of a tornado. I'm so fucking angry right now; apoplectic with rage is more like the right phrase to use. The adrenalin is still kicking through my system, making me shake from head to toe. I can't believe she knows where I live, and how the hell does she know I'm seeing George? The only one that knows about that at work is Joyce, so how did she find out?

I really need to tell Tristan about her behaviour, but I don't think he'll believe me. She's worked with him for too long, and she's got him thinking the sun shines out of her backside. Once I clear the corner, I lean against the wall and take a few minutes to try and calm myself down…

CHAPTER SIXTEEN

FEELING A LITTLE better, I carry on walking. I have no idea where I'm going. All I keep thinking about is the fact that Susannah knows things about me that she shouldn't, and I don't like it, I don't like it at all – And that's when I get a light bulb moment, two can play that game! I remember those guys from Starbucks talking *'Got a P.I on it, she's the one that found it all out for him'* and at that moment I know that is what I have to do. I wonder if that's what Susannah's done to find out about me?

Grabbing my mobile, I get straight onto the web and search P.I's in Brighton. Choosing the first one that comes up, I put my bag down and plunge my hand inside to find my little notepad so I can write the number down, I locate a pen, but no pad. My tiny little notepad has disappeared. I search again. *Nothing!*

I see a bench nearby so I walk over to it, sit down and take everything out of my bag. Nope, it's definitely gone….and so have my keys! *Holy crap! This isn't happening!*

I feel all the blood drain out of my face. I swallow hard and try to think back to this morning. I definitely put them in my bag after I locked up. So where are they now? I feel the tears bubble up to the surface, but I push back at them. I have to think logically about this. Ok, so as far as my notepad goes, maybe I dropped it at Tristan's or something? But as for my keys?…I feel a strange tingling sensation start at the top of my head and wonder all the way down the length of my spine – *Susannah has them!* – I shake my head at that thought. No, no way, I would have seen her take them out of my…*Oh shit! I had a bathroom break while she was still at my desk.*

No. I close my eyes and push the thought away, I can't even bear to think about it. *I'm sure I'll find them*, I tell myself trying to ease the panic, but I know deep down inside, my suspicions may be right. Shaking my head, I shove everything back into my bag and get back to the task at hand.

Re-awakening my mobile, I commit the number to memory then check out the address, it's not far at all. Calling them up, I check to see if I can come straight over, I'm told I can, but I'll have a half an hour wait. I put the call on hold and make a call to Joyce; she agrees to give me the extra time. I thank her and hang up, then going back to the call, I tell them I'll be there in twenty minutes.

As I'm stomping through town, and trying not to freak out about Susannah, and my keys, I get a call on my mobile – Tristan! – *Oh, no, no, no! Really bad timing!*

I actually feel reluctant to answer it. I'm worried, and I don't want my voice to give me away. I know I need to tell him what's going on, but I'd rather do that face to face, so I take a deep breath and press answer.

"Tristan," I pant, as I'm walking so quickly.

"Coral is everything ok?" he asks.

"Um...yeah. Why?" I ask.

"Susannah just called me' – my heart sinks and a lump forms in my throat – 'she's gone back to the hotel." I clear my throat.

"Really, why?" I ask trying to sound nonchalant.

"A migraine, she gets them now and again'– I feel myself instantly relax –'but she did say that your training isn't going too well?" he adds – *Cheeky Bitch!*

"Well maybe if she had a little more patience'– I stop myself from going on a rant –'I'm tired Tristan, I haven't been sleeping well," I say hoping he'll believe me.

"Me neither," he says. "Can't stop thinking about my beautiful wife to be." I smile for what feels like the first time in a long while. "I miss you," he says all huskily.

"Me too," I croak, feeling melancholy again.

"Don't cry baby," he soothes.

"I'm sorry," I choke again, pushing back the lump stuck in my throat. "I'm just...I want you here with me," I whisper.

"I know. I wish I were there too baby," Tristan softly says.

I stop walking and close my eyes. "Where are you?" I ask.

"Leeds, hold on baby' – I hear him talking to someone in the background – 'I've got to go, I'll call you tonight," he tells me.

"Actually I'll be at Gladys's, I don't know how late it'll be," I say.

"Call me anyway," he says. "I want to know you got home safely," he adds.

"I will," I answer softly.

"Bye gorgeous," he croons.

"Bye baby," I croak. I hear the line go dead.

Taking a deep breath, I carry on walking, determined to complete my mission...

AS SOON AS I'm back at work, I run through reception, up the stairs, and along the hallway. The only thing I have on my mind is searching for my keys, as I reach my desk, I'm about to wrench open the top draw when I spy a post-it note, and underneath the note are my keys. FOUND THESE ON THE FLOOR. SUSANNAH. *Yeah right!* I rip the note of them and place the keys inside my bag. Just at that moment, Joyce comes out of her office.

"Susannah's gone home," she tells me.

"I know," I answer. Joyce cocks her head to the side. "Tristan called me," I add.

Joyce smiles warmly at me. I try to smile back and sit at my desk, expecting Joyce to go back into her office, but she's hovering, I look up at her and see she seems miles away.

"Joyce. Are you ok?" I ask.

Joyce nods once. "Susannah was acting really oddly again today. She came in a couple of minutes after you left, and said she was going on lunch, twenty minutes later, she was back telling me she was leaving for the day? She looked all worked up, she really is an oddball," she says with her hands on her hips, staring down the hallway. "Well, she's gone, for now, I suppose," Joyce adds.

I nod silently as I half listen to Joyce. I'm too busy thinking about my keys and trying to work out how they magically jumped out of my bag onto the floor.

"Are you alright Coral?" Joyce asks, pulling me from my musing.

"Of course," I answer. "Can I get you anything?" I quickly add as Joyce is gazing quizzically at me.

"Yes. Tea please Coral." I nod in reply and watch Joyce walk back into her office.

As I'm in the kitchen preparing her tea, I wonder if my keys really did fall out of my bag. Maybe I didn't do the zip up properly or something. Sleep deprivation can do that to a person. I shake my head at myself, no good trying to work out what happened, the point is, I have them back safely. The rest of the afternoon goes by swimmingly without Susannah here. I decide not to tell Joyce about Susannah threatening me, I think she will freak out about it, and I don't want her to. If Joyce is right, and Susannah is playing some sort of game, the last thing I'm going to do is let her get one over on me.

I stay past finishing time, all this training has meant I've gotten behind with my usual work, and I like feeling as though I'm on top of things – *Control freak!*

FINALLY FINISHING UP for the day, I decide to get a taxi and head straight over to Gladys as it's already 6.30pm, there's no point going home. I must remember to have it out with Gladys tonight. I want to know what's being hidden from me. I will find out tonight, by hook or by crook, she will tell me.

Walking up St James's street, I locate a taxi and head over to Gladys's. As I reach the front door, I knock three times – I don't want to catch Gladys and Malcolm at it again!

The door flies open, Gladys beams brightly at me and throws her arms open wide.

"Darling!" She gushes, pulling me into her for a bear hug.

"Hi," I squeak.

"Come on in. Why didn't you use your key?" she asks.

I cock one eyebrow up at her and grin.

"Oh, well, yes. That was a little embarrassing I suppose." *She supposed right!*

We walk through the hallway with our arms linked and head into the kitchen.

Malcolm stands and walks over to me. "Hello Coral." He

leans down and kisses my cheek. He smells good, which makes me think of Tristan, my stomach twists in response, I miss him so much.

"Hi Malcolm, how are you?" I ask.

"Very well thank you, your nose has cleared up nicely," he says, smiling broadly.

"Yeah, I know," I say feeling tired and weary.

Last night's nightmares and today's shenanigans have exhausted me, plus I haven't really been able to relax since Monday night. I keep picturing someone breaking in and walking up my stairs, and I'm trapped and – "Sit down darling, drink?" Gladys asks, pulling me from my musing.

"Yes please," I say, taking a seat at the kitchen table.

"Coral you look pale. Aren't you sleeping?" Gladys asks, looking concerned. I shake my head, too tired to answer. "Well you should go to the doctors," she tells me.

"It's nothing," I say, waving my hand.

Gladys sighs at me. "Alright Coral, have it your own way."

I roll my eyes at Malcolm who smiles in return.

"Coral, what would you like? Wine? Juice' –"Wine please," I interrupt. I think I need the alcohol.

Malcolm hands a large glass to me, and I take a couple of gulps, I want to feel it swishing around my system, relaxing me. Looking up, I can see Gladys looks apprehensive and a little sloshed, her cheeks are very pink, then I look at Malcolm, he smiles tentatively at me; they both look nervous.

"How's work?" Malcolm asks.

"Great," I answer sarcastically. Malcolm nods and purses his lips together. They both sit in unison at the table, Gladys with her wine, Malcolm with his G&T.

"Now, we have something very important to tell you," Gladys says, then takes a gulp of wine, Malcolm takes her hand and squeezes it. Seeing him do that is reminding me of Tristan, of the way I feel when he takes my hand in his.

I really miss him, the dull ache in my stomach blooms to a full-blown empty crater; I glug more wine to try and make it disappear.

Gladys takes a deep breath in, slowly blows it out then turns to me. "So I suppose you're wondering why we asked you here?" she says.

I nod as it's all I can manage. Gladys takes my free hand in hers and pats it gently, then fighting back the tears, she pulls her hanky out and dabs her cheeks.

"The house has sold," she manages to choke out. *What!*

"Sold?" I repeat breathlessly, blinking rapidly at her.

I shouldn't feel shocked, I knew this was coming. I feel like all the blood is slowly draining from my body. My head feels foggy, and my ears are ringing…*Sold!*

"Oh, darling!" Gladys pulls her chair closer to me and hugs me awkwardly around the shoulders.

"It's ok," I assure her patting her hand, my mind completely blank.

She kisses me hard on the cheek several times. "We have to be out in two weeks, so we're renting for a while until we find what we're looking for," she squeaks, hugging me tighter.

I nod, throw in a fake smile for good measure, pull out of her hold and take another drink.

"Malcolm," she says holding her hand out to him. He passes her a small white envelope, smiling broadly as he does. "This is for you darling," Gladys softly says and hands me the envelope.

I have no idea what it is. Which is why I don't understand why my heart has started banging rapidly against my chest, I swallow hard and put my wine down. "What is it?" I ask.

"Open it up Coral, we'll explain everything," Malcolm suggests kindly.

I frown slightly and rip open the seal. There's a thin piece of paper inside, it's a little bigger than a cheque, when I pull it out I see it says Bankers Draft. On the first line is my name, then I read the second line. Two Hundred & Fifty Thousand Pounds – I blink twice, then re-read it. *Nope, that's definitely what it says!*

I look up at Gladys, then Malcolm, my mouth pops open to say something, but no words come out.

"It's for you," Malcolm explains. *I already gathered that part.*

"Why?" I gasp.

"Why not?" Malcolm retorts.

I shake my head, unable to comprehend what's going on.

"This is my gift to you darling," Gladys explains. *Huh?*

"I don't understand?" I whisper staring at the slip of paper in my shaking hands. Malcolm and Gladys exchange a look, I'm immediately suspicious. "Why are you giving me this?" I ask.

"Well, as you know we'll be moving away, and I wanted to make sure you are taken care of darling. You're all on your own, you don't have a husband to support you like Debbie, and I just can't stand the thought of you struggling…" Gladys sniffs and dabs her eyes again. *Husband? That may come sooner rather than later!*

I debate for a split second on whether I should tell her then change my mind. "But I'm not struggling," I answer, pushing the thought of marrying Tristan aside.

"Well yes, I know but' –"I think what your mother is trying to say, is that this is spare cash for her. I'm in a position that allows me to support us both, so she has split the money from the sale of the house between you and Debbie." Malcolm takes a drink. *Whoa!*

"Oh!" I swallow hard and look up at Gladys. "T-thank you. I...I don't know what to say?" I stutter. "That's...that's really generous," I add as it slowly starts to sink in. *I'm rich – not Tristan rich – but I'm rich!* I can pay off my mortgage I can...well do so many things...

"We have more news," Gladys says taking a large gulp of wine.

I knew it was too good to be true.

Placing the envelope and the Bankers Draft on the table, I pick up my wine and take another gulp. I've nearly finished the glass, and I'm starting to feel tipsy; I've only eaten a Chocolate swirl today.

"News?" I question, looking across the table to Malcolm.

"Well, it's not really our news. It's Debbie's," Gladys says.

I snap my head to the side and glare at her. "If it's Debbie's news why couldn't *she* tell me?" I snap.

"Because it also concerns Malcolm and me," she scolds.

I instantly feel guilty for snapping, considering what I've just been given. "Sorry Gladys, I didn't mean to…" I drift off.

"It's alright," she says, patting my hand again. She takes another deep breath, looks at Malcolm for reassurance then her eyes meet mine. "Well you know Scott got a promotion?" she says.

"Yeah?" *I don't like where this is going.*

"Well...well, the job is in Spain. Barcelona to be exact," she says taking another gulp of wine. *Spain? They're moving to Spain?*

"So they're moving to Spain," I say numbly.

"Y-yes," Gladys stutters watching me carefully.

I nod my head. I feel a little pissed that Debs didn't tell me but other than that – "And we're going with them," she chokes out and bursts into hysterical tears.

My mouth pops open, my mind feels numb – *They're all moving to Spain!*

Malcolm jumps up from his seat and wraps his arms around Gladys.

"When?" I ask Malcolm, my voice flat.

"Not until January. We'll all be together for Christmas and New Year." I nod as I listen to his answer, and then totally unexpectedly, I start to laugh. I don't know if it's because I'm way past tired if it's the alcohol or the fact that Gladys is sobbing like a baby, but the whole situation seems hilarious to me. They turn in unison and gape at me. Gladys stops blubbering, her eyes red and tear-stained, Malcolm's eyes widen with surprise.

"But...but..." Gladys wipes her eyes and blows her nose. "Aren't you angry?" She asks incredulously.

"Why should I be angry?" I ask my sense of humour dissipating.

"Well' – "Gladys," I interrupt. "I've already accepted you are leaving, you told me you were, besides Spain sounds wonderful, much better than this country. I can really see you there, lounging by the pool in your costume and sunhat."

Her mouth pops open in shock. I instantly picture her asking Malcolm to go get her another cocktail as she soaks up the sun.

"What?" I chuckle.

"You're taking this all very well," Gladys admits.

I roll my eyes at her. "Look, if you told me you were all moving to Australia or Africa, or somewhere on the other side of the world then no, I wouldn't be very happy at all. But Spain is only a couple of hours on a plane, isn't it? That's no hardship." I take another drink. "Besides, it means I get a free holiday each year," I chuckle. *Yeah, that'll be cool!*

I've never been abroad, hell I've never even had a real holiday, but I don't feel worried about that anymore, not now I have Tristan to go with. I look up and see they are both still gawking at me, which is really starting to annoy me.

"Gladys you deserve this. You dedicated a large part of your life to us. Raising Debs and me can't have been easy, especially on your own, and I know I was a very difficult child, but like I said before, it's your life, and you should do what you want with it. I think it sounds fabulous, wait till I tell Rob and Carlos!" I beam.

I actually feel quite excited about it all, although I don't quite understand why. Gladys is right, I should be freaking out about this.

"Oh, darling!" Gladys screeches. Standing up, she pulls me to my feet and into her large bosom, hugging and kissing me as she wails with delighted tears. I chuckle and hug her back, wrapping my arms tightly around her. She really does deserve this, she's been an awesome parent to me, but I'm all grown up now, I know I can let her go.

Then I think back to last week and the confusion she has put me through by not telling me in the first place, which instantly pisses me off. Pulling out of her arms, I take a step back and put my hands on my hips. "So this is the big secret you've all been keeping from me?" I snap.

Malcolm shakes his head slightly, and Gladys has the decency to look guiltily at me.

"Now that I'm pissed about," I growl. "I knew you were all keeping something from me! How do you think that made me feel?" I add, gritting my teeth.

Gladys' mouth pops open to a perfect o, and she turns to Malcolm, for back-up I think, but he just purses his lips at her then mouths, 'I told you so' she looks back at me, with wide eyes.

"I'll tell you shall I. Excluded from the family, that's how it made me feel! You made me feel shut out Gladys, it felt really awful, you kept the fact that you were dating Malcolm from me, and now this?" I pick up my wine and gulp what's left back in one go.

Malcolm hasn't stopped shaking his head. "I told you to tell her!" he barks. I feel like he knows me better than Gladys and Debs.

Gladys falls into her seat, I follow suit because I don't want to lose it, and to be quite honest; I'm tired of feeling pissed off all the time. And I have to remember, I have just been gifted two hundred and fifty grand.

"Look, Mom," I softly say, and reach for her hand. "You've got to stop keeping things from me. I'd rather deal with it than feel like I'm the one being left out, it really hurts, sucks actually. I could understand your apprehension of telling me if it was somewhere on the other side of the world, but Spain? Come on..." I say, shaking my head in annoyance.

"I'm so sorry darling, I..." she sniffs loudly, then looks at me with big round, guilty eyes. "Can you forgive me?" Gladys croaks.

I roll my eyes and sigh. "Yes, of course, I can, just don't do it again!" I lean forward and hug her. "Malcolm!" I bark. "From now on, I am making it your responsibility to keep me informed, about everything." I look up at him and smile.

"Absolutely," Malcolm agrees, nodding his head approvingly.

"Good, let's eat. I'm starving." *I'll be pissed as a fart if I don't eat something!*

"Yes, lets. You look like you've lost weight Coral," Gladys says, really scrutinising me now.

"I haven't had much of an appetite lately," I answer wistfully, thinking about Tristan again.

Gladys takes my hand and gives me a knowing smile, I try not to smile back at her, but my face has other ideas, and I grin from ear to ear.

Gladys leans forward and whispers in my ear. "I'm so happy for you darling," then she kisses my cheek, picks up the wine and refills our glasses.

"Thanks," I whisper, praying she doesn't ask me anything about it.

I wait patiently for Gladys to walk over to the stove and get dinner ready because my belly is rumbling at me, but when she doesn't, I decide to push.

"Gladys, aren't you getting dinner ready?"

Gladys beams at me and then looks up at Malcolm. As my eyes follow hers, I'm shocked to see Malcolm tying an apron around his waist. It has a logo on it. **Danger! Man Cooking. Proceed With Caution** – I giggle out loud as I read it.

"I didn't know you could cook Malcolm?" I say, he opens his mouth to respond but Gladys cuts in.

"Oh, he's a wonderful cook, he's got me eating all sorts darling, you'll be very proud of me. I've had curries and spices and well, all sorts, right Malcolm," she looks up at him adoringly.

"Indeed my darling." Malcolm slowly bends down to Gladys and kisses her lightly on the lips. I look away feeling a little uncomfortable. *Tristan….I miss you so…*

"Shall we sit outside?" Gladys asks as Malcolm stands and turns to the stove.

I nod, pick up my wine and follow Gladys out to the patio.

"So," Gladys says sitting next to me and squeezing my free hand. "Tell me all about Tristan."

I choke on the sip of wine I have taken. "Um…we're just friends," I answer staring down at the table. I really don't want to get into that one. I already feel lost without him, talking about him and how wonderful he is; it's just going to make me feel worse.

"Nonsense, come on!" I look up at Gladys. I can see her eyes are full of excited anticipation.

"Really, there's nothing to tell." I take another gulp of wine.

Gladys frowns and looks down at the table. "Alright darling, you don't want to talk about it. I understand," she says, looking a little forlorn, which makes me feel guilty because I haven't shared. But I can't, not now. I have too many things swimming around my head, and I just want to forget it all. At least I know the big secret now, at least that's something I can cross off my list.

"Have you fallen out?" she asks softly.

"No," I say shaking my head. "It's not like that," I add. "I can't talk about him, I miss him terribly, and I've still got two more days to go until' –"It's alright darling," she says interrupting. "I understand." Reaching out she gently strokes my cheek. "But there's something else, something you're worried about?" *Crap, how can she tell?*

I shake my head at her. "There's just a lot going on at work, Rob's having problems, and now you, Debs and Joyce are leaving…" I trail off and take a breath. "It's just a lot to handle in one go." I shrug and drink more wine.

She narrows her eyes at me. "Yes, it is a lot to deal with," she pauses for a moment. "But if something were really wrong, you would come and tell me wouldn't you Coral," she says in her firm, not to be messed with voice, that always scared me as a child.

I swallow hard. "Yes, I would," I whisper, trying to put on my poker face, my mask.

Gladys stares back at me for the longest time. "Alright," she says firmly. *Phew!*

"Gladys, are you sure about the money?" I ask, trying to sway the conversation.

"Of course darling," she replies.

"It's such a large amount though, don't you' – "Hush," she scolds, instantly silencing me. "It's what I want to do for you, I won't have it back Coral," she adds, reading my expression.

"Ok," I whisper, wondering what the hell I'm going to do with that amount of money. "Thank you," I add, "I really mean it."

"I know you do darling," she replies in a softer tone.

I smile at her and drink more wine, trying to think of something to say. *The Wedding!*

"So you have the Wedding soon, have you found a dress yet?" I ask…

WE SPEND THE rest of the evening chatting about the move and the different places that they're looking to buy. Gladys tells me about Lily joining her new school, and that she's very excited about learning a new language, and that the place Scott and Debs are looking to buy is right near the beach – *That's another free holiday!*

For the first time since Tristan left, I feel relaxed. I've even managed to eat a big plate of Paella; turns out Malcolm *can* really cook, but I have to wonder whether it's being in the comfortable surroundings of my childhood home that's making me feel this way.

As I sit in the kitchen listening to Malcolm and Gladys banter with one another, I suddenly realise I will really miss this place, it's filled with so many warm and happy memories. I feel blessed to have been raised here, blessed to have had such a wonderful person like Gladys with the patience of a saint to raise me. To teach me wrong from right and shower me with love and affection. I've also learned that life has to move on, move forward that change has to happen. Otherwise, life becomes stale and stagnated.

As the evening draws to a close, I feel myself start to become tense about going home, I feel angry that I do, that someone has made me feel like that – that Susannah has made me feel like that – *You don't know it was her*, I castigate myself.

I reluctantly call a taxi, and as I'm waiting for it to arrive, I have to keep convincing Gladys and Malcolm that I'm fine – I think they can see I'm on edge.

"Why don't you stay darling?" Gladys asks for the fifth time.

"I'll get you home early tomorrow," Malcolm adds.

I plaster a fake smile on my face. "I'm fine, really I am," I say, wondering who I'm trying to convince.

When the taxi arrives, Malcolm walks out the house and waits by the taxi.

"Bye Gladys, thank you again," I say as I hug her tight.

"You are more than welcome my sweetheart." Gladys kisses my cheek several times.

I reluctantly walk down the pathway to the waiting taxi, and Malcolm opens the door for me.

"Thank you, Malcolm." I lean up and kiss his cheek then slide inside.

I watch him lean inside the open window and pay the driver. "Make sure she gets back safely," he says in a firm tone. *Oh!* Tears pool in my eyes. How sweet, I love that Malcolm is so protective of me.

"No problem." The driver answers.

Then I'm hit with a wave of melancholy – I wish he had met Gladys earlier, and he had been my Dad. I swallow hard, I can't think like that right now. The taxi pulls away, and I wave heartily to them both, and for the first time tonight, I'm hit with the enormity of what they have told me.

They are leaving…and I'll never get to have this when they are gone.

I push back the tears that threaten, the last thing I want to do is start blubbering in front of a complete stranger…

AS WE REACH the Marina, I thank the driver, step out of the car and head down the concourse. I don't know why – maybe it's because it's dark – but I feel nervous, apprehensive, I can't stop looking over my shoulder. I have the strangest feeling that I'm being watched. Reaching my studio, I unlock the door, step inside and lock it behind me. It's dark inside, and I can hear the faint noise of a television. *I guess next door is up late!*

Flicking the main light switch on, I stare at the room, it feels so empty without Tristan here. Shaking my head at myself, I walk over to the sofa and place my bag down with my keys securely inside it. Taking off my wedges, I head over to the kitchenette. As I lean down to open the fridge, I notice something odd, something that shouldn't be there.

Standing back up I eye the empty bottle of beer, cocking my head to the side, I stare down at it, trying to work out if I had one yesterday, and I've forgotten about it. Reaching my hand out, I curl my fingers around the bottle – *Fuck! It's cold!*

I whip my head around and quickly analyse my studio. There's no sign of a break in, no windows smashed, and nothing seems out of place, so why is there a bottle of beer on the side? - Then it hits me – *Bob!*

I sag with relief. Yes, it's bound to be him. He has a spare key, and I've always told him to help himself if he ever wants anything, he's too old and doddery to go walking all the way up to the shops for just one bottle of beer, and he has helped himself to one before.

Laughing nervously at myself, I open the bin and throw the empty bottle inside. Then I go back to the fridge, pull out a bottle of wine and pour myself a glass. I know I shouldn't, but all the alcohol seems to have left my system on the drive home – I feel stone sober.

I take a sip of wine and look up at the clock – 11.45pm.

I should call Tristan and tell him my news, but I don't want to, not yet. I need to get changed, relax with a glass of wine, and then get cosy in bed so I know I'll sleep dreamlessly. I take a gulp of wine, put down my glass and head up the stairs. Halfway up, I glance into my bedroom and freeze – *Fuck!*

The A4 photographs that Tristan had printed of us are scattered under my bed – *What the hell!* – I swallow hard, I know for definite that I had them stowed away in my top bedside drawer. Ok, ok, ok. Let's think about this logically. Maybe I've looked through them and thought I put them away? I tentatively walk up the last few steps and look around my bedroom, nothing else seems out of place. *See, there's always a logical explanation!*

I shake my head and walk over to the bed. Getting to my knees, I stretch under the bed and gather all the photos together. Standing back up, I put them on the bed and notice they seem a bit dusty – *Oops! Guess I better get the vacuum out tomorrow!*

As I'm placing them all back inside the folder, I realise something's not right. Frowning deeply and blaming my bad counting skills on the wine I have had this evening, I count through them again, horror laces through me – *There's one missing!*

Flinging them all back on the bed, I pull my hand to my mouth to stop the garbled noise from becoming a scream and fall against the chest of drawers. Sinking slowly to the floor, the hideous, sickening truth screams loud and clear in my head – *Someone was in here!*

Ok, Coral! Keep it together – DO NOT PANIC!

I slowly turn my head to my built-in wardrobe, as I do I notice the door is cracked open. *Fuck! I always shut the doors!* I silently crawl across the floor and pick up the baseball bat. Then, being careful not to make the floorboards creak, I slowly rise to my feet. I hold the bat in my hand, ready to swing it as hard as I can.

"Hey!" I shout, whacking the door with the bat, it leaves a really big dent. "I know you're in there!" I shout, my voice cracking as my heart pummels against my chest – *Deep calming breaths Coral!*

When I don't get a reply, I take a step back and bash the door again. No one jumps out trying to surprise me. Deciding to be brave, I take another step back and using my balance, I lift up my leg, wrap my toes around the handle and slowly pull the door open. All my clothes are there, where they should be, nothing seems out of place.

I move my position, but I keep the bat in my left hand, just-in-case. Switching on the bedside lamp, I notice a mark on my bedside cabinet, a round, wet mark, like condensation. Getting to my knees, I lean forward, it looks like a...I suddenly realise it looks exactly like the rim of a beer bottle – *There's no way Bob would have been up here, no way!*

Reaching my shaking hand out, I use the tip of my forefinger and press down on the mark. It's cold and wet, and definitely fresh. *Holy fuck!*

Someone has been in my studio, drank my beer, been up in my bedroom and stolen a photograph, without breaking in!

My teeth clamp together in anger because I think I know exactly who it is. Launching myself up, I run down the stairs, baseball bat still in hand, get my keys, unlock the patio door, yank it open and take the couple of steps needed to reach Bob's door.

All the lights are off – *Crap!*

I don't want to wake him or worry him. He might fall down the stairs trying to hurry to me, but at the same time, I want to know if he saw anything suspicious tonight. *Damn it!*

I walk back into my studio and lock the door behind me. Then I set the magnetic door sensors. Evidently, they alert you if someone gets in and you're home, but they are useless if you're not! Maybe I need some sort of alarm? As I pace the room, wondering what to do, I suddenly notice something else, something odd.

The cushions on my sofa are not in their usual place. I always have two at each end, but one of them has been moved and is sitting in the middle of the sofa. I cock my head to the side, and as I continue to scan the room, I notice one of the cupboards on my large elongated wooden T.V unit hasn't been closed properly.

Stepping forward, I walk over to the unit, get to my knees, and carefully pull the door open. This is the cupboard I keep my photo albums in, I've been meaning to get them all scanned, so I have a digital copy of them all, some of them are so old. Gladys always insisted on lots of photos, not just for birthdays or Christmases, so I have a very large stock of photographs.

The first album is from when I moved in with Gladys, to starting senior school. The second is from the age of eleven up to my 21st, including the birthday party she threw for me, and the third is all the photos I've taken since then. As I stare at the albums, I notice they are not in their usual place either. *Why would someone have been interested in a bunch of old photographs?*

I frown deeply, pull them all out of the cupboard and open the first album up. It's the one from when I moved in with Gladys. I never told Gladys this, but when I was taken away from my mother, I had a photograph that I kept of my old family. I was four when it was taken, and I remember it well. It was Kelly's birthday, and we'd all gone out to Alton Towers for the day, someone took a photo of the four of us. Mom, Dad, Kelly and I are all smiling together, we all look so happy. I don't know why I took it with me, and I don't know why I still keep it, a reminder of a happier time maybe.

Reaching into the secret compartment of the album, I slip my finger inside. I frown hard as my fingers search for something that is evidently no longer there.

I gasp aloud. "No!" I grab the album and shake it upside down, hoping that the photograph will fall out, but it doesn't. I place it on the floor and frantically start flipping through the pages, I don't stop until I reach the last page – *It's gone!*

I rapidly shake my head, refusing to believe that. I go through the same process with the second and third album, only to find nothing. *No!*

I fall back, my bottom hitting the hard flooring, and clench my hands into fists. Tears bubble to the surface, so I fight them back. I shouldn't be so upset about it, I don't know why I am. I should be more concerned with the fact that someone has been in here, taken it from me, but I'm devastated.

It was the only photo I had of us all.

Heavy sorrowful tears escape me. I don't know how long I sit there for, trying to soothe myself by rocking back and forth, but the pain I feel at losing it is something I can't describe and don't understand.

Falling to the floor, I curl up into a ball and rest my cheek against the laminated flooring. I cry deeply for what I have lost, for my father, for my mother, and for Kelly. I'll never get to see them again, not like that, never again...

CHAPTER SEVENTEEN

MY MOBILE BUZZING in my bag pulls me out of my stupor. Sitting up, I slide along the floor, still choking back the tears, and take my mobile out to see who it is – Tristan – *Shit!*

Now is not the time, but I know I'd better answer it, or he'll just keep calling.

"Hey," I croak, then sniff loudly. I really need some tissues.

"Coral? What's wrong, what's happened?" he sounds alarmed. I try to think of something to say that will placate him, I can't tell him the truth, not yet. Then I remember my news from this evening – *They are leaving!*

"Gladys and Malcolm are leaving," I choke out, sniffing loudly.

"I-I thought you already knew that baby," he says, his voice a soothing tune.

"Um…no, I mean yes I did, it's just…." I take a ragged breath. "They are all leaving Tristan, and moving to Spain." I hear his sharp intake of breath and swallow hard, trying to stop the tears.

"I'm coming to you baby, I'll be a few hours but' – "No!" I bark loudly.

"Why not?" He softly says.

"Because it means you'll have to go back next w-week," I choke out.

"So' – "I don't w-want y-you to," I cry.

"Coral!" Tristan admonishes. "You're upset. I want to be there for you," he adds.

"I…I know you do," I warble. "But please, just stay, get

what you need to be done then you won't have to go back...y-you can b-be here with m-me then," I say, squeezing my eyes shut. *I want him here with me!*

Tristan sighs heavily. "If that's what you want," he says reluctantly.

"Y-yes," I stutter.

"I don't like it," he tells me firmly.

"I know," I sniff, trying to calm my erratic breathing. "T-tell me about your day," I add.

"Coral'– "Please, it will take my mind off things," I croak.

"Fine!" He huffs. I instantly picture Tristan pinching the bridge of his nose in frustration. I smile weakly. Just hearing his voice, picturing his face makes me automatically feel better.

Tristan tells me all about his meetings, funny moments that happened and how much he has missed me. I feel a wave of melancholy hit me again. I swallow hard and try to fight against the feeling. I try to swing my emotions towards love instead, and how I will feel when I see Tristan again, but it's no good, no matter how hard I try I truly ache for him; so much so that it feels like physical pain.

"Better?" Tristan asks when he's finished.

"Much better," I answer, trying not to sound too sombre.

"I still want to come and see you," he whispers.

"Don't," I tell him firmly. "We only have one more night and two days," I add trying to comfort him, or me, I'm not sure which.

Truthfully, I want him here with me right now. I want him to drive down, run towards me and wrap me up in his arms. But on the other hand if he does come back, it means he has to go away again next week, and in all honesty I don't think I can do this again. I would have to go with him, even if it meant quitting my job I would, if it meant we weren't apart.

We talk for a little while longer. I feel much calmer as the minutes, hours, I'm not sure tick by. I don't know how he does it – how this calming effect works on me – but by the time we say our goodbyes, I am already up the stairs and curled up under the quilt, listening to him hum Some Enchanting Evening to me...

THAT NIGHT I dream of Susannah stalking my studio when I'm not in, I try to work out what she's looking for, but I can't put my finger on it. Then I dream *I am* Susannah and I'm walking around my darkened studio. I walk up the stairs and across the bedroom, I see myself asleep in bed. I see something glisten in my hand. I look down and see it's a knife, a really big Rambo style knife. I grip my hand on the handle and pull it up ready to plunge it down on myself, but another hand appears, grabbing hold of my wrist. I glance to my right. My mother's warm eyes from when she was well, healthy, glare back at me.

"Leave her alone!" She growls and hits me hard around the head.

I fall to the floor in pain – Then suddenly I'm not Susannah anymore, I am me, in my bed. I look down and see Susannah knocked out on the floor. My mother sits on the edge of my bed with me. I notice she looks strange in the darkness, like a ghost, she smiles tentatively at me.

"I'm sorry," she whispers, tears filling her eyes, then she glances at Susannah, turning back to me, she leans forward and kisses my forehead. "You're safe now baby girl. I'll protect you," she whispers.

Baby girl! – She always used to call me that. I stare up at my mother in disbelief; she looks so healthy, so normal.

"Sleep now," she softly tells me, stroking my hair, and making me feel sleepy, safe, loved.

I close my eyes and allow the protective feeling to wash over me...

WHEN I WAKE the following morning, I'm aware of how strangely calm I feel. I sit up in bed for a moment, reliving the dream of my mother. That was weird, weird because of how comforting it felt to have her near me like that, and to have her protect me in that way.

Shaking my head at that thought, I think about coming home last night, and someone getting into my place. My instincts are screaming at me it's Susannah, and I know in that very moment that I will kill her if she harms one hair on Tristan's head.

I know this instinctively. I can't help myself. It sounds

over-dramatic and a little crazy, I know that. But like it or not, Tristan has a crazy person – that may or may not, but most likely has got access to my home and taken possessions of mine – and she's working in close proximity to him, I will annihilate her if she so much as looks at him.

With that thought in mind, I get out of bed, wrap my robe around me, head down the stairs and go straight into the shower. I don't have the energy or the inclination to swim today. All I can think about as I'm showering is Susannah. I am bristling with rage!

God help me, how am I supposed to work with her today? I hope she calls in sick. I hope her supposed migraine is still going on. Then I think if she is in, I hope she has an accident or something on the way to work, not to kill her, I want that part – *Coral! Ok, ok! You're scaring the shit out of yourself.*

I sigh heavily. I just...I don't want her there today. That's not so much to ask, is it? Then I think maybe *I* should ditch, but I know Joyce will think I'm avoiding her, and I want to protect Joe, she's not as tough as me, in fact, she's a sweet little walk over that Susannah will no doubt continue to threaten. No, I have to be there.

Switching off the shower, I wrap my hair in a towel and dry myself off. As I'm creaming my skin, I make more plans. First thing first, as soon as I'm in work, hopefully, crazy lady won't be in yet, I'll go straight into Joyce tell her about Susannah threatening me, about my keys and my notepad going missing, and my late night visitor, who has stolen belongings of mine. I know I need to check with Bob when I see him if it was him, but I already know it wasn't.

I feel my soul die a little again, whoever it was, took the only photograph I have of my old family, tears threaten again – I push the thought out of my head and try to get back to what I need to do.

Right – Secondly, I need to figure out a way of telling Tristan all of this without him flipping out; after all, it is going to be my word against hers. I think for a moment about heading to the police station before work so I can tell them what happened, but I already know what they will say. No evidence, so they can't really do much about it. I shudder slightly, the very thought of her, or whoever it was, trespassing inside my studio when I wasn't here gives me the chills…I shake my head to try and push the sickly feeling away.

I towel dry my hair, run my brush through it then my Coconut Oil. Grabbing my hair bobble and pins, I make a bun and smooth it over, so it looks neat. Next, I start with my makeup. As I'm applying my mascara, I wonder how I'm supposed to keep calm if she is there, the amount of venomous anger I have flowing through me right now is…overwhelming. It's going to take all my strength not to blow up at her. *Think logically Coral.*

Yes. I must. I must think like Spock. If I blow up, it will make me look like the crazy person, not her, and she will have achieved what she wanted. I take several deep breaths and calm myself down.

I think about Tristan coming home, and how I'm going to feel seeing him again, I've had my second hypnotherapy session with Cindy, so I should be able to wear my new dress on Friday. A nervous bubble ripples through my stomach, and I'm pleased it's half nerves, half excitement. I know the exciting part is what Tristan's reaction will be when he sees me in the dress. Hopefully, I'll get a good reaction, the nervous part is me freaking out that it won't work and I'll fall apart. No, I must not think like that, I must be positive. I picture myself in the dress, the bubble ripples again making me smile, I want to look sexy for Tristan.

I start to feel a little better. The anger I feel for Susannah seems to be dissipating so I carry on with the positives – I am now two hundred and fifty thousand pounds richer, I feel a strange flutter head down my spine. *What the hell am I meant to do with that amount of money?*

I turn and look out into the living room of my tiny studio – I guess I could get a bigger place? I shake my head at that thought, I can't really think about that at the moment. I put my mascara back in my make-up bag, adding a little lip gloss I nod at myself – You are ready.

Putting my robe back on, I walk out the bathroom and pour myself a large vegetable juice to take to work with me. Marching up the stairs, I hang up my robe and dress in my work clothes, black trousers and my light blue short-sleeved fitted blouse. I slip my feet into my black wedges and head back down the stairs, noticing as I reach the bottom step that my photo albums are still sprawled across the floor. *Damn it!*

I swallow hard against the lump that's formed, take a deep breath, bend down and put them away. Switching off the air-con, I pick up my handbag and my keys from the sofa and head out the patio door, locking it behind me.

"Morning," Bob pipes up cheerfully. I try to smile, but it just doesn't happen. I pull my sunglasses out and pop them on; at least they will hide my eyes.

"Got a little thirsty last night?" I ask as chirpily as I can.

Bob puts his paper down and looks up at me quizzically. "You've lost me?" he says.

"The bottle of beer," I say half laughing, trying to make light of it all.

"What beer?" He counteracts – *Fuck!*

"Oh it's ok, it must have been Rob," I say, my voice wobbling.

"What beer Coral?" he asks again.

"The empty bottle that was left on the kitchen sink," I say putting on a fake smile. "Not to worry Bob, I'll call Rob later," I say and turn to walk away.

"Well it was probably that friend of yours," he says matter-of-factly.

I freeze then slowly turn back to him. "S-sorry?" I stutter.

"I heard something last night…let me think…yes, about nine-thirty it was. I thought it was you, so I came out to see if you were ok, and this blonde girl was unlocking your door. She said you'd asked her to pop in and pick up your music player or something…." Bob says waving his hand. *Holy fuck!*

I blink rapidly at Bob. I feel frozen in place. That's why my keys went missing, Susannah got copies. Then I think about my MP3 Player, shoving my hand in my bag I feel it's shape between my fingers. Not wanting to panic Bob, I try to smile and nod my head as though I'd forgotten.

"Oh right yeah…" I say. "I remember now," I add. Bob smiles at me and goes back to his paper. "Well, I'll see you later," I say, my voice low and quiet.

"Are you alright darling?" he questions looking up at me. I nod silently. "Sure?" he adds.

"Yes," I whisper, tears pooling in my eyes – *God damn it, my make-up!*

"Alright then," he smiles and goes back to his paper.

"See you later," I squeak.

Bob nods and smiles at me again. "Have a good day sweetheart."

I turn, feeling like a complete zombie, and start walking down the concourse. All I can think about is the fact that my suspicions were right, it has to have been Susannah. I don't have any friends, and the only other blonde I know is Debs, and there's no way she would have been in place without telling me. Besides, she doesn't have keys.

I grit my teeth as I try to think of a way of getting my photo back, as odd as it sounds, that's all I care about. I don't care that Susannah broke in, I don't care that she took one of the photos of Tristan and me, and I don't care that she drank one of my beers – I just want my photo back!

As I'm walking to work, I decide I have to think more logically. I can't allow my emotions to override any rational thoughts. So I decide once I'm in work to locate a locksmith, I need to change all the locks, then I think if I keep them as they are and buy some sort of CCTV, I might be able to get some evidence of her breaking in. Deciding that is my best option, I head to work with renewed vigour and a spring in my step.

I will win this battle. I will not fail. Susannah will go down for this. I will make it my destiny to take her down, get her arrested, and out of Tristan's life, out of my life…Forever.

WHEN I GET into work, Joe hands me a message from Joyce, advising me that Susannah won't be in all day as her migraine is still bad and that she will be out most of the day too. Apparently, Gladys and Joyce are going to play a round of golf. As soon as I reach my desk, I jump online and search home security systems. I know I need it to be discreet, it can't look like a camera because even if she did get in again, she might see it and hide her face. And without a clear picture of who she is, I have no proof, and I really want to catch her at it!

The first site I go to is Argos. It's in town, and hopefully, if they have what I'm looking for, I can pick one up at lunch, but when I take a look, I see they are all pretty bulky. I need something smaller. I'm about to click on Amazon when I notice a security company that is based in Brighton.

I click on the website, and to my delight, they have loads of small, discreet cameras, and they come and install the cameras for you too – that sounds more like what I want. Picking up the phone, I dial the number. I speak to a really pleasant lady who listens carefully to what I am asking for and my reasons for it, she understands my concerns but advises me that they are booked up and can't get me in until next week. *Bollocks!*

I thank her for her help and advise her that I will buy something online, and attempt to install it myself, citing I can't take the risk of it happening again without proof. She tells me she understands and will call around all the engineers to see if she could get one over to me tonight. I thank her, give her my number and hang up.

I clamp my hand down on my leg that is jigging up and down. I really hope she can get me in. I want those cameras installed – today! Checking my inbox, I see I have a few letters to get done for Joyce. Clearing my mind of all things Susannah, I click the first one open and begin my work…

TWO HOURS LATER, I get a call from the woman at the security company telling me there has been a cancellation, and they can get someone over to me at five o'clock tonight. I agree wholeheartedly, which means I need to leave at four-thirty so I can get back to my studio in time. With nothing else to do, I feel myself getting antsy. *Why couldn't Joyce have left me more work to do? Grrrrr!*

Waking my screen up with the mouse, I start searching the internet. There's something that's been bugging me, something that's been at the back of my mind since I had the dream about Susannah. Typing in what I need, I hit enter and wait for the choices to come up. I'm about to click on the first choice, then I remember I know someone who might be able to tell me more about it, or at least head me in the right direction. Picking up my handbag, I start fishing around. Finally locating what I need, I pull out his card and dial his number, my foot starts tapping involuntarily.

"Dr Andrews office, how may I help you?" A posh sounding lady answers.

"May I speak to Dr Andrews please?" I ask politely.

"Are you a patient?" I don't know, am I? *Lie Coral!*

"Yes, yes I am," I tell her.

"May I take your name?" She asks.

"Coral Stevens," I say, my voice high pitched because I'm nervous.

"One moment please Miss Stevens." The line goes quiet. I'm pretty sure she's going to come back and say he's out on rounds or something.

"Coral how are you?" Dr Andrews's deep voice startles me for a moment.

"Well thank you, and yourself?" I answer a little breathlessly.

"Very well thank you. How is your nose?" *Whoa!* I'd forgotten all about that! So much has happened since then.

"Nicely healed thank you," I say.

"No headaches, blurry vision?" He asks.

"No, healthy as a horse," I tell him. I swear I hear him mumble that's a shame – *Hmm me and Dr A?* I shake the thought away.

"What can I do for you Coral?" he asks.

"Well I have an a...um situation," I mumble.

"Ah, well I don't work in that field, it's antenatal you need," he says. I think he's smiling. Antenatal? Where have I heard that from before...Debs having Lily? *Holy crap he thinks I'm pregnant.*

"No, no I'm not pregnant," I gush. "I wanted to ask if you know anything about...well psychotic people...I mean patients, their behaviour and such," I stutter.

"Ah, again not my field. Are you alright Coral?" he asks, sounding concerned.

"Yes, I think so," I answer.

"You think so?" he asks. *Say something Coral!*

"Well, it's just there's someone new at work, and I think she may be psychotic. I've had close contact with a mentally unstable person before, and she's well...showing the same signs," I say, hoping he'll come up with some answers.

"I see. Have you talked to your employer about this?" He asks.

"It's complicated," I answer glumly.

"It always is," he sighs. "Well, I have a colleague in the field, an old University friend – I hear him taping his keyboard – 'Let me see…yes, Dr Simon Handler, do you have a pen?"

"Yes." I reach forward to pick a pen up from the holder, but they're all gone – *Weird!*

"Coral?" Dr Andrews prompts.

"Um, Dr Andrews, I…all the pens seem to have mysteriously disappeared from my desk, I'm sorry," I say feeling embarrassed.

"No need to apologise," he softly says. "Do you have an email address?"

"Yes, I do."

"I can get Penny to email the details to you."

"Yes please, that would be great." I smile down the line. He really has a nice voice. Not as nice as Tristan's though.

"I'll put you back through to Penny. A pleasure to speak to you," he says.

"You too Dr Andrews, and thanks for taking my call," I tell him softly.

"You're very welcome, anytime Coral." *Anytime, Whoa!* The line goes quiet again. *I think I have an admirer.*

"Hello, Miss Stevens?" Penny's voice is back. I give her my email address and end the call. *Hmm, well that didn't really give me any answers!*

Wiggling the mouse to wake up my screen, I decide to go back to my original idea. Clicking on the first search result, I lean forward and start reading through…

Symptoms of Psychosis

There are four main symptoms associated with a psychotic episode. Hallucinations/Delusions/Confused and disturbed thoughts/A lack of insight and self-awareness. These are outlined in more detail below.

Hallucinations – A hallucination is when you perceive something that does not exist in reality. Hallucinations can occur in all five of your senses.

Sight – someone with psychosis may see colours and shapes, or imaginary people or animals.

Sounds – someone with psychosis may hear voices that are angry, unpleasant or sarcastic.

Touch – a common psychotic hallucination is that insects are crawling on the skin.

Smell – usually a strange or unpleasant smell.

Taste – some people with psychosis have complained of having a constant unpleasant taste in their mouth

Delusion - A delusion is where you have an unshakeable belief in something implausible, bizarre or obviously untrue. Two examples of psychotic delusions are paranoid delusion, delusions of grandeur. These are described below:-

Paranoid delusion - A person with psychosis will often believe an individual or organisation is making plans to hurt or kill them. This can lead to unusual behaviour. For example, a person with psychosis may refuse to be in the same room as a mobile phone because they believe they are mind-control devices.

Delusions of grandeur - A person with psychosis may have delusions of grandeur where they believe they have some imaginary power or authority. For example, they may think they are president of a country or have the power to bring people back from the dead.

Confusion of thought - People with psychosis often have disturbed, confused and disrupted patterns of thought. Signs of this include:-their speech may be rapid and constant, the content of their speech may appear random, for example, they may switch from one topic to another mid-sentence, their train of thought may suddenly stop, resulting in an abrupt pause in conversation or activity

Lack of insight - People experiencing a psychotic episode are often totally unaware their behaviour is in any way strange, or their delusions or hallucinations could be imaginary. They may be capable of recognising delusional or bizarre behaviour in others but lack the self-awareness to recognise it in themselves. For example, a person with psychosis who is being treated in a psychiatric ward may complain that all of their fellow patients are mentally unwell while they are perfectly normal.

Postnatal psychosis - Postnatal psychosis, also called puerperal psychosis, is a severe form of postnatal depression (a type of depression some women experience after they have had a baby). It is estimated that postnatal psychosis affects one or two women in every 1,000 who give birth and most commonly occurs during the first few weeks after having a baby. Postnatal psychosis is more likely in women who already have a mental health condition, such as bipolar disorder or schizophrenia.

As well as symptoms of psychosis (see above), symptoms of postnatal psychosis can include: a high mood (mania)–for example, talking and thinking too much or too quickly. A low mood–for example, depression, lack of energy, loss of appetite and trouble sleeping Postnatal psychosis is regarded as an emergency. If you are concerned someone you know may have developed postnatal psychosis contact your GP immediately.

I FINISH READING, take a long deep breathe in and slowly blow it out. I don't think I need to speak to that other doctor, I think this explains it all. I can't say if Susannah has any paranoid delusions, but I think she has delusions of grandeur, after all, she did say to me that she and Tristan are engaged, in love, and couldn't help themselves.

I think for a tiny split second that she may be telling the truth, that Tristan has gone through all of this with her – *Coral, what are you talking about, that's ridiculous!*

Deciding I'd better delete the search history, I press print then delete all the sites, just-in-case Susannah takes a look. If she's back in tomorrow, I don't want to raise her suspicions that I might know something, and I really don't want her finding out that I know she was in my place last night, and that I'm determined to catch her at it, by getting her on camera. Picking up the paperwork, I fold it over three times, stuff it inside a small envelope, and carefully stow it away in my bag...

AS I WALK HOME along the busy Brighton streets, I look up and see it's yet another blue-skied, warm, hazy evening. I wonder how long it will last? I hope it's this nice for Gladys and Malcolm's wedding. I take a deep breath in, and slowly blow it out, feeling glad there's only one more night and day to go until I see Tristan again.

Although I have to say, it feels as though the closer it gets, the more time slows down. It already feels like it's been weeks not days, and today seems to have passed by in a blurry haze. With Joyce out for the day and Susannah doing whatever she's doing, I've had a lot of time on my hands. I kept catching myself staring blankly at the computer screen, daydreaming about Tristan.

Reaching my studio, I see there's a chap waiting in a pair of dark blue combats, and a light blue t-shirt that has Brighton Security Inc. slapped across the front of it. *Great!*

I hope Bob hasn't seen him. I don't want him to know what I'm up to.

"Miss Stevens?" The guy questions as I reach him. He looks like he's in his fifties, has a balding head, bright green eyes and a pleasant smile.

"Yes," I answer meekly and quickly unlock the door.

He follows me inside, and I instantly feel nervous, so I start rattling off at full speed, telling him what has happened and what I want. He nods as he listens and then comes up with a plan of where the cameras need to be, I agree wholeheartedly, and he gets to work.

My good manners kick in, and I offer him a drink, he smiles pleasantly at me, as I hand him a cold glass of lemonade. When he's fitted the two tiny wireless cameras, one in the living room and one in the bedroom, and connected them to my laptop, he sits me down and shows me how they work.

I listen intently as he shows me the view of my bedroom and the two of us in my tiny living room. A huge grin starts to spread across my face, if Susannah gets in again, she'll be caught red-handed, and the cameras are so tiny, there's no way she would spot them.

"Happy?" He asks as he minimises the screen on my laptop.

"Very," I say. He hands me a card with his name on it and tells me to call him if I have any questions. I thank him, pay him and see him out the door. Then I scuttle upstairs, get changed into my training gear, and head to the gym. I really feel like I need the workout session tonight, I need to get rid of some pent-up rage...

WHEN I HEAD back to my studio, it's with a long face and a trampled heart. Training with Will totally sucked, I couldn't concentrate at all. In fact, he put me on my ass so many times; he almost sent me home again. As I drag my tired butt down the concourse, I actually debate going over to Tristan's so I can have a long soak in the bath, but decide against it. There are too many memories there, and I'll only get melancholy about him not being here, I'm missing him far too much for that, and I already feel emotionally raw today, much more than usual.

I'm not sure if it's the prolonged amount of time that Tristan and I have been apart, the fact that all my family are going to up sticks and move to another country. I don't think it's quite sunk in yet. Or the fact that Susannah is more than likely a lunatic, that has broken into my home and stolen possessions of mine that's making me feel this way.

Either way, I feel like I could cry at the drop of a hat, and I hate feeling like that.

I wish Rob were here, he would know what to say to me, he would know how to make me look at it all from a different angle, make me laugh about it all, or take the piss out of me for crying. I miss him so much. I wish he would call me. I'm worried about him, even though I know I shouldn't be, but I can't help thinking the worst.

Then I think back to last night and Gladys telling me about them all leaving, and how I blew it all up to be some big secret, which it kind of was, but it was nowhere near as bad as the thoughts I had whizzing around my head. So I take a deep breath and push any worrying thoughts about Rob away.

CHAPTER EIGHTEEN

I AM SITTING CROSS legged on the sofa feeling much better about being in my studio with my new security system installed. I look up at the clock on the wall, it's 10.10pm, and I'm wide awake. I sigh heavily. I wish I weren't feeling so fidgety and restless. I spoke to Tristan a couple of hours ago, and it was brief as he was off out for the evening.

Apparently, one of his team won a really big case, one that had gone on for a couple of years, he wanted to take them out for a meal to celebrate and say thank you. We spoke briefly about the money Gladys gave me, and the fact that they are all moving away, it was far too short a conversation, so to occupy my time I've been trying to read Captain Corelli's Mandolin.

The day after Tristan quoted a passage from it, I went online and purchased it, but I can't concentrate. I keep losing track, and I hate it when that happens. I know it's going to be a good book, so I put it to the side, hoping it can be my first-holiday novel when I go and see Gladys in Spain, or maybe Hawaii, if that happens with Tristan.

Hearing a strange noise, I glance across the room at the front door. I have checked it three times tonight, even though I know it's locked and the door sensor alarm is set. I pick up my Eskrima sticks and hold one in each hand, ready to pounce if Susannah turns up at the door again, but then I hear laughter and realise it must be next door getting home late.

Earlier today, after the morning dragging like crazy, I decided to take an early lunch. I couldn't stay cooped up in the office any longer, so I headed into town and strolled the streets in a daze. I was about to turn back when I came across a martial arts studio that I'd never seen before, it had a big shop connected to it selling everything from punch-bags to Nunchucks.

Looking around the store, I was shocked to see they were selling real Eskrima sticks. Will's been introducing this ancient form of Filipino Martial Arts to me, and in my haste, and need to protect myself, I purchased a pair today. Will would go crazy if he knew I'd bought a real set, we've only been training with foam ones. I remember the first time Will introduced me to it. I was jigging up and down like a kid in a sweet shop. I love using weapons, but before he would let me practice with him, he told me about how this art came about…

It was on the Mactan Island that the local chieftain Lapu Lapu and his men repelled the Spanish conquistadors in 1521. Ferdinand Magellan, the Portuguese navigator who led the expedition on behalf of the King of Spain, paid with his life at the battle of Mactan.

It is believed that Lapu Lapu's men fought with spears, swords and sharpened sticks, and this is the first reference to the existence of the ancient art of Eskrima. Before the coming of the Spaniards, Eskrima was an art of war taught to warriors to use in the constant tribal wars of that period. Being an art of war each tribe would evolve its own distinctive techniques, based on the type of weapon it preferred and the environment it lived in. Each tribe would jealously guard it's techniques, strategies, and tactics. During this period, Eskrima was classified as a tribal fighting art…

I run my finger across the smooth bamboo finish, they are only small, around twenty-eight inches long, and blunt at each end. I smack them against each other, they make a strange popping sound, getting whacked with one of these would really hurt – break an arm if you hit hard enough. I decide to do some practising, hoping it will help me feel less restless. I stand up and take my stance, then start gliding into a kata. Whacking the sticks with as much force as possible, imagining each time I bring one of the sticks down, I'm defending myself from Susannah...

Ten minutes later, I sit back down on the sofa wishing I hadn't done that, I feel buzzed up and full of energy. I decide the best thing to do is to put a film on that I know, that way it won't matter if I start daydreaming again, I won't feel so bugged about it. Plugging my hard-drive in, I decide on a Martial arts film. I can't bare romance, not now I've met Tristan. It will only remind me of the fact that he's not here, and make me feel melancholy about it, so I pick Way of The Dragon, my favourite Bruce Lee film.

With the film ready, I grab a beer from the fridge and curl up on the sofa. Pressing play, I tune out all things Tristan & Susannah and watch in wonder as the magnificent Bruce Lee does his thing. *Yeah, baby!*

WHEN I WAKE the next morning in bed, I open my eyes to sunlight streaming in through the window. I smile and stretch deeply. I feel energised after a good night's sleep. Having a baseball bat, a pair of Eskrima sticks to protect me, and CCTV obviously did the trick.

Then I realise it's Friday – *Tristan's coming come!*

And even though I have had a really crappy week, I feel so happy that I literally bounce out of bed –I guess that's being in love for you. Running down the stairs, I check the front door, all is well. I wander into the bathroom to wash my face and clean my teeth so I can head out for my morning swim. As I reach the sink, I take a good look at myself in the mirror – *Uh-Oh!*

I look ill, my cheeks have sunk, even more, my eyes have dark rings underneath them, and I can see my collarbone. I didn't think I had lost that much weight, but then again, I haven't really eaten much while Tristan's been away. I hope he doesn't freak out, not that I should be worrying about what he thinks, it's not like I can help it.

I decide to ditch swimming. I don't want to burn off any more calories. I quickly clean my teeth and wash my face. Pouring myself a glass of veggie juice, I head back upstairs and start packing my weekend bag, my stomach does several backward flips as I'm doing so.

Just thinking about seeing Tristan in the flesh makes it happen. My heart gallops against my chest as I picture his face, which makes my breathing accelerate like I've been running up a hill. *Whoa! Calm down Coral!*

I sit on the edge of the bed, trying to slow down my frantic heart. I turn and eye my new dress hanging up in my closet, it's still in the white bag. Standing up, I walk over to it, take out of the bag and lay it on the bed. Yes, I still like it. I think I made the right decision. Then I think about how I'm going to feel wearing it, I hope I don't freak out.

Carefully placing it back in the bag, I lay it on the bed then picking up the bag with my new lingerie, I place it next to the dress. I'll be in a rush when I come back later to pick it all up, and I don't want to forget anything. Heading back down the stairs, I wander back into the bathroom and take a shower...

HEADING OUT THE patio door, I lock it up then put on my sunglasses. It's sunny and warm again today, which makes me smile even more. I decide to take a moment and soak in the view, there are lots of boats moored today, no doubt getting ready for the weekend; it's supposed to be a blinder. I close my eyes and take a deep breath in, the smell of the sea fills my nostrils. God, I love living so close to the water. Opening my eyes again, I take in the view of the sea, I love how it sparkles when the sun shines on it.

I wonder for a moment about my studio, and what I'm going to do about it now Gladys has given me all that money. Then I think about Tristan and his flippant way of asking me to move in with him, as though it was the most natural, easiest thing in the world to do. I wonder if he's ever lived with anyone? I sigh inwardly. I guess if I am going to marry him, he will want me to live with him.

Then I think about an article I read a few years ago about couples who married but kept their own place, it's definitely something to think about, it's not like I need to sell. Tristan's got enough money to keep us both, and now I'm two hundred & fifty grand richer, I have the luxury of doing what I want with it – The thought is quite sobering.

I think back to Wednesday night, and Malcolm's offer of opening a high-interest savings account for me so I can start earning even more money, which I agreed to. I'm sure he would have banked the money by now. I shake my head in wonder. I have no idea what I'm actually going to do with that amount of money – *Buy a car!*

I snort sarcastically at myself. Then I think a nice little

F-Type to race around at the weekends could be fun – *Or maybe a sailing boat?*

My mind instantly drifts back to the nightmare of Susannah – *Ugh!* Maybe not, I think I'm off the idea of boats for now.

Shrugging it all off, I pop my headphones in and start walking down the concourse. I hit shuffle, and One Republic's Secrets starts playing. I can't help bobbing my head to the beat as I walk along. As I listen to the words, I'm taken back to what Tristan asked of me, to tell him about myself, to tell him my secrets.

My throat goes dry just thinking about it, and my heart starts to palpitate. Part of me wants to tell him, open my heart and let it all out, but the other part wants nothing more to do with the past. I buried it a long time ago, and I don't want to drag it all back up. I decide it's far too nice a day, and way too early to be thinking such heavy thoughts, so I push it away, far away to the back of my mind.

Just as I'm passing the gym, and waiting for the traffic to clear so I can cross the road, my stomach suddenly pangs with hunger, I know I should eat something, but I really don't have any appetite. *Coral!* – Ok, ok, I'll eat something!

As I cross the road, I decide to get a chocolate swirl for breakfast and maybe one for lunch too, so I head towards St James's Street. Just as I reach Starbucks, Semisonic's Secret Smile starts playing, it makes me think of Tristan and his broad, sexy, deep-dimpled smile.

My stomach instantly fills with butterflies, and my pelvic muscles clench most deliciously. *Oh boy! I can't wait to see him.*

As I walk into the coffee house and join the queue, I can't help giggling to myself. I really do feel as high as a kite today. I shake my head in wonder, what a difference to the week I've had, and I drift into another daydream about Tristan…

"Miss! Hello Miss?" *Shit! Not again!*

"Sorry," I smile apologetically at the server who has been trying to gain my attention, place my order and take a seat to wait for it, trying my best not to start daydreaming again.

I try to concentrate on work, and what's going to happen today.

Hmm, I wonder if my package will turn up this morning from the P.I Company? I hope so, although they did say it might not be until Monday. Biting my lip, I wonder what it will reveal. I'm determined to find out the truth. I will do anything to keep Tristan safe and out of harm's way. *Don't think about that!* I castigate and try to concentrate on something else.

Blink 182 starts singing Miss You, reflecting how much I've missed Tristan this week. *Yes, I have, badly!*

The member of staff waves at me, bringing my attention to her. I smile at her, pick up my order, and take a seat next to the window. As I start chewing on my swirl, I wonder for a moment how I'm actually going to get through today, without regularly jumping up and down with excitement about Tristan coming back – I guess I'll have to have lots of bathroom breaks.

I suddenly panic. When I spoke to Tristan last night, he told me he wasn't sure what time he would arrive in Brighton as his last meeting starts at lunchtime, and he's not sure how long it will take. I swallow hard – *Crap!*

I hope he doesn't come to the office. That would be like torture, I won't be able to kiss him or hold him, and I already have Blondie watching every move I make. Pushing that thought away, I finish off my swirl, pick up my Cappuccino and head to into work.

UNFORTUNATELY, I WHEN I walk into reception, Joe tells me that *she's* back in today. Feeling myself tense up, I slowly make my way up the stairs and along the corridor. As I reach my desk, I see Susannah is sat at the spare desk with her laptop open, and she's frantically typing away, then I really look at her – *Whoa!*

I don't know why, but Susannah looks totally dishevelled today. Her hair is greasy and slapped back into a messy ponytail, she has no make-up on, and she looks like she's been in the same clothes all week, and as I walk past her, I get a whiff of alcohol – *Not good!*

As I sit down at my desk, I glance across at her and say good morning, but she completely ignores me. Gritting my teeth, and trying my best to hold my tongue, I stare back at my screen. Opening my inbox, I start on the letters Joyce has sent across to me...

THE NEXT TWO hours pass by in complete silence. I try not to, but each time I have looked up and glanced her way, I have felt a shiver of fear run down the back of my spine, then I have felt overwhelmed with rage. She was in my place, I know she was, but it's not like I can simply come out with it and say that Bob saw her, I know for a fact she'll deny it. It has taken all my willpower to stop myself from dragging her sorry ass into the ladies and beating her until she relents and tells me where my photograph is!

And something keeps nagging away at me. It's like, the way she looks today is similar to the dream I had, and I can't help thinking about the fact that she might move here. It's like my inner voice is telling me that she's up to something, I just don't know what it is. I clench my jaw and stare at the screen, castigating myself – *I must not let my imagination run away with me!*

However, as hard as I try, I can't push the fear away that I'm feeling like this because deep down inside, I know she wants Tristan, loves him even. For some strange reason, she's got it into her head that they are together and I have to wonder – *Does Tristan have any idea who this woman really is?*

As eleven o'clock comes around, I ask her if she wants a coffee – just to cover myself and seem like I'm the one that's acting normal – but she turns and looks up at me in such an odd way, it makes me take a step back. Shaking my head at her, because I get no reply, I storm off to the kitchen, trying my best to reign in my escalating temper…

AT LUNCHTIME I head into town, feeling utterly grateful for the break. The atmosphere in the office has been less than desirable, tense even, and it's all coming from Susannah, well at least I think it is. It's been very odd for me too, being in the same room with a woman who has threatened me, trespassed in my property, and is trying to steal my very reason for existing, has felt extremely uncomfortable, especially given my anger issues.

If this had happened five years ago, I would have had no self-control. I would have beaten the crap out of her, so I guess she's lucky it's happening now. Shaking my head at myself, I continue north along St James's Street and pick up Tristan's present.

When I return to the office, I ask Joe to hide the present behind her desk. I can't risk Susannah seeing it – I'm sure it'll be safe in reception.

The rest of the afternoon drags like crazy.

How can a few hours seem like months? It almost like someone has got hold of the atomic clock and slowed it right down. Time, I'm discovering, is a weird thing when you're in love. Almost as though it purposely tortures you, passing too quickly when you're together, and slowing almost to a stop when you're apart…

AT EXACTLY FOUR O'clock, Susannah suddenly jumps up in a frenzy, shoves her laptop into her bag, throws it over her shoulder, grabs her handbag and without saying a word to me, she runs out of the office. I stare open mouthed at her retreating figure. *She is one crazy woman!*

Joyce comes out of her office and stops when she sees the look on my face.

"Coral, are you ok?" she asks. "You're very pale," she adds.

I turn and look up at her. "Yes Joyce, I'm fine. Susannah's just gone," I muse.

"She has?" Joyce says, peering down the hallway to reception, tapping her long manicured fingernail against her front teeth.

"Yes, she just got up, grabbed her stuff and ran for the door, without so much of a goodbye." *Ha! That will definitely make her out to be the weird one!*

"Yes, she did look a little bewildered today. I wonder why?" she muses. "Well at least she's gone now," she adds, sounding a little relieved.

I nod and smile up at her. Joyce frowns down at me, then cocks her head to the side. *Uh–Oh!* I know that look. What am I in trouble for?

"Are you sure you're alright Coral? You look like you've dropped a stone in weight. Are you feeling unwell?" I swallow hard. *I can't have lost that much weight, surely?*

I suddenly feel nervous about seeing Tristan. I really don't want him to give me a hard time about it. *What the fuck am I talking about?* When has a man ever told me what to do?

Never– *Exactly, tell him to take a hike if he hassles you* – I nod my head in agreement with myself.

"Coral?" Joyce says, still peering down at me.

"Sorry, no, I'm not ill, I'm fine – really," I add seeing the worried expression on her face. "There's just been a lot to deal with this week."

I almost tell her about someone – *Susannah!* – Getting into my studio, but I decide against it. Joyce would completely flip, and I want to handle this my way. I need to handle this my way. Otherwise, I might lose Tristan altogether, and that...that is something I cannot even imagine. It's too horrifying to even think about.

Joyce narrows her eyes. "Alright then, off you go young lady, home time." Joyce smiles at me, but it doesn't reach her eyes.

"Are you sure you don't need anything finishing off before I go?" I ask. I hate leaving work undone.

"No, it can wait until Monday," Joyce answers waving her hand at me, but her attention has gone back to staring down the hallway, her eyebrows pulled together as though she's concentrating really hard on something.

Picking up my handbag, I stand up, walk over to Joyce and kiss her goodbye.

"Have a great time tonight," she beams.

"Thanks," I squeak and smile like a love-struck teenager – *Tristan's coming home!*

Joyce chuckles at my reaction then turns and heads back into her office.

I take a deep breath then head down the hallway. Reaching reception, I see that Joe's already gone, walking around the desk I pick up Tristan's present. As I reach the doors to the building, Tom wanders over and holds it open for me.

"Thanks, Tom, have a great weekend," I tell him.

"You too Coral," he smiles fondly at me.

Stepping into the warm afternoon sunshine, I begin walking towards the main road, almost dropping Tristan's present twice, it's so big and cumbersome. I definitely need to get a taxi home tonight. As I attempt to get my mobile out of my bag, while keeping a grip on the present, it slips from my hands again – *Shit!*

As I reach down to catch it, strong hands encase mine,

stopping the present from hitting the floor. My eyes dart up – *Tristan!*

"Hey beautiful," he croons. *My Hero!*

Tristan smiles widely at me, I feel all the air leave my lungs. His eyes crinkle making his dimples deepen as his enigmatic smile captures me, making me swoon up at him. *God, he looks good!* – His crisp white shirt is folded up at the sleeves, with the top three buttons open, giving me an eyeful of his strong masculine chest, and he's wearing those dark blue suit trousers that make his legs look long and lean, and his aviators are tucked into his shirt pocket.

My heart has stopped, then restarted at a ridiculous rate – *Oh I'm so in love with you Tristan so in love…* Like an idiot, I just stand there, totally paralysed. Then my brain fires up. "Hi," I squeak, reflecting his deepening grin.

Tristan's smile gets broader, his dimples are on full wattage. "Need some help?" he asks all husky and sexy.

"Yeah, I think I do," I chuckle. Tristan takes the present out of my hands and leans it against his leg. "Thanks," I whisper.

"You're welcome," he teases.

"Shall we go?" I ask. Hoping he'll say yes – *I want him, and I want him now!*

Tristan shakes his head at me and softly caresses my cheek. "First, I want a kiss," he murmurs, his thumb tracing my bottom lip. He slowly leans down to reach my lips, and as he does, I'm instantly overtaken by his hypnotic scent, it invades my senses again, making me lose all thoughts.

Then softly, and slowly, his lips meet mine – All the worries, the anxiety, and the fears I've had over the past week, simply disappear as his warm lips brush tenderly against mine.

I close my eyes and surrender to it.

"Tristan," I whisper against his lips. *I'm so glad he's home.*

"Missed you," he whispers against my lips.

"I've missed you too," I answer softly, tears pooling in my eyes – *Fucks sake!*

"Hey." He gently wipes a stray tear away. I shake my head and laugh at myself. "That's better," he coos.

I smile up at him, but as we stand gazing at one another, I'm suddenly gripped with the fear that Susannah may have seen us – *We need to get out of the public eye!*

"What's wrong?" he asks, taking my free hand in his and squeezing it tight.

I shake my head, I can't tell him about Susannah, not yet. "I just want to get you home, so I can have you all to myself," I tell him.

"Ditto," he breathes leaning down for another kiss.

I smile against his lips. "You really have missed me," I say, wrapping my arms around his neck.

"More than you will ever know," he answers softly, embracing me tightly. Then he pulls back, and we smile broadly at each other like two loved-up fools. "Come on," he says and picking up the present, he tugs on my hand, and we start walking.

I grip his hand even more tightly and hope that Susannah or any of the other secretaries aren't around to see this.

"I didn't think you'd be back this early?" I say. Glancing across at him - *Damn he looks too good to be true! So sexy!*

"I managed to leave early," he answers, smiling broadly at me.

"Oh!" I murmur.

"What have you got in here?" he asks, struggling a little with the awkward shape of the present.

"You'll see," I say sweetly, batting my lashes at him and wondering what his reaction is going to be.

He chuckles at my vain attempt to be flirtatious, and we head down towards the coolness of the multi-story carpark. Reaching his F-Type, he places the present in the boot of the car, then opens my door for me – *He's such a gent.*

Smiling broadly at him, I take his hand, and he helps me slip into the low seat. I watch him walk around to the driver's side, and sliding gracefully into the driver's seat, he starts the engine. I feel its low rumble vibrate beneath me. Tristan slips his aviators on, pulls out of the dark car park and heads into traffic.

Taking my hand in his, he squeezes it tight. "Do we need to stop at yours?" he asks.

I nod at him, then start giggling.

"What?" he chuckles.

I shake my head. "Nothing, I'm just really glad you're back."

He brings my hand up to his lips and kisses my knuckles. "Me too," he says.

When we reach the Marina, Tristan parks the car at the

gym, turns off the engine and comes around to help me out of the car. We walk hand in hand down the concourse, stealing glances at one another. Finally reaching my studio, I pull my keys out and unlock the patio door.

"Have you packed for the weekend? Tristan asks as we step inside.

I nod shyly at him and smile, his answering grin is infectious.

"Where are your bags gorgeous?" he asks, pulling me into him.

"Upstairs, on the bed," I whisper.

"Ok," he says. He kisses me briefly and goes to move, but I stop him. "You ok?" he questions.

I swallow hard against the lump in my throat, being back here in the studio with Tristan next to me, it all comes crashing down on me, everything that's happened this week. I shake my head and crush myself against him, my head on his chest, my arms wrapped tightly around his back. Tristan doesn't say anything, he simply wraps his arms around my shoulders, squeezing me tightly, and resting his cheek on my head. Then I feel him kiss the top of my head several times, I close my eyes and surrender to the feeling.

This is what I need, what I've missed. I sigh blissfully – *I could stay here forever.*

"Baby," he croaks, rubbing his hands across my back.

I don't want to open my eyes, but I do. "Yeah?" I croak.

"It's really hot in here," he says. I look up at him and see he's melting. His cheeks have flushed, and tiny beads of sweat have formed on his brow. Then I realise he's right; the studio has got toasty hot without the air-conditioning on.

"Oh, sorry," I chuckle and release him from the hug.

"Don't be," he laughs. "That was really nice, let's get going so we can do it again," he adds tracing a finger down my cheek.

"Ok," I giggle. I reach up, briefly kiss his lips then head up the stairs, with Tristan following.

"Now there's a site I could look at forever," he says with delicious delight.

I stop halfway up the stairs and turn to him. "What is?" I chuckle.

Tristan cocks his head to the side, leans forward and bites my right butt cheek, making me yelp in surprise.

"Tristan!" I scold in laughter.

"What? You have the most amazing ass, it's the perfect shape," he tells me.

I shake my head at him and feeling a little self-conscious, I run up the last few steps, Tristan laughs even harder as he follows me.

"Now what?" I chuckle.

"Looks even better bouncing up and down," he chuckles cheekily.

My mouth pops open in shock. I go to lightly punch his shoulder, but he grabs my wrist, twists my whole body around and pulls me into him, so my back is against his chest.

With his arms wrapped tightly around me, he leans down and whispers into my ear. "If we don't get a move on, I'm going to take you in here woman," he says, his voice low with sensual promise.

"Then do it," I challenge and lean my head back, giving him full access to my neck.

"Don't tempt me," he growls huskily and pecks my neck, then releases me.

I cross my arms and pout; I hate it when he says no.

"Hey," he softly says. "I want to, but not here ok?"

"Why?" I question.

Tristan runs a hand through his hair, he looks frustrated. "Because it's hot, I need a shower, and I'm hungry," he says, frowning down at me. "And you need to eat," he adds, his eyes full of some emotion I can't name.

"Oh," I sigh.

"Yeah, oh," he titters – I can't help it, I smile back at him.

Tristan picks up my weekend bag and the bag of lingerie. I'm so glad it's folded over so he can't see what's inside, I pick up my dress.

"What's in the bag?" he asks gesturing to what I have in my hand.

"You'll see," I smile then peck him on the lips, and head down the stairs with Tristan following me.

"Got everything?" he asks as he reaches the bottom step.

"Yep." Reaching up onto my tiptoes, I peck him on the lips again.

Tristan smiles, readjusts my bag on his shoulder and scans

the room. Suddenly his gaze stops, and his body goes rigid, I watch in horror as his face falls and his eyes darken.

"What's that?" he asks in a deep, low voice as he gestures with his chin to the alarm on the front door – *Shit! What do I say?* I don't want him to know what my real fear is, that someone broke in and I think I know who it was.

"N-nothing, one of the neighbours had a little trouble with a drunken idiot, so I got one of those," I stutter. He turns and glares at me for a moment, his cheeks have blushed red, and his eyes have gone really dark; he does not look happy – *Shit!*

"Is that an alarm?" he asks, his voice low and dark.

"Yes," I answer smartly.

Tristan closes his eyes, takes a deep breath and slowly shakes his head. I can tell he's mad, and he's trying to reign in his temper. "If there was some trouble, why didn't you go and stay at ours?" He snaps, glaring down at me, frustration rolling off him.

I sigh heavily and look up at him. "Because there are too many memories there Tristan, and I didn't want to be rattling around that big house on my own, besides I was fine," I gripe and swallow hard, I hope he can't tell I'm keeping something from him.

Tristan frowns and narrows his eyes at me, scrutinising me – *Shit!*

"I can take care of myself, Tristan!" I huff.

"I don't doubt that," he says between gritted teeth then he looks at the door again – *Great!*

"Come on," I try to usher him out the door, but I can't budge him.

"What are those?" he asks, his chin pointing towards my Eskrima sticks that are lying on the sofa.

I roll my eyes at him purposely. "Will's teaching me a new technique," I say nonchalantly. Tristan's eyes narrow as he looks back at me. "I thought you said you were hot," I add, trying to get him out of the studio before he puts two and two together.

Tristan's lips purse disapprovingly, he hesitates for a moment then turns to walk forward just as Bob comes walking through the patio door.

"Hey Bob," I smile, glad for the interruption; but he doesn't smile back at me. Instead, he makes a beeline for Tristan and shakes his hand – *That's odd!*

"You tell your fella about someone trying to get in?" he asks.

Tristan's head whips round to me. I feel my heart sink to the pit of my stomach, and all the colour drain from my face. *God damn it, Bob!*

"No Bob," I sigh in resignation – *The cat's out the bag!* "Not yet," I add.

"Oh!" Bob looks a little embarrassed. I stomp out of the studio and wait for the two of them to follow. Bob is first to step outside, he mouths 'sorry' to me as he passes me, I shrug and try to smile at him, I guess he didn't know I'd be keeping it a secret.

As Tristan follows Bob, I see he looks mad, really fucking mad, but he's hiding it well –*Oh well that's just bloody wonderful!*

With fumbling hands, I lock the patio door and turn to Bob. "See you Sunday," I tell him.

"Coral, you don't need to do that," he tells me. "Gladys is having me over," he adds.

"Oh...well, ok then. I'll see you soon." Bob smiles apologetically at me. I lean in and kiss his cheek, then turn and start walking along the Concourse, I hear Tristan's footsteps easily catching up with me.

"You weren't going to tell me?" he snaps, almost shouting. *Damn it!*

I keep my eyes forward and shake my head.

"Why not Coral?" *Oh boy, he's fuming!*

"Because I knew you'd worry," I answer, staring straight ahead.

"When we get back to the house, you're telling me everything!" He's practically bouncing from one foot to the other, he's that mad. I stop walking and glare up at him, he silently glares back at me – two angry fools neither wanting to back down.

"No-one tells me what to do Tristan! I get you're upset about it, but I'll tell you in my own damn time when I'm ready!" I shout, feeling like I want to stamp my feet.

"You should have told me' – "I'm going back to the car. Are you coming?" I interrupt. *Ok, he's seething!* – Shaking my head at him, I stomp off in the direction of the car park.

Tristan silently follows me. Reaching the car, he opens the boot and places my bags next to his. I lay my dress across the top, then he shuts the boot, we glance at one another at the same time. Tristan shakes his head, takes two quick strides and crushes me into him, squeezing me so tight, I almost can't breathe.

"I'm alright," I say trying to reassure him.

Tristan leans back and looks down at me, he places his hands either side of my cheeks and searches my face for an explanation, his expression is one of confusion. Then his eyebrows knit together, he sighs heavily and looks up over my head, as though he is searching for something when his eyes reach mine again, he frowns even harder, his eyes boring into mine.

"What's wrong?" I whisper.

He shakes his head at me, clenches his jaw and stares out to sea.

I swallow hard – *Fuck he's changed his mind about us!*

"I wish you would tell me," I say. "You know how I worry, and right now I'm thinking you're changing your mind about us. I will tell you what happened. I just didn't want you to worry at the time. Besides, you were away, and there was nothing you could have done." I end in a whisper.

Tristan's gazes down at me, his eyes still searching, he shakes his head once, then sighs heavily. "You've lost weight," he softly says, his brows still knitted together, his hands still holding my face in place.

I stare back at him in wonder. I got that wrong. I thought he was still mad about my not telling him. Then when I really look at him, I see he's lost weight too. His face looks slightly thinner, and back at the studio, I noticed his trousers were hanging a little lower.

"So have you," I answer back.

Tristan nods then smiles, my favourite cheeky grin appears, he chuckles once his dimples deepening then he frowns again. "Not as much as you. You look like you've dropped a stone in five days Coral," he admonishes.

I shrug and smile, not really much I can do about it.

"Coral, please try' – "Tristan, I can't help that I've lost my appetite!" I glare back at him. Are we really going to start fighting already, can't we at least have some more kisses and sex first?

"No…" he sighs. "I suppose you can't, I haven't had much of one myself," he says, running his thumb across my bottom lip.

My stomach muscles clench as I get a vivid image of us, naked, having hot steamy sex – *Whoa! I want him, and I want him now!*

I look down at the floor in an attempt to calm my beating heart. "We can make up for it tonight when we eat out," I tell him, but now he's here I don't want to go out and share him with the rest of the world. I want to stay inside, eat Chinese food, drink wine and have all night sex – *Yes, that's what I want* – "Or not," I snort nervously.

"No?" Tristan's fingertips pull on my chin, so I have to look up at him. He leans forward, so our lips are almost touching. My breath catches; the sheer proximity of him is enough to make my legs tremble, I instantly moisten down below.

"What do you want to do?" he asks brushing his lips softly against mine, teasing me.

I close my eyes, fully expecting him to kiss me, but he doesn't, I open my eyes and frown up at him. *Why won't he kiss me?*

"What do you want Coral?" he asks more forcefully, trying to read my expression.

"You," I gasp and tug on his open shirt, so he has no choice but to lean in. "All night long," I add panting heavily.

His lips reach mine, and I feel it right down there, instantly. I gasp against his lips, and he groans a low, deep sexy sound. His lips part, then his tongue is in my mouth, kissing me with exquisite skill. My hands knot in his hair, and I pull him harder against my lips, kissing him back, claiming him, possessing him, binding him to me...*oh, Tristan, I have missed you so...*

His arms wrap tightly around me, one around my shoulders, the other around my waist, pressing me forcefully against the length of his body. I can feel his erection growing against me – *Whoa!* – It makes we want him, instantly. I want to bed him. I want him to take me over and over until I can't take anymore. I need to get this raging, passionate feeling out of my system.

Unfortunately, we hear a bunch of kids whooping and laughing, so we quickly pull away. I look across and see they are school kids still in their uniforms. A couple of the boys start clapping and laughing as they pass us – *Not good, now I'm embarrassed.*

I smile shyly up at Tristan, my breathing heavy, blood pumping loudly in my ears. He is staring down at me.

"You want to stay in?" He pants.

"Yes." I stare up into his wide eyes that are heated and filled with desire. *Yes!*

"You don't want to go out?" he questions.

I shake my head. "No." *Screw the dress!*

"Alright," he says, measuring my expression. "But don't think you're getting away with not eating," he admonishes. "Your frame is too small," he adds, his eyes blazing.

"Ok," I whisper.

"Your word?" he growls deeply.

"Yes, I give you my word, I will stuff my face tonight," I say trying not to laugh.

"It's not funny," he tells me sternly.

"No, it's not!" I say shaking my head, still trying not to laugh.

He can't help it; his lips start to twitch as he fights to hide his smile. I bring my hands up to my mouth and try to hide the laugh bursts out of me.

He shakes his head in mock horror. "You are so frustrating," he sighs, pulling me against the length of his body again, holding me tight. I close my eyes and breathe in his scent. "But you have enchanted me, Coral Stevens," he whispers. "I am under your spell, and I have missed you so." *Oh, Tristan!*

"I'm under your spell too Tristan," I whisper back.

He pulls back and gazes adoringly at me. "Let's go," he softly says, taking my hand in his.

CHAPTER NINETEEN

TRISTAN BRINGS THE car to a stop outside his house. Stepping out of the car and walking around to my side, he leans down and gives me his hand. Taking hold of it, Tristan pulls me with such a force that I almost fall to the floor, I scream with delight as he catches me in time. Shutting the car door and pushing me against it, he presses the length of his body against mine. I can feel his erection digging into my belly, the hard sinew of the muscles in his lean legs, his toned chest pushing against my breasts.

"I want you," he growls huskily and kisses me hard. I have to fight the urge to wrap my legs around him, undo his zipper and have him take me there and then.

"Then take me, here…now," I challenge.

"No," he growls sexily, running his hands through my hair – It feels so good now it's out of the bun. Grasping my hand in his, Tristan marches to the front door, unlocks it, pulls me inside, slams the door shut with his foot, punches in the code for the alarm, then turns to me with dark, devilish eyes.

Butterflies start zooming around my stomach like spitfires in an air battle. Tristan walks over to the breakfast bar, removes his jacket and hangs it across the bar stool. Then, reaching into his jacket, he pulls out his wallet, opens it up and takes out a condom.

Then he slowly turns and smiles back at me with such a dirty, sexy smile, I feel a frisson of excitement tingle throughout my body. He starts waggling the condom in his hand as he slowly saunters towards me, his look heated and sexy as hell…*holy crap!*

I tremble inside, god I want him so badly. I throw my

handbag on the floor, just as Tristan pulls me into his arms and his mouth swoops down on mine, kissing me hard. He pushes me up against the wall with his one hand, while the other shoves the condom in his trouser pocket.

I kiss him back with all the burning passion that's been building up for the past five days, our tongues passionately lash against one another. I moan and whimper as he continues to kiss me, he growls in response, a low sexy sound. Then quickly stripping him of his shirt and tie, I lift my arms so he can get rid of my blouse, followed swiftly by my bra.

Taking my breasts in his hands he stares down at them in awe, sucking each of my nipples, in turn, my head falls back as I cry out with longing – *Has it only been five days?*

"God I've missed you," he breathes, echoing my thoughts.

Falling to his knees, he opens the button on my trousers and gazing up at me, he slowly pulls down the zip. "What do we have here?" he teases, pulling my trousers further down, past my pelvic bone, across my backside, revealing a pair of my new black lacy thongs.

He looks up at me, with appreciation written all over his face. "Very nice," he says his voice all deep and husky. *Damn his voice is so fucking sexy!*

My stomach flips and everything south of my waist clenches in delicious anticipation. My lips part, I am panting with want and need. Tristan suddenly stands up, takes a step back, crosses his arms and just stands there, admiring me.

"Tristan!" I scold – *You can't just stop like that!*

He smiles a sexy smile at me, his eyes blazing, then slowly, he sinks down and unties his shiny shoes, not taking his eyes off mine the whole time. Taking off his shoes, he then yanks off his socks and stands. His eyes smoulder as he drinks me in, then stepping towards me, he kneels in front of me again and takes my wedges off, one at a time.

Then he quickly strips me of my work trousers leaving my knickers in place and stands, we take a second to gaze at one another in appreciation. Stepping forward, I lean my forehead against his chest, inhaling his scent, then I snap open the belt on his trousers.

Opening the top button and pulling down the zip, I plunge

my hand inside his boxers, his erection feels hot and heavy in my hand as I gently tease him.

"Christ..." Tristan's head falls back slightly, his mouth gapes open as his eyes close in response. It makes me want him instantly. I yank his trousers down with his boxers, so they slide freely down his legs. Tristan steps back, so he's free of his clothing, then taking him by surprise I fall to my knees and take him in my mouth.

"Coral!" he gasps. *Oh, I want this, I've missed this.*

"No baby," he protests. "I want to be in you, come on," he hisses between his teeth as I take him deeper, sucking harder. "Coral!" He admonishes.

I take one last suck and stop, but keep him in my hand, teasing him still. I gaze up at him trying to look all innocent and bat my lashes at him, then smile. He shakes his head in frustration, or joy, I'm not sure which and pulls me to my feet. Then, reaching down he takes the condom out of his trouser pocket and taking me by the hand he silently walks me over to the large u shaped sofa.

"Take a seat," he says. "On the edge," he adds.

I smile up at him and slowly sit, with my knees pressed together, so that my backside is the only thing on the sofa. Kneeling in front of me, he places his hands on my knees, leans forward and softly kisses me, he's so seductive – *I never had a prayer of avoiding this man, I realise that now!*

His hands slide to the back of my knees, and he yanks my legs apart, it makes me gasp aloud, he's turning me on, big time. He starts a trail of soft, wet kisses along my inner right thigh, stopping when he reaches my sex...*no, don't stop!*

Then he does the same with the other leg, teasing and taunting me until he's right there again. He smiles up at me with his most sexy smile – *I would walk over hot coals for that smile.*

"I don't think we'll be needing these," he croaks in that sexy voice. "Lie back baby," he adds, so I do. He slowly peels my knickers off me. "Oh I do approve Miss Stevens," he teases. "Very sexy choice." My heart leaps with joy...*he likes them...*oh, I hope he likes everything else I bought.

Then his mouth is on me, in me. I cry out in response, and hiss at the contact, it seems like it's been so long. "Tristan," I moan breathlessly as he sucks and flicks his tongue across, and up and down my clitoris, and I'm building…so quickly…*oh crap!*

Then I feel him slip a finger inside me, pulling in and out…*oh god*…then another finger, as his tongue continues to do its dirty work, and I can't hold on any longer.

"Tristan!" I mewl.

My eyes close, my head cranes back and my body bows as I erupt, like a volcano, hard and fast, squeezing relentlessly against his fingers that are still inside me, as the most mind-blowing orgasm rips through me. I cry out a garbled version of his name as I try to reign in my shattered thoughts, I feel like I've left my body again.

"Oh baby, you never fail to amaze me." I hear him rip the foil off the condom packet, and feel his erection there, against my sex. "Open your eyes baby," he softly demands.

In my hazy state, I manage to blink both eyes open. He's leaning over me, his weight resting on his forearms.

"Do you have any idea what you mean to me?" he questions. His eyes darkening, burning into mine with an intensity I haven't seen before; it makes me catch my breath.

"No," I whisper.

He leans his forehead against mine, his eyes boring into me. "You are everything to me…everything," he breathes.

"Tristan," I whisper and softly stroke his face. Then suddenly he moves again, leans down and plants a soft, gentle kiss on my clitoris.

"Ah," I cry out. I'm too sensitive there now.

He slowly traces soft kisses up my belly, as his hands squeeze my breasts and tease my nipples. Then he trails kisses up my neck, nibbles my earlobe, then sends soft kisses across my cheek until he reaches my lips. They part automatically for his tongue to reach mine, but Tristan hovers above me, staring down at me with that same intensity like he can see right down to my dark, twisted soul.

I feel his hands leave my breasts, his eyes do not leave mine the whole time, and taking my face in his hands, he moves forward, and I feel his hot, heavy length enter me, inch by inch, slowly filling me up. His tongue softly licks my bottom lip as I gaze up at him in awestruck wonder.

Taking both my hands in one of his, he pushes them up

above my head...*whoa that feels sexy*...then he starts to move, slow at first, in and out, quickening everything inside me, his other hand is skimming up and down my body, sending tingles in every direction. Then he really starts to move, faster and faster, and I feel it build so quickly, that there's nothing I can do to stop it, to slow it down.

I feel like my insides are exploding as I come hard, screaming his name. "Tristan!" I screech as the most amazing orgasm rips through me.

"Oh baby," he pants. "You fit me like a glove." He thrusts into me, twice, three times, then stills as his orgasm ripples through him.

He sinks down on top of me, his head buried in my neck. I wrap my one arm around his shoulders, while my other hand runs through his soft hair, and I drift, basking in the glorious feeling spreading through me...

AS I LAY ACROSS Tristan's torso, catching my breath from round two on the sofa, I can't help wondering to myself if it's really possible to love somebody this much. Sighing blissfully, I stare at my fingers tracing soft circles across his chest.

"Coral?" he croaks.

"Hmm," I murmur.

"You want to tell me what happened at yours?" Tristan asks huskily. *Shit!*

I close my eyes. What the hell am I meant to say? I open them up, lean my chin on his chest and look up at his face. He's staring up at the ceiling, his eyes are dark and wide with worry.

"It was nothing Tristan," I lie.

"I wish you wouldn't do that," he gripes.

"Do what?" I ask innocently.

"Lie to me. I know you're trying to keep me from worrying about you, but you're fighting a losing battle there." Tristan moves us, so we are facing one another. I avoid eye contact and stare at his chest. "Look, I get that you have this self-protecting thing down to a T, but you can't be that strong and courageous all the time, surely?" he softly scolds.

I laugh nervously at him. Tristan takes my chin and lifts it, so I have to make eye contact with him, his look says it all – he wants to know.

"Fine!" I huff and start blurting it all out. "It was Monday night. I'd fallen asleep on the sofa when a strange noise woke me up. I looked up at the patio door, I thought for a split second it might be Bob in trouble, you know…then…well, I could see a shadow coming in from the window of the front door when I turned around someone was stood there' – "Male or female?" he interrupts.

"I…I'm not sure," I answer, hoping he can't see through me and my own suspicions.

"Go on," he urges.

I take a deep breath. "I didn't think much of it…then they tried the door handle' – Tristan's sharp intake of breath is not a good sign – 'obviously it was locked, a second later they disappeared." I break off, shivering slightly and sit up.

Tristan pulls the throw off the side and wraps it around me.

"I'm not cold," I tell him.

He cocks his head to the side and gives me a 'don't argue look' I take another breath and look out through the window.

"Has anything like that ever happened before?" he asks.

"No." I run my hands through my hair. Tristan nods once, then drifts off, trying to figure it out – *Maybe he has some suspicions of his own?*

"What did you do?" he asks me. "Please tell me you didn't open the door and follow them?" he adds in horror. I glare down at him, although, I do remember thinking about seeing who it was, I quickly quash that line of thinking.

"Do you think I have a death wish?" I gush. "Jesus Tristan, give me a little more credit than that!" I scold.

"So what did you do?" he asks.

"I called the police, and they said there wasn't anything that they could do. I hadn't been attacked, and they hadn't broken in. The woman on the line made a point of saying it could have been someone who was drunk, you know, got the wrong door."

Tristan frowns as I tell him this, but I keep going.

"And she was right Tristan, I wasn't going to freak myself out about it," I say pulling the throw tighter around me as another shiver runs down my spine.

"Of course not," he spits sarcastically. "That's why you

bought some alarms, a baseball bat and some kind of freaky weapons!" *Shit, he saw the baseball bat in my bedroom!*

"Tristan' – "Don't," he warns. "Do not sit there and try to convince me that it didn't scare you!"

I go to argue then change my mind.

He sighs heavily. "Coral," he softly says, moving closer to me as he does. "You know you don't have to be strong all the time. You should have told me' –"And what would you have done?" I snap, interrupting him. Tristan goes to answer, but I butt in. "You'd have come straight down to me, I know you would have, which meant you would have had to cancel all your meetings and end up going back next week," I add, then I think about what I've just said. "You're not going back next week are you?" I question, feeling panic-stricken.

"No, but' – "Then I'm right aren't I?" I interrupt.

Tristan shakes his head in exasperation, runs his hand through his hair and falls back onto the sofa. As he stares up at the ceiling, I silently wait for him to say something, but it doesn't come. Climbing on top of him, so we're face to face, I pull on his chin like he does with me, so he has to look at me.

"You would have come back," I repeat, knowing I'm right.

He closes his eyes and sighs heavily. "Yes," he breathes. "I most certainly would have."

"Then I'm glad I didn't tell you," I say and lean my head against his chest.

"That's not the point Coral," he argues.

"I know it's not. But how could I have assured you that I was ok, without you being the hero and coming down to rescue me when I didn't need rescuing?" I say.

"I'd have asked you to stay here, at least it's safer," he tells me sternly. "I don't like the fact that you kept it from me," he snaps.

I roll my eyes in exasperation. "But I've proved my point," I snap back.

"Not necessarily," he bites. *Grrrrrr!*

Sitting back up, I stare down at him in all his naked glory. "You know, we could argue about this till the cows come home!" As he looks up at me, I can't help the grin that starts to form. I don't know why I'm starting to find it all very funny.

"This is not funny Coral!" he barks.

"No!" I laugh sarcastically, shaking my head as I do.

"Coral!" Tristan snaps as I try to hide my tittering.

I glance across at him and see his lips are twitching too. "Oh come on! If we can't see the funny side' – "Don't make me laugh," he smiles. "I'm still mad at you!" But I know I have him, so I let the laughter burst out of me.

He leaps up, grabs hold of me and pulls me onto his lap. "You are one frustrating woman, you know that!" he growls, trying not to laugh.

"Yes!" I say, giggling uncontrollably.

Tristan shakes his head at me and starts to laugh. I feel it vibrating through me, warming my very soul. I love his laugh… and his smile…and well, all his different smiles. Wrapping my arms around his neck, he rocks me gently as we both chuckle away and I hope that Tristan doesn't really feel mad at me, I couldn't stand that.

"Hey." He pulls back to look at me sternly, all traces of humour gone. "Next time' – "Next time?" I squeak interrupting him. "I really hope there isn't a 'next time'," I shudder.

"Point is," he scolds, his eyebrow raised sardonically at me.

"I know, I'll tell you," I answer. *Thank heavens for that, we've reached a compromise!*

"Good girl." He says kissing my forehead – I freeze in his arms. *Oh no! He's said it, one of my worst triggers - This is what I was afraid of!*

They come at me full force, the frightening memories, I try to push them away, but they darken and cloud my vision. I'm a child again, and he's inside me, and he won't stop, and he keeps telling me I'm a good girl. *And I can't get him to stop!* All the hairs on the back of my neck stand on end and my stomach rolls.

"Coral?" he says, his stature freezing underneath me.

I bring my hand to my mouth trying to stop the sickly feeling, but I know it's too late, I can feel the swishing of saliva that comes right before you throw up.

"Coral? What's wrong?" He says, looking extremely worried.

I scramble out of his arms, run full pelt to the kitchen sink, and I'm violently sick. Tristan is next to me in no time at all, holding my hair back for me, and turning on the tap. When my stomach is empty, and all I'm doing is dry-retching, I cough and spit trying to get some air into my lungs so I can speak to him, he needs to know – *He can't ever say those words to me!*

"Would you like some water?" he asks, his voice low and sombre.

I nod vigorously as I rinse my mouth out. In my peripheral vision, I see him trying to hand me a towel. "Here baby." I take it off him and dry my mouth.

Standing up tall, I take the glass of water from him and glug it all back – *Yuck, my stomach feels like it's full of battery acid.*

"Baby, you didn't have to tell me if it was going to upset you this much," Tristan softly says.

I shake my head, squeeze my eyes shut for a second, and take a deep, steadying breath. "Tristan, you can't ever say that to me," I say hoarsely, my throat feeling burned.

He frowns back at me in confusion. "Say what?" he asks a little bemused.

I swallow hard. I can't even bring myself to say it out loud, the memories it brings back are too horrific. I close my eyes and shake my head in a vain attempt to stop any visions forming in my mind.

"What you just said when you kissed me," I whisper, opening my eyes.

Tristan cocks his head to the side, his face contorted as he tries to figure it out. Then his face falls as the penny drops, he swallows hard. "Why?" he questions, his face going pale.

"Just…please, I'm begging you don't say it to me again." I choke, staring up into his wide, worried eyes, mentally pleading with him to drop it.

He frowns deeply at me and takes a step back. I can see the frustration, see the anger starting to dwell inside him, he runs his hands through his hair then shakes his head at me.

"No," he answers, crossing his arms.

"What?" I squeak – *He has to drop this!*

"I'm not going to just let this lie Coral. Why can't I say that to you?" He asks.

I clench my teeth in anger. I feel like screaming at him. I can't believe he is questioning me about this, we are stark naked in the kitchen for god's sake!

I stomp past him, back into the living room, and grab the

throw. Wrapping it around me, I walk back through the kitchen towards the stairs.

"Where are you going?" he barks as he starts to follow me.

"Upstairs, I need my Gaviscon out of my bag!" I shout back, my stomach rolling again.

"Coral!" Tristan shouts, reaching out he grabs me by the arm, instantly stopping me. "Your bags are still in the car." He states.

Feeling frustrated, I yank my arm out of his hold and stomp towards the front door.

Tristan reaches me again, and steps in front of me. "Baby?"

I instantly freeze. "Please move," I tremble, feeling nauseous. *I really need that Gaviscon!*

Sighing heavily, he reaches out to me, I take a step back from him. I don't want him to touch me right now. "Please… don't…don't touch me," I croak, keeping my eyes to the floor.

"Jesus fucking Christ Coral! What happened to you?" he bawls.

I shake my head and cower away from him.

"Coral!" he shouts, frustrated.

"No!" I shout back, and with trembling legs, I walk over to the sofa, curl up into a ball, and hide my head under the throw, so I don't have to look at him.

"Fuck!" I hear him hiss. Then I hear the front door opening, a few moments later I feel Tristan take my hand and place something in it, looking down I see the bottle of Gaviscon.

"Thanks," I whimper.

Opening the bottle, I take two swigs of it. It instantly numbs the burning sensation, soothing my oesophagus as it makes its way down to my empty burning stomach, then I take another gulp, just to be sure it does the job.

Tristan sits on the coffee table in front of me, he's put his boxer shorts on, and he's leaning forward with his elbows resting on his knees. He has his face in his hands, and he's staring down at the floor. "I can't do this," he says, his voice trembling slightly. *What!*

I stop breathing and stare back at him with wide, terrified eyes. I feel my soul crack in two, and the newly made stitches in my heart rip open.

"What?" I whisper, my voice is barely audible. *No, no, no this isn't happening!*

He looks up at me, his expression torn. *Oh, fuck!*

"I can't keep doing this, pretending like it doesn't matter why you're the way you are. You have to let me in Coral or' – "Or what?" I whimper.

Tristan shakes his head and holds his face in his hands again – *Oh fuck…No, Tristan!*

"Tristan," I whimper. "You said you wouldn't' – "I know what I said Coral," he snaps, exasperated – I feel like I'm spiralling out of control, my hearing has gone, my head feels woozy, and my body suddenly feels numb. Yet, I'm filled with dread, I know what's coming, what I always knew would come – *Eventually!*

Finally meeting my terrified gaze, he stares back at me with wide, dark, ominous eyes. "You're leaving me no choice Coral, I don't want to lose you, and I certainly don't want to end this, but I'm not going to spend the rest of my life walking around on eggshells, constantly worrying if I'm saying or doing the wrong thing. I can't live like that…I thought I could but..." Tristan's eyes fill with tears as I stare back at him in horror. *I can't believe I'm hearing this!*

"So I'm giving you an ultimatum," he says swallowing hard. "I love you baby, more than I've ever loved anyone else," he closes his eyes in desperation. "So please, I'm begging you, tell me what happened so we can move forward, otherwise..." He slowly shakes his head.

"Otherwise?" I squeak.

"It's over…I'm done," he croaks. *No!*

I try to swallow, but I have no moisture left in my mouth. Closing my eyes, I try to push the terrifying feeling away – *This is not happening, I'm dreaming, I must be!*

I hear movement, opening my eyes I see Tristan slowly stand in front of me. "That's it then," he trembles.

"Tristan," I whimper. Reaching out, I take hold of his hand and entwine our fingers, but he stops me with his free hand and gently parts our fingertips.

"I'm sorry Coral…I can't," he chokes. *I don't understand, how did it get to this?*

My eyes fill with unshed tears. I look up at his tall, dark

stature staring down at me in complete bewilderment. *Coral! You have to tell him!*

"Tristan please...don't do this," I whimper.

He sniffs loudly, takes a deep rasping breath and finally looks down at me. "I'm sorry," he chokes out. *No!* – I watch him slowly turn, and stagger away from me.

I want to die. I'd rather be dead than lose him.

I squeeze my eyes shut, trying to block out the unbelievable pain that's lancing through me. The empty hole that was once filled with love for Tristan suddenly fills with emptiness, there's nothing but a black hole, a deep dark black hole; it fits perfectly with my dark, twisted soul. I feel so full of anger and hatred that I want to scream at the top of my lungs!

I shake my head in horror. I don't know how it got to this? *Tell him!* – I know I have no choice now if I don't want this to end, I have to tell him, I may lose him anyway, but at least I can say I tried, I have to try!

"Tristan!" I screech, hoping his retreating figure will stop. His steps falter, then he stops and slowly turns to me, his eyes hooded, his breathing matching mine. *Fuck!*

I can't believe I'm about to tell him this. I feel so sick, and my throat feels so dry, I'm not sure I'll get the words out.

"Ok," I croak closing my eyes. "I'll tell you, but can I please have a glass of water?" I hear Tristan's footsteps patter across the tiled kitchen floor.

You can do this! I repeat to myself over, and over again.

I jump in shock when Tristan takes my hand, I hadn't heard him reach me. I open my eyes, he places the glass of water in my hand and sits on the coffee table opposite me.

I take several gulps. *You can do this!*

"I hate you for this," I mumble and take a deep breath. I know I can't look at him while I get this out, so I fix my stare blankly ahead and begin.

"When my Dad left, and Kelly died, it was just my Mom and me." I take a breath and blow it out slowly. *I don't want to remember!*

"She…did I tell you she was a nurse?" I ask glancing across at him. Tristan silently nods his head at me then stares at the floor.

I fix my gaze on the fireplace. "She worked a lot of shifts, so the lady next door would take care of me," I say. I feel numb like I'm not in my own body like someone else is telling the story, I take another deep breath.

"You see, it wasn't long between my Dad leaving and Mom quitting work, so the babysitting only went on for about six months. I didn't know that back then my Mom was already dependant on prescription drugs," I take another drink of water.

"And I didn't know that she'd become an alcoholic, I guess that's why she became so abusive towards me. She would have violent mood swings, her behaviour became more and more erratic, and sometimes I would find her curled up in a ball rocking herself, constantly mumbling' – "How old were you?" Tristan softly interrupts.

When I look up at him, we lock eyes for a second. "Five, I guess."

Tristan's jaw clenches. "Go on baby," he softly encourages.

I stare back at the fireplace. "So the nice lady next door used to look after me, they had a son that was my age called Martin, we became really good friends, and his Mom was great…you know, just one of those women that were a natural at it, born to be a Mom." I take a drink of water and swallow hard. "I think she knew something was wrong, that my Mom wasn't taking proper care of me. I was always so hungry when she'd come around to pick me up. Then shortly after that, they upped and left, I don't know why I was too young to know I guess…" I take another breath.

"But for some reason, I remember this day so clearly. It was a Sunday, My mom was going to cook my favourite meal, a beef casserole with dumplings because she was having a 'good day', which I found out many years later, meant she was high. The lady next door came around that day and gave my mom the news that they were leaving. When she left the house, my mom started freaking out at me, trying to hit me and blaming me for it. I remember she was furious because she'd got to find another babysitter. So she leaves the house, slamming the door behind her, and I'm left alone. It's night time, the house is dark, I'm tired, and scared and hungry, and I have no idea if she's coming back," I take another drink.

"I don't know what time she returned, but I was asleep upstairs. I was woken up by the music playing downstairs, and the noise of many people, laughing and joking. I remember her coming up the stairs, falling over god knows how many times as she did, and she tells me to come downstairs because she's found me a new babysitter…" My hands start to shake uncontrollably, the water sloshing about in the glass giving me away.

Reaching out Tristan gently takes the glass out of my trembling hands. I close my eyes and try to push the images away. I pull my legs up to my chest and wrap my arms around myself.

"So I follow my Mom down the stairs, she staggers into the living room, and I follow her in. There are adults everywhere, on the floor, against the wall, on the sofa, I can hear them in the kitchen too, and they are naked….there are naked bodies everywhere. My mom shouts to some woman who looks up and smiles at me, then my mom passes out on top of some naked guy."

"So the woman comes over to me and tells me she's my new babysitter, she smelt so bad, of stale booze and cigarettes, and she had really nasty yellow teeth and a deep rasping cough. This went on several times, my mom would go to work, at least I think she was at work, and the babysitter would come around with a bunch of her friends. I didn't know what they were doing, she always sent me to my room, but there was always loud music playing, and I could smell a funny smoke coming up the stairs, and they were always noisy, in and out of the kitchen," I glance across at Tristan. "They were getting pissed, smoking crack and weed, and having orgies."

Tristan looks horrified. I stare back at the fireplace and try to control the sickening feeling in the pit of my stomach. "Not ideal for a babysitter right, but what harm were they doing?" I close my eyes again.

"Anyway, this one night I was woken up by the noise, so I crept downstairs to peep into the living room, I wanted to see if my mom was home because whenever she came back from work, she would join in with them, she'd stopped bothering with me altogether. But I still loved her, she was my mom, I was a kid…" I take a moment because I can hear how badly my voice is trembling.

"That night a man caught me watching, I thought I would be told off and taken back to up to my room, but he just stood there completely naked in the doorway, I hadn't seen him before. He called back to everyone in the room, some looked up at me others didn't. He smiled down at me and held his hand out. I didn't know if I should take it. My dad had at least taught me not to speak to strangers, but he knelt down and started talking to me, he asked me my name and stroked my hair, he told me I had pretty eyes and that he liked my pretty white dress that I still had on. My dad always used to say that I had pretty eyes, so I thought he was ok…you know. When you're a kid, you don't know any better…but that was the first night I was sexually abused."

I hear Tristan's sharp intake of breath. I lie down on the sofa, curl up into a ball, and wrapping the throw even tighter around me, I continue.

"I don't know how many times it happened in those six months. And I haven't worn a dress since, except for Debs' wedding. George said I repressed the memories of it, but I still get flashbacks. I remember his hairy chest, his nasty smell, and how he would always be telling me 'good girl' when I did what he asked.

"At first it was just him, then this other guy started joining in, then the babysitter bought a camera in, and they would film it. George said they were probably a paedophile ring. I remember once they brought a boy over and made me do it with him. He was so scared, but I told him to 'do what they say, or they hit you hard' – In my peripheral vision, I see Tristan's hands ball into fists. "They hurt me so badly sometimes that I wouldn't stop bleeding. I knew how to turn the shower on so I would stay under it until the blood stopped, I didn't want to bleed on my bed-sheets. I was so scared that my Mom would find out, and completely lose it with me because I thought *I* was the one in the wrong, I thought *I* must have done something wrong for them to be doing this to me.

"I used to cry out at first, tell them to stop, but that just made them angry and physically abusive. So I found a way of blocking it all out so whenever they would start on me, I would just go numb as though I wasn't even there. It all stopped when my mom was put on psychiatric leave, she was supposed to be seeing a shrink, but she didn't, she just faded away. Sometimes she would sleep for days on end, no doubt knocked out by the concoction of drugs she was taking. I was so hungry and scared. I wanted to call my dad, but I didn't know his number.

"Then one day, I woke up feeling really ill. I was sick, I needed my mom, but she wouldn't wake up. She'd been like that for a couple of days, so I went downstairs picked up the phone and dialled 999. I remember the lady that answered had a kind voice, she talked to me until the police and the ambulance came. I can remember the policeman trying to pick me up, but I didn't want them to touch me." I swallow hard, remembering it vividly. "I screamed the place down, but they just grabbed me, and we all left the house. They took my mom away, and I lived with my Nan for a while until Gladys adopted me," I say numbly.

I close my eyes, feeling completely drained, mentally, physically, emotionally, metaphysically; just like I did when I told George. "Tristan," I mumble sleepily. "Are you going to leave me now?"

I feel him take my hand in his and squeeze tightly. "No," he trembles. I feel him kiss my temple. "Never," he adds – I exhale in relief like I've been holding my breath the whole time.

"Ok," I mumble. He tightens his grip, almost to the point of pain. "If you want to talk to George, his number's in my mobile. The lock code is 1987, it's the year I moved in with Gladys."

Tristan doesn't say anything, but I hear him sniff.

"I need to sleep now Tristan," I tell him keeping my eyes closed. I hear him move, I feel his breathe on my face as he gently kisses my temple again.

"Ok baby," he whispers. "Sleep as long as you want, I'll be here when you wake up." I feel my heart stutter madly against my chest – *He's staying, thank-god he's staying!*

Sighing heavily, I let the darkness take over, and I drift away into unconsciousness...

WHEN I WAKE, the first thing I notice is that it's gone dark outside. The only light is from the glow of the fire, the rest of the house is in darkness. I sit up slowly, feeling dazed and confused, looking down I see I have a quilt draped across me. *Tristan!* My eyes search the living room and the kitchen, but he's nowhere to be seen.

"Tristan?" I call out, but I get no answer. I need to find him. Standing up quickly, I wobble slightly, so I take a second to let my blood pressure adjust. My stomach growls loudly at me, but I ignore it.

I see my knickers on the floor, reaching down I pull them on, then I spy Tristan's work shirt. I pick it up and inhale his scent, it's still as potent. Slipping it on and doing up the buttons, I pad quietly into the kitchen. Looking around, I see my handbag on the kitchen table, with my mobile sitting next to it. I wonder if Tristan has spoken to George?–*I have to find him. I need to know we are still ok!*

Walking through the kitchen to the hallway, I call up the stairs for him, but I get no reply, and with all the lights off, the house suddenly feels dark and eerie. As I go to turn around, I suddenly realise the real reason why I didn't want to be here without Tristan. I don't like being in big houses on my own, there are too many rooms, it reminds me of my childhood, of being in that house alone. A shiver runs down my spine, I actually feel a little scared – *I need Tristan, and I need him now!*

Running back through the kitchen and into the living room, I pull the throw off the sofa and wrap it around me, I decide to check his office first. Flinging the door open, I see the lights are all off, not in here. Dashing down the stairs to the basement, my steps falter as I hear some kind of music playing, it's haunting and makes me slow my pace down.

Padding along the hallway, I follow the sound of the music and come to a stop at the cinema room. The door is cracked open, and peeking through I see such a sad vision before me. Tristan is sat on the sofa, soft lighting illuminating the room, the woman, whoever she is, is singing a haunting melody around him; it sounds like opera. He has a large glass of amber liquid in his hand, and I can see he's been training, his t-shirt is soaked with sweat, and he still has a towel wrapped around his neck.

I watch him take a drink then wipe the sweat from his brow, but it's his haunted look that worries me, his expression is so… so sad. He looks so lonely as he sits there sipping his drink… *Oh, Tristan!*

CHAPTER TWENTY

Hesitantly stepping forward, I push the door open, and as I do, I see he's on his mobile. I didn't realise, so I go to turn around, leave him to it, but his head snaps up, and our eyes meet, they look dark and broody. As I look closer, I see the rims of his eyes look a little red like he's been crying –*Oh no! Tristan!*

As he gazes up at me, his eyes take on a warm, melting, lighter shade of brown. He puts down his drink and holds out his hand to me as he continues to listen. "Yes...I understand..." he says.

I tentatively walk towards him, then reach out and place my hand in his. Tristan tugs me forward and pulls me onto his lap. He wraps his free arm around my waist and squeezes me tightly against his body. I cradle my head under his jaw and inhale his scent – Even his sweat smells good. I sigh inwardly and close my eyes – *He hasn't gone!*

"Can we continue this later?" He asks and listens for a moment. "Yes, she's woken up." My eyes dart open. "Thank you, George." Tristan hangs up and puts his mobile down on the table. "Hey," he croaks, wrapping his other arm around me, squeezing me tight.

I close my eyes again and surrender to the safety of his arms. "Who's this?" I ask.

"What?" he asks, bemused.

"Singing?" I whisper.

"Oh...it's called Lovers, by Kathleen Battle," he tells me.

"It's beautiful...and kind of sad," I say.

"I thought you'd be out all night," he says, kissing my hair.

"I'm sorry I wasn't next to you when you woke like I said I would be, but I wanted to speak to George, and I was afraid I'd wake you."

For some reason, I feel shy again like I did when we first met. I don't know what to say to him. I wrap my arms around his body and squeeze him tight. I don't want to move, I don't want to let go.

"Baby?" He prompts.

"Hmm?" I answer, snuggling even more into his body.

"You don't want to talk?" he guesses. I shake my head. "Ok. Hungry, thirsty? What do you need baby?" he asks.

I open my eyes and tilt my head back. "You," I whisper. "Are the most wonderful man I have ever met," I tremble, softly touching his cheek with my fingertips.

"You're cold," Tristan says. Grasping my fingertips between his warm hand, he gently blows on them to warm them up... *oh, he is so sweet...*

I shake my head. "I don't feel cold," I dither. *Ok, maybe I am, I probably need food.*

Tristan leans down and gently kisses my lips.

"You've been working out?" I question.

"Yes." I see his pupils dilate.

"You were angry," I guess.

"Yes." Tristan blinks a couple of times at me.

"And sad," I say tracing my forefinger under his eye.

"Yes," he croaks.

"Don't be sad for me baby," I whisper.

Tristan turns his face away from me, clenches his jaw and shakes his head in frustration. "Kind of hard not being sad, now I know what...what happened to you," he answers looking back at me. I take a deep breath and exhale. *What do I say to that?* If this had happened to Tristan, I would cry for him, I know I would.

"I know we have a lot to talk about," I tell him staring at his broad chest. "And I'm sure you have a lot of questions, but just for tonight, can we pretend like it didn't happen?" I ask.

Tristan smiles at me, but it doesn't reach his eyes. "Baby, we can do whatever you want," he tells me, leaning down and kissing my forehead.

"I did warn you," I tell him, remembering how I pleaded with him to stop pursuing the subject, and me.

"That you did." He answers.

"I guess we're not eating out tonight," I chuckle.

"Seriously! You're laughing?" He chokes.

I frown back at him. "Um...yeah," I mumble. Then it hits me – *Tristan needs time, time to process what I've told him.*

"Sorry," I mumble apologetically. "I guess it's all just so fresh to you, I've had it forever...." I stare back at him. He's broody again, which I guess is understandable. "I did something very brave," I tell him proudly, trying to pull him out of it.

"You did?" He questions, his brows knitted together.

"Yes, I bought a dress," I say smiling broadly. Tristan's face falls, his eyes darkening. "George told you," I guess.

"Yes," he whispers, his voice breaking slightly.

"So now you know why I wouldn't wear dresses?" I whisper back.

"Yes." He swallows hard.

"And why I have Hypnotherapy to fix it?" I add.

"Yes, and for what it's worth, I think you're the bravest person I have ever met. But you don't need to do that for me baby' I place my fingers across his lips. "I'm not, well I am, it's complicated," I croak.

"I'm all ears baby if you want to say," he softly says.

I gaze back at him, debating. Oh well, it's not like I need to hold back anymore. The worst is over, yet here I am, wrapped up in his arms.

I nod and start speed talking. "When I met you, it wasn't something I would have even considered Tristan, but you brought me out of my shell, out of the safe little bubble I'd placed myself in. George has been trying for ages to get me to work on it with him, but I kept telling him I was fine, happy with the way things were. Of course, I was in denial," I laugh, Tristan frowns again.

"I wanted to look nice and sexy for you, but I started to realise that I'd been holding *myself* back, by blocking it out instead of taking a risk, and taking the steps I needed to get better. I realised I didn't just want it for you, I wanted it for me too. I want to feel feminine and sexy, but most of all, I want the freedom to wear whatever I want, whenever I want to, without freaking out about it. Does that make sense?" I breathe.

Tristan pulls me into him and kisses my cheek. "You're so sweet baby," he kisses me again. "And yes, it makes sense," he adds.

Feeling thirsty I lean forward, pick up Tristan's glass and take a sip, instantly wishing that I hadn't, the Brandy burns like crazy.

Pulling a face, he takes it off me and puts it on the table. "Not going down well?" he surmises.

"No," I wince. Then I remember my initial fear about telling Tristan. That once he knows, he won't want me the same way, won't look at me like he used to.

I stare down at the floor – *I wonder if he still feels the same about me?*

"What is it?" he asks, lifting my chin with his fingers.

I gaze back at him trying to read his reaction to me. "I...I had my reasons for not telling you about my past," I whisper.

"I know baby, you told me. You were afraid to lose me," he answers.

I shake my head. "No, I was afraid you wouldn't want me anymore...I mean sexually...I was afraid I'd never see you look at me again with the same intense, passionate, burning look in your eyes. It would kill me if that were gone," I mumble.

"Well it's not gone," he tells me firmly, and I can see a flicker of it burning behind the sadness in his eyes. "I'll always want you like that Coral, we just need to sit down and talk about the dos and don'ts, so I don't fuck up, in or out of the bedroom."

I take his gorgeous face in my hands and kiss his full, warm lips, trying to reassure him.

"You won't, I know you won't. Besides you already know them, don't say, good girl, no tickling, no cameras in the bedroom, and well...you don't have a hairy chest so..." I close my eyes for a moment, trying not to remember.

Tristan nods then drifts off again.

"I don't like people touching me that I don't know," I whisper.

Tristan's body stiffens, so I stop talking. *Do I really want him to know the depravity of it all?*

"Can I ask you something?" He asks wearily. I nod in reply.

"George said…the first time you were abused, you were in a dress?" he says with difficulty.

"Yes," I whisper. "My favourite dress," I add.

"What happens when you put one on?" He questions. I squeeze my eyes shut. "Shit, Coral I'm sorry you don't have to…" He stops and sighs heavily.

I open my eyes, take a deep breath and blurt it out.

"I feel…well I kind of…it starts with trembling like my body is going into freefall. I feel faint and nauseous, but the worse part about it is the vulnerability. Like…I just feel exposed, like…like any man could slip his hand under my dress and…" I break off and look up at Tristan; he looks like he's going to throw up. "Tristan, I'm so glad you know, at least you can share it with me as I try to get better, and hold my hand through it all."

Tristan takes my hand in his and tenderly kisses the back of it. "Always," he softly whispers.

My heart melts, I think about making a move, then I remember we can't as there are no condoms, my heart sinks just thinking about it, that's something else I need to tell him.

Sighing heavily, I gaze back at Tristan, debating again.

"I was thinking," I tell him nervously.

"That's dangerous!" He softly teases, smiling boyishly at me.

"Tristan!" I scold, playfully slapping his shoulder, but I'm glad he's got his sense of humour back, it would kill me if he were all moody and depressed about what he now knows.

"I'm sorry. Please continue," he says, tucking my hair that's fallen against my cheek behind my ear. It's such a sweet gesture. "I'm really am sorry," he says. "Now is not the time for laughter," he adds, his hand gently rubbing up and down my back – It's so soothing.

I swallow hard and look up at him – *Come on Coral!*

"Well, I thought I should tell you that I don't like condoms," I whisper. Which I don't, can't stand the things, but I'm dodging the issue here, I know I am.

Tristan frowns down at me, his hand stilling on my back. "Ok," he says warily.

I look away from his eyes and stare at his chest. *Come on Coral be brave!*

"We don't have to use them," I whisper nervously, keeping my eyes fixed ahead.

"No?" He questions. "You...you want to try for a kid?" he asks a little hesitantly.

"No." I laugh nervously, glancing up at him and fixing my eyes on his chest again.

"You want to use another form of protection?" he questions quizzically.

"I can't conceive," I croak, swallowing hard against the lump that's formed.

Tristan's frame goes rigid. He takes my face in his hands and brushes my cheeks with his thumbs. "How do you know that?" he asks softly, his eyes searching mine.

I chicken out again, and close my eyes, I'm not sure if either of us can take much more.

"Coral, look at me baby," his calm voice commands. I open my eyes and look up into his warm, soulful eyes. "How do you know?" he asks again.

"How do you think?" I tremble.

Tristan's eyes widen with horror as he adds it all up.

"I'm sorry," I sniff, trying not to cry. "I should have told you when we talked about it, but I chickened out. I was so afraid you'd say you wanted children and because I can't, I thought I'd lose you."

Tristan sighs heavily, closes his eyes and rests his forehead against mine. "You're not going to lose me," he tells me firmly, opening his eyes as he does. "Baby, I told you before, and I'll tell you again. You have me darling, and I want you to be my wife, kids or no kids. I want to marry you, and I want you to feel proud to call me your husband." *Oh, Tristan!*

"Are you sure though, have you had any tests done?" he softly adds.

I nod my head at him. "Two years ago, after..." I stop, and we both look away from one another, then I take another deep breath and continue.

"I went to the clinic, used a false name, I had to make sure I was ok, that I hadn't caught anything from *him*. The gynaecologist that examined me was concerned, he said I showed massive internal scaring, he...he questioned me about it, of course, you know me, I wouldn't give anything up, but I was concerned, you know. So I made an appointment with the nurse, told her very briefly that I was abused as a child and asked if it would affect me having children. She said in most cases it's psychological problems that actually prevent the woman from conceiving, but you know me, I stamped my feet and demanded an internal scan." I squint as I remember the internal examination.

"They examined me, scanned me and took x-rays." I stare down at my twisted fingers. "The doctor told me that he's never seen internal scarring like it." I feel the tears start bubbling up to the surface, my vision becoming more blurry. "He said my chances were one in a million of conceiving, and that if I wanted children, I should look into adoption." I sniff loudly, and swipe at the silent tears, feeling angry that I'm crying again.

"It's not so much I can't have them because I actually think that everyone should adopt or at least foster one child. Especially when you hear about how many couples are desperate for kids and spend thousands on fertility treatment when there are millions of kids out there that are desperate for a good home, for loving parents. It's more the fact that they took that option away from me you know, that's the part that hurts the most," I manage to croak out.

The tears start rolling down my cheeks, thick and heavy, one after the other, dropping like rainfall. I try to fight it, to get angry about it instead of tearful, but it's too late. I let out a strangled sob.

"Baby, oh baby…" Tristan crushes me into him, wrapping his arms tightly around me.

I've never allowed myself to really let it in before, what it meant to have that honour taken away from me, and for the first time in my life, I cry like I've never cried before about it.

Tristan rocks me gently, keeping his arms securely wrapped around me. "I'm so sorry baby," he whispers over and over again, which makes me cry even harder, long cathartic sobs.

I finally let it all out; everything. I cry for the father that abandoned me, for the mother that neglected and abused me, for my sister, my abusers and the guy who raped me. I cry so hard I don't think I'm going to be able to stop, it feels like it's a lifetime of unshed tears coming out in one go.

I don't know how long we sit there for, but Tristan doesn't move an inch, he just cradles me in his arms, and I fall deeper in love with him than I ever have before. And I know in that moment of complete vulnerability, that he's the one, my soul-mate; and that I'm going to marry him, sooner rather than later...

WHEN I WAKE up in our bed, the first thing I see is Tristan gazing down at me. He's sitting cross-legged next to me, and he's in his sweats and a t-shirt, looking fresh and clean. He's evidently showered as his hair is still wet, he smells divine.

Reaching down to me, he softly strokes my cheek.

"Hey beautiful," he softly says.

"Hi," I croak and close my eyes to the feeling of his hand touching me. I feel so lucky to be with such a sweet and attentive man, then I realise something. My eyes dart open. "Were you watching me sleep?" I whisper.

"Yes." He answers firmly.

"Why?" I choke incredulously.

Tristan's eyes darken, he leans down to me, his face inches from mine. "Because I wanted to," he tells me firmly. "Did you sleep ok?" He adds his voice a worried whisper.

I narrow my eyes at him. "Why would you ask that?"

Tristan's brows pull together. "You know why," he whispers – *I need to change the subject!*

I stretch out, sit up, and wrap my arms around him. "What time is it?" I whisper, staring out at the night sky.

"Half past nine," he says.

"How did I get up here?" I question, looking up at him.

"I carried you of course," he chuckles sarcastically.

I chuckle back. "What?" I say, seeing the look on his face.

"Well it was either that, or I used magic, or I have a teleporter device secretly hidden somewhere," he answers dryly.

"Oh ha, ha," I banter back. Tristan reaches out, and tenderly touches my cheek. "Thank you," I softly add.

"For what?" he asks, his eyebrows knitting together.

"Everything…" I breathe.

"Everything?" He questions, his head cocked to the side.

I nod solemnly at him.

He smiles his sweet boyish smile at me. "Want me to run you a bath?" he asks sweetly.

"Yes please, that would be nice," I say, gazing up at him.

"I'll go get it started," he says, leaning down he pecks me

on the lips, then walks across the bedroom to the bathroom. I hear the bath start to fill, and a gorgeous, sweet scent starts to fill the room, I get up off the bed and pad into the bathroom to find out what it is.

Tristan is leaning over the bath, pouring something into it. He suddenly turns and sees me watching him, feeling awkward and geeky in his work shirt, I smile shyly at him.

"Hey," I whisper. He smiles sweetly at me, then stands and walks over to me.

"I got this for you," he says passing me a large, heavy, red bottle with Champneys written across the front. "I was going to give it to you earlier…" His lips set into a hard line, and he turns away from me.

"Tristan," I pull on his hand, he turns and looks down at me with big, wide eyes. "Are you ok?" I ask.

He stares down at me for the longest time. "Getting there," he finally says.

I nod and stare down at the floor. A part of me wishes he didn't know, but the other part is glad it's over, that it's out there. I can only wait and see what he does with it.

"Thank you," I gush. "For being so patient, so kind and loving with me," I whisper.

He closes his eyes for a moment, I think in annoyance when he opens them they are blazing brightly for me. "I love you Coral, that's what you do when you love someone," he slowly tells me, as though he's speaking to a child.

I nod again, smiling shyly at him. I still can't believe that he does, but maybe, over time, I'll come to believe it.

"So this is for me?" I say lifting the bottle in my hand.

He nods solemnly at me – *He definitely needs time!*

"It smells gorgeous," I say, and turn the bottle in my hand so I can read what it says.

'Champneys Spa Indulgence, Oriental Opulence Bubble Heaven'…*ooh, I already like it* – I turn the bottle around and read the description. 'Inspired by traditional oriental recipes this wonderfully indulgent bubble heaven leaves your skin feeling soft and pampered. The oriental blend of aromatic ylang-ylang, calming sandalwood and exotic patchouli essential oils, encourage feelings of well-being and tranquillity.'

My heart melts, he really does care. *But why, I don't know?*

"Oh Tristan," I croak. "That's so sweet, thank you, baby."

He leans down to me and kisses the tip of my nose. "You," he kisses my cheek. "Are," he kisses my forehead. "Very," and lastly he kisses my lips. "Welcome."

I throw my arms around him and squeeze him tight. I have no words. At least none that would explain the depth of feeling I have for this man, I am so in love with him. I would do anything for him, anything, lay my life down for his.

"Hurry baby, your bath is nearly ready," he softly says.

"Ok," I squeak and pad over to the mirror. *Oh my god!*

I cringe with embarrassment; I cannot believe Tristan has seen me like this. *Ugh!*

My makeup is all gone, well apart from the smudged mascara, and I have red cheeks and bloodshot eyes. I quickly cleanse my face, removing all traces of makeup, clip my hair up on top of my head, and turn to Tristan, who is patiently waiting for me.

"May I?" He asks.

"What?" I say.

Tristan chuckles at me. "You still have my shirt on. I meant, may I undress you?" he says.

"Oh!" I smile up at him and nod, feeling like a complete idiot.

Tristan steps forward and starts unbuttoning his shirt when he's done, he slowly pulls the shirt across my shoulders and lets it fall to the floor, then he bends down and gently peels my knickers off me. Standing back up he smiles at me, then his eyebrows pinch together, he swallows hard, and holds his hand out to me. I place my hand in his open palm, and he gently guides me over to the bath. As I step into the warm water, I find it's the perfect temperature, he keeps hold of my hand as I slowly sink down into the bath.

I look up at Tristan and smile broadly at him. "Thank you, baby," I softly say. Releasing my hand, Tristan leans down and kisses me, then turns to walk away. "Don't leave me!" I squeak. "I don't want to be alone right now," I whimper.

"Ok," he says, turning to take my outstretched hand and squeezing it tightly. "Want me to join you?" he asks, his voice low.

"Yes," I whisper. "If you don't mind, I can see you've already showered."

Tristan smiles at me, but I can tell it's forced. I pull my legs up and wrap my arms around them as I watch the strip show… *Hmmm, yummy!*

"Don't look at me like that Coral," he scolds, slipping in behind me.

"Like what?" I breathe, turning to look at him.

"Now you *are* being obtuse," he says, frowning down at me.

"Your kind of hard not to look at you know," I huff, turning away from him. I guess he's not ready for anything like that.

"Baby, I want you too," he whispers huskily in my ear. "I just want you to eat first, ok?" *Oh!*

I swallow hard. "Ok," I whisper back, my belly clenching.

"Would you like a massage?" he asks, kissing my hair, damp from the steam.

"If you don't mind," I softly say and turn my head to look up at him.

He leans forward and softly kisses my forehead. Then his hands begin their tender massage across my shoulders, up and down my neck. As I lay my head against his broad chest and let the warm water relax my tense muscles, I can't help thinking about all that's gone on tonight. I still can't believe that he knows and he's still here. Even after telling him about not being able to conceive, he's still here.

What did I ever do to deserve this?

"I know it's trivial," Tristan says interrupting my musing. "But how did your week go? Did you enjoy spending time with Susannah?" *Damn it!*

I purse my lips together, trying to prevent any brain to mouth blurting. "Um, sure yeah, it was ok," I say lightly.

"Then why am I not convinced?" Tristan says, his hands stilling against my neck. *I was enjoying that massage!*

"Tristan," I moan petulantly. "I don't want to be talking about work right now. It's not really important in the scheme of things," I say hoping to placate him.

Tristan is silent for a moment – *Fuck!*

Then he kisses my hair and continues massaging me – *Phew!*

"You're right baby, not tonight," he softly says.

I sigh inwardly, glad for that conversation to be over. If he knew what I was up to, if he knew what Susannah has done…I close my eyes and push the anger away.

"Ok, well how about what you're going to do with the money you've been given from Gladys. Any plans?" Tristan asks, his voice sounding all deep and husky – My insides swim with desire.

"No, I'm still thinking about it," I say my mouth dry.

"Coral." Tristan pulls me to the side so we can look at one another. "Do you still want to marry me?" He asks, his expression stark.

"Yes," I gush, even though I've been so confused about it, but since tonight…and telling Tristan…I feel different about it. I really want this. I want him, always.

"Sure?" He questions. *Tristan, you have no idea how much I do!*

I nod, grinning like a fool.

"Then will you move in with me?" he asks nervously.

"Um…yeah, I suppose so…I…I haven't really thought about it," I say.

"You haven't?" He asks, a little surprised. *Shit!*

"Not really, I've had a very busy week and not much sleep and…" I gasp aloud – *I haven't given Tristan his presents!*

"What's wrong?" he asks, his hands frozen in place.

I can't believe I've forgotten about it, but then again, with what's gone on…I decide later when I'm done in the bath, I can give him them then.

"Nothing, I just remembered something. Why do you ask anyway?" I say, trying to change the subject.

Tristan sighs heavily. "Do you want to move in with me Coral?" he asks in a firmer tone.

I close my eyes and ask myself the same question – A clear, resounding yes echoes around my head. "Yes, yes Tristan I do." Leaning up, I kiss his lips.

"What do you want to do about your studio?" he asks.

"I'm not sure, keep it I think," I muse.

Tristan looks heartbroken, but he's trying to hide it. *Shit!*

"I know it sounds strange but having somewhere that's just for me, that I can go to whenever I want' – "You want an escape," he interrupts, his voice low, his eyes boring into mine.

Hit the nail on the head, again! *How does he keep doing that?*

"You feel like you'd be trapped, living here with me?" He adds.

My mouth pops open. *I wonder if that's come from George?*

"I...Tristan, I love you, more than..." I sigh heavily. "It's not you, it's me, and it's not necessarily that I'm escaping," I say, then shake my head. I'm not explaining myself very well. "I guess it's more...I don't know...that it's just for me. A place where I can just sit and be still, do my meditating and yoga and try to sort out what's going on in my head, and I have Bob too. I feel like he's my responsibility now. Besides, you know what they say 'absence makes the heart grow stronger' right?" I look up at Tristan feeling slightly guilty.

He smiles down at me, but it's off. Which begs the question, would I like it, if the person marrying me wanted to keep their own place, and the answer is no, I don't think I would.

I turn back around and stare at our naked feet.

"But I'll sell it if it makes you unhappy," I add. "I don't want to hurt you Tristan, and I don't want you to think that I love you any less because I want to keep it..." I slap my hand to my forehead. "I'm not really making much sense am I?" I shake my head in frustration.

"Coral, nobody thinks straight when they're tired," Tristan whispers into my ear. "Besides, I think it's a good idea to keep your place," he adds.

I whip my head around. "You do?" I squeak.

"Yes," he says. "It's an excellent investment, you could make a killing over the summer renting it out," he adds.

"Really?" I squeak again.

"Yes." He chuckles wrapping his arms tightly around me.

I close my eyes and surrender to the feeling. *Hmm... Investment...renting it out, I've never thought about that!*

"You are so understanding, Tristan," I whisper. "That's one of the many things I love about you," I add.

Tristan squeezes me even tighter and kisses my temple. "Made for each other," he whispers.

"Yeah...I think we are," I whisper back.

We sit quietly, both deep in thought.

After a while, the water starts to cool, so of course, I shiver. "Come on, out you get. You need food," Tristan firmly states – He's not to be argued with.

"No, I want to stay in here a little longer," I argue – Because I can.

"Coral, your body temperature is dropping because you haven't eaten," he states, running his hand through his hair, as he gently pushes me forward and steps out of the bath.

"What's wrong?" I whisper.

"I'm going to get dressed, then I'm going downstairs to order a Chinese. If you want a say in what to order, I suggest you get out the bath and meet me downstairs," he says sharply. *Ok, maybe I shouldn't be winding him up right now.*

"I don't mind what you order Tristan," I humbly answer.

He turns and glares at me –*Boy he's moody tonight!*

"But I'm getting out," I add.

Tristan storms off into the bedroom, I lay my head back against the bath. Why am I trying to wind him up when he's been so good to me, so understanding, so sweet; he deserves better. Feeling awful for being argumentative, I get out the bath, wrap a towel around me and walk into the bedroom to make amends, only when I get there, he's already gone – *Damn it!*

Stomping back into the bathroom I cream my face and put on a little make-up to try and hide my red, puffy eyes. My skin feels really soft from the bath cream, so I don't bother creaming. Hanging my towel up, I pad back into the bedroom. I quickly dress in my sweats and a vest-top, unclip my hair, run my fingers through it, and skip down the stairs to find Tristan, thinking if I give him his presents, he may cheer up. *I wonder if he'll like the idea?* I push the thought away, I'm sure he will.

Walking into the kitchen, I see Tristan opening a bottle of wine, I feel shy again, and I don't know why. "Hi," I smile shyly.

Tristan walks over to me, pulls me up against the length of his body and tenderly kisses me. "Hi." He smiles down at me. "I've ordered the Chinese," he adds.

"You're hungry," I say, realising Tristan probably hasn't eaten since lunchtime.

"Very," he says, smiling down at me. Releasing me, he walks back into the kitchen. "Would you like a glass of wine?" he asks smiling back at me, his dimples deepening.

"Yes please." I look around me and see Tristan's present propped up against the wall. Silently walking over to it, I pick it up and start walking, awkwardly, back into the kitchen.

Tristan glances up at me, he looks mad. "Coral!" He scolds. "You could hurt yourself," he admonishes, rushing over to me and taking the weight of the present.

"It's for you," I softly tell him.

"Me?" he smiles. "You've got me a present?" he says a little shyly.

"Yes," I giggle. "I'll pour the wine, you open them up."

"Ok." He smiles shyly at me again, making my heart flutter, so I kiss him lightly on the lips. Tristan picks the present up and follows me as I walk back into the kitchen, then he stops in front of the breakfast bar, by the table.

I really hope he likes them. I wasn't sure when I walked into that photography shop that they'd be able to do what I wanted. The black and white photo of Tristan's folks is really old, but they scanned the image, sharpened it up, and now it's blown up and framed, it looks really good. Just like the one of Tristan with his folks, and the one that I picked of the two of us. I watch him open the top of the large flat box and peek inside. I pour a little wine into our glasses, trying to watch what I'm doing, and watch Tristan at the same time is a trying feat.

Reaching his hand inside, he pulls the first one out. I'm glad to see he's picked the one of his Grandparents on their own first. His head whips round to me, and he just stares at me, open-mouthed – *Shit!*

I stop what I'm doing and stare back at him. I don't think he likes it. *Double crap!*

"Coral!" he gasps, swallowing hard. "When did you' – "I stole the photos out of your wallet, sorry," I whisper feeling a little guilty. "Don't worry though, the originals are upstairs, they're safe. I took good care of them," I add.

"I...I don't mind that you did that," he answers his eyes wide with surprise, his arms stretched out as he holds the frame out in front of him. "They look great," he adds, his cheeks flushing.

I walk over as quietly as I can, I don't want to spoil the moment for him, and place our glasses of wine down. After a while, Tristan turns to me with bloodshot eyes, his cheeks have flushed, and I think he's trying to choke back tears.

"Tristan!" I gasp, feeling tears bubble to the surface for him.

He opens his mouth to say something, but no words come out. Instead, he swallows hard, quickly turns, so he has his back to me, and places the frame down. I don't think he wants me to see him upset. Then I notice his body start to shake, I think he's actually crying. *Tristan!*

Without a word, I wrap my arms around his front, squeezing him tight. He places his hands on top of mine, and lets out a couple of sobs – *Oh no! I shouldn't have done this now!*

"Tristan…I'm so sorry," I say, kissing his back several times.

He chokes out another couple of loud sobs, I squeeze him tighter. "I miss them…" He manages to choke out, gripping my arms tightly.

"I know baby, I know…" I want to take his pain away, I hate that he's going through this. My heart constricts for him, but I don't move because I think he needs this, so I hold him for the longest time.

After a while, he seems to gather himself together again. He squeezes my hand, sniffs once, then slowly turns to face me, he takes a deep breath and slowly blows it out. "I'm sorry," he whispers, placing his hand on my cheek.

I instantly think of George's words – 'crying is a release' – I shake my head at him, and reaching up, I place my hands on his cheeks. "Tristan, I'll always be here for you, to comfort you. You know that right?"

His jaw clenches. "Yes," he whispers.

"Then whatever you do, do not be sorry. If you ever feel like crying and letting it all out, then please…come to me, I'll comfort you, hold your hand…whatever you need," I whisper. "You don't have to be strong all the time either," I add.

He squeezes his eyes shut for a second when he opens them, they are blazing brightly. "God I love you," he breathes, as he picks me up, and wraps his arms tightly around me, burying his face in my neck. "T-thank you Coral," he chokes out.

"Here for you, always," I whisper as I wrap my arms around his shoulders, and hug him tightly.

We stay like that for what seems like a long time. I finally come to the startling realisation that through losing his folks, and now grieving for them, he's had no-one to comfort him, no-one to hold him, no-one to kiss it better and make him feel safe, loved, cherished, which just makes me love him even more. And I fall in love, all over again, for this brilliant, sweet, heart-broken man.

Tristan finally lifts his head. I take his face in my hands and kiss his lips lightly, as I gaze at his choked up expression. "Are you ok?" I ask, as I stroke his cheek.

"Yeah," he breathes. "I just wasn't expecting that." Putting me down, he turns us around, so we are both looking at their smiling faces. Then he wraps his arm around my shoulder and kisses my temple.

"There's more in there," I tell him, but he doesn't move he just squeezes me tighter around the shoulders. I step forward, squeeze his hand, then walking over, I pull out the one of Tristan with his folks. "I'm sorry Tristan. I...I didn't think it would upset you," I add guiltily.

Pulling another chair out, I place that photo against it, then I do the same with the one of Tristan and I. Seeing it again, I'm glad I chose the one where Tristan and I are facing one another and smiling broadly, the look on our faces says it all. When I turn around, I see him run his hand through his hair, messing it up a little – *I like that!*

"Coral...I...I'm amazed, thank you, baby," he says, his cheeks flushing. I think he's shocked.

I walk over to him, wrap my arms around him, and just hold him again.

He wraps his arms around my shoulders, I feel him kiss my hair. "You smell so good," he breathes.

"Ditto," I tell him back, smiling as I do. "Are you ok?" I ask, hesitantly looking up at him.

"Yeah...just a little shocked, but I love them. I can't believe you got this done for me," he says, surprising me.

I swallow hard – *Why would he say that?*

"Where are we going to put them?" he asks, interrupting that thought.

"Wherever you want," I tell him. "Here, one of your offices, or your other homes. It's up to you," I add.

"There not homes Coral, there just houses. Besides I've put them on the market," he tells me, still gazing at the photos.

"You have?" I squeak in surprise.

Tristan nods once, still staring ahead. "My home is wherever you are Coral," he says taking me by surprise again, and I melt.

I feel like all the bones in my body have liquefied, I feel my heart repairing that little bit more, my soul expanding again for this wonderful man that has entered my life, and I know he's right, he's felt like home since I met him.

"Me too," I say.

"I want them here," he tells me firmly. "This is where you are and where I'd want my folks to be too if they could be; besides they should be here because you got them made. They're not just smiling at me anymore they're smiling at you too." *Oh, Tristan!*

"Tristan, I got them made for you," I tell him again. "Not for me, or us, for *you*."

He squeezes me even tighter. "I still want them here," he tells me.

"Ok," I squeak.

Releasing me, Tristan picks up our wine glasses and hands one to me. "To us," he says.

"To us," I click my glass against his and take a welcome sip.

"Thank you, baby," he adds leaning down to kiss me.

I welcome it, parting my lips for his taste…his tongue.

He groans loudly as our lips connect, and our tongues find each other, and as they do, something deep within me clicks into place. I don't know what it is, I just know it feels different with Tristan now, much deeper than it did before. I didn't think it could get any deeper, I feel like my soul has a different, warm, homely feeling inside it.

The worst is over, I feel like I can let myself be loved, and love Tristan back too, with my whole heart. I wrap my free hand around his neck and deepen the kiss, and I'm glad that Tristan doesn't pull back, in fact, he reciprocates, kissing me harder, a deep sound of longing rising up from his throat – It is desire.

He pulls back, places our wines down, takes my face in his hands and kisses me, forcefully, passionately, pushing his body against mine, squeezing me tight, moaning and grunting as we get lost in the moment.

Hearing him moan like that is a beacon of light to my libido.

I moan in response and run my fingers through his hair, then I pull back for a second and stare up at him, I need to see it in his eyes, I need to see that same hunger that was there before. To my utter amazement, I see that not only is it still there, but Tristan is looking at me more passionately than he ever has before. *Oh, Wow…that look could be responsible for global warming!* – It heats my blood and sets my pulse racing, I feel like I'm on fire, my heart swells with love again for this amazing man, I feel so blessed to have him in my life.

"What is it?" he asks gazing back at me.

"You still want me like that?" I ask.

Tristan nods and leans down to kiss me again. "Of course I do. Always," he whispers against my lips. "But food will be here shortly, I want us' – I press my lips against his then pull back.

"You want us to eat first?" I say, smiling broadly.

He nods once and leans down to kiss me again…

CHAPTER TWENTY-ONE

THE BAD MEN are back. *No, please don't! Mommy, Daddy, where are you?* The bad man is on top of me, he smells bad, I can feel his hairy chest on me, his hands squeezing me.

"Good Girl, just like that." *Mommy, Daddy, make him stop! He's hurting me! Get off me, I don't like it, please stop!*

He turns me over and slaps me hard. I cry out. "Quiet!" he shouts.

I stop crying. When he finishes, he stands and walks away. I keep still and lie on the floor, my belly hurts. The other man comes over, he pushes something inside me; it really hurts... *Make him stop, Daddy, make him stop...*I'm wriggle free from him, and I run...

I run all the way through the house, out into the back garden, through the gates, and outside onto the street. I run as fast as I can. I can't stop running, running away from the bad men...then I am in the hospital that Mommy is in.

I look around at the white walls. I need to find Mommy, so I start running again. There's a lot of grown-ups here in white coats, but they don't see me. I call out for Mommy, and she calls my name. I run towards her voice. I hear her in a room, so I push the door open.

Mommy and Daddy are there, Mommy is kissing Daddy. I don't understand? They don't love each other anymore.

They both turn and smile at me. "Come on baby girl," they both say. Daddy kneels down and opens his arms to me. I run to him, he picks me up and hugs me. "I've missed you baby girl," he tells me.

I hug Daddy tightly.

The door bangs open, we all turn and look. Susannah is in the room, she looks like Mommy used to; she is wearing orange pyjamas, I scramble out of Daddy's arms and point at Susannah.

"Bad lady," I tell them.

Mommy puts her hand on my shoulder. "I'll protect you baby girl."

I don't understand. Mommy hurts me.

Susannah runs to us, she has a big knife. She falls on top of Daddy, and they fight, then suddenly he stops moving.

"Daddy. What's wrong?" He doesn't answer me.

I start to cry. Susannah turns to me, she tries to reach me with the big knife; it has something red all over it.

"No!" Mommy jumps in front of Susannah, they roll around on the floor and then she stops moving too.

I kneel down next to them both. "Mommy, Daddy, wake up." I try shaking them, but they won't wake up. Susannah laughs. I cry even harder and shake them some more, but they won't wake up.

Susannah reaches out for me. "No! Leave me alone," I cry out, she tries to catch me, but I'm too fast. I run and run and run.

I see the sea. I'm here in Brighton. I realise I'm on the beach and I'm not a child anymore. It's cold, and the air is thick with white fog, I search the beach, trying to locate the Marina. The fog suddenly lifts, and I can see Tristan, he's stood a few feet away from me.

"Tristan?" I want to walk towards him, but something about his expression stops me. I wrap my arms around myself and just stand there staring at him, then Susannah suddenly appears next to him. They turn and look at one another, smile, then take each other's hand…*No!* Susannah looks perfect in her pencil skirt and heels, she smiles wickedly at me, and then she pulls Tristan into her and whispers something in his ear, he smiles enigmatically at her. *No!*

"Tristan," I call out, showing him my open hand.

He shakes his head at me, then turns and starts kissing Susannah. His hands are all over her body…this is torture to watch. Susannah throws her head back, Tristan leans down, and his lips graze down her neck, she lifts up her leg. Tristan's hand skims up along it, then squeezes her thigh....*No please not her, anyone but her!*

As he continues to kiss her neck, she turns and smiles at me, a steely resolve in her eyes. "He's mine," she mouths at me, and then she raises her hand behind Tristan, the knife glints and shimmers against the sunlight as she hovers it above his back.

He is totally oblivious... *Tristan!*

"Tristan!" I scream, but my voice makes no sound. I violently shake my head at her in horror, I try to move forward, but I'm being held back by an invisible force. "No! Not Tristan. Please," I beg.

Susannah bares her teeth at me. "Mine," she mouths again, then without a word, she plunges the knife into his back.

"Tristan!" I scream again. I try to run towards him, but my legs won't move. "No!" I watch in horror as he gasps for air and falls to the floor. Susannah walks towards me, the knife dripping with blood. I am frozen, watching Tristan writhe in pain on the floor. I can't move...I can't get to him... He suddenly stops moving, I see a deep red pool of blood ooze out from underneath him... *Tristan?*

Suddenly, he looks up and glares at me. "Run," he garbles, blood spitting from his mouth.

"No," I cry out. "Not without you." I choke back tears of despair...*He can't die...he can't!*

"Run," he chokes. Then I watch in horror as he takes his last breath, and his head hits the pebbles, he's not moving anymore...Suddenly Susannah is right in front of me, the knife held up, ready to plunge it down on me. I will gladly take death now. I don't want to live in a world without Tristan, I close my eyes, ready for inevitable – Something tugs on my hand. I turn and see Tristan's ghostly figure.

"Move, you have to move," he tells me. I see my parents behind him, pale and grey.

Tristan smiles a sad smile and brushes an icy cold finger down my cheek. "Go," he whispers.

"No," I cry, shaking my head. I don't want to leave him.

"Please baby, please...for me, go now," he whispers. Then he slowly starts to fade away from me, heading out to sea. I realise as I try to follow him that I can move again, so I run towards him, into the sea, my feet and legs feeling heavier, colder as I try to race against the current, the waves hitting me, one after the other…

"Coral wake up!" I hear Tristan's voice shouting at me, I try to find him in the dream.

"Tristan!" I scream out, my hands searching for him.

"Wake up!" He shouts again, and I realise someone is shaking me.

My eyes dart open. *Holy Fuck!*

Tristan is on top of me holding me down. "You were thrashing about," he pants, releasing me, his eyes wide with alarm. "You ok baby?" He adds, searching my face.

My heart is hammering against my chest, and I'm covered in sweat. I stare up into his eyes, he's alive, he's here… *Oh god, that was so horrible, so awful…*

"Tristan!" I crush myself against him and burst into tears.

"Shhh," he soothes, wrapping his arms around me. "It's ok, it was just a bad dream," he whispers, rocking me gently.

I repeat those words to myself – *Just a dream*. I grip onto him tighter, not wanting to let go, then I think what if I'm still dreaming? I instantly stop crying and pull back searching his face. I start frantically checking him, my hands searching for any sign of damage, my breath coming in sharp gusts.

He takes hold of my hands in his, brings them up to his mouth and gently kisses them. "It's alright baby, I'm right here," he softly tells me. "I'm not going anywhere."

I blink back the tears again, and before I can stop myself, it's out of my mouth. "I dreamed you were dead," I choke.

His eyes widen in fear and disbelief. "Oh baby," he breathes.

I pull him to me and kiss him hard. I need this. I need to feel him. I need him to wash it all away. He is my balm, my healer, I realise that now.

"I'm here," he says. "I'm ok baby."

"Take me," I croak. "Please…" I beg.

He stares down at me for a moment, debating, then his lips swoop down on mine.

I hold him to me and lose myself in him, kissing him back, relishing every touch, every move, the feel of his skin, his body moving in perfect symmetry with mine, breathing in his scent, and I drift away, forgetting all about the horror I just witnessed…

I AM LYING cocooned in Tristan's arms after our lovemaking. My head is gently resting on his shoulder. I feel sated, calmer and more in control. I know the bad men have come back because of telling Tristan about my past, I don't dream about it that often, but I don't understand the part with my parents or Susannah. Why would she want to hurt any of them? Why would she want to hurt Tristan? I shudder slightly recalling the horrific dream.

"Hey." Tristan turns his head and gazes down at me. "You ok?" he asks, frowning down at me.

"Yeah..." I breathe, he tightens his arms around me, making me feel safe, loved.

"Coral, talk to me," he pleads. "You looked so frightened," he adds.

"I was," I whisper, but I can't tell him that Susannah killed him; he'll think I'm a complete lunatic. Besides, I don't want to argue about her, which is what will happen.

"Want to talk about it?" he asks.

I shake my head at him.

Tristan gives me a look that tells me he wants to know, he wants me to talk to him.

I pull his head down so I can reach his lips and softly kiss him. "I don't want to talk about it," I whisper.

"Was it them?" he asks, his voice low and dark.

I frown up at him. *How does he know?*

"You were mumbling, telling...telling them to stop," he whispers swallowing hard, as he answers my unspoken question. *Oh!*

I feel my face pale as he stares down at me. "S-sorry," I stutter.

"Don't be. Are you ok?" He asks again, as he softly strokes my hair, his face full of concern. I think about what he's asked, and run my hands through my sweaty hair.

"It was just a b-bad dream," I stutter.

"Want to talk about it?" he asks again, I smile weakly at him. "You can tell me anything baby, you know that right?" he adds.

I hesitate, wondering whether I want him to know, surely he doesn't have to live through the horror of it too, then I think differently, he wants me to talk to him, and I shouldn't fear letting him in, surely?

"Yes it was them, but it was other stuff too," I sigh heavily. "I was dreaming about my parents," I add. I'm not sure if I want him to know that Susannah was involved too.

"Your parents?" He questions softly.

"Yes," I whisper.

"What about them baby?" he asks.

I think of all that happened last night, Tristan getting the truth out of me about my past, and crying in his arms. Tristan crying in my arms, in those moments we connected, our bond grew deeper. I think about how easy going and funny he was as we ate Chinese food and drank wine, talking until the early hours of this morning. Then I think about how wonderful he was when we came to bed, and he made soft, slow love to me.

"Baby, talk to me," he pleads. "After last night..." He breaks off his jaw clenching. "You should know that you can tell me and I'll still be here," he adds, his eyes penetrating right into my soul.

I push him onto his back and lie on top of him, my chin on his chest. "I know...it's just...." *Tell him Coral!* "Ok, I'm worried if I tell you something about my mother, that you might think the same could happen to me or..." I shut the hell up, and shake my head at myself. "She was put in a Psychiatric Hospital," I whisper.

Tristan's face doesn't falter. "And you thought I would think that you may have some of her...tendencies?" Tristan says, reading me easily.

I squirm, feeling embarrassment. "Yeah..." I mumble staring into his beautiful brown eyes.

"You're nothing like your mother Coral," he tells me firmly.

I frown deeply at him. I'm not so sure.

"Before Gladys took me in. I was with my Nan for a couple of weeks, who seemed to think it would be good for me to still see my mother, keep that connection, she didn't know what she'd done to me. I told all the social workers that she was a good mother, I was so afraid of losing another parent, and I knew by then that my dad was never coming home, that he would never come back for me. So I went to the hospital, only a couple of times though," I laugh sarcastically as I recall the memory. "She was completely deranged of course, tried to attack me. I never went back again." I gaze at Tristan, trying to read his reaction.

"I'm so sorry Coral," he softly says, gently stroking my cheek.

"I haven't dreamt about that place for years. I think the last time I did I was a stoned teenager," I say laughing at myself. Tristan smiles at me. "What?" I question, smiling up at him.

"The rebellious teenager," he chuckles. "Oh, I'd have loved to have seen that," he laughs.

I frown deeply, remembering how lost and confused I was back then. "No, you wouldn't," I argue.

Tristan cocks one eyebrow up at me, his cheeky grin appearing. "Yeah, I would. You know why?" he says, flipping me over, so my back is against the mattress, his body pressed against mine, his erection digging into my belly – *Yes!*

"Why?" I smile, feeling my blood igniting inside me – *I want him!*

"Because we'd have fallen in love," he says his voice soft and sexy.

"No, we wouldn't have," I argue petulantly.

"Yes…we…would," he growls, kissing me in between each word.

"Ok, we would." I relent, flipping him over so I can straddle him…

IT IS YET another beautiful Saturday morning. The sun is shining, and the sky is blue. I don't know why, but weekends always seem so much better when the sun is out. We are in Tristan's car heading over to Gladys', part of me is dreading it. I really hope Gladys and Debs keep a lid on it and don't embarrass either of us.

"Are you really ok about your family moving away?" Tristan asks as we wait for the traffic lights to go green.

"Not really much I can do about it," I say smiling back at him.

"That doesn't really answer the question," he states taking my hand in his, and kissing my knuckles.

"I know," I sigh and look out the window.

I don't know why I'm feeling so moody today. I can't work out if it's the fact that I have to share Tristan or the fact that it hasn't really hit me that Gladys will no longer be here for me, close to me, or if it's the fact that I had such an awful nightmare. Dreaming about the abuse is always bad enough when it happens, but seeing my parents, then watching Susannah kill Tristan was…horrifying – I swallow hard and try to shake the thought away.

I try to concentrate on something else, but I can't get Susannah out of my head, I'm trying not to freak out about her. Part of me wants to tell Tristan, but I want to wait for the P.I results. It may come up with something that I can show to Tristan, to prove to him that she is crazy. At least then, I can tell him about what Bob told me and about someone (Susannah) entering my property. Thinking about her makes me want to ask Tristan if he's spoken to her, and whether she's told him what she told me about moving here and getting divorced, so I decide to be brave and ask the question.

"Did you speak to Susannah last week?" I ask as we head east along the A259.

"Briefly. Why?" Tristan asks.

I shrug. "No reason," I answer keeping my gaze out the window, there are so many boats out on the water today.

"Coral." Tristan admonishes. "Look at me." Reluctantly, I turn my head, and our eyes briefly meet. "Why did you just ask that?" I sigh heavily, running my hand through my hair. I decide if I am going to talk to him about my concerns, it can't be now, not here in the car.

"Later," I say smiling back at him, trying to lighten the mood, my mood.

He looks frustrated. "Why can't you just say now?" he asks.

"Because…" I clench my teeth unable to get the right words out, I decide to plant a seed, let him know I know something. "There is something you should know about, but I'm not sure if I should tell you or not. I'm not sure it's my place to say," I answer.

"Is it about Susannah?" he asks. I nod my head. "Then you should tell me," he states, sounding very much like a boss, not a future husband.

"I will, but right now we have a whole day of happy families to get through. Can you trust that I'll tell you when we get back?" I ask, praying this won't come back and bite me on the ass.

Tristan pulls my hand to his lips and kisses my knuckles again.

"Of course, it can wait," he says. *Thank God!*

AS TRISTAN PULLS up outside my childhood home, I realise how nervous I am. My stomach twists as I watch Tristan exit the car and walk around to me. Opening my door, I take his hand and step out of the car. Tristan shuts the door, and I'm about to walk off when he stops me by tugging on my hand.

"Coral," he softly says.

I turn and look up at him, wearing flip-flops was not a good idea, he's so tall compared to my short arse, but I didn't feel like making too much of an effort today, so I opted for my white linen trousers, my light-blue vest-top and my flip-flops.

"What are you so nervous about?" he asks.

"Everything," I choke, sounding just as nervous as I feel.

Tristan grimaces. "Spill," he says watching me vigilantly.

"Ok, first off I have to meet new people. Malcolm is nice, so I'm sure his family will be too…I just…I'm not very good at it, I get tongue-tied." I blurt running my hand through my hair. "And I get embarrassed and shy, and now everyone is going to meet you too and…" I stop and take a breath. "I told Gladys, well she kind of guessed we're seeing each other, but I played it off as friends," I add, hoping he'll just go along with it.

"Why?" Tristan asks in astonishment.

"Because you don't know what they're like when they get together. It's like they enjoy watching me squirm," I say, scowling at the floor.

"Hmm…" Tristan pulls me into him, leans down and kisses me forcefully. I lose all other thoughts. "Feeling better?" he breathes against my lips.

"Yes," I squeak.

"Good. Now, I'm not going to walk in there as your 'friend' Coral. So be brave, take my hand, and walk with me," he tells me firmly.

"Ok." I take a deep breath and place my hand in his.

We walk the few steps towards the garden path and stop. Tristan takes a deep breath, squares his shoulders then looks down at me and smiles shyly. *Holy crap! He's nervous, I never thought he would be!*

"You're nervous?" I guess.

"A little, I want your family to like me," he answers.

"Oh, believe me, Tristan, they already do," I blurt, laughing as I do. He cocks his head to the side, quizzically. *Ok, explanation needed!*

"Debs thinks you're hot, and Gladys thinks the sun shines out of your backside, so believe me, baby, *you* have nothing to worry about," I say.

His face bursts into his cheeky schoolboy smile – Then I think about Tristan's proposal. *Fuck, he doesn't know I haven't told anyone!*

"Tristan, they don't know you proposed to me," I whisper, feeling bad for not wanting to tell everyone. "I just thought...it's you know, a little early and I don't want...." I break off, feeling stupid.

"It's alright Coral, it'll be our little secret," he says winking at me. My heart raps against my chest, and my stomach blooms with that strange, soulful feeling.

"Thanks," I whisper in relief. Leaning down, Tristan takes my face in his hands, and kisses me so softly I feel my legs wobble in response.

"Wayhey!" I hear Debs shout from behind me. *Crap!*

I pull back in surprise and embarrassment, just as Tristan starts laughing, evidently he doesn't care that we just got caught kissing. I turn and glare at Debs as she struts her stuff across the road, her hands full of games for the children. Then I double take when I see she's wearing a skin-tight beach dress, it doesn't leave much to the imagination, at least she's wearing a bikini underneath it.

I grit my teeth feeling slightly jealous. Debs has always known how to flaunt her body in the right way. She looks very tall, slim and tanned; I guess she's been making the most of the good weather.

"Debs!" I snap, scolding her for embarrassing me. She stops in front of us, completely ignores me and smiles up at Tristan, batting her eyelashes at him as she does. *Oh god, this day is going to be hellish!*

"Well hi there handsome," she says blatantly flirting with him.

Tristan chuckles at her. "Hi Debbie, nice to see you again," he says leaning down to kiss her cheek.

"Ooh, don't you smell nice," she says, her cheeks flushing. *Oh god!* I can just imagine what fantasy is bobbing around that head of hers.

"Can I help?" Tristan asks politely, ignoring her flirting.

"Well sure you can handsome!" Debs winks at Tristan and starts to pile all of the games in Tristan's open arms, then she flicks her long blonde hair and smiles up at him.

"Debs!" I scold. *This is beyond embarrassing!*

"What?" She turns and titters at me. I narrow my eyes at her. I swear there's smoke coming out of my ears, and I have a whole day of this to look forward to.

"Come on Tristan, let's introduce you to everybody," she says, manhandling him down the garden path. As he reaches the steps to the front door, he turns to me – I think it's going to be in desperation – but when our eyes meet, he winks at me then smiles his cheeky grin.

I chuckle at him and shake my head. Debs leads him up the steps, and through the open front door. Walking forward, I feel myself relax a little; at least Tristan is taking all this in good humour. As I step inside the hall, I can hear Debs introducing Tristan to all the people in the kitchen – *As my boyfriend!* – He sounds happy, animated.

As I continue down the hallway, it suddenly dawns on me, maybe there's a reason why he's taking this all so well. Tristan doesn't have this anymore, no folks to introduce me to and no other family. I finally realise how lonely he must have been since his folks died, I try to imagine what it must have felt like to be him, being totally alone in the world. It makes me question what it's going to feel like when my family move away.

"Darling!" I look up and see Gladys gliding towards me – *What is she wearing?*

"Hi," I squeak as she reaches me, squeezing all the air out of my lungs. "You look nice," I say questioningly.

"Oh! Do you think so? Malcolm bought it for me," she says twirling around. I think Malcolm may have bought a size too small! *What is this wear next to nothing day?*

"Um...yeah it's...it's a lovely colour," I say gazing at her breasts that are nearly popping out of the lemon halter-neck-see-though-dress that just about covers her backside – *Thank god she has a costume on underneath it!*

Gladys giggles in delight. "Tristan looks nice," she says linking her arm in mine.

"Yeah he does," I agree, picturing him in his cream t-shirt, his navy blue combat shorts and flip-flops – *Very casual, very summery, and very sexy!*

"So how are you two getting along?" I smile shyly at her –*Why do I feel so awkward talking about it?*

"Gladys, you know he's not' –"Just a friend?" she interrupts. "Darling I knew from the moment he took you home after Lily's party," she says, patting my arm.

I gape at her –*I didn't even know we'd be together back then.*

"Some things are transparent," she whispers, smiling knowingly at me.

My mouth pops open in shock. I don't know what Malcolm's doing to Gladys, but she's really changing, she never would have said something like that to me before.

"Soul Mates," I whisper. Gladys gasps and turns to me with wide eyes. I quickly bring my finger to my lips. "Shhh, don't say anything," I plead.

Her eyes fill with unshed tears, and she unexpectedly pulls me into her chest, her bosoms suffocating me again– *Oh god!*

"Darling!" she chokes. I try to say something, but it just comes out all muffled. "What was that?" she asks.

I pull back from her. "I said...it's early days," I whisper. "So please don't make a big deal out of it," I beg.

Gladys pouts at me then resigns when she sees the look on my face. "Alright, alright, I won't ask when you're tying the knot!" she teases. I go to argue, but she continues before I can. "Now come along darling, lots of new people to meet," she says as she walks down the hallway.

I take a deep breath and follow her through the kitchen door...

TRISTAN HAS BEEN kidnapped from me. Everyone wants to speak to him, so I make myself useful by helping Malcolm in the kitchen. He's wearing his funny apron again – I should rephrase – he's only wearing his funny apron and a very scanty pair of white swimming trunks. I really don't think it's ideal for barbecuing!

As I watch Tristan entertaining Lily from the kitchen window my heart pangs with sorrow, he'd have made such a good Dad. Brushing the thought away, I look around the garden at all the other people I've got to meet today.

Malcolm's identical twin daughters are lovely, but it's hard to tell which one you're talking too. But I know that Ellie is a beautician who is married to Darren, and they have identical twins Matthew and Martin, and Erin is a Graphic Designer who is married to Ed, and they have twins, Aimee and Katie. I know that they both married their Uni sweethearts and got pregnant at the same time and that their kids are eight years old. They all seem really close which is nice, and Malcolm seems to adore his girls, as a father should – I halt that line of thinking, I don't want to get emotional today.

Looking out the window again, I see Lily take Matthew's hand and lead him into the paddling pool that's been erected for the occasion. Scott, Darren and Ed are chatting animatedly about football, personally, I can't stand the game, but each to their own, I'm so glad Tristan doesn't like it though; he'd go to a lot of games on his own if he did.

Tristan is sat next to Joyce, chatting freely with her. I think she has mind reading skills because just as I think that she looks up, catching me staring at them both. Joyce smiles teasingly at me and waves. Feeling embarrassed, I smile and wave back, and as I do, I see Tristan chuckle to himself, no doubt at me.

Erin, Ellie, Gladys and Debs have done nothing but sip cocktails, and lie on the sun loungers for the last hour. No wonder Gladys and Debs weren't wearing much, I can't help giggling aloud; I think Spain is going to suit them.

"Share the joke!" Malcolm booms making me jump – I'd forgotten he was there.

"Nothing…" I chuckle. "Just…" I turn and look up at him. "I'm really happy you met Gladys," I tell him. "She seems like a different woman. Like she's…she just seems so happy, so thank you, Malcolm, for making her feel that way." I smile up at him, his bright blue eyes smile back at me.

"She makes me very happy too," he says, smiling broadly. "Ready with the salad?" he adds.

"Yep, all done," I answer.

"Good. Let's get cooking!" He says.

I giggle as I follow Malcolm outside; he's so funny and likeable. I feel that melancholy feeling try to wash over me again; he really would have made a great Dad…

AN HOUR LATER and we are all tucking into Malcolm's delicious meal. There's marinated steaks, sausages, burgers, chilli salmon, king prawns, and an array of barbequed vegetables. *I'm in my element!* – I am sitting next to Tristan who's tucking into a steak.

I smile up at him. "Nice?" I ask as I take a forkful of salmon and veg.

"Very nice," he answers leaning in to kiss my cheek. I don't know why, but I feel shy again.

"They all like you," I whisper.

"Shame they're all moving away," he says, his eyebrows knitting together. I wonder if he wants them to stay too, now that his family is gone, poor Tristan.

I feel my heart sink a little. "Yeah…" I mumble and carry on eating.

SOMETIME LATER AS all the adults sit under the veranda, taking a break from the afternoon sun, and the kids are playing and splashing about in the paddling pool, the conversation changes to the news. I drift off as they talk politics, economics and such; Tristan seems to know what it's all about, giving an opinion every now and then. I find it all so boring, so I scoot down in my seat, rest my head against the back of my chair, and have a little afternoon siesta…

"Isn't it just awful news about that Jimmy Savile!" Gladys pipes up loudly, waking me from my snooze. I don't have a clue what they are talking about, I rarely watch the news, and I never pick up newspapers.

"He always gave me the creeps." Debs shudders, my ears prick up in response. In my peripheral vision, I notice Tristan tense up beside me.

"I think it's frightening," Erin says. "You just don't know who you're safe to leave your kids with anymore," she adds. *Shit! This is not good!*

Saliva swims in my mouth, I swallow hard and try to blank it all out, but my heart starts pumping against my chest, making my breathing accelerate. I try to control it because I don't want anyone to see this conversation is affecting me. Thankfully, Tristan casually places his arm around my shoulders and gently strokes my right shoulder with his fingertips, comforting me, then he gives my shoulder a gentle, supportive squeeze. I turn and smile weakly at him, he leans into me and gently kisses my temple, but unfortunately, the conversation continues.

"You're right Erin, it is scary," Debs says. "I must admit though when Scott and I had Lily, we promised to tell her from an early age about that kind of thing." Scott clutches Debs' hand.

"Yes, we've all done the same. It just seems as though it's rife, it's everywhere," Ellie bellows. "I hated taking the boys to nursery when they were due to start, you just never know!"

"It's just awful," Gladys cries. "Especially a man in that position, all those children, they trusted him." I pick up my wine and take a good couple of gulps. I feel Tristan's fingers enclose around my free hand and squeeze gently, but it's no good, I don't want to hear any of this.

"Coral are you alright?" Malcolm asks. "You're as white as a ghost," he adds. Everyone stops talking, and they all turn in unison and stare at me. *Crap!*

"Yeah..." I breathe. "I think it's just the heat. Excuse me," I say standing up from my chair.

Tristan clutches my hand to stop me. "Want me to come with you?" He whispers.

I look down at Tristan and very subtly shake my head. "I'm good, I just need a bathroom break," I whisper back. I throw a fake smile in for good measure, but Tristan's brows are still knitted together in concern.

As I walk around the table, I turn to see Gladys watching me with concern, her expression worn, and something else... Grief? No, that's not it...Pain? Yes, that's what I can see in her eyes, looking away from her, I head indoors...

CHAPTER TWENTY-TWO

BYPASSING THE kitchen and going straight to the utility room, I yank the downstairs bathroom door open and stepping inside, I fill the sink with cold water. Scooping my hair up, I cup the water with my hand and soak the back of my neck, closing my eyes to the cooling sensation.

"Coral?" My eyes dart open. I'm not surprised to see Gladys standing in the doorway.

"Hey." I look down at the sink and scoop up more water, dabbing each cheek.

"Coral," Gladys's voice is soft as she carefully steps into the bathroom. "You know you can talk to me, about anything darling," she says, holding my hair up for me as I cool my neck once more with water.

"Yes," I answer staring blankly ahead.

"Well why can't you tell me this?" she asks, holding my chin up, so I have to look at her.

"It's nothing," I say, hoping my eyes don't give me away.

"Did somebody hurt you darling?" she asks.

I sigh and close my eyes. "Yes, my parents, my sister…" I open my eyes and stare back at her. "The only one that didn't was you," I whisper.

"That was my job darling. To keep you safe, to help you recover, to show you that you deserve so much love and affection," Gladys takes a deep breath. "Everyone in your life had let you down. It was my responsibility to show you that it's not always true, that there are people you can rely on, that you can trust." She softly strokes my cheek. "I remember how long it took you to trust me, to believe I would be there for you when I said I would. You were such a withdrawn little thing, so tiny, so precious…" she drifts off, tucking my hair behind my ear.

Unwelcome tears start to fill my eyes. This is all Tristan's fault, he's turned me into a blubbering wreck!

"I know something happened to you darling, something much worse than your father abandoning you, or your mother neglecting you. I could tell, and I always thought when you were ready to tell me, you would, but you never did. I often wonder if I did something wrong, or didn't do something right, I wanted you to feel as though no matter what you told me, it wouldn't make any difference to how much I loved you, cherished you…." Gladys drifts off.

"Don't," I warn. "Gladys don't you dare doubt yourself, you were wonderful to me. I wake up every day feeling truly blessed that it was you who raised me." I add more water to my neck. "And I didn't purposely keep things from you…I just …I didn't know how to tell you," I add.

"Can you tell me now?" she asks. I turn and gaze at her wondering if I should, I can see from the look in her eyes she's desperate for the answer.

"I think you've already worked it out," I whisper.

"Abuse?" she whispers back.

I nod silently as I watch her face fall, and her eyes brim with tears. So Gladys always suspected which makes my love for her bloom within me, she never pushed for an answer, never badgered me or shoved me off to a shrink.

"Sexual?" she questions, she can barely get the word out.

I nod again.

"Oh Coral," she sniffs. "Why didn't you tell me, darling?"

"Don't feel sad for me," I say. *This is supposed to be a happy day!*

"Coral, how can you say that?" she croaks.

"Easily, I don't want you to look at me differently, like you feel sorry for me…I'd hate that," I whisper.

Gladys nods once. "I can understand that," she says. "I always had my suspicions it might be that," she adds her voice full of remorse, and old painful memories. "You never acted like other children around adults; you would always withdraw and hide behind me. I think I knew it was something along those lines when I asked you to put a dress on. Do you remember?" she questions.

I close my eyes briefly and shake my head.

"We were off to see the ballet with Joyce. I wanted you, girls, to look pretty for the occasion, but when I asked you to wear it, you shook your head at me and hid in the corner. You curled up like a feral child and started whimpering. I was mortified to see you like that, so broken…I never asked you again," Gladys sniffs loudly.

"Mom, it's in the past. Please…don't feel guilty about it," I whisper.

Gladys sniffs loudly again. "You didn't have anything like that happen here or at school did you?" she questions.

"No!" I bellow. "Not at school, and nothing bad ever happened to me here. This house is filled with warm, loving memories; you were my safety back then Gladys. This house was my sanctuary, you were my sanctuary. I know I never showed you that or told you, and I'm sorry I didn't, but I had no idea how to communicate it to you."

Gladys smiles warmly at me. "Oh darling girl," she says, tucking my hair behind each ear, then taking my face in her hands she gently kisses both my cheeks. "What an awful start in life you had. I'm so proud of you Coral, of all you've achieved," she says.

I snort with laughter. "I don't think becoming a secretary is an achievement," I answer dryly.

"It is for you," she argues. "I knew as you went through your teenage years I had a fifty-fifty chance you would go one way or the other. You chose the light, not the dark and no one else could have made that choice for you. You made sure you kept yourself on the straight and narrow. So yes, it is an achievement, a very big one. Keep that head held high young lady, high with pride, you made it when so many others haven't." *I'm speechless!*

Gladys has never talked to me like this, not honestly about what it was like for her to live with me, or how she dealt with raising me. I'm so happy she's proud of me.

"Oh Mom," I whimper, my voice cracking on me. I wrap my arms around her and hug her tightly.

Gladys rubs her hand up and down my back, comforting me. "Ah, there's no need for tears," she tells me.

"I know," I sniff, trying to pull myself together. "I just...I just want you to know how much I love you, and how much I appreciate everything you did for me," I sniff. "I'm going to miss you so much," I croak, hugging her harder.

Pulling back, she takes my face in her hands, her expression serious. "Be honest darling. Do you want me to stay?" she asks scrutinising me.

I sigh heavily – *Of course I want you to stay!*

"Yes, I want you all to stay. But not for me, because you want to," I say. Gladys gives me her stern look. "Ok, if I hadn't met Tristan I'd be begging you to stay, but I have met him and...I don't know it's weird, like...he's helping me grow up in a way, stand on my own two feet." I shake my head, wondering if I'm making any sense at all. "I want you to go to Spain, I really do. You...you deserve it," I add.

"You don't feel like I'm abandoning you?" she questions. *Shit!*

"No, I don't," I answer firmly. "Don't stay because of me, I'll be fine," I add.

Her eyebrows knit together as she tries to read my face, so I put on my best smile and start chuckling. Gladys smiles at me and pulls me in for another hug. We stay like that for a while, although I'm not sure who's comforting who, maybe we are comforting each other?

"Shall we go back?" Gladys asks appraising me. I nod and smile at her. "Tristan will be wondering where you are," she adds, linking her arm in mine.

We head out the bathroom and into the kitchen, suddenly Gladys stops and turns to me. "Does Tristan know?" she whispers. I nod, unable to say anything. "That's good darling," she says patting my hand. *I need to get off this subject!*

"Bob said you're having him over tomorrow?" I say. Then I panic, what if he tells her about someone trying to get in? Gladys will be beside herself – I must remember to call him.

"Yes, darling. Would you and Tristan like to join us?" She asks.

I think about it for a moment and decide no, I want him to myself, I haven't seen him all week, and I want to devour him for the rest of the weekend.

I start to smile; a really goofy smile.

"No, maybe not," she adds reflecting my ear-splitting grin.

"Oh Gladys, he's so good to me," I swoon.

"I know, I can see that darling." She says.

"I love him," I whisper.

"Yes darling, I know. Tristan loves you too. It's written all over the two of you," she adds.

My ear-splitting grin widens, we both giggle in unison.

The moment we are back outside I search for Tristan and find him sat next to Malcolm, having what looks like a very serious discussion. He glances up and sees me, our eyes lock, and he frowns at me. I nod slightly letting him know I'm ok, he smiles back at me, but I can tell he's still worried. Gladys walks over to them and sits the other side of Tristan, interrupting his conversation with Malcolm.

Honestly, she's like a bull in a china shop sometimes, but I love her so. Tristan looks up and winks at me, making my heart flutter as fast as a bird, then I notice Debs come teetering over to me in her heels. *Uh-oh!*

"What's up with you?" she whispers.

"Nothing," I whisper back.

"Could have fooled me," she argues.

"Alright then, I'm upset," I bite back.

"What about now?" she drawls.

"Spain!" I hiss keeping my eyes locked on little Lily – *I'm not going to see her grow up, not properly.*

"Oh!" she answers somberly.

"Yeah oh!" I mock, just like Tristan does with me. "You could have told me, Debs warned me. I'd have spent more time with Lily' – "Oh don't give me that!" she snaps interrupting me. "Besides its best this way, she hasn't got too close to you, so it won't be so hard for her."

"Nice. What are you saying, she won't miss me?" I bite.

"Probably not," Debs retorts.

I grit my teeth and glare down the garden, if I look at her I swear I'll lose it. At least Gladys had the decency to tell me to my face.

"Why didn't you tell me?" I ask, crossing my arms in defiance.

"Mom said she would," she answers sharply.

I shake my head at her. "Chicken shit!" I blurt because she is a chicken.

I'm not that scary, and it's not like we have an amazingly close relationship like Ellie and Erin, but she should have said something. She finally has the decency to look guiltily at me.

"I...I'm sorry Coral. Mom told me how it made you feel. I didn't think you knew something was going on, I would have told you if I'd known. I really am sorry. And if it makes you feel any better Scott's really mad at me, he said we should have told you straight away."

I turn and look at Scott, he and Malcolm got it so right, but I'm tired of feeling pissed off all the time. Tristan's made me realise how much I still feel like that, and I'm done with it, I want a different life, a happy one!

Debs continues. "I'm really sorry Coral, Scott was right, I should have told you' – "Chicken!" I blurt. Debs snaps her head round to argue, but when she sees that I'm grinning at her, she starts smiling too.

"Are you going to come and see us?" she asks, linking her arm in mine.

"Try keeping me away," I answer. She nods her head and smiles back at me.

"That's good. Lily will miss you Coral, we all will," she says, resting her head on my shoulder, it's such an unlikely thing for her to do.

"I know, I'll miss you all too," I say.

I try not to think too deeply about that, I know it's going to be a very emotional day when it happens, but I'm trying to think like George has taught me, it's in the future, so there's no point dwelling on it.

"I'm going to check on Lily," she says.

"Later Alligator," I chuckle, remembering how we used to say that as kids.

"Stay loose Bull Moose," Debs retorts grinning widely.

We laugh heartily with each other, hug briefly, and I watch my big sister go check on her little girl...

WE ALL SPEND another hour outside chatting away with one another. I feel happy, contented, relaxed, but there's one thing that's really bugging me – *Dresses!*

It's a beautiful hot sunny day, and for the first time in my life, I wish I was in a dress, tanning myself freely like Gladys and Debs. All the women have them on, Joyce, Erin and Ellie and so do Erin's little girls and Lily.

I decide at that moment that I want to go out tonight. I want to be brave, put that dress on and go out for a nice meal with my sexy man. I still feel vulnerable and nervous about it, but I know I can handle that because I have Tristan with me and he's not going to let any freaky pervert anywhere near me.

"He just can't take his eyes off you can he?" Joyce says pulling me out of my reverie.

I smile shyly at her. "No, but he's hard to resist too," I say feeling proud.

"Yes, I heard all about that," she says smiling coyly at me – *Huh?*

"Heard about what?" I whisper, my face falling.

Joyce chuckles. "Coral, it's one of the most brilliant ways to get a man, tell him it won't work. Men love challenges, so they go for it with everything they've got." Joyce adds.

I gape at her. "No, I didn't do it to get him…" I squeak.

"I know Coral," Joyce says. "I was just teasing you," she softly placates – *Phew!*

"Ok, good. I don't want to be cast like that," I mumble.

"So, how did it go?" she asks. *Go? What go?*

"Hmm?" I can't help watching Tristan.

"The date and the dress?" Joyce asks a little bewildered by my reaction – *Oh that!*

"Oh, we're doing that tonight. Tristan got back late last night, so we stayed in." I lie.

"Well, have fun darling. Don't get too drunk," she teases.

We both chuckle, then I think about the talk Tristan, and I are going to have about Susannah when we get back. "Joyce, did you speak to Tristan about Susannah by any chance?" I ask.

"No, darling. Now's not the time. I will speak to him on Monday though, in private."

"Did he say anything to you, ask you anything?" I question.

"No, darling he spent most of our time talking about you."

I gape at Joyce again. "Me?" I squeak.

"Yes, he told me all about the wonderful gift you had made for him. You really are very sweet Coral," she adds.

"Oh." I smile shyly at her, not really knowing what to say to that.

Turning to look at Tristan I see he's looking a little worn out, Gladys has been talking to him for at least forty minutes now, and she's tipsy, so she's got her jabbery head on. Tristan could be there all night. I'd better go rescue him!

"Well, it's getting late. We'd better get going." I say to Joyce.

"It's been lovely seeing you two together," Joyce says smiling at Tristan. "You really do suit each other," she adds.

"Thanks," I say gazing adoringly at Tristan. He's done very well today, he's not faltered once, even when Gladys and Debs harped on at him over lunch about the two of us.

After saying goodbye to Joyce, I wander over to Tristan. Standing behind him, I lean down, wrap my arms around his shoulders and kiss his cheek, feeling completely and utterly in love with him.

"Ready to go?" I ask, wondering if I'm saving him.

"Darling, so soon…" Gladys slurs.

"Yes." I giggle, leaning down to kiss her goodbye, wondering if Gladys is seeing me through different eyes.

"Well alright then, I want you both to come and see us again soon," she says standing to hug me.

"We will," I say, savouring the feeling of her arms around me.

Once we've said our goodbyes to everyone, Tristan takes my hand in his, and we walk down the hallway with Gladys following so she can wave to us from the front door, she's always done that.

"Well that was interesting," Tristan says as he helps me into the car.

I'm about to question him on it but decide against it, it might be something I don't want to hear about, so I divert to what I was thinking about earlier.

"I want to go out tonight," I say as he gets in the driver's side.

"Yeah? Where to?" he asks starting the engine.

"I know a place," I tell him. It's perfect, it has sea-views,

Freed By Him

great food and it's up-market enough so I won't feel silly in a dress.

"Your wish is my command," he tells me. Pulling out into the road, we both wave goodbye to Gladys.

Taking my hand in his, Tristan asks me, "Are you alright? I can't believe they started talking about that fucker," he growls.

"Who?" I ask.

"Savile!" He bites menacingly.

"Oh, well I don't really know…but I can guess," I answer, shivering slightly.

"You don't want to know baby, trust me." I look up at Tristan; he's caught the sun, his face has bronzed, and his hair looks a little lighter.

"You've caught the sun," I say. I reach up and run my hand through his hair.

"Yeah?" I nod and smile back at him, he places his hand on my knee and softly squeezes me. "So what are we doing? Get ready, go straight out?" he asks.

I look down at the clock on the dashboard, it's only four o'clock.

"I have a better idea…" I say as seductively as I can.

Tristan instantly reads my mind. His smiles his most sexy smile. He quickly accelerates making me giggle in delight as he zooms in and out of traffic, getting us home as quickly as possible…

"WAKE UP SLEEPYHEAD." I blink my eyes open. *Shit! I fell asleep!*

"Oh no!" I moan sitting up in bed. "What time is it?"

Tristan is lying next to me, completely naked. "Half five," he answers squeezing my inner thigh.

"Did you fall asleep?" I ask.

Tristan smiles deeply and stretches out his body. "Yes, you're wearing me out woman!" he chuckles darkly.

I snort with laughter. "Er…I don't think so," I add dryly. "You're the acrobat," I blurt.

Tristan howls with laughter, so much so that he can't get his words out. "Acrobat?" he finally chuckles with raucous laughter.

"Yeah," I chuckle back shyly.

He smiles warmly at me, leans down then kisses the tip

of my nose. "Do you still want to go out?" he asks. I have to seriously think about it, Tristan and all night sex, or getting that dress on and going out with Mr Sexy Mogul. It's a tough decision to make.

"Yes, you want to spoil me, and I want to wear my new dress." Tristan's mouth pops open. I quickly stop any reply by placing my finger against his lips. "Let's get ready gorgeous." Jumping off the bed, and taking Tristan's hand in mine, I lead him into the bathroom…

AN HOUR LATER, I am stood in front of the gigantic mirror in Tristan's bathroom. Picking up my lip liner, I start to trace the outline of my lips; then I put on my lipstick. I feel excited, really excited, which is unexpected – I'm going to go out tonight with my sexy man. Standing back to look at myself, I nod at my reflection with approval. I have styled my hair into big sexy waves and pinned it up on the one side. My make-up looks good, and I have my favourite perfume on.

As I walk back into the bedroom, I take my robe off and hang it up. Then I walk over to the walk-in closet and collect my dress and the underwear I have chosen, which is a dark blue shiny corset, with matching half thong knickers, and a pair of nude silk hold-ups; walking back into the bedroom, I place them all down on the bed.

Taking a deep breath, I shimmy into the knickers and clip the corset on, turning around I take a quick peek in the full-length mirror. *Whoa! My boobs look massive! Shit!* The corset really pushes them up. Maybe I shouldn't wear this? *Get on with it Coral!*

Turning away from myself, I sit on the edge of the bed and open the packaging for the nude silk hold-ups. I have never worn anything like this before, I'm nervous to know what it feels like. Pulling the first hold-up on, I'm amazed by how nice it feels…*ooh so soft!*

I quickly pull on the other. *Hmm, really nice…I have to get more of these!*

Taking a deep calming breath, I pick up the dress. *Here goes nothing!* Undoing the zip, I step both feet in and carefully slide it up my body. Zipping it back up, I take a moment and sit on the edge of the bed. I look down at my hands and see they are steady, no shaking. My throat hasn't dried up, and my heart rate is normal, as is my breathing. I continue to sit on the bed, waiting for the moment to come, a feeling, an image…. anything, but nothing happens, so I launch myself up, and do a little celebratory dance! *I'm so happy!*

Stepping into the Roland Cartier heels I bought, I smile as I remember being so excited that I found them. They match the dress perfectly in colour, and they glitter all over, plus, the ankle strap makes me feel secure enough that I won't fall flat on my arse with nerves, and I like the peep toes.

Picking up my bracelet from Tristan, I clasp it shut around my wrist, it goes perfectly with the dress. Closing my eyes, I turn around in front of the mirror. I peek with one eye first, then both. Ok, boobs don't look so big now I'm in the dress – *Phew!*

I gaze back at myself in wonder. *I'm in a dress!*

I twirl around so I can see how the dress fans out, very pretty. Feeling ecstatic with my choice, I grab my powder and lipstick from the bathroom and head back into the bedroom. Picking up the navy blue clutch bag that I purchased, I pop my make-up, some cash and my mobile inside, then head down the stairs to find Tristan.

As I turn to take the last flight of stairs, I hear music playing, sounds soulful, almost haunting. I stop when I see Tristan standing outside on the patio, staring out at the view. He has his hands in his pockets and seems deep in thought.

My nerves re-appear – *Come on Coral!*

I take a deep breath and head down the stairs. Tristan hears my heels clicking against the flooring and turns around, seeing me his mouth pops open just like it did when he caught me dancing. I notice his cheeks instantly flame, and his eyes dilate as he drinks me in. *Boy, he looks good!*

My blood heats in response. Damn, he looks over the top sexy! He's wearing a pair of light mocha suit trousers, and a crisp white shirt. The top three buttons are open, revealing his muscular chest, and his sleeves are turned up to his elbows.

"Hi," I squeak, cautiously approaching him. Tristan swallows hard. I laugh a little nervously and walk towards him, and taking his outstretched hand he pulls me into him.

"You look...wow." He reaches up and lightly traces his

thumb across my cheek, then leans down and kisses me softly on the lips. I think he's being careful not to ruin my makeup.

"Anyone would think you've never seen a woman in a dress before," I titter, trying to lighten the intensity of the moment.

"I haven't until now," he retorts, my breath hitches at his words. "Coral, you look stunning," he says earnestly, stepping back he assesses me for a moment, then frowns deeply. "I'm going to have to keep a close eye on you, every man in the room's going to want you looking like this," he growls.

I roll my eyes at him and smile. "Who's this singing?" I ask.

"I Love You by Sarah McLachlan." Tristan stares down at me, his eyes intense, then pulls me into his body, wraps his right arm around my waist, takes my right hand in his left, and starts dancing us around on the patio, keeping his eyes locked with mine. I smile up at him. How nice this is, dancing outside as the evening sun gently warms us.

Unfortunately, the song ends far too soon for my liking.

"That was beautiful," I say. "Thank you."

Tristan smiles, lifts our hands up in the air and twirls me around. "*You're* beautiful. Would you like a drink before we go?" He's so gentlemanly, I really love that about him.

"Please," I answer shyly. Tristan keeps hold of my hand and walks us into the kitchen. The music has changed track; it's really nice and mellow.

I turn to Tristan. "Who's this?" I ask.

"Rogue Wave," he answers. "The songs called Eyes." I nod my head along to the plinky plonk of the guitar.

"It's good," I say still nodding away. Tristan smiles, picks me up and twirls me round in his arms, in big swaying movements.

"Tristan!" I giggle, keeping my hands planted on his shoulders.

"God, you smell so good," he murmurs against my ear.

"So do you," I say as he puts me back down. "So you like my choice?" I ask fanning the dress out, feeling girly and feminine.

"Yes, you look breathtaking," he says. Bringing my hand up to his lips, he kisses my knuckles.

I swallow hard. "You look really hot too," I tell him breathlessly.

"Sorry," he says. "Took the jacket off, got a little warm."

I shake my head at him. "Tristan, you look great."

He smiles warmly at me. "Thank you, baby," he says, holding his hand out to me, and I notice he looks nervous.

I clasp mine within his. "You ok?" I ask.

He smiles a little crookedly at me then blows out a deep breath. "I was going to wait but…" I watch him walk away, I hear his office door opening, moments later, he returns with a small box in his hand. *Seriously, another present?*

Reaching me, he smiles shyly at me then drops down to one knee – *Holy fuck!*

My heart starts pumping rapidly. Is this what I think it is? Tristan opens the box, but I can't take my gaze away from his loving expression.

"I know I've already asked you, but I wanted to do this right. And if you don't like what I've chosen, we can pick another," he says swallowing hard. "Coral, I want to spend the rest of my life loving you, only you. You make me so happy baby, I can't imagine spending the rest of my life with anyone but you. Would you do me the extraordinary honour of marrying me?"

I manage to pull my gaze away from his eyes and look down at the ring.

"Tristan!" I gasp, bringing my hands to my mouth.

Bending down to look at it more closely, I can see he has chosen another antique, and the design is beautiful. Elegant flowers are entwined around the main band which holds a large single square diamond, on each side of the stone lies a beautifully crafted butterfly, above and below are intricate scrolls, it's simply breathtaking.

"Tristan it's beautiful," I gush, tears pooling in my eyes – *Crap!*

"Is that a yes?" He asks, laughing nervously.

I feel giddy. "Yes," I squeak.

Tristan leaps to his feet and stands beside me, then carefully taking the ring out of the box he takes my left hand in his and slides the ring down my wedding finger – It fits perfectly.

"It's Victorian, platinum. There's a background story, want to hear it?" He asks, gazing at the ring sitting on my finger.

I nod shyly at him as I have lost the power of speech again.

"The chap who had this ring made fell in love with a woman he knew he wouldn't be able to marry without an occupation. He wasn't wealthy, and she was high society, but she was madly in love with him too, so when he asked her, she said yes. He commissioned this ring to be made using the last of his small inheritance, then he joined the navy, so he could become a prosperous gentleman, but two years into the voyage, the ship was sunk in high seas.

"She got the letter, of course, telling her of her fiancé's unfortunate end, but she refused to believe he had died. She had many other offers of marriage but turned them all down believing he would come home to her. Eleven years later she gets a letter from a chaplain based on a Caribbean Island. Apparently, a fisherman had rescued a man from a distant island.

"They thought he was mad at first because all he kept mumbling was her name, he was sick when they found him. She wrote back explaining who he was and that he was her long-lost love. The man recovered and was shipped home by the navy."

I swallow hard. "And they lived happily ever after?" I whisper. *This better have a nice ending.*

Tristan smiles down at me, reaches out and softly strokes my cheek. "She was there, at the dock, waiting for his return. They embraced lovingly after so many years apart. He couldn't believe she had waited for him, and she couldn't believe he had survived, that he was still alive. They went straight into town, announced their wedding, and a week later they married."

I feel the tears well up in my eyes again – *Shit!*

"That's beautiful Tristan, I'm so happy you picked this ring," I gush.

"You are?" He asks, his eyes are wide, cautious.

"Yes," I smile.

"Good, because I had a difficult time choosing, there were two that I thought you might like, but when I was told the story that went with this one, it made the decision for me. I just thought their love was timeless, and it best represented you and me." *I'm speechless!*

"Do you really like it?" he asks firmly. I've seen rings like this on the Antique Road Show; this must have cost a fortune!

"Yes I do, it's beautiful Tristan, thank you," I say. I wonder for a moment how much it cost, but I know it's rude to ask. "Tristan, you haven't gone over the top have you?" I admonish.

He face contorts, his cheeks flush, and his eyes dilate – *Uh-oh!*

"I'll spend as much as I want on my future wife's engagement ring!" he scolds. *Crap! It did cost a fortune!* Yet, as I gaze down at it sitting perfectly on my finger, I couldn't care less. It's the most beautiful thing I've ever been given.

I feel tears prick my eyes again – *Damn it, my make-up!*

"I love it," I tell him, sniffing loudly as I do. I reach up, and wrap my arms around his neck, holding him close to me. Tristan chuckles then pulls me back, he gazes down at me for a moment then he kisses me, softly at first, but growing deeper with passion and love. When he pulls back, we are both breathless.

"I love you," he tells me solemnly.

"I love you," I choke, gazing down once more at the ring.

"I really chose the right one?" he says a little smugly.

"Yeah, you did," I chuckle leaning up and kissing his cheek, leaving a light lipstick mark there.

Tristan looks relieved. "We have a few minutes before Stu gets here, shall we have that drink now?" he asks.

"Stuart's here?" I ask a little surprised.

"Yes. I didn't want to drive, I can't drink if I'm doing that," he answers.

"Oh," I nod. His boyish smile appears, his dimples deepening.

"Oh!" he mocks. I slap his shoulder. "So drink?" he asks again.

"Yes please," I answer sweetly, still thrown by his romantic, sweet proposal.

"Champagne? I bought some with me. I was going to ask you last night..." He stops and swallows hard. I don't think my revelation has quite sunk in yet. *I need to change the subject, now!*

"I don't like champagne," I say, smiling sweetly at him.

Tristan cocks his head to the side and shakes it in laughter. "I should have known," he titters, I smile back at him. "Wine?" he asks.

"Yes please." I watch Tristan get a bottle of wine out of the fridge and pour two half glasses. As I watch him walk over to me, all my insides feel like they have liquefied, he really shouldn't be allowed to wear suits; he just looks too good in them – *My future husband!*

"To us," he says handing a glass to me and holding his up.

I clink mine against his. "To us," I repeat, we both take a sip.

"I was thinking...did you want to choose the wedding bands together?" he asks casually. I almost spit my wine out – *This is really happening!*

"Um...." I don't even know if that's what people do?

"You can choose your own," he tells me, laughing at my expression.

"Um...no, I don't mind. I just...Is that what other people do, choose them together?" I ask my voice a few octaves higher than I would like.

Tristan shrugs. "No idea," he says.

I think about it for a second. "Do they have to look the same?" I ask – *I mean, how would I know? I've never done this before!*

"No, I don't think so." He takes my hand in his. "What are you really worried about Coral?" he asks.

I swallow hard and stare at the floor, then start blurting out in one long breath, how I really feel. "Just...you know, going off and choosing rings together it just...seems so real like it's really happening you know. I can't pretend it's a dream or a strange fantasy I'm having any more, this is real, this is it, I'm soon to be Mrs Coral Freeman. It just feels so surreal, that's all."

I finally look up at Tristan, he's gazing quizzically at me.

"And I'm scared," I say breathlessly.

Tristan looks crestfallen and panicked all at the same time.

"Not of marrying you," I quickly say. "I know that now, it's more the concept of marriage, it's scary you know, but like George keeps on telling me, a life without risk is no life at all. So I'll take that risk of marrying you and give it one hundred percent. I want to build a future with you, Tristan, not because it means I'm no longer alone, but because in the short amount of time I've known you, you've come to be my best friend, my lover and my confidant. I want to be the best wife I can possibly be, a good wife to you.

"I trust you like no other, and I love you more eternally than I ever thought possible. I didn't think I could love at all, you opened my eyes and made me realise the life I had, wasn't a life worth living. I'll always be grateful to you for that." I take a gulp of wine hoping I haven't hurt Tristan by being so honest.

"Thank you," he whispers and softly kisses my neck.

"What for?" I ask my voice wobbling.

"Being honest," he answers.

"Are *you* scared?" I ask looking up into his deep chocolate eyes.

He shakes his head. "Not one bit. I completely and utterly believe that we will grow old together. I'm fearless about this. I've never wanted anything more. So keep telling me when you're scared, and I'll give you my word that I'll do everything within my power to ease your fears, and make you see that you're doing the right thing, that us being together is exactly where you are meant to be." I exhale loudly. He says the sweetest things.

"I will," I squeak and gulp back some more wine. Tristan laughs heartily at me. "You're mocking me," I scold, half laughing as I do.

"Yes!" he chuckles. "Don't ever change baby, I love you like this."

"What? You always wanted a freaky wife?" I tease shaking my head at him. "You know what they say it's always the quiet ones!" I add dryly.

Tristan laughs at me again then kisses my temple. "I like the way you've done your hair," he tells me softly.

"Thanks," I say, feeling a little shy again.

"So where are you taking me?" He asks taking a sip of his wine.

"You'll see," I smile smugly. *I really hope he likes it!*

Stuart announces his arrival by honking the horn. Tristan grabs his jacket, and I pick up my clutch bag, noticing my engagement ring as I do. As I stare down at it, my stomach flutters wildly. *Mrs Coral Freeman…Whoa!*

Taking my hand in his, we head out into the balmy summer evening…

CHAPTER TWENTY-THREE

ALFRESCO'S IS built out over the seafront in a ship-like design. It's a very quirky kind of place, which is one of the reasons I chose it. When you enter from the street, you really do feel as though you are walking down a gangplank, ready to set sail. The decor is very minimalistic and elegant, with a contemporary design set in a rich palette of deep reds and dark browns.

The open plan Rotunda dining room is surrounded by a wall of windows, which gives a panoramic view of the shoreline and looks directly over the historic ruins of the West Pier. During the day the place is flooded with sunlight making it a light and airy place to dine, once the sun sets and the soft lighting comes on, the place takes on a completely different feel, very intimate and romantic.

Stuarts pulls up on King Street, next to the restaurant. I only took us ten minutes to get down here – I really don't know why we didn't just get a taxi. As usual, Tristan helps me out of the car and tightly clutches my hand in his. I smile widely at him.

"We're eating here?" Tristan asks staring up at the strange looking building.

"Yes," I chuckle.

"It looks like a ship," he says in mock horror. I can't help giggling.

"I know," I chuckle. "Are you ok eating here?" I add.

"Sure, why not," he answers sarcastically.

"The sunsets are amazing from here, I thought it would be nice," I say, pulling him down the gangplank. "Food's good too,"

Freed By Him

I add looking back at his face, I can see he's not so sure about this place.

I stop walking and face him. "Do you want to go somewhere else?" I ask as a couple walks past us, the guy blatantly staring at me. Tristan must have caught on because he wraps his arm around my waist, and throws me back making me squeal with delight and kisses me, hard.

"Yes, we'll eat here," he says, bringing me upright.

As we walk through to the Rotunda Restaurant, I can hear soft music playing; I think it's Norah Jones. The restaurant isn't too packed, but I guess that's because we're early. I can see couples sitting face to face, girlfriends enjoying cocktails, and families outside on the decked terraces. It's certainly warm enough tonight.

"Good evening welcome to Alfresco's." We both smile at the hostess. "Do you have a reservation?" *Shit!*

"No," I answer guiltily.

"No problem, where would you like to eat this evening. The Rotunda, outside on the decking, or the Shoreline restaurant downstairs?" she asks.

Tristan turns to me. "Coral?"

"In here please," I say. "Like I said, amazing sunsets," I whisper to Tristan.

We silently follow the hostess to our table. Tristan pulls my chair out for me, and I take a seat. He goes to sit opposite me, but I shake my head and pat the seat next to me. Smiling deeply, he moves around the table, places his jacket on the back of the chair and sits next to me.

"Good idea," he says taking my left hand and kissing my engagement ring...

THE TIME FLIES by as we enjoy a couple of starters and some bread and olives, drinking far too much wine as we talk the night away, thoroughly enjoying each other's company.

"You said you would tell me," he says.

"Tell you what?" I ask staring blankly at the menu, unable to make my mind up what main meal to choose, it all looks so yummy.

Tristan puts his menu down. "What you had to tell me about Susannah," he says.

I swallow hard and put down my menu. "I still don't know if it's my place to say," I whisper.

"Well I'm giving you permission," Tristan says sharply – *Whoa!*

"Alright, keep your pants on!" I squeak.

"I don't like things being kept from me," he states firmly.

"Well *she* should have told you," I snipe back – *Stupid Blondie has us arguing already.*

"I'm asking you," he says.

"Fine!" I snap frustratingly. "She's getting divorced." I glare back at Tristan, he looks shocked. "Now can we drop talking about her?" I plead.

"When did she tell you?" he asks. *Why is he so bloody concerned about her?*

"I don't know, I can't remember. She said she was thinking about moving areas," I blurt – *Keep a lid on it Coral!*

"Moving areas?" he says darkly.

"Yeah...what's the big deal, Tristan? A member of staff wants to leave, so what?" I snap feeling annoyed.

Tristan ignores me and gazes out to sea. "I wonder why she hasn't told me?" he mumbles to himself.

"I don't know," I gripe, picking my menu back up so I can hide behind it. I don't want Tristan to see that I'm keeping more from him, so much more.

"Is that all she said to you, that she's getting divorced?" he questions.

I pull my menu down and roll my eyes at him. "Yes. Actually no, she did say she likes the sea air and how it must be nice to live by the coast," I say with as much sarcasm as I can.

"Do you think she wants to move here?" he asks.

"I don't know," I answer dryly. "I don't know her," I add.

"Well, it's pretty obvious you don't like her," Tristan snaps.

I glare back at him. "No, I don't," I answer sharply – *Shut up Coral!*

"Why?" he asks incredulously. I purposely do not reply. "She's a nice girl Coral, I just don't understand' – "Tristan, I really don't want tonight to be ruined by us disagreeing about a member of your staff," I say softly, trying to placate him.

He looks uncomfortable for a moment, then nods in agreement – *Phew!*

"You're right. I'll speak to her on Monday. Strange she hasn't told me though…" he says drifting off again. *Grrrrr!*

"You know, it doesn't make me feel comfortable knowing your thinking about another woman while sitting here with me," I say staring down at the table.

Tristan sighs heavily and takes my hand in his. "You're right, again. I'm sorry," he says softly, leaning in to kiss me.

Now I feel utterly guilty for making him feel guilty. I can't wait to get the P.I. Report about this woman so we can put an end to all of this and get her out of our lives.

"Don't be sorry Tristan," I say leaning into him and returning the kiss. "Let's order and enjoy the sunset." Tristan agrees, and we both go back to perusing our menus, but now I can't stop thinking about Blondie, and all the things that have happened. As I run through the strange week I've had with her, I suddenly remember the suicide.

"Tristan, she told me about the chap who…who committed suicide," I whisper then swallow hard, instantly regretting bringing it up.

"She…she did?" he stutters in shock.

"I'm so sorry that happened," I softly say.

Tristan nods once and stares down at his menu. I can see it's not something he wants to discuss. *I need to change the subject.*

I frown deeply trying to think of something else to say. "I spoke to Karen," I pipe up chirpily. "She's really nice," I add taking a drink of wine. Tristan smiles weakly at me. *Great!*

"Wish you'd have sent her to train me," I mumble getting up from my seat.

I need a bathroom break, and some time away from Tristan, his broodiness about Blondie is starting to get on my nerves – *I hate her so much! If he only knew what she's been up to, what she's said.* I wonder for a moment about telling him everything that's happened, maybe then he will shut the hell up about her!

"What was that?" he asks staring up at me.

I purse my lips and shake my head at him. "Nothing Tristan, it was nothing," I say sulkily. I don't want this night ruined – *Then keep your mouth shut Coral!*

"I'm going to the ladies." I smile sweetly at him.

Feeling totally frustrated with myself I march off to the restroom. While in there, I come up with a plan. I've been throwing the idea around my head ever since Gladys made me rich in my own right – I decide to tell Tristan about it, maybe it'll take his mind off Blondie and work.

"Hey," I say sitting next to him again.

"Mrs Freeman," he teases – My heart stutters hearing that said. *Whoa!*

The waiter comes over for the fourth time asking if we are ready to order, I think he's getting impatient with us. Tristan offers for me to go first, picking up the Menu I blast off the first thing that catches my eye.

"I'll have the Langoustine & Scallop Ravioli," I say glancing at Tristan; he seems to have recovered and is back to his old self.

"I'll have the pan-fried Beef and a side of Pont Neuf Potatoes," he says in a firm, authoritative voice.

"Any sides for you madam?" the waiter asks.

"No, no thank you," I say.

"And for you sir?" Tristan is gazing at me with the most ridiculous smile on his face. He shakes his head at the waiter. "Very good." The waiter takes our menus and walks away.

"I was thinking," I say. "About what you asked me," I add.

Tristan looks intrigued. "Go on," he prompts as he tops up our wine.

"Well, since I have the money from Gladys, I was thinking about what you said about what career I really want."

"You have?" he smiles, my heart starts to beat rapidly.

"I just thought...as I'm so interested in cooking, maybe I could take a course or something?"

"Or go back to school," he suggests.

"Give up my job?" I question.

"I thought that's what' – "No Tristan. I was thinking more of a hobby, you know a couple of nights a week or something." *Blondie is not getting my job!*

"Not full time?" he clarifies.

"No," I bite, wondering if he's suggesting that because of what I've just told him.

"Hey," he says softly. "I was only asking."

I smile nervously at him, laughing a little as I do. "Sorry, I like my job, I don't want to give it up," I say hesitantly.

"Then don't," Tristan chuckles lightly, I relax in my chair. That was a bad idea, I'm obviously still reeling about Blondie – I need to get her out of my head.

"But I think you should take the classes, I think you'll love it," he tells me.

"I'll look into it," I tell him, then my other idea comes up, but I'm not sure if Tristan will want to do it.

"There's something else too, something I've wanted to learn for a really long time. I was going to ask Rob to go with me, but with everything he has going on with Carlos...." I drift off feeling a little melancholy. I've missed my friend, badly, and I've missed Carlos too. It's been really strange not having them around, it's like they're my family.

"What is it?" Tristan asks pulling me from my musing.

"Salsa dancing," I blurt, but I don't think he'll want to do it. Tristan starts chuckling. I sigh inwardly. "It's ok. I guess I can go on my own. I just don't want to end up with some creepy dance partner!"

"You're not going alone," Tristan snaps. "The last thing in the world I want is another man's paws all over you," he adds. *Oh!*

"You…you want to...to go?" I squeak in amazement.

"Hell yes! Seeing you in one of those little dresses, salsa dancing around the room' – Tristan's cheeks have flushed – 'I can just imagine how well you'll do, and how gorgeous you'll look." Tristan's eyes dance with hunger. *I did not expect that!*

"Really?" I laugh excitedly.

"Yes," he chuckles.

I lean forward, take his face in my hands and kiss him hard. "Thank you," I say, then clap my hands together in glee.

Tristan laughs hard at my expression. "Like a kid in a sweet shop," he says. "So you're going to have some pretty busy evenings, cooking and dancing?" I nod in excitement. "That's good baby," he says his eyes all warm, melting me into the seat.

Our meals arrive taking us by surprise. As we tuck in and try a little of each other's dish, I ask Tristan what he fancies doing tomorrow. Apparently, he already has something planned. My heart flips with excitement, and no matter how hard I try I cannot get him to tell me, much to Tristan's amusement and my annoyance. I'm still not too comfortable with not knowing what's going to happen. As we both finish our meals and sit gazing out at the setting sun, Tristan turns, smiles adoringly at me then looks down at my engagement ring, the diamond sparkling brightly at us both. I lean forward to kiss Tristan, but his sharp intake of breath stops me.

"Susannah?" He breathes. I whip my head around and see her kissing some man on the cheek as they both sit down at a table. *What the hell is she doing here?*

I immediately hide my left hand. I wonder for a moment if she somehow knew we were in here? *Maybe she's been following me?* I swallow hard at that thought. I can't help glaring at her. Susannah is immaculately dressed in a long black evening dress, with a split along the right leg that goes right up to the thigh – *Ugh!*

She looks amazing. Her makeup is perfect, and her long blonde hair is shining brightly in the soft lighting. *Maybe divorce suits some people!*

"I'd better go and say hello," Tristan says. *What?*

"Fine!" I mumble childishly. I watch Tristan stand, then walk across the restaurant to Susannah, my heart in my mouth the whole time.

When he reaches her, she smiles warmly at him, her eyes shining brightly. They kiss on the cheek, and she gazes adoringly at Tristan as he talks to her, suddenly her head whips round to me. I glare at her, then Tristan looks my way, so I quickly throw in a fake smile. Susannah nods and smiles at Tristan and then takes her seat again. As Tristan walks back over to me, I see her glare at me with that really weird look she had on Friday.

I subtly shake my head at her – *Now we both know who's playing games.*

"Who was she with?" I ask Tristan before he's even sat down.

"Her solicitor," he says sitting back down. "For the divorce," he adds. *Yeah right!*

"Why isn't she using someone from the company?" I ask.

"I have no idea Coral," he answers dryly.

"Shouldn't she be back in London?" I ask feeling more and more irritated by the minute.

"She's free to do whatever she wants at the weekend," he tells me firmly. "Would you like a dessert?" Tristan asks, trying to change the subject.

"No thanks. You?" Tristan shakes his head – *I want to get out of here.*

"What's she still doing in Brighton?" I ask as calmly as I can.

"I don't know Coral." Tristan's answer seems sincere.

I don't want to argue about her or have her come between us, especially after Tristan's proposal, this should be a special night.

"Shall we go?" I ask softly, moving my hand towards his arm, trying to act as though I'm not bothered that she's there.

Tristan pulls his arm away and leans back in his seat looking uncomfortable. "She thinks I've taken you out to say thanks for your hard work, purely platonic." I frown deeply at him.

"Why would you say that? Surely she just caught us kissing?" I say feeling bruised. Tristan says nothing. "What! She can't keep a secret for you?" I add snorting sarcastically at him. *Maybe he does have feelings for her?*

"Coral' – "I'm going to the ladies then I'd like to go home," I say, trying to sound normal but my throat is thick with unshed tears. I calmly walk away, I don't want anyone to see we've been arguing – especially not Blondie. I storm into the restroom and stand in front of the mirrors. I take a deep breath and stare back at my own reflection.

Keep it together Coral!

I shake my head at myself in exasperation. Ok, let's think about this logically, there has to be are several options as to why she is here. I nod in agreement with myself and begin my assessment. Ok, firstly, it could be that she really is getting divorced, and that's why she's got a solicitor with her, but I've never heard of a solicitor taking a client out for a meal to discuss their divorce?

I shake my head at that one.

Secondly, it could just be a coincidence. I have to question that. Could it be she just happened to be in the same restaurant? Somehow, I doubt that. No, no, no, I shake my head, remembering what she said – *'Tristan and I are engaged…we just couldn't help ourselves'* I think there's a real possibility that she knew we were here. I shake my head again. She can't be feeling too good right now seeing me with Tristan. I can't help smiling at that one.

Ok, so the only option left is that she knows we were here,

so she followed us. A shiver runs down my spine at that thought. *Ok, I'm definitely going with stalking.* There isn't another explanation for it, but how did she know we were here? I picture her in my studio again, rifling through my belongings…stealing my belongings – *Get back to Tristan Coral!*

Sighing heavily I stare back at myself in the mirror. It's no good, I need to tell Tristan everything I know, everything that's happened. I need to trust that no matter what, he'll believe me, stay with me, and choose me, not Susannah. I instantly picture his face, his angry face, ok, not tonight, but definitely tomorrow. *Forget her Coral, take a deep breath and get back to your man!*

I stare at myself in the mirror again. I decide to be brave, walk out there and take my man home. I look down at myself, I have a dress on for the very first time in my life.

Don't let Susannah ruin this night!

I nod in agreement with myself. Then I think about the sexy underwear I have on, and what Tristan's reaction will be to it. I picture us going home, Tristan stripping this dress off me, his eyes lighting up when he sees the sexy underwear I have on. I instantly imagine him making love to me, on the floor, in front of the fire.

My stomach flutters wildly with desire. *Whoa!*

With that idea firmly set in my mind, I quickly wash my hands, being careful with my new ring and head out of the ladies. Rounding the corner, I look down the restaurant to where we are seated, Tristan is gone, and so has his jacket – *Fuck! He's left me….*I feel all the blood drain out of my face. I frantically search the room, looking for him, and when I locate him, I feel my heart drop into the pit of my stomach. He's sat next to Susannah, and she looks like she's crying – and he has her hand in his!

I take two steps back, shaking my head in disbelief – *No, no, no, no, no! This is not happening!*

Susannah glances up, I know she's seen me, she purposely starts choking back tears, Tristan looks a little lost and just as I thought, he tries to comfort her. He puts his arm around her shoulder, she leans into his chest and puts her arm around his waist.

That's it, I'm done!

I stomp out the Restaurant, down the gangplank and head

in the direction of the Marina, my heels clicking loudly against the pavement. I should feel nervous, it's gone dark, and I'm on my own, but I'm too mad to think about that. Besides, they are loads of people out tonight, enjoying the warm evening, and the street lamps are lighting up the pavement and the roads. *At least there are no dark alleyways I have to walk down!*

A slight breeze kicks up, it makes me shiver slightly, I wrap my arms around myself and quicken my pace. I'm so mad at Tristan. I can't believe he would do that with any woman, let alone Susannah. *This is supposed to be our night, he just proposed to me for Christ sake!*

Five minutes into my walk, I hear my mobile buzz in my purse. I know it's going to be Tristan. I wonder for a second if I should answer it, I instantly picture him holding Susannah and change my mind. *He can just stew for now!*

Just as I pass Brighton Pier, I notice a bunch of men walking down the pier towards me, they are loud and definitely pissed up. My mobile buzzes again, I picture Tristan's face, his frantic look as he searches for me – *God damn it!*

I stop walking, open my purse and pull my mobile out – *Yep its Tristan*. I feel torn, on the one hand, I want him to stew, on the other, I don't want to worry him, I don't like causing him pain.

Reluctantly, I answer it. "What?" I snap.

"Where the hell are you?" he snaps back.

"I'm going back to my studio," I bark.

"Coral' – "Don't," I say, my voice shaking.

"I don't understand' – "You're a smart man Tristan, I'm sure you'll figure it out!" I say hanging up on him.

"Alright sexy!" I hear a man shout, slurring his words.

Keeping my head down I glance to the right and see the bunch of men have nearly reached me. Ignoring them, I carry on walking.

"Ah don't be like that." A different one shouts. *Just keep walking*, I tell myself, but I hear them all laughing, egging each other on, their footsteps following me – *Shit!*

I search the roads, hoping I'll see a taxi that I can flag down, but wouldn't you know it, not one passes me by. My heart starts to hammer against my chest, and my mouth feels as dry as a bone. I wonder for a second if I should call Tristan. I'm starting to feel a little panicky, and I have every reason to, because just as I think that one of them grabs my arm.

"Come on sexy, come out with us." Spinning round to face them all, I yank my arm out of his grasp.

"Don't touch me," I threaten, feeling my blood boil within me.

They all look at each other, and smirk. There's five of them, and I notice two of them can barely stand up straight, they are so pissed – *Ok, stay calm!*

I go to turn around so I can walk away from them, but they surround me, like a pack of wolves ready to take down an injured animal.

"Don't be like that," the leader says. I try to shove past one of them, but he laughs and pushes me backwards. *Shit!*

All the training I've done with Will has disappeared, literally fallen out of my head, my mind is completely blank. I try not to panic, but I don't think I would if it was just one of them, but how the hell am I meant to protect myself from five?

"What's your rush?" the other one asks, mock punching the leader. They both start laughing again. *I need to get out of here!*

The leader takes a step closer to me. I take a step back and come up against the chest of one of them. I spin around, and using both my hands I slam into his chest, he staggers backwards, leaving an opening. I push past the other and out of their circle. *Thank god!*

I want to run, but I don't want to show them how threatened I feel, quickening my pace, I make the stupid mistake of looking behind me. I see the leader laugh and slap his friend on the back, then they both start jogging towards me – *Shit!*

"What's your name?" the leader asks as he reaches me.

I keep my eyes forward and ignore him.

"Oi! I'm talking to you," he shouts and grabs my arm again.

"Get off me!" I screech and try to pull my arm out of his grasp – Right at that moment he's yanked away from me, and I'm pushed to the side. *Tristan!*

Tristan growls and punches the guy so hard I think I hear bones crack. The leader crumples into a heap on the floor. His friend launches toward Tristan, but he's taken down just as quickly, then Tristan's head whips round to me.

"Get in the car Coral," he growls and turns back to glare

wildly at my would-be attackers. I hear him say the words, and I know I should, but I feel frozen to the floor.

In a daze I turn and see Stuart get out of the Jag, he walks around the car and opens the back passenger door for me; he doesn't seem to be concerned about Tristan at all.

The leader stumbles back up, his eye is split, blood pouring from it, and I think his nose is bleeding too. He wipes his nose with his hand, sees the blood and bunches his hands into fists.

"I wouldn't," Tristan warns.

The guy turns and glares at me. "Fucking dick tease," he spits. *Dick Tease?* I'm a dick tease for saying no to you! Anger rears up inside me, I feel livid. My training comes back into play, and all I want to do is hit the guy. I drop my bag, clench my fists and take two steps towards him, but Tristan steps in front of me, effectively blocking me. *No!*

"Come on then!" He shouts, stepping towards me. I try to step around Tristan, but he yanks me behind him, keeping his eyes locked on the guy.

"Stay where you are," Tristan hisses at me.

"Fucking whore!" The attacker spits, blood splattering the ground in front of us.

Tristan hits him again, it happens so fast it's almost a blur. I stare at him, lying face down, out cold on the floor. The other guy stumbles up onto his feet, just as his other friends start making their way over to us – *Uh-oh!*

"Move," Tristan growls yanking me by the arm, he quickly bends down and picks up my bag. My steps falter as I try to keep up with him marching us over to the car. With the door already open, Tristan shoves me inside and slides in next to me –*Holy fuck!*

Stuart slams the door shut, jumps into the driver seat and instantly drives away, tires squealing as he does.

We drive back up to the house in complete silence.

Stuart pulls up in the driveway, keeping the engine running. Tristan steps out, and then he leans inside with his hand. I silently take it, sliding across the seat in a daze. Tristan helps me to my feet, and then he leans down and nods to Stuart who pulls away.

We silently walk to the front door. Tristan unlocks it and gestures for me to go first. I take a step and stumble in my heels.

My legs don't feel like my own. Tristan wraps his arm around my waist and slowly walks me inside. I hear him shut the door, and punch the code in for the alarm.

"Coral," his voice is firm and sharp. He comes and stands in front of me, assessing me. "Are you alright?" he asks frowning down at me.

I don't have any words, but I'm shaking from head to toe.

"Coral?" I go to speak, but my mouth just opens and closes, I feel really weird. "You're in shock," he says, then scooping me up into his arms, he walks over to the sofa and gently sits me down. "Please don't move," he adds.

I watch Tristan walk into the kitchen, removing his jacket as he does. Returning to me, he places a can of Pepsi in my hand, I shake my head at him. He rolls his eyes at me, takes the can off me, opens it up and places it back in my hand.

"Drink it," he orders. "It will help with the shock," he adds.

I take a sip, then another. Then I realise how thirsty I am and glug back several mouthfuls. *Whoa! That's fizzy and cold!*

I shiver slightly, Tristan is instantly on his feet, pulling the throw around me. I go to hand him back the can, he reaches his hand out, and that's when I see it – *Holy fuck!*

"Tristan," I gasp. "Your hand!"

"It's fine," he states firmly.

Ignoring him, I take his hand in mine and inspect it. The three knuckles starting from his forefinger are split, with a small amount of dried blood caked to each one. I instantly forget about how I'm feeling. Standing to my feet and yanking the throw off me, I take his hand and march him into the kitchen. I turn on the tap and put his hand under the water.

"Keep it there," I tell him. Finding the small first aid kit we bought. I unlock it, yank it open and find what I need. Antiseptic wipes, antiseptic cream, a bandage and some tape. I quickly rip open the antiseptic wipe, take it out and unfold it.

"Give me your hand," I tell him firmly, he reluctantly does so. "This might sting," I say and start gently wiping across his knuckles.

Tristan hisses a couple of times as I go deeper into the cuts. I can feel him watching my face as I do this. Keeping my eyes firmly fixed on what I'm doing, I throw the wipe in the sink. Opening the antiseptic cream, I pinch a little onto my finger and smooth a little over each knuckle. Then I open the bandage and start wrapping it around his hand, when I'm satisfied it won't come off, I cut the end, and add a little tape.

I finally look up at him. "Ok?" I ask.

"I am now," he answers, his broody look is back. "What happened?" he questions. "Why did you leave Coral?" I look at the floor and hesitate for a moment. "Coral!" he bawls.

My eyes dart up to his, I can see he's mad, well so am I.

"I left because you were busy feeling Susannah up when I came out of the ladies!" I shout.

"What!?" he bellows. "I can't believe you just said that. You know I have no feelings for her," he adds, shaking his head.

I grit my teeth feeling guilty I said it like that, then I question it. "How would you feel if the moment you disappeared, I was like that with Stu or one of your team?" I bark back.

"That's not the point," he bellows.

I shake my head in disagreement. I can't believe this is happening on the night Tristan proposed to me, gave me a ring – *It's all her fault!*

"I hate her," I mumble.

"Let me guess, Susannah?" Tristan barks at me, crossing his arms.

"Yes!" I screech.

"This is fucking ridiculous," he shouts, running a hand through his hair.

"Well, she's got us fighting already, hasn't she," I say wearily.

I suddenly feel bone tired. His face falls as he catches my expression, then he shakes his head and stares down at the floor, deep in thought.

"Tristan, I don't want to fight," I tell him softly. "And I'm sorry, I didn't mean for it to come out like that. I just…I walked out of the ladies, and there you were, holding her hand," I start to choke up. "Comforting her, touching her, being close to her," I sniff loudly. "I know it sounds stupid, but I don't want you being close like that with another woman, no matter who she is. It really twisted me up inside, I didn't know how to react, so I just ran." I say feeling totally deflated.

Tristan gazes down at me with wide, cautious eyes. We stare at each other for the longest time, neither wanting to back down. Then he runs a hand through his hair and sighs deeply.

"Jesus Coral, I never looked at it that way. I don't want you being like that with another man either. It won't happen again," he tells me firmly, I absolutely believe him. "I'm sorry I made you feel like that," he adds.

I sniff loudly. "I'm sorry too, for running," I croak.

Looking down at me with his brooding look, he pulls me into his body and crushes me against him. It's almost painful, but I don't care. I feel safe, protected.

"Thank you," I whisper. "For saving me," I add, pushing back the tears.

"I didn't scare you did I?" he asks.

"No, not at all, you're my hero," I tell him. Then I think about what could have happened, and grit my teeth, feeling angry at myself. "I can't believe I panicked. All that work I've done with Will, all that training…" I shake my head in disgust. "What's the point if I'm just going to freeze?"

I close my eyes and swallow hard, I dread to think what would have happened if Tristan hadn't turned up. I start to tremble all over as all these scenarios start running through my mind. What would they have done to me?

"Coral," Tristan breathes, tightening his hold on me. I feel him kiss my hair. "Most people freeze baby," he adds.

I look up at Tristan…*my hero…my love, my future husband.*

He takes my face in his hands. "Baby, no matter how mad you are with me, don't ever do that to me again, don't disappear on me. For a start look what happened, what could have happened…" Tristan shakes his head and grits his teeth. "You had me worried sick. I had no idea what had happened to you, or where you'd gone' – "I'm sorry," I say interrupting him. "It will never happen again," I add staring up at him.

Tristan closes his eyes and lets out a long deep breath. I rest my head against his chest again.

"Lucky for me you really can box," I squeak, looking up at him.

"Yes, Gramps did well," he says, sighing heavily.

"I've never seen a boxer hit so fast though, it looked more like martial arts," I say. Tristan frowns looking guilty. "Was it martial arts?" I question.

He nods once. "You…you know martial arts, and you never told me?" I squeak.

We've talked about this, he knows I love Bruce Lee and martial arts films. I don't understand why he hasn't told me!

"Coral I…" Tristan looks lost again and runs a hand through his hair. "I didn't want you to have any reason to fear me," he says. *What?*

"That doesn't make any sense?" I say.

"I still train in boxing and mixed martial arts, but for all I knew it could have been something that would have scared you away, so I kept it to myself," he tells me softly.

"So I wouldn't have any reason to fear you?" I clarify.

Tristan nods solemnly, his eyes bleak.

I shake my head at him. "We could have done some sparing you know," I scold.

He gazes down at me again with his broody look. Raising his hand, he softly strokes my cheek. "I'm sorry you had to see that," he says. I think back to the guy out cold on the floor.

"You don't think he's…" I stop, I can't say the word.

"What?" Tristan questions and rolls his eyes at me. "Tell me Coral, what are you thinking?"

"You don't think you k-killed him do you?" Tristan's eyes go dark. "Tristan?"

"He attacked you, so I don't give a fuck! But I doubt it, I didn't hit him as hard as I could have," he growls.

"Oh," I whisper. The enormity of it hits me again, and I start to choke up. "It's not fair, why me? Why do I feel like I'm walking around with a big sign on my head, all fuckers this way," I croak.

Tristan squeezes me even tighter and kisses the top of my head. "Well, nothing like that is ever going to happen to you again Coral. You give me your word you won't run, I'll give you my word I'll always protect you," he tells me firmly.

I look up at him. He closes his eyes and rests his forehead against mine.

"Deal," I say feeling a lot better about it all. Tristan's right, if I hadn't run off…

"Deal," he says, opening his eyes and smiling down at me. "Let's not allow it to ruin our evening," he adds.

Then lifting my hand with the ring, he brings it to his lips and gently kisses it. I feel all the frustration, the fear, and the anger drift away, I'm not mad at him anymore.

"You know, when I first came out the ladies, and I couldn't find you, I thought you'd ditched me," I smile nervously at him.

Tristan cocks his head to the side then shakes his head at me in wonder. "Let's get a drink," he says…

CHAPTER TWENTY-FOUR

AS I WATCH Tristan pour us both a Brandy, my heart swells with love for him. I still can't believe he can punch like that, and he was so calm about it too, I wish I'd have been that calm. Tristan hands me a glass, clinks his against mine and knocks his back in one go. *Whoa!* He leans down to me, his lips almost brushing mine. I feel the room charge, the atmosphere change.

"I want you," he whispers against my lips.

Oh, Tristan, you had me the moment you met me!

"You know what I was thinking in the ladies?" I say, trailing soft kisses down his neck.

"What were you thinking?" he asks, his hand moving slowly up my leg, right to my thigh, his breath catching as his fingers reach my lacy hold-up. I slowly snake my way down his torso and reach his erection, it feels hard and heavy against his suit trousers - *I want him, and I want him now!*

"I was thinking about you making love to me in front of the fire. I was thinking about you discovering what I'm wearing under this dress." I lean back and gaze up at his dilated eyes. "I want you," I whisper squeezing his erection just a little harder, his breath catches again as he groans deeply with desire, then he leans down and kisses me, hard.

"So you want the fire on," he whispers seductively.

"Yes," I whisper back breathlessly.

He smiles sexily at me, steps back and marches off into the living room. I take a sip of brandy, and turn towards the living area; I see flames start to flicker. Moving around the breakfast bar, I see Tristan standing in front of the fire. He silently beckons me with his long forefinger; his look is so hot, so sexy. I feel my blood instantly heat.

With trembling legs, I walk over to him. As I take his outstretched hand, he pulls me into him and kisses me hard again. I moan with pleasure as his hands work their way up my legs, past my hold-ups, finally gripping my backside.

"Damn you're one sexy woman," he whispers.

Stepping back, I unhook the back of my halter-neck and shimmy out of the dress.

Tristan gasps loudly. "Dear God," he breathes, swallowing hard.

"You like?" I smile holding my arms out for the offering.

"Oh yeah baby," he says in his deep husky voice, it sends shivers to all the right places.

Pulling me into him, he kisses me passionately as his hands caress the lace across my hold-ups, working their way across my lacy panties and up across my new corset.

"I didn't think they could look any sexier." He says gazing down at my bulging bosom. I smile in delight at his reaction and reach down for his erection.

"I'm yours, take me, fiancé," I whisper.

He gazes at me in awe for a moment, then gently takes me in his arms and lowers me to the floor. I close my eyes and surrender to the sweet sensation...

"WAKE UP SLEEPY." I open my eyes to sunlight pouring in through the floor to ceiling windows and instantly squeeze them shut, it's too bright, and my head hurts. Wine at lunch and dinner, sipping Brandy by the fire till the early morning, and god knows how much making up sex, was too much in one go.

"What time is it?" I groan, still feeling sleepy.

"Eight o'clock," Tristan answers.

"Why so early?" I grumble, my head really starting to bang.

"Because we are booked for ten o'clock, and I knew you'd need some time to get ready. Baby, open your eyes." *Booked? For what?*

I do as Tristan asks, and see he's got a big glass of veggie juice in one hand, and two painkillers sitting in the palm of his other – *How sweet!*

"Thanks," I smile sweetly at him and swallow the tablets with several gulps of juice. Putting the glass down on the bedside cabinet, I close my eyes again and rest my head on the pillow.

Tristan chuckles at me. "You want to go back to sleep?" he surmises.

"Uh-huh," I answer, feeling myself drifting back off.

"Ok, I'll come and get you in a while." I hear him say, but it's already muffled as I lose consciousness...

WHAT FEELS LIKE moments later, I'm rudely awoken by Tristan jumping on top of me, and I hear music blasting. It's Phil Collins, Find A Way To My Heart – I know it well, it's my favourite song of his.

"You like Phil Collins?" I giggle.

"Yes," Tristan chuckles back, playfully kissing me all over.

Checking my headache has gone, I smile at Tristan, and without a word, I jump out of bed and start dancing to the amazing beat. Tristan joins me and starts dancing too, I laugh aloud as he pulls some sexy moves. I twirl and sing along to the words, moving my hips to the beat, and as the song comes to an end, he pulls me into him.

"I think we just found our wedding song," he tells me. "I can't wait to see you in your wedding dress, walking down the aisle towards me," he says his voice all husky, his eyes deep and intense.

My throat goes dry, and my heart pounds against my chest. I hadn't thought of that. Where the hell am I going to get a dress from? *I really need Rob right now!*

"Really?" I pant as Phil starts to sing Come With Me.

"Yes," he states firmly.

I wonder for a second why I haven't thought about any of these things – *Because you're a freak of nature!* – I laugh sarcastically at myself.

"What?" Tristan chuckles.

"Nothing," I chuckle then frown. Why haven't I thought about the kind of wedding I want, or dress or wedding song?

"Tell me," he pleads.

I feel panicky just thinking about it and start squeaking it all out rapidly.

"I just don't understand why I haven't thought about any of the stuff you keep bringing up, like wedding rings and dresses and songs'– "Ok, take a breath," Tristan says and walks us over to the bed. Sitting us both down, he wraps his arm around my shoulders. "Does it matter that you haven't?" he asks softly. "All I care about is that you want to marry me. Still, do?" he asks questioningly.

I roll my eyes at him.

"Ok," he laughs. "So don't worry about the rest. I know I keep mentioning certain things because I keep thinking you're thinking the same. Most women would have loads planned by now, I'm sure, but that's one of the many reasons I want to marry you because you're not like them, you're so different." I look up at him feeling sceptical about what he's saying.

"It doesn't matter to me that you're not running around ordering this and that for the wedding, or planning where and what date. All that matters to me is what's most important, that you want to marry me."

I somberly shake my head, I feel so guilty. "I have no idea what I want Tristan, except you. I have no idea what kind of wedding, or dress or rings or any of it. I just want to marry you," I whisper.

"Well that settles it then," he says.

I frown back at him.

"We hire a wedding planner," he adds. *What?*

"Really?" I squeak in surprise. "Aren't they for people who have huge weddings?" I ask.

"I don't think so," Tristan frowns.

I chuckle at him, he has no idea, but I like his plan, I'm already feeling less nervous.

"Leave it to me," he says confidently. "Now, I've moved our appointment to an hour later," he tells me. "So, how do you feel, headache gone?" He questions as his lips quirk up at the corners.

"Why are you trying to hide your smile?" I ask.

"I'm not," he says, grinning broadly.

"No," I answer sarcastically, shaking my head. "Of course you're not!"

"Headache?" he asks sharply, trying not to smile.

"Gone," I smirk. "What – Are – You – Laughing –At?" I ask mock punching his arm with each word.

Tristan really starts tittering and falls back onto the bed. "I was thinking," he chuckles. "About when you came with me to view this place, you were so ill. I think I knew back then that you don't handle hangovers very well," he says.

So he did find my suffering amusing, bastard!

"Who does," I answer dryly.

"Well it's a good job you're feeling better," he tells me.

"Why?" I question hesitantly. I may not like what I'm about to hear.

"You'll see," he answers smugly. I look down at his hand, remembering last night, the bandage is gone, and the cuts look like they are already healing.

"How's your hand?" I ask, taking it in mine. Feeling on top of the world that I have such a gentle, yet masculine man who loves me – *Who knew!*

"Fine. Now come on, shower Mrs, and I'll get your breakfast going."

Mrs…Hmm, I like the sound of that!

"*My* breakfast?" I question.

"Oh, I already ate," he tells me jumping up from the bed. *How can he have so much energy?* We were both pretty slurry when we climbed into bed this morning. Glaring grumpily back at him, I huff loudly, pick up my veggie juice and stomp into the bathroom…

AFTER DRESSING IN my jeans, t-shirt and trainers at Tristan's request, I make my way down the stairs. The moment I reach the top step of the first flight of stairs, I'm hit with the smell of smoked salmon and eggs. *Hmmm,* my stomach rumbles loudly in appreciation.

As I skip into the kitchen, I see Tristan whisking something at the counter.

"Just in time," he says. "Take a seat," he tells me, so I do.

Picking up my orange juice, I take several gulps. *Mmm… it's so refreshing.*

"Close your eyes," he requests politely, so I do, I hear him place something in front of me, it smells divine. "Open your eyes," he whispers.

I look down and see he's made Eggs Florentine on a bed

of spinach with smoked salmon, all neatly stacked on a toasted muffin.

I gaze up at him. "You made this?" I ask in astonishment – *I think Tristan should be the chef!*

"Gran taught me," he says shrugging his shoulders. "Come on, eat up," he tells me.

I pick up my knife and fork and cut through it, taking a bite I moan dreamily.

"Perfect," I say sweetly, because it is, just like Tristan, just like his proposal, and just like last night's lovemaking.

My pelvic muscles contract just thinking about it. It wasn't perfect, it was damn-hot-sexy-sex, not lovemaking. I pick up my orange juice and take several swigs, trying not to picture what we got up to, clearing my throat and taking a deep breath, I smile sweetly at Tristan, quiet my mind and tuck into breakfast.

"I could get used to this," I say, feeling a tradition in the making; Tristan making breakfast, me cooking our evening meal.

"Me making you breakfast?" he questions, laughing lightly.

"Yeah," I chuckle. "I think that's fair, especially if I'm cooking on an evening."

Tristan seems deep in thought. "I could get someone in to cook and clean for us," he says.

I can't help smiling.

"What?" he chuckles.

"Nothing," I laugh.

"Tell me," he pleads.

"It's just...I never imagined myself with someone' – "With money?" he questions, interrupting me.

I nod feeling shy. "I just think it's going to feel weird you know…having people to do stuff for me. I've always been so self-sufficient," I say.

"Well I don't know about you, but cleaning bores me to death, and this is a big place. I'd rather pay someone to do it," he says. "And if you're going to be busy in the evenings, maybe we should get someone in to cook for us too – I don't always have the time myself," he adds.

I think about it for a second, maybe it's not a bad idea. I can cook when I'm home early, and when I'm not the chef can do it, at least I'll know Tristan's getting a decent meal in him. I look around the huge expanse and decide a cleaner would probably be a good idea too. Tristan and I could spend all weekend cleaning this place, and we still wouldn't get to every room.

"Ok, let's do it," I say.

"Glad you agree," he says. "But I was going to do it anyway." He adds, grinning broadly at me.

"Really?" I say sarcastically.

He chuckles at me. "What do you think about a live-in housekeeper?" he asks.

I shrug, unable to answer as I'm eating, but wouldn't that be weird, other people living in the house, but there's something about the way he's smiling at me.

I quickly swallow. "Do you already have one?" I ask.

"Yes," he smiles. "In London," he adds.

"You do?" I squeak in surprise.

"Yes," he chuckles. *Hmm, I've never asked him where he spends most of his time.*

"Are you there a lot, you know compared to Birmingham and Leeds?"

"Yes, I consider it home…well, I did," he says his thumb skimming my cheek.

"Male or female?" I ask, frowning at him.

"Female." *Hmm, not sure about that!*

"Will you ask her to come here?"

"Yes."

"Do you think she will?"

"Yes, I think so. Her daughter is in Devon, so I think she'll jump at the opportunity."

"Oh," I nod. "How long has she worked for you?"

"Ten years." He raises one eyebrow as he reads my expression – *Crap!*

"She's sixty-three," he says, smiling broadly.

"Oh," I say, feeling stupid.

"Oh baby," he chuckles. "Edith is lovely when she came for the interview, I hired her there and then," he says, his eyes going all warm with memories.

"Why?" I ask.

"She was by far the best candidate," he says, but I can tell he's hiding something.

"Why don't you just tell me the truth?" I say between mouthfuls.

Tristan sighs then smiles warmly at me. "Alright, ten years ago I had my folks move in with me, they were both getting on, and I didn't want them rotting away in a care home. My London pad has its own studio, so they were happy with that. Edith knew her duties would be mainly taking care of them, keeping the house clean, grocery shopping, and cooking meals, you know stuff like that…" he trails off, his cheeks flaming.

"What's wrong?" I whisper.

He turns and stares down at me with sad eyes. "I…I just… sometimes it hits me so hard that they've both gone and I'll never see them again. It feels like I've been hit by a truck like it's just happened all over again, but that's grief for you I guess." He takes a deep breath and slowly blows it out. "I miss them Coral, sometimes…it's really hard to think about them," he adds, swallowing hard.

"I know baby." I wrap my arm around his waist and lean my head on his shoulder, and I can tell he's fighting back the tears. Tristan rests his head on mine and puts his arm around my shoulders, I try to think of something to say, something to take his mind away from the grief.

"Tell me about Edith," I prompt.

He kisses the top of my head and seems glad of the change of subject.

"Ok, well Edith had never worked a day in her life, but she knew how to run a home. Her husband had always done well, and she wanted to be a full-time mother to their daughter, so she was a stay at home mom, but her husband had died suddenly of a heart attack, the very same month her daughter had gone off to university. She said to me that she had to re-evaluate her life, and with them, both gone she knew she couldn't stand being in the house on her own, the other job she applied to was cabin crew on a cruise-liner."

"She was brave," I say.

"Yes and determined, I immediately liked her, and so did my folks, she really was the mothering type, which was exactly the kind of women I trusted to take care of my folks, you hear such horror stories about abuse in homes-" Tristan stops dead and looks down at me.

"It's ok Tristan, I know what you meant, believe me, I've thought about it often enough with Gladys, there's no way I'd let her go into a home."

Tristan nods once then continues. "Well as you know, I like giving good jobs to good people," he says.

"Yes Tristan, I know, you're very sweet like that," I say.

"Well, she started with me, and after three months she put her house up for sale, it quickly sold, and she has that money invested for when she retires," he says.

"So, was she there?" I question. "At the funerals? Did she help you, Tristan? Help you get through it all?" I softly ask.

"Yes," he breathes. "Without her, I think I would have fallen apart," he adds, his eyes darkening as he remembers.

"Oh Tristan," I whisper. I kiss his cheek and hold him to me. "Then she must come here, she can't stay in London on her own, not after everything she's done for you," I say. "And I like her already," I add, knowing it's true. Edith helped Tristan through a painful part of his life.

Tristan pulls back and gazes down at me. "You are so sweet," he whispers.

"Tristan' – "You are," he interrupts.

"So will you ask her?" I say, trying to get off the subject of me.

"You're keen?" he observes.

"Yes, aren't you?"

"Yes," he smiles. "I have a question?"

I swallow hard. "Ok."

"Next weekend, can we move you in, I mean officially. I'm dying to tell everyone Coral, I don't think I can contain it much longer. I want the whole world to know that you, beautiful you, have consented to be my wife."

I frown down at my empty plate.

"You don't want to?" he says.

"No…it's not that…" I whisper, still frowning at my plate.

He places his hand on my cheek and turns my head, so I have to look at him.

"What is it Coral? What are you hesitant about?"

"I just…the moving in part yes, let's do that, but announcing we are getting married after such a short amount of time together…I don't know about that. And I think we should still keep our relationship quiet…at least until…" I stop, frowning deeply.

"Until what?" he whispers.

Ugh! Susannah, Susannah, Susannah…If she weren't a possible psycho, I would have him announce us, our relationship, our engagement to the world, but he can't, because of her!

Argh! That is so annoying!

"I just don't think anyone should know about us yet, not until the take-over has happened."

"Alright," he whispers frowning down at the floor. I think I have hurt his feelings.

"Tristan, I want to shout it from the rooftops…tell the whole world about you, about us. I just think with everything going on, it's best to wait. Besides, I don't want to give Gladys a heart attack, I've never lived with anyone or had a real bona fide boyfriend. I just think she'll freak out, and I don't want her thinking I'm rushing into this because she's moving away. I want her to know – eventually, that I moved in with you and married you because I fell in love with you."

"Oh baby," Tristan grasps my face in his hands and kisses me forcefully, I feel giddy by the time he's finished. "You're right," he murmurs against my swollen lips. "We know how we both feel, let's give others time to adjust."

I smile up at him. "So, if I'm secretly moving in next weekend, will Edith be with us by then?"

"More than likely," he answers.

I'm excited to meet her. I fast forward to next weekend, to packing boxes and moving them here – I instantly get an image of Bob, looking sad and lonely, eating junk food – *No!*

Then I remember that I need to call him anyway, he can't tell Gladys someone tried to get in!

"What is it?" Tristan asks.

"I just…" I quickly pull my mobile out of my bag and call Bob, letting him know I don't want him to say anything to Gladys about my late night visitor. Tristan raises an eyebrow at me as he clears away the plates. Bob assures me he won't say anything, so I say goodbye and hang up.

"Tell me, baby," Tristan says sitting next to me.

"Tell you what?" I ask.

"Why you looked upset before you called Bob?" *He doesn't miss a thing!*

"Bob," I whisper, remembering the image. "Who will look after him when I'm gone?" I muse.

"Well, we could always ask him if he wants to be here with us?" he casually says.

"You would be ok with that?" I squeak.

"Yes Coral, of course, I would. I know you consider him as your adopted granddad, he may not agree though," he adds.

"Where would he sleep?" I ask.

Tristan shrugs. "We'll sort it if he says yes," he softly says.

"Thank you, Tristan," I whisper – *He really is a wonderful man.* "I guess we'll be filling up the bedrooms after all," I murmur.

"What do you mean?" he chuckles.

I smile shyly at him. "Well, when I came here with you on the viewing, I didn't understand why a single man would want to buy a place with so many bedrooms," I say.

Tristan frowns down at me. "Kids," he whispers, reading my mind.

I shrug. "Yeah, I guess I was thinking like that," I gush.

"Coral, you do know don't you?"

"Know what?" I ask.

"That I'd be very happy to adopt, that's if you want a family one day?"

"Are you trying to tell me something?" I whisper with wide eyes.

"No baby, I'm just putting it out there," he shrugs.

"Oh, ok," I whisper.

Tristan quickly stands and holds his hand out to me. "We'd better get going," he says.

"Ok," I place my hands in his, and we head out for Tristan's surprise...

AS WE HEAD back to the car, Tristan drapes his arm over my shoulder. I reach out and squeeze him tightly around his waist. Tristan's surprise was Go-Karting, I didn't know there was a place in Brighton you could do that, but it's actually closer to Worthing, so that's probably why. I wasn't really sure if I wanted to do it, but once we were inside the massive building and got kitted up, I was bouncing about with excitement, which Tristan found really funny.

There were eight of us (I was the only girl) a small stag doo and Tristan and I, they seemed a nice enough bunch, but there was one that was a little flirty, well, until I showed him my engagement ring, and introduced him to Tristan. It was quite comical as he looked up at Tristan's tall stature and wide shoulders, he immediately gave up with the one-liners.

The track was awesome. It had a sweeping double apex, a twisting flyover and a most impressive Monaco-style tunnel. At first, we were all given a few goes at getting to know the track. Tristan instantly picked it up and overtook me several times. I gritted my teeth and pushed harder, trying to beat him, then we all raced individually.

Tristan won, and to my complete surprise I came second, I had to wonder if it was because the other guys were hung-over, or if it was because I was actually good at it. Tristan told me in no uncertain terms that I was brilliant and he was very proud.

After the individual races, we all teamed up. Tristan was like a kid at Christmas, of course, he had a strategy, and after five laps the scores came up on the board. Tristan was totally overjoyed that we won. His free spirit and laughter were infectious, I don't think I've ever had such a good time on a date. I still can't believe we got so close with our scores, maybe there's a racing driver in me after all? *I wonder if it should be my new career?*

Laughing at myself, I shake off the thought.

"Was that fun, or was that fun?" he laughs.

"It was great fun," I chuckle, squeezing him tight.

"So what would you like to do now?" Tristan asks as we pull out of the car park. "I don't know about you, but I'm starving," he adds.

I roll my eyes at him. *He's always hungry!* As I think that, inspiration hits.

"How about the beach?" I say, feeling last night's shenanigans and this morning's racing catching up with me. My muscles are sore and aching, and I feel like I could sleep a good couple of hours. *What better way to do it than soaking up some Vitamin-D!*

"The beach?" Tristan questions, glancing at me behind his aviators – *Damn he looks sexy in those!*

"Yeah, I know this great little cove. Hardly anyone ever goes down there, it's a great little suntrap." Tristan is silently nodding in approval.

Hmm Tristan in nothing but a pair of swimming trunks, I hope they're tight fitting!

I shake my head at my wayward thinking. "We could take a picnic," I say a little high pitched and clear my throat.

Tristan glances across at me and smirks. "A picnic?" he says his voice low and husky.

I grin like a fool. "Yes," I chuckle. "And I'll need my bikini, from my studio," I add, wondering if my place will still be in one piece.

"Do you own one?" he asks.

"Yes," I giggle. "Why would you ask that?"

"Because you've never been abroad," he simply says.

"Oh," I say. "Well, it's pretty ancient…it might not even fit me anymore," I muse. Last time I wore it…I can't remember the last time.

"I'll buy you a new one," he says, smiling down at me.

"You will?" I squeak in delight.

"Yes," he chuckles. "Where should we go to get one?" he adds.

I think about it for a moment, then I remembered a few years ago, Gladys, Debs and I took little Lily down to the beach for the day, we actually had a sunny Saturday. I remember Gladys mentioning that she'd got this ready-made picnic hamper from M&S, and I know the one I'm thinking of is open on a Sunday.

"I have an idea," I say.

"You do?" he teases.

"Yes," I chuckle. "Head back towards the Marina baby," I say.

"What's your idea?" He asks.

"Well, I thought we could pop into M&S and pick up one of those ready-made picnic hampers," I say.

Tristan lets go of my hand and very slowly, starting at my knee, he starts to slide his hand up in the inside of my leg. "Get you a bikini while we're at it," he says, his breathing getting heavier. *Whoa!*

"Good idea," I say, swallowing hard as his hand continues to travel up my leg. "Tristan," I warn.

"Yes," he answers playfully.

"If you don't stop doing that I'm going to jump on you and I don't care who sees!"

"Well, I do," he says, his voice low.

"Concentrate on the road," I admonish. "We don't want to have an accident," I add.

His hand is still travelling, teasing and tantalising me, so I reach across and place my hand on his crotch, and to my great surprise, I find he's hard underneath his jeans.

"I was just picturing you in a bikini," he says a little breathlessly, explaining the reason why.

"Oh!" My heart is trying to claw its way out of my chest.

Tristan laughs and stops just as he reaches my sex – *Bastard!*

"You're a tease," I admonish, pulling my hand from his lap and crossing my arms. Tristan laughs at my little hissy fit. "You can't just turn me on like that and leave me hanging," I scold, staring out of the window.

"No?" he questions.

"No," I pout.

"Shall we make a quick detour home first?" he questions. *Yes!*

"Yes, before we go shopping," I say.

"Your wish, my command," he says and puts his foot down. The car zooms in and out of traffic, and we sit silently, heading east back to Tristan's mega-pad…

WAKING FROM MY peaceful snooze, I turn onto my back, lean up on my elbows, and put my sunglasses back on. We are on the beach, and as I look out, I see the sea is sparkling like diamonds under the glare of the afternoon sun, and I notice there are loads of boats out today, they look so tiny out there in the distance.

"Hmm…" I feel so content, so relaxed – *That'll be the hour's worth of sexual antics you got up to before shopping!*

I grin like a fool. Is it really possible to feel this happy?

"Hey, beautiful." Tristan's deep husky voice pulls me from my musing.

I turn and smile sleepily at him…*boy he looks good, so sexy!*

He's wearing a pair of Oakley wraps and he looks just as sexy in them as he does in his aviators. He's sat on his lounger – Of course, we had to buy loungers, we couldn't just put a couple of towels down on the sand – with his e-reader in his hand.

"Hi," I croak reaching down for the big bottle of water we bought, and taking several gulps. *Ugh!* I still feel stuffed from lunch. Even though the picnic basket we bought had several mini sub rolls, two strawberry tarts – which I didn't eat, I don't like short-crust pastry – and two goblets of chardonnay, Tristan insisted on buying extras, citing it wouldn't be enough to keep him going – *Boy he can put it away!*

"Need anything?" he asks.

As I turn and gaze at him through my sunglasses, I see his chest is starting to look a little red, even though he's browning up nicely.

"You're burning," I scold.

He has the decency to look a little guiltily at me, especially after our argument in M&S about what sun lotion to buy. I wanted the highest factor Tristan wanted the lowest. I told him it makes no difference to how quickly you brown, and that the higher ones protect your skin, he argued some more until I stamped my feet, and told him I wasn't going unless we bought the one I wanted.

"When was the last time you put some sunscreen on?" I say questioningly.

He smiles wryly, shrugs at me and returns to his reader – Must be a good book – I roll my eyes and pick up the lotion, holding it out for his hands.

"But I don't want to get my reader greasy," he grumbles.

I roll my eyes again, sit next to him on his lounger and squirt some into my hands. As I rub the sunscreen across his mighty fine chest, I see a smirk start to play across his lips.

I shake my head at him and start laughing. "You did this on purpose!"

"Of course," he answers smugly, watching me cream his skin.

I squirt more sunscreen into my hands and rub it across his shoulders – they really do look a bit too red – I'm about to ask him to put some on my back, but I stop myself, I want to tease him. Squirting more cream into my hands, I head south, rubbing the lotion across his toned abdomen, keeping my eyes fixed on his gorgeous bronzed body.

My nipples respond all by themselves, trying to break through the thin material of my new bikini. Tristan's one eyebrow cocks up in response, as I head further south to the edge of his swim trunks. I sigh blissfully as I reach his hardened erection.

"Here?" he questions, reading my thoughts.

"Yes," I whisper, leaning in to peck his open lips.

"Someone on one of those boats could have binoculars," Tristan growls.

"They won't see anything," I argue.

Handing him the bottle of lotion, Tristan puts his reader on the hamper, and I step my one foot across the lounger, so my legs are wide apart, then slowly sink down and straddle him. I rub myself against him. His lips part as I lean in and kiss him, his tongue lapping gently against mine...*Hmm, sex on the beach*...

"I don't like this," he growls, looking up at the cliff face behind us.

"Like anyone is going to turn up!" I argue.

"Let's make this quick," Tristan grumbles.

I pull his shorts down so his erection can spring free. Then placing my one hand on his shoulder, I lift up, pull my bikini bottoms to the side and take his erection between my other hand. I feel his tip reach my opening, and slowly but surely, I slide down over him, until he's completely filling me. *Mmm... skin against skin, it feels so good.*

With both hands on his shoulders, I start to move, up and down, my leg muscles protesting, but really grinding into him as I come down. I want to feel his full length, buried deep inside me.

"Quickly," he moans, his mouth slack as I pump up and down, gaining a rhythm.

Tristan grasps my thighs, his fingers digging in, and then he's lifting me, and pumping up into me as I come down on him – *Christ I'm close...so soon...so quickly.*

"Come on Coral," he says, staring down at my pert nipples underneath the material.

I take my hands from his shoulders, reach down and move

the material of my bikini top to the side, so my nipples and half my breasts are on show for him.

"Fuck!" he hisses and pulls me closer, sucking my right nipple.

"Ahh…" I feel it right down there, deep inside me. He moves across and sucks the other, then leans back to gaze at me.

"Jesus," he hisses and pumps even faster. "You are so fucking sexy," he groans.

"Oh god…Tristan," I moan as everything tightens and quickens inside me. He is hitting my sweet spot. I fall spectacularly, squeezing him, over, and over again, as my orgasm ripples through me. "Tristan," I call out, my head lolling back, my mouth slack.

"Christ," he growls. I feel him thrust into me once more, then still, his hands gripping my thighs tightly. I open my eyes and see he has his eyes shut, his head craned back as he pours himself into me, this man, this wonderful man; who will soon be my husband.

What did I ever do to deserve him?

He opens his eyes and blinks up at me. "Jesus Coral," he whispers, looking frantically around him, replacing the material back across my breasts, I start laughing at his worried expression.

"It's not funny!" he growls.

"Your face is a picture," I say chuckling even harder.

"Right!" Standing up with me in his arms, I wrap my arms and legs around him and kiss his bronzed cheek; I can still feel him inside me. Then he starts to march down the beach, towards the shoreline, as he reaches the water, he smiles wryly at me, and I know exactly what he's going to do.

"Tristan, no!" I shout, "It's freezing," I screech.

He wades into the water, stopping when it reaches his waist, instantly freezing my legs and soaking my bikini bottoms – I really don't like the Atlantic, it's too cold. I grip him tighter, scowling angrily at him.

Tristan pecks me on the lips and then smiles his cheeky grin.

"Don't you dare!" I threaten, but it's too late.

Tristan wraps his one arm around my shoulder, the other around my waist, gripping me tightly, and plunges us both down into the icy cold water – *Oh my god!*

Moments later, he launches back up, and I cough and spit sea water.

"Bastard," I dither, my teeth clashing together.

Tristan laughs at me, and then I feel his fingers tease my clitoris, before pulling himself out of me. Then he deftly hides his manhood back in his shorts and puts my bikini bottoms back in place.

"That was cruel," I say, pouting at him.

"Ah, poor baby," he soothes. "But we're both clean and fresh now," he says his eyes glinting wickedly. "Besides, I needed to cool down," he adds.

He pulls me to him and kisses me passionately, gripping me tightly. I welcome his tongue, his lips, as they skim along mine making me want him all over again. Then, out of the corner of my eye, I think I see something glinting in the water. I may like the sea, but it doesn't mean I like being in it, I start frantically searching around me looking for any signs.

"What are you looking for?" He laughs, keeping a firm hold of me.

"S-s-sharks," I whisper fearfully, my teeth clashing together.

"Sharks?" he laughs. I nod my head. I've never looked at the sea the same since I watched Jaws. "Ah baby, I won't let a shark get you," he titters.

"Very funny," I scold. "But if a shark comes and bites you in the ass, then takes me with him, you won't have much choice," I blurt.

Tristan bursts into raucous laughter and starts wading out of the water. I keep my legs firmly wrapped around his waist, my arms almost choking him.

"It's ok," he teases as we finally reach the shore. I grip him even tighter. "Hey," he says calmingly. "We're back to dry land baby, relax," he soothes.

I take a deep breath through my chattering teeth. "Let's get you warmed up," he says. I nod vigorously in agreement – *I'm friggin freezing!*

THE FOLLOWING DAY as Stuart drives us into work, I can't help thinking how magical the weekend has been – well apart from Friday – but either way, Tristan has been wonderful, sweet,

Freed By Him

thoughtful, fun. He was amazing at the barbecue; everybody loved him, and his proposal that followed...*his sweet, sweet proposal...*

Then I think about Saturday night, our romantic meal, his gallant way of protecting me when I stormed off, our sexy hot make-up sex, and then our amazing fun day out yesterday. My mind drifts back to having so much fun and relaxation on the beach, and we both look better for it, healthier, happier and more relaxed.

I'm surprised I don't have Monday morning blues, but I think that's because Tristan and I seem to have come so far in such a short space of time. And this time he's not leaving, he's here all week, well, he's actually here now for good, apart from the odd meeting he needs to go to. I can't wait to see him tonight. I could definitely get used to this, seeing my sexy man every night after work, and to top it all off, Rob is back today; my best friend, my awesome best friend. *Oh, I have missed him so...*

I can't wait to see him. I have so much to tell him. I push the sinking feeling away that something bad has happened, and try to think positively. *Everything's going to be fine*, I tell myself. Everything feels like it's finally falling into place – well except for one thing.

"Ready for another working week?" Tristan asks, pulling me from my musing.

"Yes," I whisper, and as we are strapped in with our seat belts, and I can't easily kiss him, I reach out and take his hand in mine.

"Happy?" he questions, reflecting my goofy grin.

"Yes, future husband, I couldn't be happier," I say and blow him a kiss.

Tristan smiles like a fool in love, but I can't help wondering what his reactions going to be when Joyce speaks to him about Susannah, and worse, what he will be like when I tell him what I know. If he listens objectively, I will tell him what Karen told me about Blondie, and I really want to tell him about all the other things she's been up to too, I feel slightly nervous about doing that. Then I remember that my package should be arriving this morning, so maybe I'll get some answers.

"I don't think it's a good idea we arrive together," I say

looking down at my left hand. It already feels strange not wearing my engagement ring. Tristan has stowed it away in his safe at home until we break the news.

"I agree. Stuart can drop you off first, I have a couple of things I need to do anyway." He says.

I frown back at him, wondering what it is. "Oh, ok," I say feeling a little forlorn.

"Hey." Tristan cups my chin. "Thank you, baby, for the best weekend ever," he says in his sexy, husky voice.

I smile back at him. "Best ever?" I tease as Stuart pulls up in the underground car park.

Tristan takes his seatbelt off, unclips mine and pulls me into his lap, making me giggle. "Best ever, let's do it again this weekend," he says, leaning in to kiss me softly.

"Definitely," I murmur against his lips, inhaling his scent. "I better go," I whisper, not wanting to leave him at all.

Tristan's eyes peruse the car park stealthily.

"I'll be fine," I tell him leaning in to kiss him once more. I pull the door handle and hop out of the car, but as I bend down to say one last goodbye, I wince in pain – Damn I can't walk properly again, poor muscles. *Tristan and his sexing!*

"Sore?" Tristan teases.

I purse my lips and frown at him. "Aren't you?" I gripe.

"Nope." He replies, smiling sexily at me.

"Who've you been practising on?" I say my voice low as I frown down at him, but I'm secretly teasing him. His mouth falls open as he sees my serious expression. *Ha!*

Just as he goes to answer me, I smile widely, bob my tongue out at him and quickly slam the door, chuckling heartily to myself as I do.

Feeling triumphant, I almost skip my way into work. Pushing through the double doors, I see Joe stuffing her face as usual. "Morning Joe!" I laugh. She mumbles something at me, but I can't make out what it is.

Then I think I'd better warn her that Tristan is in today. I walk over to her desk, lean forward and immediately spy *two* blueberry muffins!

"He's coming in today," I whisper raising my eyebrows as I do.

Joe frowns at me as though I've gone mad, then I see the

penny drop. She gulps hard, goes bright pink and silently nods, swallowing again she whispers, "Thanks, Coral."

"No worries," I tell her. "Joyce in yet?" I ask.

"No, not yet. You look nice," she says. "You've really caught the sun, look how dark you've gone! You're so lucky, I just go pink then burn," she grumbles.

"Yeah? Well, I don't like it, Gladys calls it dirty brown, I'd much rather go bronze," I say.

"Who's Gladys?" she asks.

"My adoptive Mother," I tell her – *I thought she knew.*

"Really, you were adopted?" she says a little surprised and eager to know more. *Uh-oh!*

"Well, I'd better get to it," I say. I'm about to walk off when she screeches at me.

"Coral!" Scrambling under her desk, she hands me an A4 DHL delivery package. "I thought it might be important, so I signed for it, he said you wouldn't get it till tomorrow if I didn't."

I smile as she hands me the package. "Joe, I could give you a big kiss for doing that!" I say, she suddenly frowns and starts fidgeting uncomfortably.

"I...I'm not into girls," she tells me awkwardly.

I burst out laughing at her. "Me neither!"

Joe starts laughing too. "S-sorry Coral" she giggles, blushing again.

I shake my head at her as the laughter still ripples through me. Then the phone goes, she runs around the desk to answer it. I whisper 'thanks again' as I hold the package up, so she knows what I mean, she gives me the thumbs up.

This has to be my package from the P.I Company. Eager to see what they've come up with, I run up the stairs and bypassing my desk completely, I go straight into Joyce's office and lock the door behind me. I look up at the clock – 8.20am – I have time.

Putting down my handbag and sinking onto the leather sofa, I rip open the package, feeling very nervous about what I might find. When I requested as much information as possible about Susannah, I also asked if I could have the details of Tristan's ex, I gave them the dates they were together, so the information was easier to find. I know I shouldn't have, but there's something I want to ask her, yet another suspicion rattling around in my head.

With shaking hands, I pull out the paperwork and lay it on my lap. I close my eyes and take a deep calming breath – *Ok Coral, you wanted to know!*

Feeling guilty for doing this behind Tristan's back, I start scanning the first page. Tristan's ex's name is Olivia Logan, was Peters, but she's now married with a couple of kids. I'm surprised to see that from the time they started dating, it was only a couple of months later that she moved in with Tristan, and then she moved out of his registered address when he ended it. My hearts sinks. I didn't think they would have moved in together so quickly, just like us, does that mean there's no distinction between us? *Enough Coral get on with it!*

I scan further down the page, and I'm shocked when I see her Driving Licence picture. Olivia is stunning. I mean really stunning, she reminds me of Penelope Cruz. Her dark hair is shoulder length and beautifully styled, her facial features are perfectly symmetrical, and her wide eyes are green and sparkling. I can really see why Tristan fell for her, and she for him. My self-esteem goes down a few notches, not only is she beautiful – and no doubt normal – but they moved in together so quickly, just like Tristan and I. They must have really fallen in love with one another – *Crap!*

Feeling guilty for doing this, I take a moment, wondering if I should continue – *You have to Coral, she knows something!*

Listening to my gut instinct, I take another breath and continue reading. I now have her husband's name, her children, their address and most importantly, Olivia's mobile number. I'm shocked at how easy it is to find this kind of information about someone. I'm about to continue reading when a loud bang pulls my attention away. *Shit! Joyce is at her door!*

Flying up from the sofa, I unlock it and pull it open.

"Coral!" Joyce says in shock, rubbing her forehead.

"I...I'm sorry," I squeak.

"What are you doing?" she asks as she walks through the door.

Feeling stumped with what to say, I pick up my package, my bag and head for the door.

"Coral!" Joyce booms. I turn and stare back at her, but I don't know what to say. "I asked you a question," she says firmly.

"Um...I was...I just wanted some privacy. I..." I rack my

brains for an excuse. "I had some mortgage papers to look through," I say hoping she'll believe me.

"Oh, well you can stay in here if you like," she tells me.

I shake my head at her. "No thanks, Joyce. I can carry on reading it later, it's not urgent," I say hoping my voice doesn't sound as shaky as it feels. Joyce frowns and stares back at me with her hands on her hips, scrutinising me over the rim of her glasses – I'm squirming inside.

"Very well then," she says, staring disbelievingly at me.

Without another word, I scuttle out of her office, close the door behind me and sit down at my desk. *Whoa! -* That was close, maybe I should wait until lunchtime to carry on, but my fingers are itching to turn the next page and read about Susannah. I have the information I want for Olivia, I just need to make the call. I really hope she will speak to me. Just as I'm about to carry on reading, Tristan comes wandering up to me. I keep my eyes locked on his and casually flip the pages over, so he can't see what's on them.

"Tristan!" I swallow hard and fake a smile.

"For you," he says passing me a small bag with Starbucks printed on it, and I'm presuming a Cappuccino to go with it.

"Thanks," I squeak in reply.

"Open it," he says sipping his drink. Opening the bag, my heart melts when I see there's a chocolate swirl inside. Last night, I told him about my survival on these while he was away, he really does listen.

"Thank you, baby," I whisper in appreciation. *They really are delicious.*

"You're welcome," he smiles. "You ok?" he asks scrutinising me like Joyce did.

"Uh-huh," I keep my eyes fixed on his.

"You look a little nervous," he assesses.

"Do I?" I squeak, laughing as I do.

Just at that moment, Joyce comes out of her office saving me from continuing. "Ah Tristan, just the man I wanted to see."

I swallow hard and stare at my blank computer screen.

"Good to hear!" Tristan swoons and smiles enigmatically at her.

Joyce blushes and titters at his reply. "Hold all calls Coral, we'll be about an hour," she says.

"Ok," I squeak again. *God damn it, I wish my voice wouldn't do that!*

Tristan follows Joyce into her office, looking back at me once before he closes the door, I can see he's still assessing my behaviour. He can read you like a book Coral. Hide what you're feeling for god's sake woman. I smile up at him, then wink. Tristan chuckles at me then slowly shuts the door.

Tentatively, I pick up the information on Olivia, fold it over several times and stuff it inside an envelope. I decide it's too risky to read through Susannah's information at my desk, so I place it in the same envelope and stuff it inside my handbag. I switch on my computer and sip my Cappuccino while I wait for it to fire up, when it does, I open my inbox, and get started on the letters Joyce sent across to me...

I AM ITCHING to read Susannah's information. I'm about to sneak off to the ladies when Joyce's door is flung open – *Uh-oh!* – Tristan looks mad.

"Can I see you in here please?" he asks firmly. He does not look happy.

Frowning at him, I stand from my desk and walk into the office. Joyce is sat at the big mahogany desk she uses for meetings. I walk over and sit down next to her. Tristan almost slams the door shut, and then takes a seat opposite us both, with a face like thunder. I've never seen him look like this before.

"Joyce has given me some...well, disturbing news," he says, his voice flat. "Can you confirm that Susannah upset Joe?" he asks.

"Yes," I whisper, swallowing hard, my eyes wide with fear.

"Why didn't you tell me Coral?" he asks, finally meeting my gaze.

"It wasn't my place to say Tristan, and Joyce told me not to, she said that she would talk to you about it," I answer honestly.

He clenches his jaw and looks once at Joyce, then stares down at the paperwork in front of him. This feels really weird, he's acting like...like a boss.

"I'm going to ask you a question, it is pivotal, so please be honest. Is there anything else Joyce and I should know about?" I look down at my hands. "Coral!" he admonishes.

I wonder if I should tell him everything, but the fear of losing him takes over. Besides, I want to read that report first, and then I'll tell him what I know.

"No," I state firmly, locking eyes with him.

"There's been no problem working with Susannah, nothing to report?"

"Tristan, you know I don't"– I shake my head – "It's not like we're going to become best buddies," I laugh nervously.

Tristan narrows his eyes at me – *Shit!*

I sigh heavily. "No. Nothing to report, well apart from what I told you on Saturday," I say.

Tristan looks deep in thought as he stares at the paperwork. Joyce clasps my hand under the table. *What's that all about?*

"Are you sure?" he questions, his head cocked to the side, his eyes narrowed, trying to read me.

"Yes," I say narrowing my eyes back at him. *Something's going on!* "What's going on Tristan, why am I in here?" I question.

He sighs heavily, looks up at Joyce then his gaze rests on me. "Susannah has put in an official complaint about you. She said that you threatened her when she found out we are seeing each other, that you have repeatedly been un-co-operative with her, and that you threatened to get her sacked." My mouth pops open, I silently stare wide-eyed at Tristan. *Is he joking?*

Tristan continues. "I have no choice but to involve H.R, they will continue this complaint." He looks mortified.

I blink three times trying to get my brain to fire. I look several times from him to Joyce, while the enormity of what Tristan's just told me sinks in.

An investigation? I threatened her?

I shake my head feeling totally bewildered. "That's ludicrous!" I snort sarcastically.

His head snaps up, our eyes meet. "Were you difficult with her?" he asks. *See, this is one of the reasons I didn't want to get involved with my boss!*

"No." I bark, feeling angry that Tristan would even ask that question. "Tristan, I haven't threatened her," I tell him firmly.

I try to get my head around why she would say that. I stand up and start pacing the room, there's no way I can say that it's her that threatened me now, that's just going to make me sound like I'm trying to save my own bacon; that I'm trying to turn the tables on her.

"Coral, please sit down." I turn and look at Tristan, it's written all over his face.

"You believe her," I say, my voice barely audible.

"Coral, I can't be seen to be taking sides. I have to pass it on to H.R."

My head whips round to Joyce. "Do you believe me?" Joyce nods once.

I start pacing again. I can't believe Tristan is choosing her over me. Then it hits me, she can get me sacked for this, and she wants to move here.

Holy crap! – This is her way of getting rid of me!

"Is she moving here?" I ask sharply.

Tristan frowns. "She's asked for a transfer," he states.

I can't help laughing sarcastically at that answer.

"What?" he questions.

"You're not going to need two P.A.'s here are you?"

"No but' – "So what is *she* going to do Tristan?" I narrow my eyes at him.

He glances across at Joyce, takes a deep breath then looks up at me. "Coral, Susannah's been with the company a long time' –

"Six years," I interrupt. "I've done fifteen," I add.

I know where this is going, she's going to get my job, well screw her!

My heart starts manically beating against my chest. I don't know why I think it or say it, but the moment the decision comes into my head, I know it's the right one to make.

Taking a deep breath, I utter the words. "I quit." Joyce gasps and Tristan looks up at me with wide eyes, then they narrow as he once again tries to read me. "You want Susannah here, you got it," I snap then I turn and look at Joyce. "Joyce if it's ok, I'd like to work with you until the end of the week, as long as Susannah's not here," I add between gritted teeth.

Joyce stands with tears in her eyes. "Coral, please…" she whimpers.

"Don't be upset. I think this is the best option anyway. I don't think I'd have liked it here once you've gone." Joyce nods despondently and sits back down in her chair.

Freed By Him

I turn my glare on Tristan and silently shake my head at him.

He stands up and starts to walk around the table towards me. "Coral," he says with his hand held out. "Don't be rash."

I shake my head at him and cross my arms. "Do you believe her?" I ask again.

Tristan stops about a foot away from me, clenches his jaw, sighs heavily and stares down at the floor. *I guess that answers my question.*

"Un-fucking-believable!" I hiss.

"Coral' – "Save it, Tristan," I snap holding my hand up to him.

Turning on my heel, I march out of Joyce's office, slamming the door behind me. Stopping at my desk, I pick up my handbag and stomp down the corridor to the ladies....*Holy hell, what have I just done?* I lock myself inside one of the stalls, then close my eyes and lean my head back against the cubicle. I try to think clearly, but my head just feels like its swimming. *What just happened?* I can't work out if Tristan was on my side or not, and how dare Susannah flip everything around, so I'm made out to be the bad one, the crazy one! Putting the lid down on the toilet, I slowly sink down onto it, tears pooling in my eyes. *Holy crap, I just quit!*

What the hell am I going to do now? Then I remember that I'm two hundred and fifty thousand pounds better off, at least I don't have to worry about money, and whether I can pay my mortgage, but I can't not work, it would drive me crazy. I decide to call Malcolm, see if he's got anything going at the moment, unzipping my bag I go to find my mobile when I'm instantly side-tracked. There, sitting in my handbag is the information that may save me. *Right!*

Taking the envelope out and ripping it open, I pull the contents out and flatten them across my legs. I may have quit my job, but I haven't quit Tristan. I love him too much to lose him, and I won't let her get between the two of us. So let her come here, let her have my job, see how she likes Tristan and I being an item…hopefully married.

Taking a deep breath, I begin reading…*Oh, this should be good!*

On the first line is her name.

Mrs Susannah Johnson–*So she is married.*
Then I read the next line.
Spouse – Sgt Samuel Johnson - Deceased 19/4/07 – Helmand Province.
Her husband died!
I stop reading. I can't help but cry a couple of tears, how awful, poor Susannah! I check the date again, 07' – So her husband dies a year before she started working for Tristan. Even though I feel heartbrokenly sorry for her, I also feel angry, she has lied to everyone, including Tristan –*And she stole from me!*

Reluctantly, I continue reading. It tells me all the kind of information I thought I would get like; D.O.B, her age, her parent's names, the schools she went to, her academic achievements, and a full employment record. I'm surprised to see that none of the places she's worked at is office based. It's mostly retail work; shoe shop, bakery and clothes store. *Not one office job?*

I find that very odd, but I don't have much time to be thinking this over, as I reach the end of the page and turn it over to the next, I'm shocked to see it says Medical History.

As I start reading it gets really scary.

7/5/07
Patient admitted to hospital. Failed suicide attempt. Anti-Depressant Paroxetine prescribed.

9/9/07
Patient admitted to hospital. Second suicide attempt. Patient grieving the loss of a husband and miscarried child. Patient placed in Psychiatric Ward for a full evaluation.

Fuck - She lost her baby too! I swallow hard and carry on reading.

20/9/07
Patient receiving Psychological Treatment. Diagnosed with Post-Traumatic Stress Disorder. Cognitive Behavioural Therapy implemented. Patient symptoms include – Severe Anxiety Attacks, Clinically Depressed, Emotionally Unstable – Patient showing signs of progression through treatment programme.

5/11/07
Patient released from programme due to greatly improved

behaviour. Patient to return home for follow up sessions with an assigned therapist.
20/5/08
Patient showing signs of increased behavioural difficulties. Sessions with therapists to be increased. Patient diagnosed with Chronic Obsessive Compulsive Neurosis.

Holy fuck!

CHAPTER TWENTY-FIVE

THIS IS UNBELIEVABLE! I mean, I knew there was something iffy about her, but I wasn't expecting this, I don't even know what Chronic Obsessive Compulsive Neurosis is, but it doesn't sound good. I swallow hard. Jesus, on the one hand, what the poor woman has been through is just awful, losing her husband, then her baby, but on the other hand, she's dangerous, and my instincts were telling me from the very start.

I look back at the last paragraph May 2008 – Tristan told me she started working for him by then –*Shit! Shit! Shit!*

I try not to freak out, but my heart is slamming against my chest, and my stomach is twisting with anxiety. What if it's not just love that she has for Tristan? What if she's turned obsessive about him? I shake my head in denial, no way. Surely someone that sick wouldn't function normally on a day to day basis? I'm instantly reminded of the film Fatal Attraction, Glen Close's character seemed pretty normal until she went loopy.

I suddenly feel really, really scared for Tristan. What if she's been stalking him, keeping potential relationships away from him, what if I'm right, and she's the one that told Tristan Olivia was cheating on him? Karen's words come into my head *'she is so different with everyone when he's around, the moment he leaves she goes back to being...I don't know....just weird."*

My mouth goes completely dry. I think about her behaviour last week, she's been up and down like a yo-yo, one minute she's nice, the next she's not. The dream I had of her comes unbidden into my mind's eye, and I know in that very instance why I had the dream about my mother – *Oh my God!*

I close my eyes and lean my head against the cubicle. They

have the same look in their eyes. I knew it, I knew all along that something wasn't right with her, I'd seen it before but, I just never put two and two together. Susannah is sick, really sick, and she needs help before she harms someone.

Then a sinking, sickening feeling washes over me, and I know it was her.

Susannah was the one outside my door Monday night.

Suddenly it all becomes very clear.

She's not after Tristan, she's after me. *Fuck!*

Shaking my head in horror, I open my eyes and read the last entry.

2/7/08

Patient no longer attending sessions. Repeated attempts to contact patient have failed.

Case Closed.

Case closed? *What the fuck!* – I close my eyes and lean my head against the cubicle. Why the hell didn't they bang down her god damn door? She was evidently showing signs of getting worse, not better. I suddenly feel really lost, what do I do? Should I speak to George, Joyce, Gladys, or should I be brave and show this to Tristan? Even though I know, I risk him rejecting me because of what I've done.

Opening my eyes, I look down at the papers in my shaking hands, and that's when I notice I still have a page to go, I turn it over. *Oh no!..No….No…No!*

I am staring at what looks like a photo of Tristan, but it's not, it's her dead husband. They couldn't look more alike if they tried; same bone structure, hair colour, even his eyes are the same warm brown. As I stare at the handsome soldier before me, I feel sick to my stomach, my head starts to swim, I think I'm going to faint. I reach out, place my hands either side of the cubicle walls and press against them in an attempt to stop the room spinning. I close my eyes and breathe deeply until I feel the cloudiness wash away. *Ok, ok, better, much better!*

Ok, decision time. I know the moment I think those words that I have to tell Tristan, he has to know everything and he needs to know now. I need to be brave, march right into Joyce's office, place the paperwork down on the desk and beg

Tristan to read it. Hopefully, he will see sense, and we can get the police involved and get Susannah away from him before she does anything stupid. But there's something I need to do first, as there's still one question I need answering.

With trembling fingers, I prize open the piece of paper with Olivia's details and punch her number into my mobile, three times I have to re-do it because my hands won't stop shaking.

Finally, getting it right, I hit call and wait for an answer.

"Hello?" A sultry voice answers.

"Um...Hi...is this Olivia? Olivia Logan?" I ask stuttering as I do.

"Who is this?" she questions. I rack my brains for what to say, how do I start?

"I'm not interested in anything you're selling, goodbye' - "Tristan Freeman!" I screech. "I-I'm calling about Tristan Freeman, I'm not selling anything," I tell her firmly.

"What about him?" she asks.

"I...he's in trouble," I say.

"Trouble?" she questions.

"Well...he might be...I'm not sure," I say. *Come on Coral!*

"What has this got to do with me? Who is this?" she snaps.

"Olivia, I'm sorry. I should explain. My name is Coral Stevens. Tristan and I...well we're engaged but," I take a deep breath. "I need to ask you about Susannah Johnson," I tremble.

Olivia is quiet for a very long time.

"Tristan is engaged to you?" she whispers.

"Yes," I answer. I wait for her to say something, but when she doesn't, I know I need to push. "Olivia, please help me," I plead.

"Help you how?" she asks a little bewildered.

"I...I know this must be hard for you. I know you loved Tristan and that it got all messed up, but I need to know, was it Susannah that told him you were with your ex?"

"How do you know about that?" she questions.

"Tristan told me a little bit about you," I softly say.

I wait again.

"Yes, yes, Susannah was the one that told him," she answers.

My heart sinks to the pit of my stomach, Tristan lied to me, he told me Susannah didn't know about him splitting with Olivia, but she did

With a heavy heart, I continue. "How do you know that?" I question.

"Because the night I was with my ex, she came over and talked to me, I even introduced her to him. I always thought it was strange she was there, but when she told Tristan, she made up a pack of lies, and he believed her, I've never forgiven him for that," she snaps.

"Olivia, Susannah was mentally ill, psychotic even, she still is, people like that can be very, very convincing. I would know, my Mother spent most of her life in a Psychiatric Hospital," I say, trying to ease her pain.

"I'm sorry," she says.

"Look, Olivia, Tristan loved you, I know he did, but he also trusted Susannah. I can just imagine how convincing she would have been with her story, and Tristan is too trusting, he would have believed her."

"He should have believed me," she snaps.

"Yes," I whisper. "He should have. That's why I've had a private investigator find out all he can about Susannah…" I proceed to tell Olivia about my week with Susannah, all the things she's done, then I read out everything that's in the report. "Do you see what I mean about him being in danger?"

"Yes," she answers. "I'd like to help, but I don't see how?"

"You have helped. I know it was Susannah that lied to Tristan. I'm going to tell Tristan I contacted you if that's ok?"

"He won't take your word for it," she says.

"I know it's a risk I've got to take, but I'm going to show him the report. I don't see how he can deny what's plainly written in front of him." *If he does, we're through…*I squeeze my eyes shut.

I hear a child cry out in the background. "I have to go," she tells me. *Babies, kids, Tristan could have had it all with her…*My heart sinks even further.

"I know, thank you, Olivia. I really do mean that, and if I need you as back up, do I have it?" I ask tentatively, even though I doubt I do, I can't blame her for not forgiving Tristan.

Olivia sighs heavily. "I may not have forgiven him, but it doesn't mean I want to see any harm come to him," she says mournfully.

"That's wonderful Olivia." I swallow hard. "Thank you," I add solemnly.

"I'd rather you didn't contact me again," she says, "Unless you really have to." *Crap!* She still sounds cut up about it. *Maybe she still loves him?*

"I understand," I softly say. "I'll let you go."

"Oh Coral...I'm not the only one," she says.

"Sorry?" I say a little bewildered.

"Tristan and I, we moved in the same circles and had the same friends. I'm not the only one that got nailed by that bitch," she spits, taking me by surprise.

"I...I don't understand?" I stutter, frowning deeply.

"Just ask him about Cathy, Rebecca and Sarah," she says, sounding exasperated.

"What about them?" I whisper.

"I have to go," she says and hangs up. I shake my head in wonder, who are Cathy, Rebecca and Sarah? – *Another time Coral!*

I sigh inwardly. I was right, it was Susannah that told Tristan about Olivia. What the hell did Susannah say to convince Tristan to believe her – a woman he's known less than a year – over Olivia, who he lived with, shared time with, loved, surely his allegiance should have been to Olivia?

My stomach starts to sink, I have a dreadful feeling he'll do the same with me, that he'll believe Susannah instead, but I have no choice, he has to know. I fold the paperwork over, stuff it back inside the envelope, place it in my bag with my mobile, zip it up and shakily stand up. Stepping outside the cubicle, I walk over to the sinks and stare at my reflection.

Come on Coral! – As I wash my hands in a complete daze, I try not to think too hard about Tristan's reaction, I try not to think about him disbelieving me, I have to stay focused, I have to stay calm. Shaking my head at myself, I quickly dry my hands at the blower, head out the ladies and storm down the hallway; feeling totally numb with fear. I walk straight past my desk, ignoring the line that's ringing, and pull my hand up to knock on the door.

"Coral!" I whip my head around and see Joe stood before me.

"What?" I ask, feeling exasperated as she's stood there looking like a lost lamb.

"I can't get rid of the woman on the line," she says. I look

Freed By Him

down at the phone on my desk. I see the red light flashing, the line continues to ring.

"I can't deal with this right now Joe," I answer sharply.

"But she won't stop calling!" Joe shrieks. I replay her last words to me. *I can't get rid of the woman on the line…*

I feel a cold sweat instantly cover my body. "What woman Joe?" I question breathlessly.

"She's from Social Services," she says, her voice trembling.

My heart calms a little. "Social Services?" I question frowning hard.

"Yeah, she...she wants to talk to you," Joe explains.

"Me?" I ask surprised. "What would they want with me?" I add cocking my head to the side, Joe looks nervous; her fingers twisting against one another. "Joe?"

She looks up at me with wide, worried eyes. "What if it's about my kids?" she chokes, tears spilling down her cheeks. *Shit, what if it is?*

I step forward, pull her to me and try to comfort her. "I'm sure it's not, but either way you know I'd give you a glowing report, right?" I pull back and smile down at her.

Joe smiles back in relief. "Thanks," she sniffs. "Shall I tell her to call back? It's the fifth time she's called."

"Really?" I say, surprised again.

"Yeah, she really wants to speak to you." *Damn it! Really bad timing!*

"Is that her?" I say pointing with my chin. Joe nods. Better get this out of the way so I can talk to Tristan. I grit my teeth walk over to my desk and pick up the handset. "Garland & Associates' – "Coral Stevens?" A woman with a Jamaican accent asks interrupting me.

"Yes," I snap looking up at Joe who's hopping from one foot to the other.

"Formerly Coral Foster?" *Fuck!*

My eyes widen with fear, and my heart starts thumping against my chest. I feel all the blood drain out of my face. That was my name until I took Gladys's.

I try to stop myself from hyperventilating.

"Miss Stevens?" she prompts.

"Yes," I murmur my voice trembling. Just at that moment,

Joyce comes out of her office, the look on my face stops her dead in her tracks.

"I'm sorry to call you at work. I tried getting hold of your Foster Mother, but there was no answer. My name is Laticia Smith, as I said I'm calling from Social' – "Why are you calling me?" I interrupt, my voice barely a whisper.

"I'm afraid I have some bad news," she says, her voice sounding sorrowful.

"Bad news?" I question and look up at Joyce.

"Yes. I'm afraid it's about your birth mother."

I close my eyes and grit my teeth. "What about her?" I whisper, the dream of her protecting me from Susannah comes into my mind's eye.

"I'm sorry to say, she passed away yesterday," she answers mournfully.

I open my eyes and blink twice, my head feels foggy, and my ears are ringing. I feel the handset slip from between my fingers and hit the desk. I hear Joyce call out for Tristan in the distance, but the fog washes over me, and everything goes black...

I HEAR TRISTAN'S voice, but he sounds like he's miles away.

"Coral, open your eyes." He says.

I know I should, but I want to stay in the murky grey haze. I feel something cool being placed on my forehead, it feels so nice.

"Coral?" I hear a different voice, I think it's Joyce. "Come on darling, open your eyes."

I don't know where I am, but it's comfortable. *Why won't they leave me alone?*

"Coral..." Tristan's voice sounds strangled, I feel his cool fingertips brush across my cheeks.

"I think we should just wait. Let her come round in her own time, she's had a nasty shock," Joyce says. *A nasty shock?*

I try to remember, but it doesn't come to me.

"Why would they contact her about that?" Tristan asks.

"Next of kin, I suppose," Joyce answers.

"You think they'd be a little more delicate. Getting news like that is bad enough at the best of times, but while you're at work...it doesn't seem right." Tristan sounds upset.

I try to remember...

"I've contacted Gladys, she's coming over to take her home."

Gladys?

"I'd rather take her back to our place," Tristan grumbles.

"I don't think it's the right time Tristan, I think she should be with her Mother."

Mother – That's ringing a bell? I search the recesses of my mind – *Mother?*

I hear a voice tell me *'she passed away yesterday'*...

Mom? – I search for some kind of meaning, but all I keep getting are flash images of my Mom and me before things got bad. Playing hide and seek, me giggling loudly as she throws me up in the air then catches me in her arms, tickling me all over. Making pancakes, kissing me goodnight, telling me she loves me...*Mom?*

The fog suddenly lifts – My Mom is dead! – *No!*

My eyes dart open, my mouth swims with saliva – *Shit!*

I only wretch once and see Tristan's blurry figure push something underneath me, and I'm violently sick.

"Jesus." I hear him hiss, as his hand gently strokes my back.

"It's normal," Joyce tells him. "Most people are sick after fainting."

I wretch several times until my stomach is completely empty. Then the burning comes, and my lungs feel like they're on fire, and my throat feels like I've gargled with a glass of acid.

"Gaviscon," I choke.

"I think I have some," Joyce says.

Moments later, she's handing me a spoon and the bottle, with shaking hands I try to open the top, but it won't budge. Tristan takes it off me, takes off the cap, carefully fills up the spoon with the thick pink liquid and spoon feeds it to me like a child.

"Another?" he asks.

I swallow and nod. He does the same again, and slowly but surely, the burning fades away. I look up at my surroundings, I'm in Joyce's office, and I'm on the sofa. Tristan is sat beside me, Joyce kneeling in front of me.

"Coral," Joyce says softly. I look down and meet her eyes. "Do you remember what happened?"

"My Mother is dead," I answer numbly.

Joyce nods solemnly at me, patting my hand. "Yes, darling."

"How?" I croak, my throat feeling bruised. Tristan passes me a glass of water, I take a tentative sip.

"They're not sure darling. There's going to be a post-mortem."

I gasp at this news and close my eyes, silent tears start to flow down my cheeks. I don't understand why I'm crying for her. Then I think about my photograph that's missing. What if Susannah killed my Mom? I shake the thought away, she can't have done, it's a secure facility.

I swipe angrily at my tears and jerk to my feet. "I'm sorry I was sick," I say to Joyce then begin to walk towards her door.

"Darling, where are you going?" she asks.

"Back to work," I answer numbly.

Tristan is at the door before I can open it, shaking his head sympathetically at me. "Coral, Gladys is coming to pick you up," he tells me softly.

"Why?" I snap, fighting back the tears that will not go away.

I feel someone's hand rest on my shoulder, I jerk it away, whipping my head round I see Joyce lower her hands and stare at the floor. I think I've offended her, but right now I don't care, I just want to go back to work.

"Coral," Joyce soothes.

I whip my head round to her. "Stop Coraling me both of you!" I shout.

"Coral!" Tristan shouts. "That's enough!"

I whip my head back round to him and swipe at the tears, glaring angrily at him. *I'm still mad at him about Susannah.*

"Let me past!" I bawl – *I want to run, far, far away.*

"Coral," Tristan pleads, reaching up to touch my arm.

"Don't touch me," I jerk it away and take two steps back.

I don't want anyone to touch me.

Tristan backs away with his hands held high looking bruised.

"Why can't you just leave me alone!" I shout just as Gladys flies through the door.

I feel my resolve falter as I stare back at her, then completely disintegrate as she envelopes me in her arms.

"I'm here darling," she softly says as I break down and let out loud, cathartic sobs.

All I can see is a picture of my Mom's face smiling down at me, she's healthy, happy, her eyes filled with love for me, and at the same time, the voice keeps telling me my Mother is dead. I want it to stop –*No!* – I can't handle this!

"Hush now darling," I hear Gladys say. "Hush now!" she squeezes me tighter as my crying slowly softens. "We need to get her home," she says.

"I can get Stuart back here," I hear Tristan offer.

"Good idea darling," Gladys says.

I'm aware Tristan leaves the room.

"Have some Brandy Coral, it'll help with the shock," Joyce softly says. I let go of Gladys feeling completely bewildered and turn to Joyce, she's smiling tentatively at me.

"I'm so sorry Joyce," I manage to choke out between sobs.

"It's alright," she says. I take the glass of brandy, she knocks one back herself and hands another to Gladys. "Drink," she tells me.

I bring the glass to my lips, open my mouth and neck it back. Joyce takes the glass off me and stuffs a load of tissues in my hand. I blow my nose several times, but no matter how I try, I cannot stop the tears.

"Is your bag at your desk?" Gladys asks.

I hear her speak, but I can't answer. I think I'm in shock.

"I'll get it," Joyce walks out of her office.

I feel waves of hollow black pain lance through me. I hug Gladys again as another set of raging tears overtake me...

I DON'T REMEMBER getting back to the house, but I do remember Gladys making me a hot chocolate, sitting me down on the sofa in the living room and helping me make sense of it all. We talked for a long, long time, she helped me understand why I felt so bad when I heard the news...

"She was your birth mother sweetheart." Gladys softly says.

I frown deeply at her. "But she's never meant anything to me before," I croak.

"Nonsense, of course, she did, it can't all have been bad. You must have some fond memories of her?" she questions.

I nod, knowing full well I do.

"It's only natural to grieve for what we have lost, what could have been," Gladys says, stroking my back.

I listen to Gladys's wise words and nod silently.

"Will she have a funeral?" I croak.

"I'm not sure darling, but I can find out for you if you like?" I nod feeling totally confused about it all if my Mother had kept her shit together...

"Do you think I should go if there is one?" I ask.

"I can't really answer that one for you darling. I think you have to look within and listen to your heart," she says.

I stare numbly out the window.

"Tristan's been calling you," she tells me. "He's worried about you, he wants to come and see you." I sigh heavily, I know I should put his mind at rest that I'm ok, but I feel drained, exhausted.

"Can you call him for me? Tell him I'm ok. I feel exhausted, I just want to sleep," I say.

"Of course, I'll let him know," she says.

"Thanks," I say numbly and head out of the room.

As I climb the stairs, I feel really weird, like I'm walking up the stairs in someone else's body. Opening the door to my old bedroom, I collapse on top of the bed, fully clothed, and fall instantly into a deep sleep...

SOMETHING WAKES ME. Turning over, I search the room. Then I hear it again. *Oh!* It's my mobile buzzing. I sit up and spot my bag hanging on the bedpost, reaching forward I find my mobile. Punching in the security code, I see I have a new message, it's from Tristan.

*Hi baby. I hope you're feeling a little better. I want you to know how sorry I am about your Mother, that must have come as a nasty shock. I really want to see you, baby, Gladys called me earlier said you were a little better and had gone to lie down. I know you're in safe hands, but please say I can come over, I want to see you for myself. I need to know you're ok.
Your loving husband (to be) Tristan x*

Oh, Tristan! You're so sweet and caring! I think back to what happened before I got the news. I work it backwards, Stuart dropping me off at work, Tristan bringing me breakfast, getting pulled into the office, being really mad with Tristan, quitting my job! Then I remember reading through Susannah's report. *Shit!*

I have to see Tristan, I have to tell him.

Launching myself up off the bed and grabbing my bag, I'm about to run out the door when I hear laughter coming from the kitchen. Gladys is with someone, and I know it's not Malcolm. Walking to the door, I open it as quietly as I can, the loudest person laughs heartily again. Hold on a second, I know that voice – *It's Rob!*

Throwing my bag over my shoulder, I dash down the stairs, run the small length of the hallway and bang through the kitchen door, making Rob and Gladys jump, and skid to a stop.

"Rob!" I squeak in delight, running into his open arms. I hug him tightly. "What are you doing here?" I ask.

"I popped into Chester House to see you and that hunk of a man of yours told me what happened and that you were here," Rob says. It's so good to hear his voice. I have so much to tell him, I don't even know where to begin. Then I remember the hell he's put me through the past two weeks, yet here he is laughing and joking with Gladys in her kitchen, I pull back from him and slap his bicep.

"What are you laughing about?" I shout.

I see Gladys's mouth pop open in my peripheral vision.

"Answer me, Rob! You've had me so worried." I slap him again, just for good measure.

"Alright, alright keep your pants on!" he chuckles.

"I think I'll leave you two to it," Gladys says, she tenderly rubs my arm. "You know where your bed is if you want to stay, oh and Tristan called again and said he's back at the house," she adds.

"Thanks, Mom." I don't know why, but I really feel like I can actually call her that now. Gladys makes a high pitched squeaky noise, sniffs loudly, kisses us both goodbye and heads out the kitchen. Turning back to Rob I narrow my eyes at him, cross my arms in a huff and wait for his answer.

"Well?" I snap, my foot tapping involuntarily.

"I'm sorry about your Mom' –"Rob!" I screech.

"Ok, ok...Carlos found a lump." I gasp in shock. I'm speechless. My heart starts thumping wildly. "We went to the hospital, got the biopsy done, then went to his parents. We were told we had to wait a week for the results." *So maybe I did see him at Montefiores?*

"And?" I whisper in shock.

"Benign, he's ok!" Rob says with relief.

I launch into his arms again. "No wonder you were so upset," I squeak, fighting back my own tears.

"Yeah well, wait for the shocker." He says teasingly.

I pull back and look up at him with wide, worried eyes. "What?" I ask.

"We are going to be parents," he says matter-of-factly.

I frown deeply at him. "But you don't want kids," I say knowing he doesn't.

"Yeah well, when you think you might be on death's door things change, and it did for both of us. We talked all week, and Carlos told me he's been thinking for a long time about having a family, but he didn't say anything to me because he knew I didn't want them. But seeing him so upset about it all, and knowing he was going to be ok, I realised I'd do anything for him, including kids.

"I don't want to lose him, and now I know how badly he wants a family and well…I love him, so I said yes, as long as he deals with the nappies' Rob makes a funny face 'I can't do that. Carlos will be at home as he always is, and I'll bring in the bread." Rob shrugs, then smiles brightly at me.

I clap my hands to my face. "No way!" I squeak in delight.

"Yes way," he laughs. "But it won't be for a while, we're adopting from China."

I launch myself into his arms again and squeeze him tight. "Oh Rob, I'm so glad you and Carlos are ok, I was so worried. That must have been, so nerve-wracking waiting for the results."

Rob squeezes me tight. "It was," he says darkly. "The worst week of our lives," he adds solemnly.

"Don't you ever do that to me again," I scold. "I had all sorts of horrible things racing through my head."

"Sorry, but Carlos didn't want anyone to know." He tells me.

I sigh heavily. "That's understandable, but you could have just told me anyway. I wouldn't have said anything to anyone!"

"I know…" Rob shakes his head. "Never mind about us, are you ok?" he asks pushing me back so he can look at me.

"Look at the state of your eyes woman!" I smile back at him. "Come on," he says grabbing my hand and leading me outside to the table and chairs.

"No!" I say, pulling on his hand. "I need to see Tristan. Can you drive me over to his place?" I ask. I have to see him now! He has to know about Susannah.

"Why?" Rob questions seeing the panic on my face.

"Please," I beg. "As soon as I've seen him I'll come straight over and see you and Carlos, tell you all about it, but I really need to see Tristan – now!" I add.

Rob frowns at me then pulls me into him for a hug. "You ok?" he asks, his voice sounding worried.

"No...yes...I don't know," I croak, feeling anxious about seeing Tristan.

"Has he hurt you?" Rob asks, his voice going deep.

"No," I pull back from him. *I really need to see Tristan.* "Rob, please can we go?" I ask jigging up and down.

"Alright, alright let's go!" he says waving his hand in the air.

"Thank you!" I kiss his cheek. "I'm so glad your home."

"Me too," Rob takes hold of my hand. "Come on let's get you over to him."

On the short drive over, I briefly tell Rob about Susannah, what's gone on and the report I'm about to show Tristan.

"Your fucking kidding me!" he gasps. "You think she was in your place?" I nod my head at him. "Jesus, you need to be really careful Coral," he warns. "She sounds like she's really lost it," he adds.

"I know," I whisper.

Rob pulls up outside the gates and whistles. "You've certainly fallen on your feet their kiddo," he says. I sardonically raise an eyebrow at him. "And he's gorgeous to boot," he says, teasing me.

"Rob!" I scold.

"Sorry," he chuckles. "Good luck," he adds.

I lean forward, and we kiss each other. "Thanks for the lift," I smile weakly at him.

"Anytime," he says.

"Rob," I look up at the house. "If this goes wrong..." I swallow hard. "Will you come and get me?" I squeak.

"You don't even need to ask that," he says.

"Ok, good," I say, taking a deep breath.

"Let's go for it does work," he adds.

I smile weakly at him and exit the car. Rob holds his hand up and waves, I wave back as I watch Rob drive away. Taking a deep breath, I head down the driveway to Tristan's house – our house – I can't get used to that. Using my keys, I take another deep breath and open the door.

The moment I step into the house, I see Tristan running towards me.

"Baby!" He breathes pulling me up and into his arms, squeezing me tight.

I don't know why I don't hold him back – maybe I'm subconsciously protecting myself from the onslaught I may receive – and I'm still feeling sore about earlier.

"Come, sit down. What do you need? A drink, something to eat?" he frantically asks as he walks me over to the sofa.

I shake my head in reply. I seem to have lost the courage to speak.

"I'm so sorry about your Mother," he says solemnly, sitting next to me on the sofa.

"I'm sorry too, for freaking out at you. I shouldn't have," I say feeling ashamed that I did.

Tristan smiles tenderly at me, picks up my hand and kisses it. "You don't need to apologise baby," he says. "And I'm sorry about what happened in Joyce's office," he adds.

I stare down at our entwined fingers. "Why did you act like that?" I whisper.

Tristan shakes his head, he looks mortified. "I was angry you hadn't told me…that I had to hear it from Joyce," he says. I keep my gaze on our fingers. "I can't be seen to be taking sides," he reiterates.

"But it was just Joyce and me, you could have given me the benefit of the doubt," I squeak.

"I know, I was wrong, and again I'm sorry. You're not really going to quit are you?" he asks.

"Well yeah…you…you've given my job to *her*," I say.

Tristan shakes his head at me, his lips twitching with a smile. "No, I haven't," he tells me.

"But you' –"No you said it, not me. I just didn't tell you, that's all," he interrupts.

"But that doesn't make any sense, why would you do that?" I ask in astonishment.

"I needed to see your reaction when I told you about the complaint." I frown back at him. "Please say you'll stay in the company."

I shake my head at him, I've quit, made my decision. In a way, I think what happened today made me realise I won't like it, that it won't be the same without Joyce.

"Can you forgive me?" he asks with puppy dog eyes. "Because I don't quite know how to live without you," he says melting my heart all over again.

"Of course I forgive you," I tell him. He leans down to kiss me, but I push him back with my hand. "I need to know Tristan…do you believe I threatened Susannah?" I swallow hard, waiting for his answer.

"No," he says after an eternity.

"Then why didn't you say that earlier?" I question.

"Why didn't you tell me she upset Joe?" he asks, ignoring my question.

"Joyce told me not to get involved," I repeat. This is getting us nowhere! "Look, Tristan, there's something I need to tell you. I don't think you're going to like it, so I'm going to ask you to wait until I'm finished before you judge me," I say scrutinising his reaction.

His cheeks flush, and his pupils dilate with worry. "Ok," he murmurs, looking down at our hands.

"Ok," I breathe. *You can do this!* "Firstly, I need you to keep an open mind. Can you do that for me?" I ask hesitantly.

"Anything for you," he tells me. *Ok, here goes!*

With shaking hands, I reach into my bag, open the envelope and pull out Susannah's report. "Here," I place it in his hands.

"What's this?" he asks, his eyes going darker.

"Just, read it," I say my heart in my mouth. I watch Tristan open the pages and start reading, then he stops, and his eyes shoot up to meet mine.

"This is a report on Susannah," he says, frowning deeply.

"Yes," I whisper.

"Why do you have this Coral?" he questions.

"Just…please read through it. You can ask me whatever you want when you've finished."

Clenching his jaw several times, he carries on reading it. "Her husband died?" He whispers.

I say nothing. I keep watching as he turns over to the next page, the medical history one, and continues to read, he looks horrified –*Good, maybe he won't think she's all holy and great anymore.*

"Jesus," he whispers running his hand through his hair. He stops reading and looks up at me. "She lost her husband *and* her baby?" he says.

I nod once. "She's really sick Tristan, she needs help," I say.

Tristan looks down at the paperwork again. He looks totally shocked. He runs his hand back and forth through his hair, messing it up. I can't help swooning at him for a moment, then I snap out of it.

"I still don't understand though, why do you have this Coral?" He asks.

"Turn it over," I say.

Tristan turns to the last page, the image of her husband. "Fuck!" he hisses.

"He really looks like you don't you think?" I say softly.

Tristan nods, totally mesmerised by what he's seeing, then he places the paperwork down next to me, and stares at the floor for a while, deep in thought.

"Tristan," – "Don't" he warns, with his forefinger. "Why do you have this?" he questions again in a deep, low voice.

"Lots of reasons," I say, not knowing where to start.

"Enlighten me," he snaps. He's mad at me.

I take a deep breath and begin. "Would you agree that men and women are different, that we pick up on different things?" He narrows his eyes at me. "Yes or no Tristan," I bark.

"Yes," he growls. *Ok, he's really pissed.*

"I could tell from the very first time I met you that Susannah liked you, I even thought you were sleeping together, you know a couple maybe. Of course, I never thought for one second that she was in love with you; that she's obsessed with you, and now I know why. Tristan, everything she said I did to her, was exactly what she did to me." Tristan's face pales.

"She deleted the Google images I had of you, and basically said I was useless and that if you found out, I would lose my job. Her behaviour was totally erratic, up and down like a yo-yo, she snapped at me, she upset Joe, and I know she said something to Joyce." I take a deep breath and continue.

"When she told me she was getting divorced and moving down here, it raised my suspicions, especially given the fact that you told me she was happily married. When I called to speak to you on Tuesday, and Karen answered, we got chatting, she's really nice by the way, I wish you'd sent her down to train me," Tristan cocks one eyebrow up at me, I look away and continue.

"Anyway, I told Karen that Susannah had upset Joe, I asked her what she thought of Susannah," I stop talking because Tristan is glaring at me like I'm the one to blame for all of this. "I only asked her that because I thought it was just me being me," I snap, he squeezes his eyes shut, so I continue.

"Karen confirmed that no one within the company actually likes her, that she's all sweetness and light when you're around, and when you're not, she's well...weird. She also said that everyone knows Susannah is in love with you, and hardly anyone believes she's actually got a husband, I guess she was right about that part…" I break off shivering slightly.

Tristan stands, wraps the throw around me and softly strokes my cheek.

"Go on," he says, his brow furrowed his eyes dark. He is not a happy man.

I shake my head remembering her words. "Susannah threatened *me,* Tristan, she said she figured we were together, she caught you winking at me on Monday before you left, she told me to stay away from you. She said *'he's mine'* and……and… and she said you would never be interested in someone like me, someone in constant therapy. And the worst part is that she said that you two are secretly engaged, mad about each other…" I stop for a moment and take a breath. "So not only does she know I'm seeing George, but she also knows where I live."

"How do you know?" he asks.

"She made a comment about my studio," I say and continue. "Then at lunchtime on Wednesday I went out, I wanted to write something down but when I searched for my little note-pad it was missing. I emptied my bag in a panic only to find my keys had gone too." Tristan looks horrified. "When I got back to the office I found them on my desk with a note from Susannah, she said she found them on the floor. When I was out Wednesday night, she entered my property, drank a beer and stole two items from me."

Tristan's eyes widen. "How do you know it was her?" he whispers, horrified.

"Bob heard a noise and went outside to investigate, he saw a blonde woman entering my studio, so he questioned her. She told him she was my friend, picking something up for me."

Tristan shakes his head at me. "That doesn't prove it was Susannah," he argues.

"I know, but who else would it have been? I don't have any female friends Tristan. Debs is blonde, but she doesn't have a key, and she doesn't drink beer." He frowns deeply and stares down at the floor again. I can tell he's trying to work it all out.

"I think it was Susannah outside my door on Monday night too," I add.

His head snaps up. "Those are very serious allegations," he tells me.

"I know," I whisper.

"What's missing?" he asks me.

I stare at the floor and swallow hard. "The one and only photograph I have of my family before things went wrong, and one of the pictures of us." I hear Tristan's sharp intake of breath. "Tristan, if she knew so much about me, you don't think she would have..." I break off unable to say it out loud.

"What baby?" he asks a little calmer.

"My mother," I whisper.

"I don't understand?" he says.

"You don't think she would have...k-killed her do you?" I manage to squeak out.

Tristan's eyes close for a moment. "No, no way," he says shaking his head.

I nod, feeling a little better about it. "Ok, well that's why I got the report. I was so freaked out Tristan, you were away all week, and she kept reminding me of someone. I worked it out in the end that it was my Mother, they both have the same crazy look in their eyes," I say shivering slightly.

"I don't believe this," he chokes, staring out the window.

"I'm sorry Tristan," I whisper. Reaching out, I place my hand on his forearm but he pulls away, I instantly feel rejected. "I know this is a lot to take in, and I really wish it wasn't true, but she needs help Tristan, and we both need to be really careful, and quite frankly, I'm scared to death that she'll just flip out and hurt someone, hurt you." I end in a whisper.

He keeps staring out the window – *I'm losing him!*

"Tristan," I place my hand on his cheek and turn his head, so he has to look at me. "I'm not doing this to hurt you, you know that right?"

He closes his eyes and shakes his head. "I…I don't know what to say," he murmurs.

"You don't have to say anything. It's up to you what happens now, but whatever you decide to do…just, be careful, please." I beg.

He nods silently, then shakes his head again. "This is unbelievable," he chokes.

"Tristan' – "Don't," he warns again. "I need a few minutes," he says as calmly as he can, although I can see the anger rearing up inside of him. I watch as he silently walks the length of the hallway, and disappears into his office.

I can't help wondering what he's up to, and why he's walked away. Maybe he's feeling foolish for not seeing through her pretences? Or maybe he's mad that none of his staff has brought any of this to his attention? Especially with the fact that he's so good to them all.

Either way, I have more to tell him, and there are more questions to ask, so I guess I'm just going to have to be patient and wait for him to come back.

I suddenly feel really cold, right down into my bones cold. I pull the throw tighter around me and begin my silent prayer.

Please don't hate me, please don't blame me, please don't leave me…

CHAPTER TWENTY-SIX

AS I SIT WAITING for Tristan's return. I can't help wondering if I'm doing the right thing here. I can't lose him, I just can't. I look up at the clock on the wall, he's been ten minutes already, another five and I'm marching in there.

I hear his office door open. I watch him storming over to me, he looks really mad. He sits on the coffee table opposite me, and without a word, he reaches forward and entwines our fingers together. Tristan frowns at me then stares down at our fingers. I know I need to continue, he needs to know what I know, and I still have unanswered questions. *Ok, I can do this!*

"Tristan, I've got to ask, how did Susannah get the job? Her employment records show no prior office-based work."

"I..." Tristan shakes his head. "It's irrelevant," he snaps.

"No Tristan, it's not," I say softly.

He gazes out the window for a while then starts to speak. "I kept bumping into her, outside work, at the cafe I used to eat at..." *Holy Crap, it's just what I thought!*

"She seemed really sweet you know, we got talking one day in the queue, she said she was looking for a job because she'd been made redundant. I had an opening, so I invited her to come over for an interview, she told me she had no prior experience, I told her that was fine." Tristan shakes his head in exasperation. "She started at the bottom Coral, worked her way up. She became one of the best employees I've ever had. I don't understand how someone with so many problems can do that well?" He looks hurt, confused, his eyes bleak.

"I know, I have a theory about that," I say.

"You do?" he says, cocking his head to the side.

"It was never about the job, it was about getting close to you, I think she planned it all Tristan. People who are sick like that, they can seem really...well normal, as though they are functioning properly." Tristan shakes his head in disbelief. "I think when she first saw you she saw her dead husband, I mean the likeness is uncanny don't you think?" Reluctantly, he nods. He can't disagree with that, they could be twins.

"I think she did everything she could to get close to you, I think *you* were her obsession, and you still are." I take a moment and let that sink in. "I think she stalked you, Tristan, that's why you kept bumping into her. Then she tells you some cock and bull story about losing her job, so you offer her one, she knows that's the best way to get close to you, in your life, and in less than a year, she's also got the woman you love out of your life."

"Jesus...Oli," he whispers. *Does he mean Olivia?* – Bile rises in my throat if Olivia still loves him…and he loves her…my stomach twists with anxiety – *No, stop this Coral!*

I take a deep breath and think about my next question.

"How did Susannah react when you turned her down? You told me she was ok about it, was she?" I tentatively ask.

Tristan shakes his head. "No she wasn't, she was a little snappy and erratic. I gave her some time off. When she came back, she was good as new."

"It was Susannah who told you about Olivia, wasn't it?" I say.

His head snaps up. "How do you know her name?" he asks his voice icy cold.

"I…I spoke to her," I whisper, instantly feeling guilty.

"You did *what*?" He growls, launching himself up from the coffee table, his hands balling into fists. "How could you Coral," he adds then starts pacing the room, up down, up down – *This is going nowhere!*

"Tristan, please sit down," I plead.

He shakes his head and carries on pacing, his jaw tensing every now and then. "How did you get her number? Did you get information on her like Susannah?" He asks his cheeks deep red.

He's not going to let this go.

I sigh inwardly. "Yes, I asked for her info, I wanted to speak to her. I was suspicious that it might have been Susannah who split you up," I say, feeling downhearted.

"You shouldn't have done that Coral," he says between clenched teeth.

"Tristan, I am sorry I did this behind your back, but my intentions were good. You have a mentally unstable member of staff who has close access to you…I…I was afraid…afraid she would hurt you, hurt me, I just didn't know. Olivia clarified it for me, I'm sorry I called her, ok?"

Tristan turns away from me, shaking his head as he does, then he crosses his arms, and stares out the window – *Now I'm getting mad at him!*

"Was it Susannah?" I ask again. He doesn't reply, he doesn't even turn around to look at me. "Fine! You don't want to talk to me about it, I may as well leave." I stand up from the sofa.

Tristan is instantly over to me. "Don't go," he pleads.

"Why not, there's no point staying," I choke. "You won't listen to me, just like you didn't listen to Olivia." I turn on my heel and storm towards the door – *I'm so mad at him right now.*

"Yes!" he shouts, stopping me in my tracks. I turn and face him. "She told me," he says hanging his head.

"You lied to me!" I bark.

"How?" he questions.

"You told me that Susannah didn't know anything about you and Olivia." I snap.

Tristan hangs his head in shame. "I know," he says staring down at the floor.

"How can you ever expect me to trust you if" – "Trust *me?*" he shouts, his hands balling into fists again. "And how am I supposed to trust you? I think that's a bit hypocritical of you darling, considering how much you've been keeping from me," he snaps. *Ok, he's got me there.*

"You're right," I say running my hand through my hair, trying to figure a way of getting us back on track.

"I *was* going to tell you," he says, surprising me.

"Oh really, and when would that have been?" I ask, trying not to sound sarcastic.

"After your training Coral, you don't like her, and I couldn't tell you something like that in case…" Tristan puts his hands on his hips and looks up at me.

"In-case what Tristan?" I snap.
"In-case you fucked it all up!" he shouts.
"What?" I screech. "That doesn't make any sense?"
"Coral, anytime her name has been mentioned you go off at the deep end, I know you do. You might not say it, but I can see it in your eyes." I cross my arms and huff loudly – *Ok, he's right about that part, but right now we've got bigger issues.*

"Fine! What did she say?" I ask, walking back over to him.
"Who?" He snaps.
"Susannah, when she told you about Olivia?" I bite.
"Why?" He asks, looking exasperated.
"Because I'm curious how a woman you'd known less than a year, could convince you that the woman you loved and shared a home with, was seeing her ex behind your back." I bite.

Tristan stares up at the ceiling for a moment then sits on the edge of the sofa with his face in his hands. "What did Olivia say?" he breathes. *What? Why does he want to know what she said?*

My heart instantly sinks into the pit of my stomach – *He does love her still, No!*

"Why?" I tremble.
"Just curious," he says.
"Can we get back to us?" I say a little harshly.
Tristan glares up at me. "You want to know what she said?" he snaps.
"Yes," I say a little exasperated.
"She didn't say anything," he snaps. "She showed me a photo."
"A-a...p-photo?" I whisper stuttering slightly.
"Yes, when she saw it was Olivia, she took out her phone and..." Tristan trails off.

I think hard for a moment, and quickly come up with a plausible scenario. *Yes, of course, that's easy to do!*

"What!" he barks at my smug expression.
"Photoshop," I answer crossing my arms in defiance. He's not going to like this.
"What?" He snaps, crossing his arms.
"Tristan, all she had to do was take an innocent picture of two people kissing each other goodbye, pull it up on her laptop, and change the image," I tell him. Tristan shakes his head in

disbelief. "That's why you were so adamant it was true, you thought you had proof," I say.

"I did have proof!" He booms stepping towards me. I stare back at his wide eyes, I can see he's angry, but I can also see pain and regret behind the anger.

"How long did Susannah wait before telling you that she loved you?" I ask, ignoring his anger. Tristan laughs sarcastically and shakes his head at me, then runs both his hands through his hair. "I know she said she was in love with you Tristan. She got rid of Olivia, and you were a free man, how long?"

He sighs heavily, wraps his hands around his neck and stares up at the ceiling. "A year," he finally whispers.

"So she leaves it long enough, so it doesn't raise your suspicions, and you have some time to get over Olivia," I mumble to myself.

"I need a drink, you?" I shake my head. He storms off into the kitchen.

I follow him. "Do you know if she's still in Brighton?" I ask.

"No, Sunday morning she called me and asked for some time off, I said yes." Is that why he was so happy on Sunday because he'd spoken to her? I shake off the stupid thought.

"Did you tell her you're moving here permanently?" I ask.

"No, not yet. Only Karen and Claire know. I was waiting to speak to Susannah," he answers.

"Then why is she making plans to move here...." I'm suddenly filled with a dreadful thought. I think I know the answer. "Can I have your mobile?" I ask.

"Why?" He snaps, totally exasperated.

"Because it wouldn't surprise me if she's bugged you' – "Enough!" he bellows.

I cower away from him. "I can't take anymore Coral." I wince at his words. "I've just found out that the girl I trust, who has been the best member of staff I have ever had, is a complete lunatic who sabotaged my relationship with Olivia, who…" He squeezes his eyes shut, his hands bawling into fists again. In his anger, he reaches up and slams both fists down on the kitchen counter.

Ok, I think I need to go!

"Look, I know this is' – "No you don't know!" he bellows. He storms off, picks up his jacket and heads for the front door.

"Where are you going?" I call out as I walk around the breakfast bar.

Tristan stops and slowly turns to me, his jaw tense and his eyes full of pain. "I need some space from you…I need to get out of here," he chokes.

"Tristan," I shout, stopping him from walking any further. "I know you need time to process this, but I'm warning you now if you walk out on me, I won't be able to trust that you'll stay if we get back on track. It'll feel just like it did when my Dad left, please don't do that to us," I tremble, praying he stays.

"You're already waiting for that to happen anyway," he snaps. *Ouch, that hurt!*

I know what I need to do. "You know what, don't bother leaving, I'll get my bags," I snap.

Running up the two flights of stairs, I grab my overnight bag, shove my toiletries and some of my clothing inside, then I pull my mobile out of my bag and call Rob.

Running back down the stairs, I wait for him to answer. "Ola' – "Can you come and pick me up?" I croak, fighting against the waterfall that's breaching the gates.

"Oh…of course," he solemnly answers.

"Thanks," I croak and hang up. I spot Tristan leaning against the breakfast bar, his head hung low. I tentatively walk over to him. "Are we through?" I tremble.

He doesn't answer me, he just stares straight ahead, his jaw clenched.

I grit my teeth and take a deep breath. "Here," reaching into my bag I place Olivia's paperwork on the counter. "Olivia's number," I tell him, his eyes shoot up and meet mine. "She's still mad at you, I can't say I blame her, maybe you should call her and apologise. Oh, and she said to mention Cathy, Rebecca and Sarah. Apparently, Susannah screwed those potentials up for you too. And now you're letting her do the same to us," I say, my voice trembling.

Tristan clenches his jaw several times and glares back at me. "Just go Coral," he snaps.

Oh my god, we're through, it's over!

I take one last look at the man that I love, that I adore, the man I was about to marry and walk silently out of the house.

I feel numb – I have no tears.

I know the emotions of anger, hate and fear so well. Where is the rage that should be pulsing through me? I have lost another person that I loved. I should have unbelievable, unimaginable pain lancing through me, just like I did when I left him, but I feel nothing, nothing at all.

I look up and see Rob's car coming up the hill. I start walking towards it, he pulls up beside me, and I get inside.

"Hey," he softly says. Reaching for my hand, he squeezes it once.

I don't look at him, and I don't say anything – I have no words.

"Back to mine?" he asks, I stare straight ahead not really registering his words. "Ok," he says, the car moves forward, and we head back into town.

I feel like I'm in some sort of weird dream, nothing seems real, not the drive over, getting out the car, or the elevator ride up to Rob's apartment. I barely register Carlos sitting in the room when I walk in, but he walks over to me and hugs me tightly.

"If he doesn't believe you, he doesn't deserve you," he tells me, but again, I feel like I'm in a completely different dimension, not of this world. They walk me over to the sofa and sit me down between the two of them.

"Do you want a drink?" Carlos asks, but all I can do is stare blankly ahead.

"Would you like something to eat? Rob asks.

I look across and shake my head. I shiver slightly, I feel so cold. I know somewhere in the back of my mind I shouldn't be because we are having a really nice summer, but it doesn't really register.

Kicking off my shoes I pull my knees up to my chest and hug myself tightly, trying to hold myself together, then I curl up on the sofa, trying to generate some heat. I feel something heavy and warm being placed on me, but I don't know who's done it.

I stare at the wall, trying to understand where I went wrong. I can't even begin to imagine what it's going to feel like not having *him* in my world. Squeezing my eyes shut tight, I try to block out the scream that's building within me, a scream of his name.

Pulling the warm blanket tighter around me, I start a mantra – *It's all a bad dream, just a bad dream* – I keep repeating this to myself, until my eyes become heavier, and I slip into unconsciousness…

SOMETIME LATER I realise I'm being moved. My eyes open for a second, I'm in Carlos's arms, and he's carrying me somewhere, he opens a door and places me on a bed.

"Do you want to get changed?" he asks. Looking down in a daze, I realise I'm still in my work clothes, I nod silently to him. "I'll get your bag," he tells me.

I watch him walk out of the room, then return with the bag I hastily packed at Tristan's, opening up the zip, he pulls out a pair of jeans and a long-sleeved t-shirt, and with a sorrowful smile, he hands them to me.

"You know where the bathroom is right?" he softly says. I nod again, still unable to speak. "And if you need anything, anytime. Just come and get us," he says, gently stroking my hair.

I blink up at him. "Carlos," I whisper. "I'm so glad you're ok."

He pulls me into his arms, and we hug for a while. "Me too, I would have missed you, and you're crazy ways," he says, pulling back to look at me. I smile weakly at him. Carlos leans towards me and softly kisses me on the forehead. "I'll leave you to it," he says. I nod again as those were the only words I could say, Carlos, stands and quietly leaves, shutting the door behind him.

I stare down at the clothes in my hands, then decide if I'm going to sleep through this numbness, I'm better off doing it in these. It takes a long time to change clothes, I keep stopping and staring blankly at the wall, I think I'm in shock. Pulling my top over my head, I collapse back onto the bed staring numbly at the wall…

"CORAL WAKE UP!" My eyes dart open. I see Rob stood over me, my mobile in his hand. "It's the police, they need to speak to you," he says in a panic. *What?*

I frown deeply, I feel so disorientated – *Police? Why would they want to speak to me?*

"Coral, take it," Rob shouts. In a daze, I take my mobile

from him and bring it up to my ear, I'm still not sure if I'm awake or dreaming.

"Hello," I croak.

"Miss Coral Stevens?"

"Yes."

"Are you the owner of studio seven on the western concourse?"

"Yes." My heart starts to palpitate.

"My name is Sargeant Phillips, I'm afraid there's been an accident." *An accident?* What's he talking about? As my senses start to come back to me, I look up at Rob.

"Um...I'm sorry what accident?" I whisper.

"Your next-door neighbour," he says.

"Bob!?" I shout– *Oh My God, something's happened to Bob!*

"We are here with him now, just waiting for the ambulance."

"Ambulance," I choke. "I'll be right there," I tell him and end the call.

Rob runs out the room. I launch myself up from the bed, grab my trainers from the bag and shove my feet into them. Running out of the bedroom and down the hallway, I see Rob already has his jacket on and his keys in his hands.

I run to the front door then glance behind me. "Thanks, Carlos," I say, "For everything."

"Anytime, I hope Bob's ok," he says a look of concern on his face.

I smile weakly at him and dash out the door...

THE DRIVE DOWN to the Marina seems like a complete blur, the only thing I notice is that it's gone dark. All I can think about is whether Bob's ok. Why does it feel like we are going in slow motion? My leg is rapidly jigging up and down, and I'm chewing my tips with nerves.

"Hurry Rob," I squeak. Rob screeches to a halt at the gym, right next to a police car with blue lights flashing. Not waiting for him, I launch myself out of the car and run at full speed across the carpark, heading straight for my studio. I hear someone calling me back, but I can't stop, I won't stop. I have to get to Bob!

Taking the steps down to the concourse two at a time, I

almost fall over I'm going at such a speed. I can see several people hanging around, and I can just make out a policeman, I can tell from his black uniform, his radio on his shoulder. Reaching my studio, I have to shout at several people to move out of the way. When the crowd finally parts and I see what's before me, I almost burst into tears.

Bob is on the floor, a pool of blood underneath his head. A female police officer is holding his head with a towel, and my studio has been completely ransacked, my music, photo albums and DVDs are all over the place. The cushions on the sofa have been slashed, my little table over-turned, and I can see what I think, are several of my work trousers hanging across the bannister, but they are in pieces like someone's cut them all up.

Bob sees me and lifts his hand in the air. *He's alive, thank god he's alive.*

I launch myself forward and sink to the floor next to him, I take his hand in mine and squeeze it gently, he smiles crookedly at me.

"Bob," I choke, my throat thick with tears.

"She was here," he whispers.

"Who was?" I ask.

"The girl…from before," he says coughing. *Susannah!*

"The blonde girl?" I ask.

"Yes," he croaks.

"What happened?" I ask softly.

"I heard a noise…thought it was you, she was upstairs…" Bob stops wincing in pain.

"Take it easy Bob," I say, and gently stroke his forehead.

Bob takes a breath and continues. "She came down when I called for you…she hit me with that," he says his eyes moving to the right, my eyes follow his, and there, lying on the floor with blood on its tip is my baseball bat.

"She attacked you?" I growl.

"Yes," he croaks – I feel such venomous hatred run through my veins. I'm going to fucking kill her, I'm going to find her, and I'm going to fucking kill her for this. Rob arrives and crouches down the other side of Bob.

"Bob," he squeaks in shock, taking his other hand.

Bob smiles crookedly again. "You kids are so good to me…" he croaks. "Coral," he winces, just as the paramedics turn up and start working on him. "She's after you," he whispers. "Go kick her butt…" he coughs, his eyes rolling into the back of his head.

"Bob!" I screech. The policewoman is shouting at me, trying to get me to move, but I am not leaving his side. Rob grabs hold of me by the waist and pulls me out of the way.

I watch in horror as two paramedics start CPR, trying to resuscitate him. *No!*

Rob squeezes me tight, trying to comfort me. I slap my hands to my mouth…*don't die on my Bob, please*…I close my eyes and start a mantra. *Don't die on me Bob, please don't die on me…*

"Coral!" Rob squeaks.

I open my eyes and see Bob's chest start to move up and down on its own again, I sag with relief, then watch as they carefully move him onto a stretcher. I walk forward, take his hand in mine and squeeze it tight. I know Rob is behind me, walking with us.

"Are you family?" The female paramedic asks.

"Practically, he doesn't have anyone else," I say, choking back tears.

She nods once. "You can ride with him," she tells me.

"Hang in there Bob ok?" I croak.

With the oxygen mask across his face, he blinks once at me and tries to smile, he's such a fighter, I dread to think what would have happened had he not been that way. I lean down and kiss his cheek, keeping up with the paramedics as they roll him along the concourse.

Bob tries to pull off the oxygen mask several times, but the paramedics keep stopping him, he looks pissed off. Reaching the ambulance they get him inside, and I follow. I feel so angry and mad at myself, I should have protected Bob, I should have demanded he stay with Gladys. A few stray tears fall down my cheeks, when I think of what could have happened, it's too horrifying to think about.

I lean down and kiss his cheek again. "I'm so sorry Bob," I choke.

Bob points to his mask. I know he wants to tell me something, so I carefully lift the mask.

"I'll be fine," he says wincing again. "But he won't," he whispers.

"Who?" I question.

"Tristan…" he croaks. "She's gone there, looking for you…" he whispers.

It takes a few seconds to register what he's said…*she's gone there looking for you…Holy Fuck, Tristan!*

I think Bob can see the horror spreading across my face. "Go," he says trying to move me. "Go…" My head whips round to Rob who's stood outside the open doors.

"Rob, can you go with him? And can I borrow your car?" I ask.

There's somewhere I need to be!

"Yeah…but, what's going on Coral?" he says, stepping inside the ambulance.

"No time!" I frantically say, holding my hand out for his keys.

Rob shakes his head at me. "Don't do anything stupid," he says, reluctantly handing me his keys.

"I have to go do this," I tell him, then I look down at Bob. "Hang in there Bob," I say kissing his forehead.

"Be careful," Rob says. I nod once at him, step outside and watch as the paramedics get ready to shut the doors.

"Rob," I shout. "Call Gladys, she needs to know," I add.

Rob nods once, looking very worried and squeezes Bob's hand and the doors to the ambulance close before me. I hear the sirens come on, and I watch as it drives out of the carpark, heading in the direction of the hospital. My blood instantly boils within me. I am going to kill her. Clenching my fists, I start running back to my studio. I have one thing and one thing only on my mind – *Tristan!*

Pushing past all the people that are being asked to go home by the police, I run into the living-room – *How the hell am I meant to find them in this mess?*

"Miss, you can't be in here." A male voice tells me.

"I live here," I snap at him, still searching for what I need.

"Miss Stevens?" He questions.

"Yes," I shout – *Found them!*

"We need to ask you a few ques'" – I barge past him, out the studio, past all the onlookers and run as fast as I can towards the carpark.

Reaching Rob's BMW 4, I press the fob, and the car unlocks, throwing myself inside, I push my foot on the brake and press the start button, the engine revs to life. Slamming my foot down on the gas, I fishtail out of the carpark, tyres squealing as they find grip. I almost collide with another car, but they slam on their brakes as I go speeding past them…. *I have to get to Tristan, no matter what!*

For some unfathomable reason, I notice Brandon Flowers Crossfire is blaring on the radio – I hadn't even realised the radio was playing on the way down here. Racing up Marina Way, I have to use the handbrake to turn right into Roedean Road, then I slam on the brakes as I take a right onto Cliff Approach, then I turn left, tires squealing as I merge onto The Cliff, and I almost lose control – *Shit!*

I slam on the brake and then back on the gas as the car powers down the road towards Tristan's pad. With the gates still open, I swing a left into them, skidding so badly I almost smash into the gatepost. When the car straightens up, I slam my foot down on the gas again and launch towards the house.

I see Tristan's car in the driveway and the front door wide open – *Fuck!*

Screeching to a halt, I pull on the handbrake and push the stop button. Opening the door, I jump out, and slamming it behind me I run a couple of steps to reach the front door.

Tristan, please be ok!

Stilling myself for a moment, I take my Eskrima sticks out of the cloth bag and take a deep breath – *You can do this Coral!*

I close my eyes for a moment and picture Tristan smiling at me. A strange calm washes over me, I don't feel angry or scared, I feel calm and focused and totally in control. Stepping out of my trainers because I know they will squeak across the flooring, I carefully step inside. All the lights are out. As I take silent steps into the hallway, I see the alarm cover is down, and there's a green light flashing on it, I remember Tristan telling me it triggers the alarm for the police. I wonder for a moment if I should call out to him, but something tells me I need to be silent, invisible.

My eyes search the living room, I can't see him in there or

the part of the kitchen I can see from the hallway, and there's no sign of a struggle. Turning around, I tiptoe silently towards his office. I open the door as quietly as I can, I half expect to see him in here, but as I step into the room I see he's not, but I'm instantly immobilised when I see what's up on the walls – *Oh My God!*

The photos from Hastings are all blown up and hanging on the walls.

On the back wall, there's a collage of four, to my right another four, to my left are the two I liked the most. They have been blown up and changed to black and white, and I can tell from where Tristan sits at his desk; they would surround him… *Oh, Tristan!*

Swallowing hard, I turn on my heel and walk back out. I feel lost for a moment. This house is so big I could spend forever trying to find Tristan. Deciding my next step is to check downstairs I silently pad as quickly as I can down the stairs, I run along the hallway and stop as I reach the cinema room. The door is open, so I lean in as quickly as I can and pull back taking a mental picture of the room as I do. *Damn, he isn't in there!*

Running to the gym, I stop before I reach the glass wall and do the same as I did with the cinema room – *Damn it!* – Not in here either.

Dashing back down the hallway, I silently run up the stairs two at a time, I turn to my right and head towards the kitchen. I check the library and the large dining room, and just as I'm running back out, I start to hear music playing, I stand stock still so I can try and work out where it's coming from. *Upstairs!*

I tentatively walk towards the stairs leading to the bedrooms, I hear Florence and the Machine playing, I've never heard Tristan play that before. I put my foot on the first step and listen again, I know the track – Shake It Out – I try to listen for any strange noises, any kind of danger, when I don't, I run up the first flight of stairs as silently as I can. I'm so glad these stairs don't creak and give me away!

Reaching the first landing, I open each bedroom door as quietly as I can and glance inside. I have a horrible feeling I know where Tristan is…*and Susannah.*

I walk over to the last flight of stairs and stop for a moment…*Ok, this is it!*

Feeling sure of what I'm about to do, I run up the stairs and then I slowly walk across the short landing to the doorway so I can catch my breath. I hear the music getting louder, but my heart is overtaking that, thumping loudly against my chest, blood pounding in my ears.

Reaching the door, I shakily reach out and place my hand on the doorknob. I slowly turn it then gently push it open. Keeping an Eskrima stick in each hand just-in-case Susannah is there, I step forward into the room. *Oh God! No...Tristan...*

Tristan is lying on the bed. His head is cut and bleeding, his mouth is covered with duct-tape with his arms tied behind him, and he's out cold – *Tristan!*

I run over to him and crawl along the bed when I reach him I try to lift him up, but he's too heavy for me. Leaning down, I try to see where all the blood's coming from, but there's too much of it, I quickly untie his arms and pull the tape from his mouth.

"Tristan, wake up baby, please wake up," I whisper into his ear.

Silent tears start to fall against my cheeks; seeing him like this is my own personal hell.

"Tristan," I whisper kissing his head. "Please wake up." I tap his face a couple of times, hoping that might do the trick.

Finally, his eyes drearily open. "Tristan, look at me," I say sharply, his eyes search for me, but he looks like he can't focus properly, then suddenly his eyes widen with fear as he grips his head in pain.

"Run," he growls.

"Is she here?" I whisper.

"Get out Coral... she has a gun!"

"What?" I gasp. *Fuck!* Where the hell did she get a fucking gun from?

"Get out Coral," Tristan says again, gripping his head and groaning in pain.

"No. I'm not leaving you, Tristan, come on," I stagger as I try to help Tristan off the bed and onto his feet. He instantly falls to the floor, taking me with him.

"Tristan!" I cry out. "What did she do to you?" I choke.

He tries to push me away from him again. "Go, run...get

out," he moans, holding his head again. I feel absolute rage flood through me. I want to find her. I want to kill her.

"Coral...move, go," he says then he cries out in pain and holds his head.

I start to cry. "No! I'm not leaving you," I croak.

I help him to his feet again, but he stumbles three times onto the bed. I lift his arm over my shoulder, and with all my might, I lift him up to his feet, blood starts gushing from his head, pooling onto his shoulder, then dripping down his torso –*Fuck, Tristan!*

I hear police sirens close by, and just as I'm about to take a step forward, I see Susannah appear from behind the door. *Shit! She was there the whole time!* – I see the gun in her hand, I think it's a small revolver; we stop and stare at one another. I decide my best bet is to try and talk her down, get her to see sense, I have to do something.

"Susannah," I whisper, swallowing hard.

"He's mine," she says robotically and lifts the gun up, so it's pointing at me. *Oh, fuck!*

I hear voices shouting from down below, it gives me a tiny glint of hope.

"Coral…don't move." Tristan's voice startles me, I turn and look up at him. He seems more lucid as he glares at Susannah.

She smiles weakly at him then she looks back at me, her lips pull back over her teeth, and she starts to growl at me, which quickly turns into an erratic scream. She holds her head in her hands and starts to shake her head. Then she starts banging the gun against her forehead, as she mumbles incoherently to herself. Suddenly she stops and looks up at me, and raising the gun in her trembling hand she points it right at me – *Holy fuck, I think I'm about to die?*

"Susannah! - Don't!" Tristan shouts.

She moves a fraction and aims at Tristan, tears pool in her eyes and start to stream down her cheeks, just as her finger starts to pull back against the trigger.

"No!" I swing myself around and dive in front of Tristan, just as I hear the deafening sound of a gun going off, and something…something painful pierce my shoulder.

"Coral!" Tristan gasps and falls to the floor with me in his arms.

Several footsteps run into the room, I hear Susannah scream in rage as she's taken down, and another shot goes off, my ears are ringing so badly. I feel a strange sensation start to trickle down my back. I'm aware of several things happening at once, an ambulance being called, lots of male voices shouting, Tristan looking frantic. I realise I can't really feel my body anymore, everything feels numb. I look up at Tristan, his beautiful face looks so clear to me.

"No baby, no!" he shouts as I lie in his arms. "Hold on ok, hold on," he pleads. I see his face change from fear to anger. "Why did you come back?" he shouts. "Why?"

I swallow once so I can tell him. "I came back...for you my love..." I reach up and place my hand on his heart. "Protect you..." Tristan starts to choke back angry tears.

"We need help!-Somebody!" he shouts, looking around the room.

In the next moment, I'm aware I'm being moved, but I keep my eyes focused on Tristan and smile up at him – I love him so much, and I saved him, I saved him from Susannah.

For some strange reason my hearing is drawn to the song that's started playing, it's Florence and the Machine again, and the song - Never Let Me Go.

I reach up and touch Tristan's face. "I like this song," I say, but it comes out garbled. I start to feel really cold, but I know I shouldn't, we are having such a beautiful summer.

"Coral! Stay with me," Tristan shouts.

I feel so tired...my eyes won't stay open anymore.

"Open your eyes," Tristan shouts, so I do. He leans down and whispers in my ear. "Stay with me...stay with me baby, you have to fight."

I try, I try so hard, but I can feel myself drifting off.

"Open your eyes," he shouts again.

I fight against the sleepiness and do as he asks.

"Don't you dare close your eyes," he shouts, I smile weakly at him, but I feel myself slipping, I feel the clouds coming over and the darkness taking me away.

"No...Coral...No!" I hear my voice tell him I love him, but no words come out. "Don't you dare leave me," he shouts. "Keep fighting, stay with me!" I feel his hand crushing mine.

"I love you," I hear him choke, and his words are my

undoing. I feel my heart thump twice then stop, the black clouds roll over me, and I drift away...

END OF PART TWO

Hi There!
Did you enjoy this book?
If so, you can make a big difference.

Reviews are the most powerful tools in my arsenal when it comes to getting attention for my books. Much as I'd like to, I don't have the financial muscle of a New York Publisher. I can't take out full page ads in the newspaper, or put posters on the subway. But I do have something more powerful than that, and it's something that those publishers would kill to get their hands on.

A committed and loyal bunch of readers.

Honest reviews of my books help bring them to the attention of other readers like you. If you've enjoyed this book I would be very grateful if you could spend just five minutes leaving a review (it can be as short as you like) or simply rating the book on Amazon. I wholeheartedly thank you in advance.

Find Out What Happens Next In…
Forever With Him
Darkest Fears Trilogy Book Three

When Coral Stevens first met Tristan Freeman, the sparks flew and fear exploded, causing her tentatively safe world to brew with defensiveness and mistrust. Tristan, for his part, somehow worked his magic and managed to break down Coral's walls, wearing down the barriers she threw between them – until Coral's heart was firmly caught in his grasp. But Coral had no idea that meeting him would lead her to challenge every aspect of her life – Including her own mortality.

Now, as she begins to recover from her ordeal, she must learn to let go of her need to control, and allow Tristan to take care of her, for he has become her best friend, her passionate lover, her bright light in the darkness, and maybe with his help, she can finally lay the ghosts of her past to rest.

Now they must prove to each other, that no matter how hard it gets, they have become intrinsically woven into the web of each other's lives – Forever. Or will fate take over again, and play a hand neither one of them can see?

Reviews for Forever With Him

"Sooo good! Beautiful story, beautiful ending. I love this trilogy. I love Coral, and I'm so in love with Tristan. This is the kind of trilogy that puts you on an emotional rollercoaster ride while transporting you to into their world, this author truly has a gift. Love, love, loved it! So sad it's ended " 5 stars - **LibraryThing**

"Brilliant third book in this well written trilogy, I loved them all. Coral and Tristan fit so perfectly together. This trilogy captures your attention, not just a load of romance. It's got intrigue, psychology and the girly stuff as well. Loved it!" 5 stars – **Amazon**

"Awesome book." 5 stars – **Amazon**

"This is the third book in an enchanting love story. Lots of good writing and suspense here that has been lovely to read. I found myself glued to the book until the very end. I was rooting for Coral and Tristan who truly make this worth reading. Thumbs Up." 5 stars – **Amazon.com**

"A wonderful series conclusion. I loved this last book, and the entire trilogy, so much. Having travelled this road with Coral and Tristan, it's heartening to find things not only work out the way you want it to, but better. An excellent romance series that I would highly recommend." 5 stars – **Amazon.com**

"I love this story – 456 pages of love, hardship and learning to trust." 5 stars – **Barnes & Noble**

'Wow…what an utterly compelling story! I found myself reading into the wee hours on the weekend and at every spare opportunity during the week. Clair Delaney will definitely be added to the list as one of my top 10 authors. I'm looking forward to reading more of her books in the near future.' **5 stars – *iBooks***

'I loved this book and I couldn't put it down. I finished the trilogy in a few days and I love the characters. I love Tristan and Coral. I'm really recommending this one and for the writer you've done a very good job.' **5 stars – *iBooks***

'Great love affair…a page turner! Glad it ended happily ever after.' **5 stars – *Scribd Library***

'Great finale that had me gripped. This author can write romance, sex scenes and suspense. Coral and Tristan are most certainly in my heart and in my head. I'm actually getting a bit weepy writing this review as I remember all that happened in this one. Heart wrenching read that I highly recommend.' **5 stars – Scribd Library**

'I can't believe it's ended, I want more…I'm a sad, sad girl right now. I love, love, loved this trilogy. I loved it was British, I loved the raw, honest style of writing that can have you crying one minute and laughing the next. I think this shows great promise in an author and I want more from her.' **5 stars – Goodreads.**

'If you are wondering whether or not to give it a go, don't, just buy it. Each book gets better and better as Coral and Tristan become more entwined in each others lives. My heart is overflowing with love after that happy ending in Forever With Him **– 5 stars – Goodreads**

Join My Mailing List

Join my mailing list via my website www.clairdelaneyauthor.com for exclusive offers and competitions and to keep updated with future releases.

Connect with me

Also, you can connect with me via social media. Or contact me via the email address below. I would love to answer your questions, or simply read your feedback and comments.

FACEBOOK - Clair Delaney Author
TWITTER - @CDelaney_Author
INSTAGRAM – ClairDelaneyAuthor
PINTEREST – Clair Delaney Author
WEBSITE - www.clairdelaneyauthor.com
EMAIL - clairdelaneyauthor@gmail.com

ABOUT THE AUTHOR

CLAIR DELANEY is a former P.A who currently lives in rural Wales in the UK. From a very young age, Clair would always be found drawing pictures and writing an exciting story to go with those picture books. At five years of age she told her mother she wanted to work for Disney, that dream didn't pan out, but eventually, she found the courage to put pen to paper and write her first romance novel Fallen For Him. She is also the author of Freed By Him, Forever With Him and A Christmas Wish, Darkest Fears Christmas Special. When she is not writing Clair loves to read, listen to music, keep fit and take long walks with her dogs in the countryside.

FREED BY HIM - Copyright © 2018 Clair Delaney

The moral rights of the author have been asserted. All characters and events in this e-book other than those clearly in the public domain are fictitious and any resemblance to real persons, living or dead is purely coincidence - All right reserved. This e-book is copyright material and must not be copied, reproduced, transferred, distributed or used in any way except as specifically permitted in writing by the author, as allowed under the terms and conditions under which it was purchased or as strictly permitted by applicable law. Any unauthorised distribution or use of this text, maybe a direct infringement of the authors rights, and those responsible maybe liable in law accordingly.

Printed in Great Britain
by Amazon